THESE DIVIDED SHORES

Also by Sara Raasch

Snow Like Ashes

Ice Like Fire

Frost Like Night

These Rebel Waves

THESE
DIVIDED
SHORES

SARA RAASCH

BALZER + BRAY
An Imprint of HarperCollins*Publishers*

Balzer + Bray is an imprint of HarperCollins Publishers.

These Divided Shores
Copyright © 2019 by Sara Raasch
All rights reserved. Printed in the United States of America.
No part of this book may be used or reproduced in any manner whatsoever without
written permission except in the case of brief quotations embodied in critical articles
and reviews. For information address HarperCollins Children's Books, a division of
HarperCollins Publishers, 195 Broadway, New York, NY 10007.
www.epicreads.com

ISBN 978-0-06-247153-6 (tr.) — ISBN 978-0-06-294202-9 (int.)

19 20 21 22 23   PC/LSCH   10 9 8 7 6 5 4 3 2 1
❖
First Edition

THESE DIVIDED SHORES

Menesia

Availability: rare

Location: beneath cypress trees in
   Backswamp

Appearance: almond-shaped brown seeds

Method: seeds are crushed and powder
   is consumed

Use: memory erasure

I

"TO ENSURE THE good of every Grace Lorayan, we, your Council, have unanimously voted to relinquish control of the island to His Majesty Asentzio Elazar Vega Gallego, King of the Pious God–Blessed Nation of Argrid, Eminence of the Eternal Church."

Even though Vex and Edda weren't on the side of the castle that faced the courtyard, the councilman's voice reverberated with perfect clarity. Last time Vex had been in New Deza's fortress, he'd come as a prisoner—and he'd rather have been locked in the dungeon again than been subjected to the pristine acoustics of the servants' halls.

He darted behind Edda, flying past windows servants had opened to usher in the lake breeze. All that the windows really let in was the stench of sweat from the crowd in the front courtyard and the bleating words of a representative from Grace Loray's Council.

"Cansu and Nayeli are sure they found her?" Vex hissed. "They *see* her? I don't want to hear this speech again. If we're dallying here on a hunch or a rumor—"

Edda adjusted the Budwig Bean in her ear. One of the benefits of running missions with the Tuncian raider syndicate was access to the magic plant, which let two people communicate across great distances. "You planned this whole mission. Having doubts now?"

"I've had doubts about every decision I've made since Elazar set foot on this island again."

Edda's blue eyes softened, but then a maid appeared in front of them. Vex and Edda slowed to a walk. Vex drew the hood of his gray cloak lower, concealing his missing eye, while Edda twisted into the shadows until the maid vanished down the hall.

"The last time we had true peace on this island was centuries ago," the councilman was saying, "when Argrid brought unity to the conflicting immigrant groups that settled here—"

"Nay heard guards outside her room mention her by name," Edda assured him. Spots of pink touched her pale cheeks. "Just because Ben wasn't here doesn't mean this mission won't—"

Vex shoved by her. "Won't be a complete waste?" he snapped. "Yeah, we didn't find my cousin. We weren't able to save the people scheduled to burn today. But here's hoping we free Kari Andreu—that'll fix our problems."

A sack of galles had bought Vex and Edda access to the list of prisoners due to be burned today after the councilman finished his speech. Ben's name hadn't been on it, but eleven other people's names were—and defensors had them lined up at the base of the councilman's platform, watched by a crowd, with no way for Edda and Vex to save them.

Part of Vex hadn't expected to find his cousin, just as he hadn't at the last three burnings he, Edda, and Nayeli had scouted. Ben had made himself a traitor after helping Vex and Lu try to escape his father's ship two weeks ago, but he was still the Crown Prince of Argrid. Elazar wouldn't let priests kill his son like a common criminal. He'd make an example of him instead.

Even so, Vex didn't stop scouting the burnings. Ben had to be *somewhere*.

But god, it'd only been two weeks, and Vex was exhausted to the bone.

Edda caught up to him. Vex expected her to punch him in the shoulder for being irritable, but she walked next to him in silence as if he was a brittle creature. Which pissed him off.

"Threats darkened Grace Loray's shore only when the stream raider syndicates rose against Argrid," said the councilman. "What we perceived as aggression from Argrid was in fact defensors countering the attacks from stream raiders. All this time, we blamed the Argridians when they were as much victim as Grace Loray. The true enemy, the cause of our combined ills, is the manipulative, evil stream raider syndicates."

ARGRID IS EVIL, Vex screamed in his head. *ARGRID IS THE ENEMY, YOU LYING SACK OF CROCODILE SHIT.*

When Grace Loray was discovered centuries ago, it became a free-for-all settlers' paradise. People from the five Mainland countries had come, filled it up, and lived in moderate tolerance until Argrid decided to seize control and attempted to regulate its magic. To counter Argrid's forceful claim, immigrants from the other four countries had each formed syndicates to protect their own.

They had been right to. Argrid had tightened its grip on Grace Loray, outlawing the magic plants that grew in the island's waterways and burning anyone who disagreed with the Church's doctrine. Rebels had fought off Argrid and instituted a democracy—but even that failed when Argrid infiltrated the Grace Lorayan government.

Now Argrid was back. Instead of forcing its standards of purity and magic-abstinence on the whole island, it had singled out one group: stream raiders. Lawless thieves hated by any who weren't raiders themselves. Which made them perfect unifying scapegoats.

"Raiders hoard deadly magic," the councilmember continued to the all-too-silent crowd. Why weren't they screaming in fury? Why weren't they *outraged*? "Raiders pillage and destroy in the name of defiance for defiance's sake. Soon, you will not have to live in fear. The Council has allied with

Argrid to purge Grace Loray in pursuit of our joint goal: a war on raiders."

Vex's lungs swelled. Variations of this weak-ass speech had introduced every execution he and his crew had infiltrated these past two weeks, as though any words could diminish the horror of people burning to death.

But *people* weren't burning, not this time. *Raiders* were burning.

A spasm swept over Vex and he stumbled. His Shaking Sickness spells were getting harder to hide, as though his body knew his one chance at a cure had been stabbed to death on the deck of the *Astuto*.

The thought of Lu hit him like scalding water, and he caught himself on a window frame. Beyond his trembling fingers, a cloudless blue sky capped the island's tangle of deep green jungle. Breaks in the trees spoke of the rivers that wound across the island, with long plumes of steam rising over boats. Below was the castle's garden.

Edda put her hand on his shoulder. "You all right?"

This was the place he and Lu had escaped from weeks ago. He had to be standing right above the window he'd yanked open and jumped out with Teo on his back. Lu had been downright furious at him for bringing the six-year-old along, but what else could he have done? She had to admit that the journey had been good for the kid—

Vex scratched at the rough indigo sleeve of his stolen servant's uniform. *Good.* Sure. If *good* meant Teo sitting in a shack in Port Mesi-Teab. Since Vex had come back without Lu two weeks ago, the only person Teo had spoken to had been Edda. But when Vex asked her what he said, she'd told him, *"He's a kid. He doesn't know how to deal with what's going on."*

Vex's heart throbbed and he shook off Edda's hand. "I'm *fine*. Let's go."

Edda gave him a look of disbelief. She fiddled with the Budwig Bean and her face got distant, as though she was listening to a voice echo down a tunnel. "We're on the third floor now. Servant's hall on the south side." A pause. "Second door? Which—oh."

Nayeli poked her head through a door, stray black curls bouncing in rebellion from the beige knit cap of her own servant's uniform. She looked at Vex, the sympathy in her eyes saying Edda had told her, at some point, that they hadn't found Ben. But she didn't press for details— wouldn't, around Cansu. The fact that Vex was Argridian royalty wouldn't go over well among stream raiders, so as far as anyone else knew, Vex was just looking for his cousin. Not his cousin, the Crown Prince of Argrid.

Cansu pushed her way into the hall. "Two guards outside her room. Easy to eliminate."

"Eliminate?" Vex gawked. "Stand down, Cansu. No bloodshed if we can help it."

"We need to take out as many enemies as we can when we have the chance. You know Argrid wouldn't hesitate to stick knives in our backs."

"We aren't Argrid," Vex snapped. "And we aren't your raiders, either. No killing."

Cansu's golden skin reddened. "You gave us the castle's layout. You gave us the *basics* of the plan. But don't you dare go getting it into your head that you're in charge of this mission."

"Oh, and you are?"

"You bet your unaligned ass I am."

White-hot loathing descended over Vex. This was why he'd never joined a syndicate—he wasn't about to follow orders with no questions asked. On a good day, he'd have laid into Cansu until someone—probably he—ended up bleeding. But with the added fury and grief and terror of Elazar's takeover, Vex couldn't have stopped himself.

Nayeli could stop him, though. She shot forward as he opened his mouth, and one hard look from her sent his insults sinking back down his throat.

"So help me," she started, "I've had enough of you two and your verbal pissing contests. Cansu's in charge because we're using her syndicate's resources, but gods damn it, we aren't killing anyone. Now let's get Kari before I change my mind on that last bit and *kill both of you*."

Cansu flicked her short flop of dark hair out of her eyes and plodded back through the door.

Vex stayed long enough to sulk at Nayeli. "Sorry," he mumbled.

She should've rolled her eyes and called him an idiot for challenging Cansu. But she gave him the same look that Edda wore, one filled with apology and sorrow.

Vex stomped after Cansu. Enough of this. Enough *pain*. He couldn't handle it.

Tall windows lit an ornate hall of marble and gold. Cansu stood over the collapsed bodies of two soldiers outside a closed door.

"Cansu! Goddamn it—"

"They're only unconscious." Cansu waved her fist. "Stop. Questioning. Me."

Vex snarled at her, but Nayeli slid between them. "Gods, *stop*." Her dark eyes went to Vex and she motioned at the door. "You want to be the one to—"

"Yeah." No. But he walked up to it and tried the handle. Locked. Which he made quick work of with picks from Cansu, and when the gold-lined door opened, he took a step inside—

Something iron-hard swung him around and trapped his neck in a vise grip.

Vex yelped, but the sound weakened into a choked gargle.

"Wait!" Nayeli shot into the room after him. "Kari, right? We're friends of your daughter! Let him go—gods, now I see where Lu gets her temper."

"Adeluna?" The grip released. "How do you know her? Why are you here?"

Vex stumbled away, clutching his neck, half certain it was indented now.

"Rescuing you," Cansu said as though it should've been obvious. She shut the door and marched across the room to yank open one of the balcony doors.

A gust of hot lake air swirled in, along with sensations that reminded Vex of memories from another life. Smoke. Fire. Screams.

"Today we commit the following raiders unto the Pious God's mercy" came a different voice. A priest, likely, to oversee the proper disposal of heretics. "Vina Uzun; Branden Axel—"

He kept reading off names. Kari must've recognized one, because she pressed a hand to her chest, rocking forward.

"Can we get out that way?" Nayeli asked Cansu, as if people weren't dying.

"The escape boat's in the lake," Cansu said. "You have that Aerated Blossom?"

No one saw Vex falter. He'd planned their way *into* the castle—steal servant uniforms and sneak in with the crowd that had come to see the burning—but all he'd known of their way *out* was that an escape boat would be waiting. But this was how Cansu planned to get to it—she'd loved his story of how Lu had used Blossoms to jump off the Schilly-Leto waterfall. Vex had been terrified. But Lu—she'd been fearless.

The crowd in the courtyard let loose a pained wail. Vex

felt a blossom of relief that the burning repulsed them, despite their silent, dangerous agreement earlier. Their complacency about Argrid's seizure of power was surface level.

"Who are you?" Kari demanded. Her face showed her calculations just as Lu's did. "Stream raiders? From the syndicate associated with Tuncay? Are you here on Cansu Darzi's orders? Has my daughter become entangled with the Tuncian syndicate?"

"We're not here on Cansu's orders," Cansu said. She turned from the balcony. "I *am* Cansu. The absurdity of a raider Head rescuing a Senior Councilmember is not lost on me, but that's why we're here. Because your daughter, along with these idiots"—she gestured at Nayeli, Vex, and Edda—"convinced me that the best way to stop Argrid from overtaking the island is to unite the Council and raiders and everyone who calls Grace Loray home. Figured Kari the Wave would be the most capable person to do that."

The Argridians had put Kari under house arrest—but she meant a lot to Grace Loray, so they hadn't killed her. She was Kari the Wave, a nickname she'd earned during the revolution because of her guerrilla-style ambushes that had whittled away Argrid's forces. The only reason the rebels had beaten Argrid the first time was because Kari had gotten the volatile, bickering stream raiders to ally with each other, becoming a force too powerful for Argrid to defeat.

Between border skirmishes, burning each other's steamboats, and other messier crimes, relations among the raiders had always been tense. Vex knew, for instance, that Cansu hated the "thieving" Grozdan syndicate with "the intensity of nigrika"—a Tuncian spice so hot Vex hadn't been able to taste anything for a solid two days after he'd eaten a pinch. If the raider syndicates had any hope of unifying to stop Elazar again, they'd need an intermediary, like Kari.

But the deeper reason Vex had suggested freeing Kari was because he knew Lu would've wanted it. It was that simple. That selfish.

Vex's vision faded. He lost sight of the room in favor of a sword, shining with Lu's blood, dripping scarlet circles on the deck of a ship—

"Other councilmembers can help." Kari composed herself, spine straight, again like Lu. "They are locked in rooms along this hall. They can be trusted to—"

"Trust? What do you know about *trust*?"

Kari snapped a look at Vex. Edda and Nayeli did, too, but Edda's focus went back to Kari, and Vex could see her thoughts spin. Should she intervene?

Vex didn't care. He hadn't meant to speak. But here he was, staring at a person who was as responsible for Lu's death as the man who'd stabbed her.

"Devereux Bell." Kari's fingers curled into fists. Last she knew, her daughter had freed him from prison and run off with him. "What do you—"

"Who do you think you can *trust*? Your husband?"

"Vex," Edda tried.

Kari's face went gray. "I only recently learned of my husband's deceit—"

"Stop acting so goddamn proud." Vex's arms shook so hard he had to cross them. "If you'd realized earlier that your own husband was a fucking *spy*, Lu might not be dead."

The last word hung on his tongue. He wanted to say it again, let it stick to someone else.

Kari's lips parted. "What did you say?"

He saw Lu's body slip to the deck of the ship. Her eyes searched for him, her face shocked and scared and alone, with just Ben to hold her, because Edda threw Vex overboard.

He'd left Lu. He'd left Ben, too.

"I said she's dead," Vex growled. "Lu's *dead*. Thanks to you and your husband."

Kari dropped onto a chair. Her silence was worse than if she'd started weeping, grief so tangible on her face that a fierce stab of guilt punctured Vex's heart.

"Or maybe you knew about your husband all along," he spat at Kari. "Maybe you're a spy too. Maybe you're glad Lu's gone. You're as guilty as—"

"Paxben!" Edda cried.

Vex's body went stiff. That name from her—that name *at all*—struck him dumb.

Edda grabbed his arm. "You have to stop. You can't drop this on someone!"

"But it was dropped on *me*!"

Vex's scream rebounded, the tremble in his voice from both Shaking Sickness and grief.

Edda's face was broken. Nayeli wiped at her eyes, her gold skin blotchy. If the two of them looked that bad, he must look like hell in human form. Cansu seemed caught between remorse and confusion about why Edda had called Vex *Paxben*.

Booted feet pounded in the hall—soldiers, coming to check on the noise in Kari's room.

Vex rolled his eye shut. *Dumbass*. They were supposed to be on a stealth mission.

Cansu barked a strand of curses in Thuti and shot to the door, dragging behind her furniture to make a barricade. "Nayeli—Blossoms, *now!*"

Edda helped Cansu stack chairs, a table, a curved divan. Nayeli pulled the Aerated Blossoms out of a bag on her belt.

"Vex—" Nayeli started, but he snatched a Blossom from her and stomped to the balcony.

The lake was a straight shot down. The wall of the castle gave way to jagged cliff and blue water, with one of Cansu's steamboats bobbing in the waves. To the left, all Vex could see of the courtyard was the back of the platform, plumes of smoke rising from pyres that were out of sight.

The screaming had stopped.

Cansu braced her body against the furniture barricade. "Andreu—you're first!"

Kari hadn't moved from her straight-backed seat on the chair, her hands poised on the armrests. But as soldiers pushed against the barricade so the furniture peeled across the floor, Kari sprang to her feet, her eyes on Vex as if no one else was there.

Maybe she wanted him to feel her own blame. Maybe she hated him like he hated her.

"No," she stated. "I won't—"

Cansu shouted in frustration and launched herself away from the barricade. She grabbed an Aerated Blossom, thrust it at Kari, and drove her body into the Senior Council-member to send her tumbling over the balcony railing.

Edda and Nayeli objected, but Cansu ignored them. She took Blossoms from Nayeli, left her one, handed another to Edda, and shoved Nayeli backward so hard she sank into the air with only a parting gasp.

The soldiers bellowed a warning. They cracked the door open enough for Vex to see them in the hall—defensors in the Church's navy-and-white uniforms. Alongside them, Vex caught a flash of blond hair. The glint of crocodile skin. Mecht raiders from the syndicate that Elazar had convinced to work with him.

"Go," Cansu ordered Edda.

Vex nodded at her, and she leaped over the railing.

The barricade tumbled, chairs falling across the marble, the divan tipping on its side. Defensors clambered into the room on a sharp cry of victory. Two furiously focused

16

Mecht raiders charged in, crocodiles seeking prey in bloody waters.

Vex dropped to the floor as a bullet pinged off a silver bowl and another lodged in the ceiling. Cansu rolled behind a couch and Vex dove after her, plaster scattering around them. She already had a pistol out and she cocked it, her eyes on the balcony.

"I'll cover you," she said.

"Like hell you will. Nay'll kill me if you—"

"STOP ARGUING." Cansu swung onto her knees and fired back at the soldiers. "For once in your life, you idiot, *listen!* Go—I'll be right behind you!"

Vex looked at the soldiers, clustered behind an overturned table. He cursed and pointed at Cansu. "I'm not making a habit of listening to you," he told her and scrambled away.

He swore he heard her laugh as bullets whistled past.

Vex didn't process how close he was to getting shot until he heaved himself over the balcony and wished he *had* gotten shot. It would've been less awful than *free-falling to his death.*

A scream tore from his lungs. The tang of salt and sweat from the crowded port consumed Vex as he fell, down, down, down, the blue of the lake opening wide to swallow him.

The Aerated Blossom made it to his lips. His body absorbed the flight-giving gases in the few seconds it took to inhale them, yanking him to a brief pause. The gases released, and he dropped into the lake with a soft splash.

Hands hauled him onto a steamboat. Vex hacked water from his lungs and straightened his eye patch as he looked up at the balcony. Rocks held the castle in the air, and the balcony—terrifyingly high up, how had he jumped that?—stayed empty for one second, two, three—

Cansu appeared, bent halfway over the railing. One hand braced on the stone, the other reached down, fingers spread toward the boat. Toward Nayeli.

Defensors swarmed the balcony.

Vex couldn't breathe.

Cansu teetered forward, airborne. She was going to make it—

Defensors caught her around the waist and hauled her, kicking and snarling, out of sight.

Even if Vex hadn't been on a boat, the world would've shifted.

"Cansu!" Nayeli tore to her feet, dripping water across the deck. "CANSU!"

"Nay—stop!" Edda grabbed her. "Don't draw their attention! We knew this could happen—she's alive, she's a prisoner, but she's—"

"A prisoner of *Elazar*," Nayeli clarified, trembling.

Vex wasn't sure how he had room for worry alongside his grief. He stayed crouched on the deck, staring up at Nayeli, realization sinking in a slow shudder down his arms.

He'd left Cansu. Like Ben. Like Lu.

"He'll kill her," Nayeli said to Edda, dark eyes red with tears. The raiders who'd been driving the steamboat stayed in the pilothouse, their faces mirroring Nayeli's concern.

"Not immediately."

Behind them, Kari's dark hair stuck to her cheeks, her eyes glassy. She was definitely where Lu got her Tuncian traits—golden brown skin, curly black hair, round dark eyes.

"I heard that Elazar holds most of his captives in Port Camden until he can decide what to do with them," Kari continued, looking to the northeastern jungle. "He only left the Senior Councilmembers here so he could make it look as though the Council had allied with him."

"Are you sure he'd use—" Vex stopped on a hard wince. He'd almost asked, *Are you sure he'd use the Port Camden prison?* But of course Elazar would. The Port Camden prison was one of the few places on the island that Argrid had held until the war's end. It was a fortress.

Nayeli flew to her feet and pointed at the raiders in the pilothouse. "To Port Camden."

"Nay!" Vex shot up. "It's a day's ride to Port Camden. We can't—"

"I'm not leaving her!" Nayeli whirled on Vex, voice raw. "I know you're hurting, and I can't make you not miss Lu. I can't make Ben safe. But I can damn well make sure Cansu doesn't suffer the same fate. I won't lose her."

Did Vex imagine the emphasis she'd put on that last

sentence? *I won't lose her.* He gasped, her words a punch to the stomach. *"I lost them?" I did, damn it, I did.*

"You know that wasn't what I meant."

"No. You're right. I let Lu die. I lost Ben. I left Cansu. It's my fault. Go—go to Port Camden. You're better off without me."

Why was he arguing? He owed Nayeli, but he couldn't feel anything.

No. That wasn't true. He felt anger. He felt rage. He felt hatred. And he loved Nayeli enough that she was one of the only people he could show his emotions.

Nayeli screamed. No words, just noise, and it scraped Vex clean out.

"He could be there" came Edda's soft voice. "Ben. He could be in that prison."

Vex closed his eye. If he hadn't been so set on being furious, he might've seen that too.

"Damn it," he muttered, tapping his fist to his forehead.

"Why?" Nayeli shot at him. "That's good, right? It's worth it to you to go now."

Vex's brain yelled at him to stop being an ass, but he ignored himself. "No, it's *not* good, because our best chance of getting into that prison is to talk to Nate."

Edda groaned. Nayeli did too. "Shit."

"Nathaniel Blaise." Vex looked at Kari. "The Head of the Emerdian raider syndicate. The prison's in his territory, built by his people. He's our best chance of making it in."

Kari nodded, her blank expression not giving away her thoughts.

Like Lu, Vex thought. His chest burned.

Nayeli fished in her pocket and drew out the second Budwig Bean—one that communicated with Port Mesi-Teab. She started to put it in her ear, but paused.

"Are we going, *Captain*?" she snapped.

Their mission was to bring Kari to Port Mesi-Teab so she could unite the syndicates and they could stop Argrid from destroying Grace Loray. But Ben could be in that prison. And Cansu was one of the raider Heads they needed to lead her people against Argrid.

Vex exhaled, drained from the day. From the week. From the whole damn year.

He looked at the raiders in the pilothouse. "To Port Camden."

2

COARSE ROPE BOUND Lu's wrists to the back of a chair. She sagged forward, each breath a wave of knives. Sweat and humidity glazed her skin in a velvet film.

Stay strong, she told herself. *Hold on. Mama and Papa will save me—*

"Croxy, sir? Make her go a little wild," a voice offered in Argridian.

Lu quivered, her raw throat burning on a swallow. Croxy, the berserker plant.

"No. I want her to break." Frustration roughened the new voice with borderline loss of control. Booted feet stepped into Lu's downcast vision. "Bring Lazonade."

Panic crawled through her. *No, please, no—*

Fingers dragged her chin up. Night blurred the far reaches of this rickety wooden room, but a single circle of light drenched Lu from above and created a halo around Milo Ibarra.

He scowled, face glistening. His uniform was sweat stained and ripped at the shoulder, a product of the battle to take this rebel safe house. When he had led his defensors here, they had wanted secrets, maps, plans—anything to quell the revolution on their Grace Loray colony. What they had found was a resilient twelve-year-old girl.

A defensor appeared at Milo's side and held out a vial filled with green paste. "You won't break," the defensor told her. "That's why you're my Lulu-bean. You can keep a secret so well it's as if you've taken a magic plant that sealed your lips."

Lu jerked back in the chair, ripping herself out of Milo's grimy fingers. The defensor wasn't a faceless Argridian soldier—it was Tom. Her father.

She had known he would come to save her. She didn't feel relieved, though. She felt . . . furious.

The world contracted, and when it released, the safe house became the deck of a ship. Defensors crowded the planks, rifles blasting, and steamboats fired magic from the sea below.

Lu staggered at the sudden discord of battle. The chair and her bindings were gone, and she spun, watching friends and defensors alike fall in the raging war.

"No," Lu forced out. "No! Get off my island! *Leave me alone!*"

That plea undid her, a croaking scream from the moment she had first heard rifles fired on Grace Loray.

I want Argrid off my island. I want to live here in peace.

But after all the things I have done, came Lu's helpless thought, *I don't deserve peace.*

Lu turned again, seeking escape. A figure caught her. Too late, she recognized Milo, and he drove his sword into her gut.

Her eyes flew open. The ship vanished. The battle, the screams, Milo—they rushed away as Lu bolted upright, gulping in thick air. Her hand flew to her stomach, not finding a wound or bandage under her baggy linen shirt. But the tightness of dried sweat on her skin, the roughness of a blanket over her—these feelings meant she was *here.* She was alive.

How? Milo had stabbed her. She should be dead.

Cautiously, Lu lifted her eyes, expecting to see Milo near her. But she was alone, on a cot tucked against a pale stone wall. The angle of a window farther down didn't let her see outside, but it filtered in white light—morning, or the wake of it. Wooden floorboards stretched into a room clogged with *things*: crates and barrels and tables overflowing with papers, vials, mortars, pestles, and more that she couldn't see. A laboratory?

Lu slid her legs to the floor and forced herself to shakily stand. Metal clanked next to her scuffed boots—a manacle that fed to a chain bolted to the wall.

She was a prisoner, then. How long? Where?

She felt one answer in the way her body ached from immobility. Her empty stomach grumbled angrily; her throat scratched with sand and dust.

Too long. She could be anywhere. Anything could have been done to her.

Revulsion clouded her vision. She wavered, wiping sweaty palms on her black breeches, wrestling each breath until she managed one long, calm inhale.

Where was Vex? Ben? Nayeli, Edda, Gunnar? She couldn't fall apart, not yet. She would figure out where she was. She was, impossibly, healed. She could escape.

The window was too far for her chain length to reach. What crates were close by, blocking her cot from the rest of the room, were sealed, and no stray magic sat on the tables. She grabbed the only weapon-like item she could find: metal tongs. If they failed as a weapon, she could use them to pick the lock on her ankle.

"We should increase their dosages."

Lu stiffened. The voice speaking in Argridian came from two places at once: from behind the crates and barrels, farther into the room; and from her nightmares. Milo.

Panic's numbness became a shield as, step by gentle step, Lu rounded the crates, the matted tail of her braid brushing her neck.

Milo, along with half a dozen Argridians, stood on the far side of the room over three more cots filled with either sleeping or unconscious patients. Raiders, Lu guessed, and she let a part of herself relax that she didn't know them. One had blond hair; another wore a crocodile-skin vest. Raiders from the Mecht syndicate.

The Mecht syndicate's Head, Ingvar Pilkvist, had stockpiled magic plants for Elazar's experiments. Were the boxes around her from his stores? Lu couldn't be in Backswamp, though—this building was too solid, unlike the dilapidated, swamp-worn structures there, and the light through the window was too pure.

"Increase the dosage," Milo repeated, impatient. He was polished to gleaming, black hair neatly tied back, blue military uniform pressed into straight lines. A perfect facade, the way the lush magenta leaves of the Digestive Death plant contrasted with its deadly poison. "Menesia is one of the only plants that is permanent on its own. Something will unlock eventually."

Confusion was a welcome counter to Lu's fear. Menesia—the memory-erasing plant?

Vex had spoken of Menesia when they had spilled their souls to each other in the *Rapid Meander*'s pilothouse. Remembering him, his outstretched hand toward her—Lu reeled, willing herself to focus on what he had said. That Elazar gave some of his victims Menesia to make them forget he had people experiment on them in his as yet failed quest for permanent magic.

Small doses of Menesia could wipe recent memories.

Larger doses, and the taker could lose a year; enough, and they could forget how to eat, how to speak.

Lu stayed behind a stack of crates, her breathing shallow. Milo was right—Menesia was, more or less, permanent, in that takers did not regain their memory over time. These people were discussing Elazar's magic experiments.

"Similar tests have not produced the desired results," said a priest in long brown robes. "We could combine Menesia with other plants to see if it imparts permanence to other magics."

"Prepare it," Milo snapped. "With double the Menesia dosage. Force the permanence."

Another Argridian rose from the bedside of an unconscious raider. "I know my daughter," he said. "If Adeluna figured out the cure for Shaking Sickness, and that cure is tied to permanent magic, then it is about precision, not quantity."

Lu's frail, beaten body couldn't fight the rage and sorrow that crashed into her.

Tom was here.

Tom and Kari had first sent Lu out to spy for the revolutionaries when she was ten years old. A child could go unnoticed, so she had obeyed to help her parents save her home.

When Tom started teaching her how to fight, it had been *"for her own protection."* She had killed two men in self-defense. But once, Tom asked her to follow him into the jungle and pull a trigger on *"an enemy. You're so good, Lulu-bean. You're doing so well."*

But while on Elazar's ship, Milo had admitted that Tom was his informant. Tom had been on the inside of most of the revolutionaries' plans during the war, and after they won—thanks to Kari's tactical prowess, moves Tom hadn't known about—he had been a trusted member of the Council. Lu had done terrible things at his request, secrets stolen and lives taken.

And it had all been for the enemy.

Lu swallowed her tight knot of agony. She had loved her father. She *did* love him. And in the five years since the war, Tom had been on Grace Loray with Kari and Lu, working to do good things for this island. He couldn't be loyal to Argrid.

Was it too much to hope that he was a double agent?

Milo glared at Tom now, arms folded across the glinting medals on his jacket. The other Argridians—priests and monxes, some defensors—fell silent, conceding to this tension.

"How do you know, Andreu?" Milo snapped. "You may have the king convinced that you were unaware your daughter healed herself of Shaking Sickness, but I'm not fooled."

Yes, Lu told herself. *See? Tom didn't turn me over to Elazar after the war—*

Tom gave a narrow squint. "Are you calling our Eminence King a fool?"

Milo hesitated. The other Argridians gave shocked looks.

But Lu hooked onto something else. "*Your* Eminence King?"

The priests' robes wafted as they spun. The defensors' hands flew to pistols. But Lu didn't flinch, too focused on her father.

Tom smiled, a blush increasing the warmth of his skin's Argridian redness. "Adeluna."

"The Eminence King will want her to start working, Andreu," Milo said, words twisted in a sickening pleasure. "Prove her worth."

His implication was heavy. *I'll incentivize her.*

Lu couldn't breathe. But Tom didn't look at Milo, didn't move his eyes away from Lu.

"Give us a moment, would you?" he said. "Let me speak to her alone."

A defensor scoffed. "Not without protection, sir."

"She won't harm me."

She wouldn't have to—because it was a lie. His allegiance to Argrid. It was a *lie.*

Lu tightened her fingers around the tongs, the metal biting into her palm.

A moment longer, and the priests relented, brown robes shushing on the floor as they left. The defensors went next. Last, Milo.

"I'll inform the Eminence King that she is awake," he said, his eyes sliding from Tom to Lu. His sickening grin lost its amusement, darkening with anger. Lu bit her tongue to stop from cowering under the realization that she was at this man's mercy. Again.

But he left. A door opened, then shut with a *click*, and she was alone with Tom.

Tom spoke before she could. "You shouldn't be up yet, sweetheart," he said in Grace Lorayan. Hearing that language from him confirmed her hope—he was loyal to this island. He was loyal to *her*. "You healed in minutes, but the internal damage was difficult to determine. The king let the prince save you, though we weren't sure of the extent his potion would—"

Ben's healing potion? Lu gawked. She didn't even feel sore. Ben's potion was powerful, and that was more terrifying than encouraging.

"Ben." Lu anchored. "He's here?"

Tom bobbed his head toward the floor. "Imprisoned. He agreed to make his healing tonic to save you, but he refuses to work on permanent magic."

Lu cast her eyes to the closed door, barely visible over the crates. "What is the plan?" she asked in a low whisper. "Is Kari waiting to help us get out? You've coordinated it with her, all this time, haven't you? How does Elazar not suspect?"

Wonder crept into her tone, that her father had upheld such a miraculous dual life.

The scarlet on Tom's cheeks deepened. He sighed. "Lulu-bean. Let me explain."

The fragile remains of Lu's foundation started to crack. "You're loyal to Grace Loray," she stated. Begged.

"My desires have never changed," Tom said. It wasn't confirmation. It wasn't anything but pain, and Lu couldn't breathe. "I want unity. Which is what you want too, and your mother. I was a spy long before I met Kari—she was a mission that . . . changed for me. I knew she wouldn't see the alignment in our goals. Yes, I misled you both. But I am still your father."

In a crash of grief, Lu's childlike hope dissolved. Tom wasn't a double agent, feigning allegiance to Elazar as he spied on Argrid for Grace Loray. He was a traitor to this island. To Kari. To Lu. To everything they had built together.

It was true. Her father had betrayed her.

Tom motioned at the Mecht prisoners behind him. "Do you know the history of Grace Loray? The Grace himself, Xoel Loray? The Church anointed him after his death to represent the Pious God's pillar of purity. He warned of magic's corruption and devoted his life to balancing magic with the Pious God's will. But we failed Xoel Loray, and this land became overrun. Criminals, disorder. This island needs to be cleansed."

Lu only half heard him. A tear slipped down her cheek. "Who were they? The people I killed for you."

Tom wavered. "People who had threatened to sell Argrid's secrets to the rebels."

Enemies who could have ended the war. *People* who could have ended the war.

"Argridian traitors," Lu stated, angling the words at him. *What you should have been.*

"You were not meant to kill two of them, sweetheart," Tom told her, his voice soft as though he could be comforting. "My superiors requested it of me. You were only meant to lure them out so I could uncover if they had betrayed Argrid. That you did kill them was . . . fate."

"Fate?" Anger spiked through her grief, refreshingly powerful. "Fate for me to have blood on my hands?"

"The Pious God chose you." He closed the space between them and reached out, fingertips on her cheek. "I never realized what you had done after the war—to heal yourself of Shaking Sickness! The Pious God is wise. If you can do that, you can unlock the rest of magic's secrets. You can make magic permanent the same way that the Mechts made their fire-wielding Eye of the Sun permanent. With it, the Eminence King will have the power to rise against the Devil and stop the evil that has taken this island."

The metal tongs in her hand grew heavier.

This man didn't sound like the father who had raised her. He sounded like the fanatical Church priests who had spewed doctrine across the island during the revolution.

Exhaustion plummeted through Lu's body. She had tried to stop war from coming. She had freed Vex from prison, paid him to find Milo Ibarra, traveled from New Deza to

Port Mesi-Teab to Backswamp to the ocean, to keep Grace Loray in a state of peace. But that peace had started cracking the moment the revolution ended, weakened by her own father and by the Council's refusal to accept that raiders were worthy citizens of the island, not criminal pests.

War was already here. It had never left. Grace Loray would return to being an island of burnings and mission-prisons, where people were guilty until they screamed their innocence under torture. If Elazar's defensors had permanent magic to make them inhumanly strong and fast and healthy, no one would be able to escape. Elazar could sort the world as he pleased.

The last time Argrid had threatened Grace Loray, Lu had relied on her parents to fight back. But this time? Would Kari alone be enough to stop Elazar—to stop *Tom*? What would it take to bring peace to Grace Loray? Why was peace such a difficult, impossible desire?

Lu leveled her eyes at Tom, not sure her heart was beating. "I will not help Elazar."

Tom drew his hand off her face. "Let us start small. You are brilliant, sweetheart, to be the only known person to survive Shaking Sickness. Tell me how you did it."

His belief in her clashed with a similar memory: watching Fatemah in the Port Mesi-Teab sanctuary cooking Budwig Beans to increase their potency. Lu had been confident in her knowledge of magic—and Fatemah had stripped her down to a questioning mass of uncertainty.

Lu bit onto the answer. That Shaking Sickness wasn't a disease, but a body's reaction to too much magic, and undoing it was as simple as taking the counter plants—which was what Vex needed. How long had she been a prisoner? How much worse had his condition gotten?

"No," she told Tom. "Even if I was willing, I am no longer so narrow-minded as to think that I could make permanent magic. The Mechts, the Tuncians—there is knowledge that I will never—"

Tom cocked his head. "The Mechts made Eye of the Sun permanent—we know that, and have spent years trying to learn their secret. But the Tuncians? What have they done?"

Lu's grip on the tongs slackened. Dread left a sour trail in her throat.

She hadn't meant to draw attention to them. The process Fatemah had used to intensify Budwig Beans had nothing to do with permanent magic . . . did it?

Lu pinched her lips in a thin line. No more. She had indulged Tom long enough.

He took another step back, face graying. "You were never supposed to be so defiant. Your mother is to blame. You're so like her."

His mention of Kari sent heartache stabbing through Lu's chest.

"I *tried*, Lulu-bean," Tom said. "Remember, sweetheart, that I tried to reach you first, and I am sorry, so sorry, for what must be done. It shouldn't have to happen."

Tom had spoken such words to her on the floor of the safe house in Port Camden, after rebels had chased Milo and his defensors from the building.

"I'm so sorry, Lulu-bean. I'm sorry this happened to you. It shouldn't have happened—"

He was putting the blame on her. *It shouldn't have happened— you should have been obedient. You should have been better.*

Lu's throat cinched closed. Reason told her that Tom was insane—but the pieces of her that loved him welled with questions.

What can I do, Papa? How can I be better? How can I bring you back to us?

The door, hidden from Lu by the stacks of crates, creaked open.

She tucked the metal tongs into her sleeve and twisted her back to a table littered with papers and books. Titles on the spines gleamed with embossed ink. *The Virtue of Grace Neus. The Holy Doctrine of the Pious God. Sermons of Grace Biel.*

Elazar swept into the room. Indigo robes spilled around him, gold trim sparkling like hand-woven treasure. Behind him, Milo watched Elazar with a masked expression.

Elazar surveyed Tom before turning his gaze to Lu.

Milo numbed her. Elazar peeled her raw.

"She refused," Elazar guessed in Argridian.

Tom winced. That was why Lu had woken up here, why Ben was imprisoned. This had been a chance for her to save herself.

Nausea flooded Lu, that Tom had thought she would give in to him.

"She has provided an idea," Tom said, straightening. "About new methods to try."

Lu's eyes widened. But resistance would confirm that there was validity to her slipup in mentioning Tuncians. She swayed, caught with inaction.

"New methods?" Milo frowned. He gathered himself and bowed to Elazar. "My king, permit me to begin testing these . . . new methods. I will not fail you."

Elazar's eyes stayed fixed on Lu. Exhaustion swarmed her again, thirst and hunger and a bright, disintegrating reminder of how alone she was.

Ben was here, somewhere. But what of Vex? Anyone else?

"Correct, Ibarra. You will not fail me again." Elazar pierced the last word. Milo cringed. But Elazar swept past him and turned his heavy focus to Tom. "Andreu. The Pious God anointed your daughter for his mighty plans. But what role are you to play now?"

Tom stared. "My king?"

"Perhaps your daughter's penchant for magic came from you." Elazar's eyes went back to Lu. "If your daughter fails to comply further, the Pious God may bless you in her stead."

Tom's mouth popped open. Milo rose upright, his face purple-red with anger.

A month ago, Lu would have laughed at the possibility that Tom could figure out permanent magic. But as she watched him now, the way he bowed again, thanking Elazar—she didn't know this man. She didn't know what he was capable of.

Elazar waved to someone at the door. "Put Adeluna with my son. Let them consider repentance together."

Defensors moved around the clutter and made for her. Terror scoured through Lu.

"My king," Milo tried again, "allow me to reason with her. I am certain I can extract—"

"Enough of your desperation," Elazar snapped. "The Pious God is not yet ready for you to regain his love. Should I banish you back to Argrid entirely? I left our country in a state of constant vigil until this war is complete, and the priests in Deza would happily guide you in prayer. Is that what you wish, Lieutenant Ibarra? To be removed from this war until it is won?"

The way Milo recoiled revealed his thoughts. To leave Grace Loray, no chance for glory? "No, Eminence. I will strive for . . . for *patience* until the Pious God sees use for me."

Milo's words were a snarl as defensors unlocked Lu's ankle manacle. *Lieutenant Ibarra.* Elazar had demoted Milo. Because of her? Which meant the glare Milo sent her way held more than just hatred for how she had resisted him in the past. It held the desire for revenge.

"I am sorry, so sorry, for what must be done," Tom had said.

"No." The plea came out of Lu on its own, and she dropped her heels into the stone floor, struggling with the defensors. Tom couldn't lock her away— "No, Papa!"

The name burned her throat, but it had its intended effect: Tom flinched and looked at Elazar. Would he help her? Would he try?

But Elazar was focused on Lu, every wrinkle of disgust intentional and deadly. "The whole of this island is as you are, Adeluna Andreu: unaware of the fact that you are drowning. Grace Loray's evil has plagued the world for too long, and Argrid has suffered because we have not stopped you. But I will cleanse this island from the mountains to the sea, and I will bring Argrid back to a state of prosperity in Grace Loray's ashes."

Lu went slack against the defensors, overwhelmed by the certainty in Elazar's eyes. He was a madman—but he was infectious, an unavoidable storm. "We will fight you," she managed. "We won't stop."

Elazar smiled. Even that looked malicious. "I am well aware of what the Devil's corruption will compel you to do. You can resist, you can wail, you can sabotage my efforts, but I have planned for every action you might take."

He stepped away, facing the unconscious Mecht raiders— no, one was awake now, sitting upright, staring vacantly at the blanket across his lap.

The man didn't move. Didn't fight. Didn't react to the Argridians around him.

Elazar placed a hand on the raider's head and nodded at

the defensors. They pushed Lu toward the door, Elazar's voice carrying as she went, helpless.

"This war will be different, Adeluna. It will not be a war at all, in fact—it will be a lesson on the blessings that come with obedience."

3

A MONXE SLID the day's supplies through the bars and retreated with tapping footsteps. Ben assumed it was breakfast—time had trickled through his fingers since Elazar had moved him, Gunnar, and Lu off the *Astuto* two weeks ago. Maybe longer.

Ben waited, arm bent under his head, eyes closed. Distantly, a door thudded, the footsteps swallowed behind it. Silence.

Then, "Thaid fuilor mauth? All is well?"

Ben smiled weakly.

Gunnar had been the only other captive with Ben on the *Astuto* while Lu writhed between life and death. When Elazar moved them to this prison, keeping Lu in that makeshift laboratory, Ben had a feeling of solidarity in seeing Gunnar across the hall. Not that they could talk much, with defensors and monxes around. But Gunnar had begun asking a question, first in his language, then in Argridian:

"Thaid fuilor mauth? All is well?"

At night, in the morning, after monxes came and demanded Ben repent. Ben had responded, even when he wasn't sure. He needed it to be true.

Ben rolled to his feet. The bed shrieked under him and he gripped the thin edge, bearing down on it to stay grounded. Floor-to-ceiling bars kept him in this cell, but across the hall, another set of bars marked a different cell for Gunnar, who hung from the rafters on chains.

Within hours of getting here, Gunnar had been deemed *"in need of restraint."* Two defensors still had bandages where Gunnar had singed them with his Eye of the Sun powers.

Gunnar fixed his furious blue eyes on the empty hall, his lips moving in a silent whisper. He swayed, shirt billowing and boots dragging against the stones. Once, they had been Argridian servants' clothes, ivory with navy and gold stripes—imprisonment had ripped and stained them beyond repair.

"Thaid fuilor mauth," Ben repeated. "All is—" His voice caught. "The monxe didn't feed you." He hadn't heard Gunnar's cell unlock.

Gunnar gave a sad imitation of a shrug. "A new punishment?"

Ben stood and crossed to the supplies that had been left for him. A bowl of porridge, a piece of bread; a fresh waste bucket; and a pitcher with water that glistened in the light of the torches between the hall's empty cells. Ben's gut twisted.

The defensors made him drink the whole pitcher. Every drop. Something about this prison was . . . *wrong*. The moment Ben and Gunnar had set foot in it, the walls themselves had seemed to move. What other prisoners they had passed, in wings close to this one, acted drugged, screaming nonsense, some with lolling tongues or wide, unseeing eyes.

Day by day, that delirium had crept over Gunnar, making him whisper to himself or cry out in his dreams. But it hadn't affected Ben. Magic, though he didn't know what or how. Likely Narcotium Creeper, the hallucinogen. Or Croxy, the plant that caused bouts of rage. The defensors were drugging the prisoners but gave Ben the antidote so he would work for his father and continue experiments to make permanent magic.

The door up the hall slammed open. Booted feet thudded in a sprint. Ben pushed back a step, eyes on Gunnar in an unspoken agreement of preparation.

Preparation for what? To *do* what? Hopelessness smelled of ash and smoke.

Ignoring Gunnar, Jakes jerked to a stop outside Ben's cell and ripped off his defensor hat. Sweat sheened his face, panic paling his bronze skin and making him look almost human. But Ben knew to see through the facade—beneath the emotion lay a man who had manipulated Ben's thoughts, his belief, his heart, to help advance Elazar's mad plans.

"Ben," Jakes panted. "You have to repent. We both know you will—do it *now*."

Ben rolled his eyes and tugged on the already unbuttoned collar of his filthy shirt. Weeks ago, it had looked like the blend of silk it was. His breeches, some supple velour; his boots, knee-high and crisp leather. All of it was now no better than the moldy, moth-eaten blanket on his cot.

"My father has resorted to having his defensors beg me? He must be desperate."

Ben's own statement caught him by the heart. If Elazar was desperate enough to have Jakes come to him, *begging*—

"Adeluna?" he rasped. The only time Elazar had allowed him out of this cell had been to give her the healing potion, with Lu's father watching his every move.

Jakes nodded. "She's awake."

Ben exhaled in relief. Jakes, though, stiffened even more.

"I said *she's awake*. You have to give in. This act has gone on long enough."

"It isn't an act. I saved my cousin. I was trying to help Adeluna as well, to free her from the despot who is my father. That is where my allegiance lies. I will not work for Elazar."

"You don't realize what this means," Jakes hissed. "Your father has two of you now—"

The hall filled with more booted feet, the clank of armor,

the steady murmur of prayers. Jakes tugged his hat back on.

Ben processed what Jakes had said. Until now, his imprisonment had been mild. Monxes prayed over him or sang hymns, demanding he repent. Elazar would visit, bemoaning what a disappointment Ben was to him, but he never entered Ben's cell and lifted his hands only to make the Church's symbol. Even so, Elazar's nearness made Ben's old injuries throb. His jaw ached constantly, his body unable to forget what it felt like to question his father.

What Ben had done on the deck of the *Astuto* had surpassed mere questioning—he had outright defied Elazar. And all he had received so far was mind-numbing monotony.

Ben had held his breath every day, waiting for this precise moment.

Lu was awake now. She and Ben—one of them would make permanent magic for Elazar.

One of them was expendable.

Three monxes and two defensors stepped around Jakes, filling the hall with more white-feathered hats and billowing navy tunics showing Argrid's curved *V* and crossed swords. The defensors held Lu, who staggered when they halted, her black hair shifting to reveal eyes bloodshot with the emotions Ben had to stomp out in his own body: fury, terror, disgust, hatred.

Ben braced himself as defensors unlocked his cell and shoved her in. All the empty cells, and Elazar was putting them together?

"The Eminence King reminds you to repent," said a defensor with a bandage around his forehead. He was one Gunnar had burned during their first failure of an escape attempt.

Lu caught herself. The door shut behind her, and the swirling fury in her eyes landed on Ben. Did she blame him for her being at Argrid's mercy, for the horrors his country had committed?

Her brow relaxed. "You're all right?"

Ben managed a smile. "Yes—are you? What—"

The group in the hall hadn't retreated. Jakes stared at the floor, his jaw rippling the short stubble along his chin.

Bumps of dread prickled the skin on the back of Ben's neck. Elazar wasn't with this group—surely he would dole out his son's punishment. But when Ben had been younger, before he had learned to hide his defiance, Elazar had given Ben's monxe tutors permission to treat him as any other pupil. To do whatever it took to banish insolence in favor of purity.

These weeks of monotony had been a ruse to lull Ben into ease.

He staggered back, heart thundering. He had endured beatings as a child—he was stronger now, harder, he could survive this, he could survive—

But the defensors turned their backs to him. And faced Gunnar.

Jakes didn't look at Ben as the defensors opened Gunnar's

cell. The one with the bandage had a brutal whip coiled at his waist, leather interspersed with shards of glass.

That Elazar had let Gunnar live should have stuck out more. Gunnar had proven he wouldn't break under torture during his captivity in Argrid. He didn't matter to Elazar— but defensors watched him and Ben. Monxes heard them talking.

Elazar knew Ben and Gunnar had bonded.

Ben's heart froze, a biting, icy knot in his chest. He stumbled forward. "Jakes," he begged, pride be damned. "You can't do this. You aren't—"

A torturer. A tool. A weapon. Every word dissolved in his mouth.

"Gunnar isn't part of this," Lu tried.

"Repent. Make the potion." Jakes almost looked sad. "And we'll stop."

The monxes started praying—"Let them see reason, Pious God, let them understand"—and it drove into Ben's mind, dredging up childhood Church services and those moments when praying to an unknown god had brought him peace.

Gunnar watched the defensors enter his cell. Smoke escaped his lips in tight spirals.

The defensors got close, and Gunnar heaved forward, fire licking one's face.

The defensor only chuckled. "You didn't think we'd come near you again without Extin, eh?"

Extin made its taker fireproof for a time. Which meant Gunnar couldn't hurt them.

A lie of surrender curled Ben's tongue like bark shriveling off kindling. His mouth opened with a primal drive to protect Gunnar, consequences be damned—

Gunnar's eyes found Ben's across the hall, blueness hardened with determination and beautiful resolve. He shook his head, once, and Ben's fire went out.

He couldn't surrender. He couldn't work for his father again.

He couldn't save Gunnar.

"You can stop this too, barbarian," the defensor said with a sneer. "Tell us how to make Eye of the Sun permanent, and we'll leave. Well, we'll leave *sooner*."

Ben yanked on the iron bars. Lu's breath came in quick gasps behind him.

He had known for six years what would happen if he revealed his true loyalties: his father would imprison him until he changed his mind. That had always been the threat, that *he* would be harmed, and it had been enough to keep him silent.

Had Ben known Elazar would break him through someone else's torture, he wouldn't have spent the past six years silent. He would have spent them comatose.

One defensor ripped off Gunnar's shirt. The other gave the whip a threatening crack on the floor.

"Stop!" Ben cried. "God, don't do this!"

Jakes turned away as though Ben's pain hurt him. As though he could *feel*.

"The Pious God doesn't hear you," a monxe spat. "Let this act chase the Devil from your hearts. Defensors, save these wretched souls."

He waved at them to start.

✤✤✤

Gunnar was a warrior. He had undergone whatever Mecht ceremony had given him Eye of the Sun; his rigid bearing said he knew how to endure pain.

But after thirty-seven cracks of the whip, he broke with a whimper.

The defensors left, satisfied by that quaking moan from the strong Mecht warrior. Monxes sopped the blood off the floor and wrapped bandages around Gunnar's wounds but left him hanging, his hands a dark purple-red from his weight on the manacles.

His hoarse breathing was the only sign he was alive.

Lu's pulse clawed at her veins. Knees to her chest on the floor, she gulped at the thick air. The metal tongs she had in her sleeve were the only thing solid in a world gone to liquid.

Ben, his back to the bars, didn't move. She couldn't bring herself to see his face, the stain of agony that would unravel her.

"Have you . . . have you tried to escape?" Lu whispered in Argridian. She knew Argridian as most on Grace

Loray did—the Grace Lorayan dialect had developed from Argridian over centuries. Lu's parents—her father, particularly—had made sure she was fluent to better serve on her missions during the war.

Speaking it so much felt like wearing an ill-fitting gown. One she wanted to rip off.

Ben was silent for a long while. "Once while we were on the *Astuto*. Once here. This prison is . . . disorienting. And Gunnar—sometimes, he seems drugged. I think my father is giving him something to weaken his mind. The defensors insist I drink certain water to stay unaffected should I choose to work. It must contain the antidote."

Lu looked at him out of a dread-laced shock. "When you came down here, did the walls move?" She hadn't noticed that when the defensors brought her from the upper room, but—

Bloodshot veins reddened Ben's dark eyes. "I thought I had imagined it."

"No. It's Emerdian." Surely the Argridian prince had heard of Emerdian masonry. Argrid was neighbors with Emerdon on the Mainland.

The horror on Ben's face said he had. "We can't be in Emerdon."

"Port Camden. The Emerdian syndicate's territory."

The city that sat in Grace Loray's northwestern corner. Thanks to its prison, the revolutionaries hadn't been able to wrest control of Port Camden away from Argrid until the war was won. The Emerdians had built it as their fortress when they first settled on Grace Loray, centuries ago. Masonry was a prized Emerdian skill—intricate brickwork made up every important building in Emerdon, its most feared penitentiaries being no exception. Walls moved to rearrange halls; doors disappeared into the bricks; whole wings could be cut off and reopened.

Three inescapable prisons stood in Emerdon. One was on Grace Loray.

During the war, the revolutionaries had intercepted people released from the prison. They spoke of a fraying place that made you question your own mind: *"Magic. In the food, the water, the air—wherever it comes from, you can't escape it."*

Lu knew Port Camden, the steep gables of the buildings that created knife-sharp silhouettes against the sky. The clopping of horses on the cobblestone roads. The tanneries on the northwest side of the city that coated the port in the stench of sour death when the wind blew the wrong way. She, Ben, and Gunnar could get out of this prison, and she could get them somewhere safe—through mildew-slick alleys like the one where she had first killed someone in self-defense. As Tom had taught her.

Her heart all but ruptured as she tried not to remember that night. But it led to other memories centered around Port Camden: the end of the revolution. The safe house two hours of travel into the jungle. The lace-edged quilt that hung over the bed where she and Annalisa had hidden as defensors stormed the building. Her nightmare, Milo standing over her. Hours, *hours*, of Lazonade and Awacia—

"Elazar isn't drugging the other prisoners." Lu tripped over her own words. "The prison itself drugs its inhabitants. There is magic, somewhere."

Ben braced his hands on his temples. "To have a prison on Grace Loray use Emerdian building techniques is one thing, but did they put plants in the construction materials? Do the guards pump toxic air in? *Where?* And more—"

Ben turned, the instinctual flip of someone seeking the counsel of another—Gunnar. But when he saw Gunnar's state, bloodied and half-conscious, Ben cried out.

"We'll escape," Lu promised them. Promised herself. She held up the metal tongs. "I can pick our locks. We'll get out."

Ben glanced back at her, tears streaking clean lines through the grime on his russet face. "How? He won't make it far."

"Go," came a gruff bark. Gunnar looked through his blood-matted hair. "Get out."

Leave me were his unsaid words.

Ben shot to his feet. "*This*"—he waved at the prison, the island beyond, the whole of the conflict—"has happened because I spent the past six years saving only myself. Don't tell me that I should leave you here. I owe you your life. I owe Argrid and Grace Loray so much more. We're not leaving without you. If it costs me my own life, I don't care."

He gagged on the weight of his admission, head dropping to his chest.

Ben didn't understand what he was saying. Lu needed to escape before she shattered over these cold prison stones, pieces of a girl abandoned by her father, pieces of a murderer, pieces of *nothing*.

She needed to get out, to find her mother. To do anything, *anything* necessary to get Argrid off this island.

As if her desperation read on her face, Ben looked away. "Give him a day. Enough for his wounds to . . ." He swallowed. "If we leave without him, my father will kill him."

Ordinarily, Lu wouldn't have challenged him. They couldn't leave Gunnar. "What if the defensors don't let him heal enough to escape?"

Ben bit his lips together. He looked at Gunnar once more, then back at Lu.

He nodded at the single cot and an uneaten tray of food. "Just one day. Give him that."

Lu hesitated. Ben insisted again. She relented, grabbing a chunk of stale bread and pulling herself onto the thin, lumpy mattress.

"A day," she agreed.

❊❊❊

The stomping of boots pulled Lu from a light, vacant sleep.

Ben stood at the cell bars. Across the way, Gunnar swayed against his chains.

Lu pushed upright on the cot, dreamlike, the world shifting.

Four defensors stopped in the hall. None had a whip. But one of them—the one Ben had fought on the *Astuto*, Jakes—cleared his throat.

"The Eminence King demands your presence, my prince. And the Mecht." His voice was rough, as if he had been weeping.

"Why?" Ben demanded.

Defensors unlocked both cells. Lu was vaguely aware of them letting Gunnar down, muzzling him, while Jakes snapped manacles on Ben's wrists. He resisted with a cry.

The defensors were taking Ben and Gunnar away. Lu would be left alone.

The horror of that possibility made her shoot off the cot as defensors relocked her cell.

"Wait!" Lu grabbed the bars. "You can't—"

"Do you want to repent?" Jakes whipped to her as another defensor led Ben up the hall.

Lu said nothing.

"I thought so," Jakes spat, and retreated up the stones.

Lu waited, seconds filling with her thundering heartbeat.

Tom could save her. He could swoop in as he had the night the war ended—

A sob ruptured out of Lu's chest. No, *no*—she wouldn't disintegrate. Elazar hadn't tortured *her* yet.

But he had. Having her wake up to Milo in shackles, facing Tom's duplicity . . .

How could Tom have done this to her? How could Lu not have seen his lies?

In the same way she had not seen the truth of the Council, and how they had ignored the poverty of the stream raiders and lower classes. She had been so blindly loyal that it had never occurred to her to question what she loved. What other foundations would prove to be rotten? What other truths that she refused to see were right before her eyes?

Lu cried out and dove for the cot. She had left the metal tongs under the blanket, and she grabbed them now in sweaty fingers. Her harsh breaths choked her as she braced the tongs on her thigh and snapped them apart. She had two metal rods now—the number needed to pick locks.

Rational thought leaked out with Lu's sobs. Only desperation remained.

Tom had taken everything from her. She would not stay here, collapsing at Elazar's feet, waiting for Milo to come. She would get out. She would make them suffer for ever setting foot on her island.

She would destroy them all.

Lu scrubbed her eyes on her sleeve and reached through the bars to level the picks in the lock. Her body quaked, but she pried apart each tumbler with delicate precision— *click*.

Lu paused. No soldiers rushed her. No alarms were raised in warning.

She shoved on the door and it opened. Her boot hit the stone of the hallway, and that single tap of leather on rock made her sob again.

What of Ben and Gunnar? Where had the soldiers taken them? No matter—she would follow their path and free them. Or find Vex. Find him, and get help. Find him, and—

Exhaustion sculpted a fuzzy, singular wish: Vex, his arms open to her. *Safe*, her heart said. Teo, too. And Kari, she hadn't forsaken her like Tom—had she?

The shakiness in that question pushed out a feeble cry. Lu ran—from her cell, from the part of herself that whispered, *Who will you run to? You cannot even trust yourself.*

Shadows blurred the hall, thrashing in the torchlight. Lu hit a fork, and a grating noise rumbled farther ahead.

Guards could shift these walls with knobs and levers. One hall could become a dead end. Another could loop her right back to the cells. Which way would lead to—

"Adeluna!"

Lu spun to the left. That voice—it couldn't be.

A raffish smile. The ripple of muscles in his neck when he tried to suppress true emotion and the glitter in his eye when he made her laugh. The softness in the brush of his fingertips, as though he believed her worthy of sweetness and respect.

"Adeluna!" His voice was coming from ahead, louder now.

You cannot even trust yourself, her mind echoed.

But I trust him, she told the broken pieces that had once been her heart.

"Vex!" Lu screamed. "VEX!"

She started again, hitting a corner and shoving off it, scrambling until she swung into a long hall. A lantern flickered at the distant end and it slowed her steps, one, another.

"Vex." The name broke through to her soul as the person lifted the lantern to his face.

Lu stopped.

It wasn't Vex. It was Milo.

4

VEX'S WORLD HAD been nonstop chaos for weeks. Getting arrested in New Deza; escaping the castle with Lu and Teo; trekking across Grace Loray on the hunt for Milo Ibarra; sneaking onto the Argridian ship; fleeing that ship; retreating to Port Mesi-Teab; tracking places Ben might be; and finally sneaking into New Deza again to get Kari Andreu.

But now, the world was quiet. Vex hated it.

Nayeli and Edda whispered beside the pilothouse. Cansu's raiders took shifts driving the boat northwest so they could find the Emerdian raider syndicate and break into the Port Camden prison. Vex sat at the bow, the evening sky brushed gray by clouds and the lake ahead of them as still as polished glass. This boat wasn't the *Rapid Meander*, docked halfway across the island in Port Mesi-Teab, but a similar lulling peace wiggled its way in.

Vex folded his arms under his chin and stared straight out from the bow, furious that Cansu's raiders wouldn't let him drive. It was their boat, after all; he'd never let them touch the *Meander*'s helm, were the situation reversed. But he was more furious that there was no other way to expel the energy in his chest. Except through the disease that made his arms shake.

But it wasn't a disease, was it? Not according to Lu. Shaking Sickness was a result of too much of Grace Loray's botanical magic entering a person's body—solved by ingesting the specific plants that counteracted the ones that had been taken in excess. But it had been years since Church priests had given Vex magic, so Lu had devised a way to cook down the counter plants, increase their potency, and maybe cure him.

She'd worked through one of the plants he'd remembered, before . . .

Vex closed his eye. Healing his Shaking Sickness wasn't the only reason he missed Lu, and he hated that he had to tell himself that not to feel selfish. As if he needed more reasons to be mad at his body.

It isn't fair, he'd wanted to scream so many times. The rational part of him knew it wasn't his body's fault, but the rest of him hated this vessel he was trapped in.

This scarred, shaky, dying vessel.

"Have you eaten?"

Vex lurched around. Kari held a sack of jerky he'd seen

Cansu's raiders dipping into. Behind her, Edda and Nayeli had stopped talking to watch them. To watch *him*, in case he did anything stupid, like start yelling again.

He shifted forward. "Yep."

Silence. Maybe he'd get lucky and she'd leave—

A crate beside him moaned. She arranged her now-dry skirts, and Vex could practically hear the creaking of her spine as she sat down rod straight.

The water shushed around the bow and the night breeze cooed in his ears.

"Your crewmate—Edda," Kari said. "In the castle, she called you Paxben."

Vex sat up, fingers curving around the railing.

"Paxben Artur Gallego," she whispered. "The son of Elazar's brother, Rodrigu. The son of the man who started Argrid's resistance."

Of course she'd recognize the name. Vex eyed the Tuncian raiders, who were out of earshot.

"Argrid's *failed* resistance, you mean," he grumbled.

A long moment passed. "Your father was incredibly brave."

Vex bit down on his tongue. That used to be the first word that flared into his mind when Rodrigu came into a room. *Brave.* Followed by *strong* and *loving* and *joyful* and—

He'd thought, if his father was brave and strong, that he had to be those things too. God, he'd idolized his father. Everyone had—when the collaborators in Rodrigu's resistance had filled his office, their faces glowed with hope. They had wanted to overthrow Elazar and put eleven-year-old Ben on the throne with Rodrigu serving as regent until he came of age. With Rodrigu in power, Argrid would pull away from the Church, legalize Grace Loray's botanical magic, and stop the burnings, torture, and fear.

Paxben had squished into a chair in the back of the room during the secret meetings, overflowing with pride that *his father* was someone who could inspire such awe.

That pride blossomed, though weak from years beaten down. Vex could rename himself, turn his back on what his father had made him—but he couldn't get rid of this pain, no matter how hard he tried.

"As are you," Kari continued, "for all you must have faced. I cannot imagine what you have endured to be alive today."

"I've done what I had to do to get by in this world. The world *you* helped make."

Kari sighed. "My daughter told you about my role in the revolution."

Vex swung on her, one hand rigid on the boat's railing. "She told me what you made her do. The way you used her to be a soldier for your cause. Your own *child*. You're a monster. How could you live that life and make those decisions for her? Didn't you see what that did to her? Couldn't you have been a normal parent? Couldn't you have made her *happy*?"

Edda stood. Nayeli hesitated, hand braced on the deck, and in the dimness of the pilothouse's single lantern, it looked like she was crying.

Kari's eyes were glassy too. "I will never forgive myself for what I let Adeluna do. But the life I chose—to fight injustices and pain—I *had* to. I never would have been able to look at her, knowing I had been too afraid to try to make this world better for her. And"—Kari stared at him as if she could see the thoughts bruising his mind—"I suspect your father felt the same."

Vex flew to his feet and spun to face the calm lake. *Shut up. You don't know a damn thing—you didn't know him at all—*

"I didn't know him," Kari said, following him up. "But I read his correspondences with our revolutionaries during the war. I worked with the refugees he sent here. He was passionately in favor of a new world full of promise and peace. Such hope could have only come from a man who was fighting for someone he dearly loved."

Vex shut his eye. *Love.* Rodrigu hadn't loved him. If he had, he would've put Paxben above his plan to depose Elazar. He would've been careful and not let Elazar find him out.

Vex hated Rodrigu for that. He hated him for dying and leaving him alone in a world of sinners and burnings. For not being on the deck of this boat, right now, in the same way he'd hated Rodrigu every minute since his death. In a way that felt too much like a love so strong it cored out his insides and made his tremors feel like they'd kill him then and there.

Vex had been ignoring so much—his father, his real identity, his illness—and now that he'd acknowledged them, they demanded six years' worth of attention at once.

"You all right, Captain?" Edda asked, her face open and sad with her own lifetime of regret, her pain coming from the moment eight years ago when she'd murdered her husband and had to flee the Mechtlands. Nayeli was silent behind her, echoing Edda's expression. Their individual wells of regret were what linked the three of them most.

Vex sniffed. *Are any of us?*

But Kari spoke instead. "What is the plan now?" She rubbed a hand over her face and folded her arms, gathering herself up. As though she hadn't lost her daughter, her husband, and her country before getting dragged into war plans.

Vex shook his head, incredulous. "How do you do that? Plunge on ahead, no matter what bad stuff has happened. She did it too."

At the mention of Lu, Kari's facade rippled. Tears rushed into her eyes, but she held on to her soft smile. "I do it for her. I do it for the people I love." Her smile slipped. "How have you been getting by all these years? Haven't you been fighting for anyone?"

The memory of Ben punched through Vex's thoughts. When Elazar took everything from him, the fact that Ben was alive had comforted him. That one day, he might see his cousin again, and convince Ben not to trust Elazar, and they'd be *irmáns*, brothers, like they used to be.

That goal had faded the more Vex had to fight just to survive. His goals became smaller, until he fought only for himself, Nayeli, and Edda.

"Who are you fighting for now?" Vex didn't realize how insensitive a question it was until he asked it. "I'm sorry. I didn't mean—"

"Lu," Kari answered. Her focus shifted back to the horizon. "I'll still fight for her, so her death isn't in vain."

Vex had never let himself think about that. That his father's death had been a waste. Nothing had come from his heresy.

Vex's focus slipped. When he came back, Edda was giving Kari a neutered explanation of the plan they'd come up with to defeat Argrid.

Well, it was Cansu and Fatemah's plan. Vex's interests had been narrow: to free Kari, to find Ben. He'd try to focus on the bigger war now, though.

"We have Cansu's syndicate based out of Port Mesi-Teab," Edda was saying. "We know the Mecht syndicate is allied with Argrid—they were all over that burning at the castle. The other syndicates, the Emerdians and Grozdans . . . we aren't sure where they fall. It doesn't seem like Argrid'd be able to convince more than one syndicate to join them, so best chance, they're both viable allies. That's the goal, anyway—to get the syndicates united, to create a strong enough force to fight against Argrid. Like you did, during the revolution."

"Fatemah said she'll send raiders to Port Camden," Nayeli explained. She slid up next to Vex. "If the Emerdian syndicate sided with Argrid, the Tuncians will back us up; if Emerdon wants to fight, the Tuncians will help us break into the prison. Either way, we'll get into that prison, grab our people, and reconvene in Port Mesi-Teab—the sanctuary is hidden from Argrid."

Kari's eyebrows rose. "Sanctuary?"

Vex eyed Nayeli, who bit her lips together and shrugged as if to say, *What the hell?*

"A refuge the Tuncians built for their needy," she said. "We've kept it . . . secluded."

Kari's eyebrows stayed up. She nodded, logging the information.

"How will we know if Cansu's in the prison?" Edda asked. "Or what if the rumors are wrong, and Argrid is using the building as a garrison, not a jail? We could walk into a trap."

Vex hadn't thought of that. God, he'd always been terrible at stuff like this, big-scheme planning. Throw him into a situation, and he could improvise his way out; tell him to get one person out of a jail, and he could coordinate enough to do it. But his father had made him play this awful strategy game when he was younger, one where players had to map out ten, twenty moves in advance while considering the moves of their opponent and different traps on the board. The memory sent a dull ache into Vex's neck—and a sharp whimper into his throat.

His father had been so damn good at the game. Vex had never won against him. Elazar's defensors had still gotten hold of correspondence between Rodrigu and the Grace Lorayan rebels, or found plants Rodrigu had illegally stashed to use against Elazar, or whatever it was that had condemned him, and Vex's world had crumbled.

What hope did Vex have of coming through this war alive?

"We're counting on Nathaniel Blaise being willing to talk," Vex tried.

"You mean instead of shooting us on the spot?" Nayeli rubbed her shoulder where one of the Emerdian raiders had shot her last time they'd been in Port Camden.

Edda faced Kari. "What'd you do to convince the syndicates to unite last time? Nate will have better information about what is going on in the Port Camden prison."

Kari sighed. "We—the rebels—spent months persuading the Heads to speak with us, and months after, trying to coordinate demands between them. Ultimately, there was one desire that appeased them: autonomy in the new government. Which many of the rebels refused, until the war turned dire."

Heaviness rippled over her face. Vex knew what she

meant now by *dire*—she meant the final battle, the night Argrid took the revolutionaries' headquarters.

The night Milo Ibarra had tortured Lu.

Rage made Vex shoot forward. "We'll *make* the raiders unify. Only . . . I realize that after that whole bill to eradicate raiders, most raiders would rather we string you up as a show of solidarity. Which, hey, might unite the syndicates anyway."

Kari gave Vex an unimpressed stare. "I was under house arrest because I *opposed* the Council turning on raiders. I can use that to my advantage, and I will find another way to win back the raiders' respect." She shifted, smoothing her skirts as she surveyed the gray-black horizon. "We go to Port Camden and meet with Nathaniel Blaise. I convince him to join our cause. We use the combined might of the Emerdian and Tuncian syndicates to break into Port Camden prison and free Cansu."

"And Ben," Vex added. Kari frowned in confusion. "Elazar has him. He'll force Ben to finalize permanent magic that would make Argridian defensors unstoppable."

Kari sighed. "That Argrid has begun using magic against us is so inconceivable, I cannot keep that piece of the war clear—let alone that the Crown Prince has defected. He followed your father's example, it seems." She gave Vex a smile he couldn't return and smoothed her skirts again, one of her few nervous tics. "After we rescue Cansu—and the prince—we gather in Port Mesi-Teab and, with Cansu and

Nathaniel, we seek unification with the Grozdan syndicate and use our numbers to push Argrid out of Grace Loray."

Silence followed, everyone digesting the plan.

"If you don't mind"—Kari sat back on the crate—"I would like to be alone."

Nayeli squinted. "How? It's a really small boat."

Edda punched her in the arm. "We'll do what we can."

Edda and Nayeli moved away, but Vex hesitated.

"You didn't know, did you?" Vex swallowed. "What your husband did. That he was feeding information to the Argridians."

Kari looked up. "I fear he may have done more than that."

Vex wanted to ask what she meant. But, just as strongly, he didn't want to know.

He'd had two weeks with the knowledge of Lu's death, and it still poked holes in his lungs, wrapping cold fingers around his heart and squeezing, *squeezing*.

He should talk to Kari. But what could he say to give her any comfort?

Vex looked down at the teak deck. "I think I loved your daughter."

Kari didn't try to hide the tears spilling out of her eyes, or the blotchy redness to her face. She bowed her head—a thanks, an offering.

Edda squeezed Vex's shoulder, and they made for the pilothouse, leaving Kari alone.

Vex had to admit that Elazar's takeover of Grace Loray had been perfect this time.

Cansu's raiders sailed up to Port Camden at midday. The last time Vex had been to this city was months ago, to steal crates of Healica for the Argridian bullies who'd threatened to kill his crew if he didn't give them what Elazar demanded. Remembering that time, when it'd just been him, Nayeli, and Edda racing around the island, trying to avoid his uncle's lackeys while planning how to hide away from any war—god, it almost seemed simple now.

Like the other main ports on Grace Loray, Port Camden had been built by a specific group of immigrants and mimicked the styles of its Mainland counterpart—in this case, Emerdon. Sharp roofs peaked over towering, narrow structures of crisscrossing timbers and white panels, compliments of Emerdon's fixation on masonry: the cobblestone roads, the arching bridges, the chimneys hugging most buildings.

But that was where the similarities between Port Camden and the fairly well-off country of Emerdon ended. Because Port Camden was a *pit*.

Every building needed upkeep, and garbage littered the streets. The Emerdian syndicate liked to blame Port Camden's deficiency on the Council—once the rebels had won the war against Argrid and instituted a *real* government, the Grace Loray Republic had taken control of magic trade with the Mainland countries. Any time the Council sold magic to the Mainland, it was *official* and sent money into the Council's coffers; any time raiders sold magic to the Mainland, it was *illegal* and sent raiders into the Council's prisons. The syndicates lost their main source of income, which spiraled all four of them into poverty.

But the Emerdian syndicate, and Port Camden by extension, had been hurting long before then. From what Vex could tell, they'd had a run of irresponsible Heads—and Nate wasn't much better, sinking money into elaborate steamboats or feeding his Emerdian obsession with fine leather goods. Rumors had it that his husband was trying to turn things around, but for now the poverty gave off a dangerous energy.

Cansu's raiders steered the boat slowly, weaving around other vessels moored on the banks, but traffic in the waterways was nonexistent. No one stood in doorways; no patrons bustled toward markets. Loose shutters banged against windows. The chirp of a child's cry cut off with the slam of a door. A stray dog shot into an alley, its tail curved between its legs.

Port Mesi-Teab had been similar when Vex and his group had left days ago. Elazar had managed to wrap up the island with familiar actions: burnings. Defensors in every city. Priests spewing nonsense about purity and cleansing. And now, the Council's endorsement.

Cansu's steamboat curved down a narrow river. Off a

branching road, five Argridian soldiers marched in the opposite direction, focused on a cluster of people farther up.

"Halt!" a soldier commanded. "By order of the Eminence King, stop for questioning!"

The people obeyed—except one, who bolted. The others cried alarm as two soldiers broke off from the group and raced after him, pistols out.

"Stop!" the soldiers bellowed. "Raider! He's a raider!"

Cansu's raiders pushed the boat on. Vex winced, a low ache cramping his stomach as the road slipped from view. They couldn't help—there were too many soldiers, and more could be up that next road, or around that corner, or waiting in a steamboat on that river.

Next to Vex, Kari didn't speak. But he could see her mind spinning with similar thoughts. Weighing possibilities. Considering outcomes.

Being around her was not making him miss Lu any less.

A couple minutes later, Cansu's raiders docked in a shack on the edge of the stream. This was Nate's main neighborhood—that building with the roof so steep half the brown shingles were slipping down was where Vex had found the Emerdians' Healica. He doubted it was still one of Nate's drop spots now, though.

They disembarked, and Vex pointed. "That road leads to one of Nate's favorite taverns. We can start there."

A group of kids stood under the awning of a closed schoolhouse. One of Cansu's raiders whistled to get their attention. "Get inside!" he hissed. "Don't take—"

The raider's command cut off with a startled yelp. Vex whipped around to a dull pain that knocked the air from his lungs. Another fist barreled into his face and stars burst across his vision—then a bag went over his head, blackening the daylight.

Terror sparked through him. Argridian defensors?

"Edda!" he shouted as hands grabbed him. "Nay—explosives! Something!"

Grunting and a shout of alarm didn't tell him who was winning, who had been subdued—

A weight slammed into the back of his head, and consciousness slipped through Vex's fingers.

5

LU DIDN'T SCREAM as the defensors led Ben and Gunnar through the prison—not that Ben could have helped her. The rumble of stone on stone was the only noise that pulled his focus back in time to see a wall close off a hall they had just passed through.

This prison was a living trap. Once Lu picked the lock, how would they get out? One wrong turn, and they would die down here, lost in a maze of shifting halls.

It was midday when defensors shoved Ben and Gunnar outside. A staircase led from the prison to a river, giving them a view of Port Camden's buildings jabbing the sky like fangs.

Ben filed down the steps after Jakes and glanced back—Gunnar was right behind him. The muzzle, his wrist and ankle chains tugged down his beaten body.

This was the closest defensors had allowed them to be

to each other since their capture.

Ben's heart cracked. He grabbed Gunnar's forearm, their manacles clanking. Gunnar's blue eyes locked on his, but his expression was distant, fighting through a fog.

Ben cursed. "I'm sorry," he panted. "I'm sorry I couldn't—"

"Thaid fuilor mauth," Gunnar murmured, the iron deadening the noise. "Remember? Thaid—" He winced. "—fuilor—"

A defensor behind Gunnar grabbed his shoulders. "Move!"

They'd reached the river. Three short docks held prison boats, fortified steamers with cages on the main decks. The defensors shoved Ben and Gunnar aboard one and into the cage.

"Even think about doing anything stupid," a defensor told them as they locked the door, "and the big one'll suffer."

Ben swallowed his nausea, his mind filling with images of shoving this man overboard.

Fingers of humidity coiled the hair around Ben's face as he hunched under the metal. He fought a wince at the sight of Gunnar huddled beside him, gripping the bars to keep himself steady against the slosh and surge of the boat.

"Clear," Gunnar said.

Ben noticed it too. Outside the prison, a weight had lifted, as though it had been night and now the sun had risen. He had assumed the guards were altering the food or water, but if that wasn't the case, where was the magic coming from?

Jakes sat outside the cage, frowning from Ben to Gunnar. The boat listed and Ben caught himself on Gunnar's knee.

A defensor started the engine, but Jakes lifted his hand.

"We're to wait for Andreu," Jakes said. "You might see what is keeping him."

Two defensors leaped off the boat while one remained in the pilothouse, out of earshot.

"Andreu?" Ben whispered. "Lu's father?"

Jakes shrugged.

With a grimace, Ben tried again. "Where is mine having me brought?"

Jakes squinted, calculation veiling his face. "How long have you hated your father?"

"You didn't answer my question."

"Answer mine." A defensor, making a demand of his prince.

"Six years."

"Six—" Jakes's whole body rocked. "You expect me to believe that you hated him in secret all this time? You were loyal. I saw your devotion."

You're right, Ben almost said. He hadn't realized how much he hated his father until recently. His hatred had grown over time, watered and nourished by every burning, every violent act, every beating and broken bone and reprimand.

This was the first time Ben had looked into Jakes's eyes

as his true self. Their conversations had been brief these past weeks, interrupted by monxes or cut off by Jakes's angry sulking. Ben hadn't had the chance—or desire—to explain his choices.

The defensor in the pilothouse looked at them, a question in his frown, but Jakes flicked his hand at his comrade in dismissal.

"All those weeks on the *Astuto*"—Jakes leaned closer—"you never intended to create permanent magic, did you?"

"No."

Jakes dragged his hand down his face, laughing in incredulity. "But you tried to make the cure for Shaking Sickness. This isn't any different—good will come of it. You don't understand how much the world needs this power."

"After the horrific acts you've seen my father do, how can you believe that giving him permanent magic will make the world better?"

Jakes jerked back from the cage, face set. He started humming that song he always fell back on when he was anxious, the one his sister had written. The smallness of the cage meant Ben couldn't get away from it.

A detail snapped into place. Ben teetered, catching himself on Gunnar's knee again. Gunnar cocked his head, but Ben only gaped back, unable to look at Jakes.

"You told me your sister and her children died of Shaking Sickness," Ben breathed.

Jakes stopped humming.

"You betrayed me"—Ben licked his lips—"to further Elazar's goal of permanent magic. But through Elazar's own attempts, he gave uncountable victims Shaking Sickness. Which you knew. Yet you allied with him, even though he killed your sister."

Ben turned. He wished he hadn't, seeing the pain that flowed out of Jakes's face. He couldn't afford sympathy.

"My father killed your sister," Ben repeated. "Didn't he?"

A deadly level of resolve set Jakes's eyes. "Elazar did not kill her."

"She died of Shaking Sickness," Ben pressed, his hand braced on Gunnar's knee as the prison transport listed. "You told me that was how she died. And—and her children, too?"

"Stop, Ben."

"Elazar *killed them*." Had he not realized? But Jakes had been in the Grace Neus's holding cells when Elazar had revealed his true intentions to Ben. Jakes had heard the same admission: that Elazar had left a trail of Shaking Sickness victims in the wake of his search for permanent magic. "Shaking Sickness comes from overdosing on Grace Loray's magic."

Jakes bared his teeth. "I said *stop*—"

"No one in Argrid has access to enough magic to overdose on their own." Ben leaned closer, drawing strength from his hand on Gunnar. "Elazar used your sister and her children in his experiments to make permanent magic. He killed your family!"

"You're wrong!" The shout tore from Jakes's mouth, ripping him to his feet. He towered over Ben, hands in fists, the brim of his feathered hat catching his face in shadow.

Gunnar seized Ben's arm, the two of them frozen as Ben glared up at Jakes, watching the nerve he'd hit twitch and writhe.

"Defensor Rayen?" the defensor in the pilothouse called. "Are you all right?"

"Yes," Jakes snapped. "Our prince's rebelliousness knows no bounds."

He crouched in front of Ben, eye to eye. "You are wrong, my prince," Jakes said, loud enough for the other defensor to hear. "The Eminence King could never commit the atrocities you mentioned. He knows best. Do you know what Argrid is doing while the king is here? He sent a missive during your first week of imprisonment, for the cathedrals across Argrid to lead the people in a constant state of prayer until his return. They will willingly obey him, because the Eminence King controls *everything.*" Jakes's voice dropped but his intensity didn't subside. "If you question him directly, you will die."

Ben gaped. In Church services where he had listened to Jakes pray, or the moments when he'd heard Jakes speak of the Pious God, Jakes had never sounded so desperate—so *imploring.*

Up on the plateau, Andreu descended the steps with the two defensors.

Jakes stomped into the pilothouse. "Prepare to depart!" he bellowed.

Ben went slack against the bars, realizing in that motion that Gunnar's hand had moved to his shoulder.

"He lies," Gunnar whispered. "Soldiers, even pious ones, do not speak that—that—"

"Pleadingly," Ben finished. "He was begging me, wasn't he? I didn't imagine it."

Gunnar tipped his head to the cage's bars, sweat glistening on his pale face. "Something is odd in him."

Ben restrained himself from throwing Jakes a questioning look. Jakes had spied on Ben for months; he had stood by while Ben was imprisoned; he had let defensors whip Gunnar.

But Lu was right. They needed to escape—they needed a plan.

Maybe Ben could reach something in Jakes.

✵✵✵

Milo grinned at Lu through the pulsing light of the lantern in his hand.

She shook her head, fingers on her temples. No—this was wrong. This prison was *wrong*, warping her mind. The magic that made the captives go mad was getting to her.

"Vex," she said again. Tears sliced down Lu's cheeks. She had heard him say her name. *She had heard him.*

"Vex?" Milo echoed, walking toward her. "My king's banished nephew? You leave a trail of disgraced Argridians in your wake. Paxben. Benat. Almost, your father. Almost, *me.*"

Sweat ran in a cold droplet down Lu's spine. Milo's tone shifted from taunting to furious.

"Do you have any idea," he said, "what you have cost me? I lost my title. I lost my command. Everything that I have done for this island, for Argrid, for my God and king—you wiped it all out when I did not recognize you as the girl who escaped me." His lips peeled back in a manic grin. "But as your dear father has a chance to redeem himself, the Eminence King has also given me the opportunity to prove my worth."

His insinuation pounced on Lu's mind, but she stayed numb in the middle of the hall, watching Milo and his lantern come closer, closer.

She was trapped. She was Lazonade incarnate.

Milo surveyed the stone walls. "Emerdians call this type of prison *Ribège*. The Snare. Prisoners try to escape, but there are dozens of pathways, countless routes that these walls can make. Where will you go, Adeluna? The hall behind you slopes upward. Perhaps that is the way out. There is a corner ahead—perhaps that way will lead to an exit. To your *Vex*."

"No," Lu sobbed. "No—you don't—*stop*—"

"No—you are right. *No*, he won't be there, he won't come to save you, for the same reason I did not recognize you and your father never turned you over to the Eminence King. You are worthless, Adeluna. But the Eminence King believes there is use for you, and it is my task to drag it out where your father failed." His face was darkness, sin, and hunger. "Repent, Adeluna. Beg my forgiveness. Beg me to stop."

Milo lunged. Lu's body threw her backward, a stunted cry ripping her throat raw—

The hallway blurred. She had eaten bits of Ben's food but hadn't drunk any of the water with the antidote for whatever magic was down here. She felt the effects of that magic now, a wistful wave that yanked her out of this prison— and into her family's apartment at the castle.

White light from the sun over Lake Regolith highlighted the tears on her father's cheeks. *"I'm sorry—you didn't need to find out—it shouldn't have happened at all!"*

Kari was in front of him, sobbing. *"She trusted you! You destroyed everything—"*

The prison's hall descended around Lu. She teetered, but her parents weren't here.

Milo was an arm's length from her. Heat palpitated off him, the air thick with his body odor and acrid hair grease. He had been this close before, holding a knife to her skin as soldiers dosed her with Lazonade to immobilize her.

Lu's strength unraveled. She fumbled, caught herself, ran.

"She trusted you!" Kari screamed. *"You've been lying to us! You've destroyed everything, and now—and now—"*

The memory, what was it? Lu couldn't recall her parents arguing like this—

Milo stalked her; his lantern light wavered on the stones.

Lu glanced back as she took a turn and smacked into a wall. Hadn't she come this way? It was a dead end now.

She spun around. No, *no*. Milo had moved the walls, with levers and knobs hidden in the stones. He was corralling her wherever he wanted her to go.

Her resolve was gone. Her determination, obliterated.

Lu hammered her fists on the wall. She had feared this moment every day since the revolution's end; she had lain in the darkness of her bedroom and imagined Milo in the shadows, and she had wept that not only would it happen again, but that she deserved it.

She had killed people. She had killed people *for Argrid*. Tom had made her betray her own country.

Fingers coiled into Lu's shoulder. A trilling echo rebounded as Milo yanked her away, her stone-warped screaming coming from a dream, from the past, from the moments she had bitten it down for fear of what it would do to her.

Elazar knew that hurting Gunnar would wear Ben into submission. He had tried, with Tom, to break Lu. But this. Milo. His arms around her as he dragged her up the hall—

Milo was her undoing.

6

THE PRISON TRANSPORT sailed through starkly different scenery than the mangrove trees and slimy darkness of Backswamp that Ben had seen from the deck of the *Astuto*. Now the jungle pressed against the river in walls of emerald vines and thick tree trunks, gold and teal macaws launching into the sky amid flurries of leaves. The water ran a brilliant, piercing blue that rivaled the sky. Each gust of a breeze brought fresh perfumes of greenery and salt.

When Elazar had moved Ben, Gunnar, and Lu from the ship to the Port Camden prison, he had done so at night, locking them in a covered wagon. Ben's first true visit to Grace Loray would have awed him if he wasn't looking at it from a cage.

The steamboat turned down a narrower river, and after chugging along to the squawks of distant birds and the gust of a strong wind, a village appeared.

The jungle wove through every part of the village, mating with it in dances of lacy moss and curtains, branches and wood. Buildings, the doors accessible by rope bridges, teetered on stilts where the river died in a mud pit. Two docks shot into the river.

The defensors tethered the prison transport between bobbing, dented steamboats. The only other activity was on the opposite dock, crowded with boats flying the Argridian flag. One boat lurched under defensors struggling to force manacled villagers belowdecks.

Ben's heart heaved. What was Elazar doing?

The buildings and rope bridges surrounded a platform of wood planks on stilts. Stalls sat at the edges, framing people who stood shoulder to shoulder in silence. Argridian defensors guarded the bridges and balconies.

Ben swallowed hard as defensors forced him and Gunnar off the boat, trailing Lu's father into the village. The thumping of their boots on the walkway echoed like thunder and drew the crowd's curious eyes.

The silence grew more potent. Lungs sucked in gasps.

Ben and Gunnar were prodded into the square, their boots at the edge of the wooden platform. Defensors stood on either side of them, pistols held in silver threats, while Andreu disappeared into the crowd.

Jakes linked one hand around Ben's forearm as though he might run. Gunnar was on Ben's other side, and when he swayed in the oppressive heat of the island, Ben jerked out of Jakes's hold to steady Gunnar with a hand on the small of his back.

"Careful," Ben whispered. "Eye of the Sun warriors probably don't fare well in water."

Gunnar eyed the water behind them. He cocked an eyebrow over his muzzle.

"I doubt dainty princes do either," he murmured.

A flush warmed Ben's face. He thanked the island's heat for hiding it when he saw Jakes glowering in his peripheral vision.

"Citizens of Grace Loray!"

Ben went rigid. On a balcony across the square, Elazar lifted his arms, robes glowing blue in the sunlight that filtered through the trees. Blue was one of the colors for Grace Aracely, the Grace of the Pious God's pillar of penance. Of contrition. Of regret.

Ben growled deep in his throat.

"Many of you have heard the rumors involving my country," Elazar continued, his voice echoing over the square. "Rumors of ruthless burnings. Senseless arrests. Bloodshed and violence. But I have personally come before you to speak the truth: your Grace Lorayan Council has allied with Argrid to rid this island of raiders, such as those arrested from your village."

A retching sob cut through the air. Ben spun toward it to see a woman and man curled together, weeping, while others gave them a wide berth and eyed the docks.

Elazar had had villagers arrested. Raiders—likely people who had resisted his presence.

"The depth of the corruption on this island is astounding," Elazar continued. "We have discovered neighbors, *your* neighbors, to be conspirators in a plot to turn this island into an anarchist, crime-run hell. I have seen this fate befall other nations who embrace magic—the evil of magic split the Mechtlands into warring factions that killed thousands of their own countrymen. Does that not sound familiar? A country, split into groups, warring over magic?"

Elazar paused. The crowd stirred, casting looks at one another, while the weeping man and woman stifled their misery. Who had Elazar taken from them? A son? A sister?

The soft padding of feet followed, and Tomás Andreu joined Elazar on the balcony.

"This is why we of your Grace Lorayan Council reached out to Argrid," Andreu announced. "The Eminence King is the only force on this earth who possesses a power stronger than the evil botanical magic of the stream raider syndicates. He saw the truth long before the world was ready to believe: that magic is the source of our ills. But the Pious God's power is pure and lasting. We must commit to it, and to the War on Raiders."

"But do not believe our words without proof." Elazar lifted a hand. "I have brought someone else who can confirm these truths."

Elazar went on to explain the destruction magic had caused in the Mechtlands. People addicted to certain plants; towns slaughtered by enhanced fires; victims unable to put up any resistance to those affected by magic.

Ben's mind spasmed. The defensors hadn't dragged the two of them here because of him.

"He means *you*," he panted at Gunnar, expecting the defensors to rip him away and escort him up to Elazar. "You have to deny it. You have to tell these people what really happened."

Redness highlighted the blue in Gunnar's eyes. "How? The things he says are true."

"More factors caused the Mechtlands' war than magic—and more is at work here."

"Yes. But will these people believe that?"

Ben looked at the crowd again. A few villagers, slinking away to the recesses, might have been raiders, but most were regular citizens trying to survive. Those people were the ones who watched the others, whispering, glaring—blaming.

"Grace Loray!" Elazar bellowed. "Your Council and I present a man who was once one of the outlaws bent on your destruction. The Head of the Mecht syndicate, Ingvar Pilkvist!"

The crowd murmured their amazement as Ingvar ascended the steps to Elazar's balcony.

Elazar hadn't called up Gunnar. But Ben didn't relax.

"Friends," Ingvar started. He had the same accent as

Gunnar, only weathered by years away from the Mechtlands. "Magic brings ruin, and I admit that the raider syndicates had planned to seize this island by force."

The crowd gasped. Some let out startled yelps of fear. Andreu nodded gravely, and Elazar put a comforting hand on his shoulder.

"Each syndicate has been stockpiling dangerous magic," Ingvar continued. "Our plans were gruesome and need not be recounted here. I beg your forgiveness, Grace Loray, for allowing magic to manipulate me into plotting atrocious acts against you." He dropped to his knees and lifted his hands in the curved *V* of the Church. "I throw myself at the Pious God's mercy. Any raiders who do not recant as I have are vying for war. We are sick from magic use, sick from obeying the Devil, and we need the superior power of the Pious God to heal us."

Elazar held his hands out over Ingvar but spoke to the people. "With the support of the Council, I will bring order to this island. I will cleanse Grace Loray of evil."

"You have our full support," Andreu declared.

Elazar nodded. "I understand the transformations I ask will not come easily. Removing the Devil's influence from your hearts can be painful, and many of you may struggle. But I am familiar with sacrifice—the Pious God taught me early that he most rewards his followers when the sacrifices we make are great. I have lost many people I love through sacrifice—some by corruption, others to a higher will—"

Ben's focus flickered. He remembered a crypt in Deza. All his dead relatives—his grandparents, from a plague; two other uncles, killed by an accident in youth; his mother and unborn sister during childbirth when Ben was small.

"Ours is a family of tragedy," Elazar would say. *"The Pious God ordained us in blood."*

Now Elazar pointed at Ben. "Botanical magic's evil has corrupted my own son."

Elazar had benefited the most when Rodrigu had burned. But every death in their family had benefited Elazar, earning him at least sympathy—at most, power.

Elazar wouldn't hesitate to burn Ben, if it suited his needs. Ben had known since he was thirteen that Elazar had wanted Rodrigu to die.

Had Elazar killed them? Everyone in Ben's family?

The crowd went silent again, absorbing the events with growing curiosity. But Ben couldn't breathe, and the heat of the day became a pyre—

Elazar cupped his hands over his head in the Church's symbol. Ingvar knelt at his feet. Councilman Andreu stood behind him, hands to his chest in the curved *V.*

"Together—you and I, Grace Loray and Argrid—we will cull the evil and step into the future born again, purified," Elazar told the village. "How, you may ask? Where to begin with undoing such deep, potent sin? The Pious God has heard your cries. He weeps to have you return to his fold. He has given me a mighty vision: a coming light bathing Grace Loray. The light will start in your outlying cities—Port Mesi-Teab, Port Fausta, Port Camden—and will culminate in New Deza. This light will chase out every pocket of evil and bless the pure who remain. Obey the Pious God and you need not fear this War on Raiders. When it is done, this island will be such a bright beacon of obedience and salvation that the whole of the world will be in awe."

Life meant nothing to Elazar. His parents, his brothers, his wife, his child—*nothing*. These Grace Lorayans meant even less to Elazar. He would strip the world raw if it served his goals. What did he want if not to save these people?

Ben looked at Jakes. "What is he talking about? What coming light?"

Jakes was gaping at Elazar. "I don't know. I don't—"

"Do not submit to the Pious God out of fear," Andreu boomed, stepping to be flush with Elazar. "I have seen the blessings that come to those who submit to the Pious God. We were wrong to fight Argrid, and our resistance is why we had misery under their previous rule—we held to evil. Had we stopped our misguided attempts at revolt, we would have seen that the Pious God is infinitely more powerful than botanical plants."

Andreu waved below the balcony. Ben couldn't see, but after a moment, the crowd pulsed with awe.

Elazar placed a hand on Andreu's shoulder, steering him out of the way. "These children suffered illness under the care of magic-using physicians. I anointed them in the name of your island's namesake saint, Grace Loray, the Grace of healing and purity. The Pious God healed them—their old wounds and scars—without magic. Only with purity."

The murmurings grew. Someone wept with joy. The crowd—the people who had once cowered under the Church's purification, the ones who had watched relatives die on pyres or vanish into holding cells—applauded.

Jakes's face went ashen. He shoved back through the defensors, making for the dock.

"My healing potion," Ben gasped. He had made more for Lu—while her father watched. Andreu had replicated his steps, and Elazar had given the potion to these children, in their water or their food, and laid hands on them to make a show of healing them through the Pious God.

This was how Elazar would do it. Trick his followers into taking magic, and claim the results were the Pious God's power. These people had never seen long-term, instant healing of new and old wounds from Grace Loray's plants, so what else could it be if not the Pious God?

When permanent magic became a factor, Elazar would give it to his most loyal devotees. *The Pious God blesses his followers with never-ending strength and permanent speed. Can your magic plants do this?"*

"These are the sorts of blessings you will reap if you obey the Pious God," Elazar declared. "As the purifying light moves through this island, those who are holy will bask in the glory of our most high God. Those who are evil will fall. Choose your side—push through the pain of sacrifice, and surrender any evil you may have today."

The villagers eyed Elazar's traitorous son. They looked at their surroundings—their battered homes; their impoverished lives under the Council's rule despite the changes the rebels had promised.

They moved forward, dropping plants, vials, magic of every kind, at the base of the balcony.

Fury charged through Ben's limbs. "He can't do this. He's manipulating *everything*—"

Defensors grabbed Ben to hold him back, but what stopped him was Gunnar, who angled into his path and enveloped him in a wave of heat.

"Not here, Benat. You will confirm that you are the traitor he has made you."

Ben hesitated. Gunnar was right. Elazar would meet any objection with dismissal.

"See? The Devil grips my son. He speaks lies."

"What can I do?" Ben begged.

Gunnar might have responded, but the crowd started chanting.

"War on Raiders!" they shouted. "Welcome the light! War on Raiders!"

7

VEX WOKE UP with a bag over his head and one hell of a headache.

Iron manacles pinned his wrists behind him and ropes tied his legs to a chair. He groaned, loudly, hoping to get the bag pulled off so he could find out who'd attacked them.

Wait. Did he *want* the bag pulled off? Maybe he should stay ignorant.

Before he could pretend to be unconscious again, light stabbed him in the eye. He let out an annoyed croak and slammed his eye shut, alarm flaring until a voice said, with the slightest Emerdian accent, "Devereux. Fucking. *Bell.*"

He couldn't stop his grin.

The room's shuttered windows meant the light was coming from lanterns and a massive fireplace in Emerdian masonry, this one a crisscross of gold and peach bricks. To

Vex's right, Kari, Edda, and Cansu's raiders were tied to chairs; to his left was Nayeli. All had bags on their heads.

Ahead of him, backed up by equally furious-looking raiders, stood Nathaniel Blaise.

Emerdians held leatherworking, equestrianism, and masonry as elite parts of their culture. Nate wore their telltale signs: a well-crafted leather jacket, gleaming riding boots, and a flared maroon leather hat with a wide brim that curved up on the sides. Two pistols sat on his hips, and when he hooked his hands around one, polished stone rings flashed on three of his fingers.

Nate had never intimidated Vex. There were two types of Emerdians—the blithe kind who served Argrid's Pious God but used that religion as an excuse to be forgiven for any sin they could think of; and the studious, manipulative kind who had taken Emerdian crafts like masonry and warped them into buildings like that inescapable prison.

Nate was the former type—the reason he'd let his syndicate flounder in poverty so long. But his husband was the latter, and god, was *that* man terrifying.

"Where's Pierce?" Vex asked. "Your husband promised he'd do a few things to me if I showed my face in Port Camden again, and I'm curious to see how he keeps those promises. Some of them didn't sound physically possible."

Nate's whole face went red. He ripped off his hat, chucked it behind him, and dove forward, throwing Vex back in the chair.

"You don't get to talk about him," Nate snapped. "Especially you, Argridian rat. I've cleaned enough of you out of my city, but you keep popping up like the pointy-faced vermin you are."

Vex's whole body went molten hot. "The hell you say?"

Nate reared back to rip a pistol from his holster and aim it at Vex's head.

"You know me, Nate!" Vex tried. "That doesn't mean you like me, but you know I'm not—"

"Don't matter. Argridian's Argridian, and if I'd followed that rule from the start, I wouldn't have had to put up with your bullshit in the past."

Vex gawked. He admitted to being a pain in the raider Heads' asses, stealing from them, blowing up their stuff—but that was the reason Nate should've hated him. Because he was a nuisance. Not because Vex was an *Argridian rat.*

The difference sank into Vex's toes. After the revolution, there had been two options on this island for people with Argridian pasts: either they gave up all ties and called themselves Grace Lorayan, or they stuck to being Argridian but got labeled *one of the enemy.* Vex'd become a raider, a pest on his own, and *that* was what he was known for.

This war had reshuffled enemies and allies. On one side, Argrid and the Grace Lorayans had unified to get rid of outsiders—raiders. On the other, raiders were justified in hating Argridians and Grace Lorayans for trying to wipe them out.

But what about Argridian raiders? What about anyone who still didn't fit into the narrow boxes this country kept trying to squeeze around people?

Being Argridian felt as volatile as Vex's Shaking Sickness. He hadn't chosen to be this way, but that didn't matter in Nate's hatred. Yet another instance of Vex's work to reinvent himself these past five years not meaning a damn thing.

Nate cocked the pistol. "Give me one good reason why I shouldn't save myself a lot of trouble and kill you now."

Vex jutted his head at Kari. "She'll explain."

Nate yanked the bag off Kari's head. She blinked, dazed by the light, and when she focused on him, Nate aimed the pistol at Vex again. But there was a desperation in his look now, a glaze over his eyes and a twitch to his lips. Was Nate crying?

"An Argridian and a councilmember." Nate laid each letter side by side. "In my city."

"Goddamn it, Nate, I'm not an Argridian! Stop saying that. The hell is wrong with you?"

"You Argridians took over my city," Nate said. "Most of my raiders are *gone*. People have been going missing for weeks, before Elazar got here, so I thought it was those damn Grozdans on our eastern border. Snatching up my raiders 'cause their own are all muscle, no brain." Nate clicked his tongue in disgust. "But when Elazar revealed he was working with the Council, I knew it'd been him all along. We put up a fight. But the Council soldiers in Port Camden knew we'd turn on 'em, because they knew Elazar was here before we ever did. Triple the number of guards met our resistance. I lost almost a third of my raiders in one day, not including the half dozen that Argrid—*the Council*, too—captured. They're being held in the prison *we* built. Shit, we should've torn that place down after the war. Not only that—"

Nate *was* crying. He lowered the pistol to his thigh with a trembling gulp and smeared the back of his hand across his nose.

Vex looked around the room. Realization smacked him in the head. "Where's Pierce?"

"Don't act concerned. I'll get him back and then I'll get you Argridian rats out of Port Camden—"

"How?"

Nate and Vex looked at Kari, who stared calmly back at them.

"Kari the Wave," Nate snapped. "Kari the Senior Councilmember. Last I saw you was more than five years ago, when you and a group of rebels convinced us raiders to rally against Argrid. You lot made promises about what'd happen after the revolution—and didn't waste no time breaking every single one when the war ended."

"Now the Council's gone and allied with Argrid," another raider spat. "Kill 'em!"

Nate stood there, fury in the lines around his mouth, in

his tight grip on the pistol.

"That is why this takeover has happened: because we did not fulfill our promises to you."

Vex's eyebrows rose. Kari straightened, as proper and regal as if she wasn't restrained.

"Had we stayed true," she continued, "Grace Loray would have unified five years ago and Argrid would never have had the opportunity to separate us by twisting prejudices and deceiving our citizens. The allegiance between Argrid and the Council was a lie to soothe Argrid's presence here—Argrid locked away many councilmembers for refusing the union. Though Mr. Bell and I"—she nodded at Vex—"have come together, that act should not be reduced to an Argridian and a councilmember machinating against you. Quite the opposite. The bills that passed in recent days to eradicate stream raiders, the terror and prejudice that have gripped the island, are not the Grace Loray I fought for. I strove from the beginning of this country to bring fairness—but I failed. I failed Grace Loray. I failed *you*. I am sorry."

Nate and his raiders gaped at Kari. Vex gaped at Kari. The bags were still on their heads, but Vex suspected Nayeli, Edda, and Cansu's raiders were gaping at Kari.

Hearing a councilmember apologize had never been on Vex's most desired list, but now that he heard it, it loosened his anger. The disgust when the Council heralded being *Grace Lorayan* as the only possible future and ignored anyone who refused to take on that nationality.

The rest of the room seemed to share his realization.

Nate cleared his throat and pulled on his *I haven't decided if I'll kill you* face, but he holstered the pistol. "We're well aware that you failed. You going around, offering apologies? Apologies won't bring back anyone who Argrid's snatched."

Nate's raiders shifted, their faces speaking to the terror that hung over every street, the innocent people who had run from Argridian soldiers. How many of these raiders had family members who Argrid had taken? Or worse?

"My apology was not meant to fix anything. You merely deserved to hear it," Kari said with a shrug. "We have come to seek your help removing Argrid from Grace Loray. This request echoes of the past, I know, but I do not come with a militia of rebels—I come as myself, surrounded by raiders from other syndicates, to ask you, a powerful raider Head, to take up the mantle of Grace Loray's freedom. I offer my knowledge of strategy, but I will follow your lead, and I will not ask you to agree to war without proof of my value. First, together, we will work to free your people—your husband—from the prison."

Nate went cherry red. "You're holding my husband as ransom for going to war?"

"No. Your decision to stand against Argrid is your own—my allies and I will attack the prison with or without you. A fleet of Tuncian steamboats is on its way to Port Camden now. We have our own plans, but we would be grateful for your syndicate's knowledge of the prison. Should our rescue be successful and you find my services of value, we can discuss taking further action against Argrid. But your husband will be free no matter your choice."

"Why do I need you?" Nate snapped. "You're tangled up with the Tuncians already—so if I went to war, I'd have to work with Cansu, yeah? Where the hell is she, anyway?"

"She's also in the prison," Kari said. "But we have Tuncian representatives with us."

Nayeli, the bag still over her head, jerked as though someone had stabbed her. Kari could've been referring to Cansu's raiders—but she had no reason not to think Nayeli was part of the Tuncian syndicate as well. Nayeli had left the Tuncian syndicate less than three years ago when she'd had enough of her aunt Fatemah and Cansu preferring to wallow in poverty rather than accept the Grace Lorayan Council's help in exchange for *being Grace Lorayan,* not Tuncian.

When was the last time anyone had called Nayeli a Tuncian representative? Probably around the last time anyone had called Vex an Argridian without it being a slur.

Vex swallowed, wishing he could share a look of disbelief with Nayeli.

Nate's eyes widened. "Argrid captured a Head? Shit. *Shit.*"

Kari nodded at Nate's raiders. "Am I right to assume

that you have not attacked the prison because you no longer have enough troops? How many has Argrid arrested?"

"I've lost forty-two raiders in the past three days, including my husband," Nate said. "Most in our initial attack on the Port Camden soldiers, but since then, anyone out past dark, Argrid takes. Anyone on the rivers, they question, and if they don't like the answers, they take. Anyone who refuses to surrender magic, Argrid takes."

Nate pinched the bridge of his nose and muttered a prayer.

Emerdon followed the Argridian Church, but Emerdians viewed the Pious God less as an all-powerful deity and more as a benevolent overseer who occasionally passed out punishments. They also didn't recognize Elazar's unquestioned authority as Eminence.

The Church for Argridians was a way of life; the Church for Emerdians was a sport. Vex repeated that to himself as one of Nate's raiders made the sign of the Church against his chest.

"Fine. Shit. *Fine.*" Nate waved his hands. "We'll help you break into the prison. But that doesn't mean I agree to ally with the Tuncians or go to war. This is a prison break. Getting my people out. Showing Argrid what happens when they mess with the Emerdian syndicate. Hell, might be enough to scare Elazar back across the ocean."

Doubtful. Vex bit his lips together—tighter when he saw Nate glaring at him.

"I'm not one of those Argridians," Vex said again, but it

lost his earlier fire. He was *one of those Argridians*, more than Nate knew.

Maybe Nate was right, in a messed-up way, and Vex shouldn't be involved. Maybe everything would be better if all Argridians backed off and hid away somewhere.

"After we free the prisoners," Kari started again (Vex noted how she hadn't mentioned that Ben would be one of the prisoners they'd rescue), "we will not be able to stay in Port Camden. The success of the attack will rattle Elazar and we do not have the numbers to retake this city. If you choose not to join our war efforts, you will be staying in Port Camden without aid. Your people may well end up back in prison."

Nate frowned. "Are you threatening me?"

"Of course not—I want you to be aware of the facts. If this is only a prison break to you, not the first step in a larger war, we will part ways after the prisoners are free. Our people will need to convene in the southeast—with the Tuncians in Port Mesi-Teab. Our ultimate goal to save Grace Loray from Argrid will, eventually, free Port Camden."

Nate sucked in a breath to counter, but Kari kept talking.

"Or," she said, "you and your people may join us in Port Mesi-Teab to regroup and press on in other attacks against Argrid. But you will be joining the war, and have to leave your city behind. Not *forever*, I promise you that."

Nate's lip curled. He held for a moment, another, before he snapped at his raiders.

"You—unlock their manacles. We're gonna plan the prison break," Nate said to Kari. "I haven't decided about any war yet. Don't get confident."

Kari stood, stepping away with Nate to discuss their attack.

"Damn," Nayeli said, rubbing her wrists where the irons had been. "One conversation, and she convinced Nate to listen."

"We might actually do this," Edda whispered on Vex's other side. "The prison, the war."

Vex started to agree but choked. He'd been in the Port Camden prison to break Edda out two years back after a misunderstanding with Council soldiers—but she hadn't been processed yet, and he'd snatched her from the atrium. He'd heard rumors about the bowels of the prison, how some of the halls moved on the guards' whims, and other levels made people go mad.

An image hit Vex, of him and his group searching the cells as Argridians streamed in. What if they missed Ben's cell? What if Elazar had already decided his son was expendable?

Rodrigu had made Ben play the strategy game when they were younger too—and, once, Ben had beaten him. Rodrigu's eyes had gone from the board to Ben's face in startled shock.

Rodrigu had never looked at Paxben like that. Like he was proud.

At the time, Vex hadn't cared. The game was stupid, and he could make his father laugh in a way no one else could—that was important too, right? That other stuff, a distant revolution and the succession of the Argridian royal family, would work itself out. Rodrigu had planned it. Paxben didn't need to worry.

Kari and Nate neared a table covered with papers and maps.

Did Vex want to play that role again? The role of errant child, letting older and more experienced people make decisions that would shape his life? When he'd done that, his father had burned to death. The girl he might've loved had gotten stabbed on the deck of a ship. He'd left his cousin to god-knew-what fate.

Vex fought a shudder and looked at Nate and Kari with renewed purpose.

Whatever his role in this war, he sure as hell wouldn't let things happen *to* him anymore.

8

THE DEFENSORS DRAGGED Ben and Gunnar to three more villages before the day was done.

In each one, Elazar gave the same speech about raiders being the true enemy; a coming light that would purify the evil and bless the obedient; unity with the Council; and the reveal of his wicked son. Ingvar and Tom gave the same supplication, and Elazar revealed sick villagers made well by *the Pious God's mighty powers.*

Each time, the crowd hesitated until the healed villagers appeared. Children, adults, elderly—the ages varied, but the results were the same: all sicknesses gone. Old wounds, bones that hadn't healed right. The potion made these people anew, and no one on Grace Loray—or anywhere—had ever seen such results. The strongest healing plant on this island cured current wounds and sicknesses, nothing from the past.

In village after village, people surrendered their magic, vowing devotion to the Pious God. Elazar's claims that raiders were servants of the Devil made sense. To most citizens, they were criminals, thieving beasts who stole livelihoods and property. The revolution against Argrid five years ago—that conflict had been the reason no one had seen the full strength of the Pious God's power before now.

When Elazar's defensors became invincible with permanent magic—unstoppable strength and lasting speed and constant healing—it would only confirm his claims. Of course *Argrid* had the strongest military—the Pious God had ordained them!

What would be next? The Mechtlands, divided and warring, primed to be overtaken? Emerdon, which already worshipped the Pious God? Grozda, small and treacherous?

Was that what Elazar wanted—the entire world bowing at his feet, crying out for the Pious God? He had tried to force that on Grace Loray the first time. Did he think having permanent magic on Argrid's side would be enough to change the outcome now?

Ben had had uncles besides Rodrigu whom he had never met. He had had a mother he couldn't remember, a little sister he had never known, grandparents he could only name. He had known Elazar was evil, but he hadn't—he had never thought—

Ben's body felt bursting with muddy waters. He couldn't get rid of the inescapable feeling of filth, inside and out.

Elazar would become the Pious God incarnate, if he wasn't already.

The defensors pushed Ben and Gunnar back into the twisting, shifting halls of the prison. The moment the stones closed over them, trading the orange sunset for gray rock, Gunnar faltered. Ben moved to catch him, but Gunnar stumbled past. The pressure of these walls bore down on Ben's soul too, leaving a metallic grittiness in his mouth.

Defensors pulled Gunnar back into his solitary cell and shoved Ben into the one with Lu. But this time, Gunnar was not chained to the ceiling—the defensors just tossed him to the floor and left.

Gunnar, braced on his knuckles, flicked his eyes blearily behind Ben. His posture changed from slumped to alert.

Ben whirled.

Lu hunched on the cot, hair across her face, head on the wall. She barely moved, her breathing stunted. Ben almost asked what was wrong when his stomach clenched.

Her black shirt acted as camouflage, but the torchlight caught it: blood coated her right arm up to her shoulder.

A hundred possibilities charged through Ben's mind. A hundred horrible torments he knew the Church inflicted on sinners. He lived every one of them, staring down at Lu.

She found him from behind strands of her hair. "Lazonade . . . wearing off . . ."

She tapped her head against the wall with a gasp that sucked the life out of Ben. When she twisted, her arm moved farther into the light—the fabric of her sleeve wasn't sliced. Just her skin beneath, methodic cuts bleeding through, like tick marks carved into a cell wall.

The Lazonade—*someone gave her Lazonade?*—would let her numb body slowly, achingly feel the pain of so many wounds. Torture, twice.

Ben sat next to her and lifted a trembling hand. She recoiled and he pulled back, pulse humming in his ears as a tear rolled down her sunken face.

Watching the defensors whip Gunnar had bruised Ben's soul. But knowing Lu had been tortured, alone—

He couldn't find nobility in resistance, nothing he could form into a speech about strength. Whatever had happened . . . Elazar had found what would break Lu. Their future played out in knife cuts and whip cracks, village parades and death threats.

"I won't leave you again," Ben fumbled. "Lu, I promise—"

"Benat." Gunnar's warning came a heartbeat before another voice overpowered the hall.

"That is not for you to decide."

Ben spun off the cot. Jakes, Ibarra, and Elazar stood in the hall.

Seeing Ibarra yanked a memory forward—in the captain's office on the *Astuto*, Ibarra had recognized Lu. He'd *hated* her.

The prison walls rippled at the edges of Ben's vision. Ibarra had been the one to hurt her.

Ben couldn't protect Lu. He couldn't protect Gunnar. His country was committing these atrocities, and he couldn't stop any of it.

A rush of blood resounded in his head, his shoulders heaving on furious breaths.

Elazar folded his arms. Here, Ben could see stains on the hem of his blue robe, a splattering of mud on Elazar's left hip. His hair was still neatly styled, the oiled black and gray strands reflecting torchlight in stabbing flares.

"Lieutenant Ibarra," Elazar said, his eyes on Ben. "I have long suspected evil would grip my son, and I prepared ways to save him. But I have kept you, despite your disappointments, because you assured me you can reach this girl. Was I wrong to trust you?"

"No, sire. You will be pleased."

Elazar sighed. He looked at Lu, curled on the cot. "Sweet girl, are you ready to confess your sins and give yourself over to the Pious God's plan?"

"No," Ben said. His heart screamed, so he said it again. "No, you'll have to kill us—"

Lu made a frail cry, high in her throat. "Yes. I surrender to you."

Ben staggered. But she looked up at him, blood pulsing down her arm, and the plea in the divot between her brows came from a place of single-minded need for respite.

Iron clanged and squealed as their cell door unlocked. Ben made himself face Ibarra.

The lieutenant grinned and pointed at the floor. "When we come, both of you will kneel to show respect for the Eminence King."

Ben staggered. In the hall, Jakes watched Elazar, who made the curved *V* of the Church with his hands against his chest.

When Jakes looked at him, Ben lowered himself to his knees so it was almost to Jakes that Ben was supplicating. Jakes parted his lips but didn't speak.

The cot shrieked. Ben didn't have time to help her before Lu slid off the thin mattress and buckled to the floor next to him. The fading Lazonade made her arms droop before her.

"Good," Ibarra said, and patted her hair. "What sins have you committed, child?"

Nausea clamped Ben's throat. Lu trembled, her bloodied arm rubbing against him.

"Defiance," Ben spoke. This was all he could do for her. He knew what Ibarra and Elazar wanted to hear. "Pride. We—" He dug his fingers into the stained, worn fabric of his breeches to hold himself steady. "We give ourselves over to the will of the Pious God."

Ben had spoken similar lies most of his life, but a long strand of fatigue hung off this one. He'd promised himself he was done, that he was *free*.

A pause, and Ibarra's hand swooped down to break against Lu's cheek. She crashed into Ben, who scrambled to catch her.

"Stop!" Ben shouted. "We gave in! You will have what you want—now *stop!*"

Ibarra pointed a harsh finger as Lu shrank into Ben's chest. No—he pointed with two metal rods that looked like plant tongs. "If you think you can trick us," Ibarra said. "If you try to escape again. Remember—you may run, but you will always end up here, cowering at my feet."

Ben lunged as if to grab Ibarra, to punch him, *something*—but Elazar was in the cell now. When had he moved? Ben yanked Lu closer, letting free an unexpected shout of alarm. The torture and games had loosened his instinct to shout when his father was near, no resolve left to keep himself strong.

"You have done well, Lieutenant," Elazar said. He paused, considering. "I will reassess your demotion. For now, you may resume your post overseeing my defensors on Grace Loray."

Ibarra let out a relieved sigh and bowed at the waist. "My king."

Face against Ben's chest, Lu shuddered.

Elazar knelt to put one hand on Lu's bowed head. With the other, he cupped Ben's face.

More than five years ago, Ben had had a nightmare about Rodrigu and Paxben's burning. He had sought out his father in his study the next morning.

"I knew them, Father. They weren't evil. Burning them was wrong—"

Elazar had curled his fingers around a marble paper-weight emblazoned with the Church's curved *V.* The rings on his fingers—one a thick ruby set in gold, the other the seal of Argrid in cobalt and sapphire—caught fire on the righteousness in his eyes.

The first blow had rendered Ben speechless, making him too numb to fight back.

"Do not question the Pious God, Benat," Elazar had said. Another strike, the paperweight cracking on Ben's jaw. *"You are incapable of seeing the evil that was in Rodrigu."* Another, another; Ben fell to the floor, crying *"Father, Father, stop——"* *"But you will not question me when I say that it was there. You will not question me, ever."*

"Stop," came a gruff voice now. "Don't— Take me— *don't hurt him——"*

Gunnar held himself up by a white-knuckled grip on his cell bars, twitching in the prison's disorientation.

Though Gunnar couldn't physically put himself between Ben and Elazar, the idea made Ben's chest go cold, hot, cold again, changing on every inhale with dizzying, centering gratitude.

Elazar looked at Gunnar, and Ben twitched forward with a panicked gasp. By the flicker at the edge of Elazar's lips, the motion was not unnoticed.

"Let their surrender inspire you," Elazar said to Gunnar. "You know how your people made Eye of the Sun permanent. Tell us, so these servants of the Pious God can fulfill

His mighty work. They may be able to remove the Devil's touch from you, barbarian."

"He isn't a barbarian," Ben snapped.

Elazar smirked at Ben. "The Devil may think himself clever in his tricks, but a true follower of the Pious God always sees the pattern. You, my son, have a habit of yoking yourself to the wrong people."

"You haven't given me many choices." Ben took pride in the harsh fury of his own response. "You killed everyone else."

Elazar's grip on Ben's face was gentle, terrifying. "I have sacrificed everyone the Pious God has asked of me," Elazar told him. His father's straightforwardness shot from Ben's head to his gut, seizing him. "But Argrid's shortcomings are punishment, Benat, for not giving enough. I have held on to the one person I believed that the Pious God would never ask for: you."

Every nerve twisted. Every vein pinched shut.

"I have wondered"—Elazar stroked Ben's jaw, lingering on the scar and bump from the long-healed bone—"if I merely did not hear the Pious God's request. If I sacrificed you, would that unlock Argrid's destiny? Our country's poverty, our loss of Grace Loray—did that happen because I kept you? Was I meant to sacrifice you?"

"Ben." Lu's voice was far away. "Ben, don't listen—"

"I almost did." Elazar stared into Ben's eyes. "I almost let the crowds in Deza take you away to burn you as a heretic. But the Pious God showed me a larger sacrifice, the one I should have made long ago, something grander than my love for you."

"The 'coming light'?" The words lifted from Ben's memory, his body numb.

Elazar smiled. "The world will change, Benat. The time for wavering between sin and salvation is at an end. You have repented, but we both know you are capable of lying. I promise you, if you are not sincere, I will do whatever I have to do to save you now."

Ben was a hundred pieces, mismatched and jagged, and he believed, more than he had ever believed anything, that Elazar would go to any lengths necessary to secure his obedience.

"Adeluna." Elazar faced her with a sad sigh. "I believe in your repentance only slightly more. You will be granted access to magic—harmless magic. If you prove trustworthy with those plants, I will consider reuniting you with your father. He has taken to the task of finding permanent magic with a zeal I wish you yourself would embrace."

Lu's father was working on permanent magic for Elazar now? Even Ben, in his stupor, noticed her recoil of disgust at the offer of being turned over to him.

Elazar hummed. "Is that not what you want? What a fitting pair you two make." He smoothed Ben's hair out of his face, another jolting caress. "Two wayward children, so certain of their fathers' misdeeds that they cannot see their own. The Pious God is poetic."

A tear toppled down Ben's face. Elazar rose, his fingers trailing Ben's temple, and when the contact released, Ben wrenched in a breath as though his father's hands had been around his throat.

Elazar hummed again, acknowledging Ben's weakness. He went into the hall with Ibarra.

Jakes took a step forward as Ibarra locked the cell. "Ben—"

"Come, Defensor," Elazar ordered. "Let them bask in their surrender."

They left, footsteps echoing—that thudding echo would haunt Ben the rest of his life.

Lu stirred against him when they were alone. "I'm sorry. If I hadn't said—"

Ben grabbed her shoulders and pushed her back. New blood streaked across her face from a cut on her forehead, her eye half-open and fluttering.

"I don't give a damn what happened." A lie, but he needed this one for his own stability.

Lu's arm streamed blood. Gunnar had gotten bandages—would monxes come with aid for Lu? Ben couldn't wait for that.

He pulled the sheet off the cot and started tearing long strips. Moving felt good. As if his father's words and touch had formed a shell on his skin, and each motion sent cracks through it, breaking it off him.

Every outcome Ben had feared had happened right there in his father's eyes.

And Ben was still alive. That was enough, now. To exist.

"You cannot give magic to them," Gunnar stated, his voice rough.

Lu rocked forward, back. "I'm going to make the magic for us. For me. I'll take it, and become the unstoppable soldier they want us to create."

Ben hesitated. "I thought you were agreeing to work on magic just to buy us time."

"Buy us time for what?" Lu gave him a look of madness and terror, of many things and yet nothing, and that nothingness planted fear in Ben's heart.

"The defensor. Jakes," Ben said. "I can reach him. I can convince him to help us."

"How long will that take?" Lu snapped. "How many whippings? How many more—"

Her words died as she caved forward with a sob, her arm limp in her lap.

Ben could try to persuade Jakes to help—or if not, then use him or trick him. Ben, Gunnar, and Lu could break out of these cells, run into the shifting halls. But how many escape attempts would Elazar tolerate before he declared them beyond salvation? He already had Lu's father at work on permanent magic too, and who knew how many other resources? Lu and Ben were the two who were closest to a solution, but others could make them obsolete.

Once a heretic, the only way out was through flames.

Lu wanted to make the magic Elazar sought, and put it in her body before he could use it. That had been their plan, back on the *Astuto*—to make magic first and show the world that such power came from Grace Loray, not the Pious God. Was it too late for that? Ben had seen how quickly the villagers of Grace Loray had surrendered to Elazar. Would they believe anyone who countered him and said, *"No, these mighty acts are not the Pious God, but your own magic?"*

Did these types of grand thoughts matter right now? They needed to escape.

Ben felt ill.

Gunnar waved at himself. He winced, his own wounds unhealed. "Eye of the Sun. Elazar—he is not wrong about that. Can you remove it from me?"

Ben finished the sheet, now a pile of makeshift bandages. Lu pushed up her sleeve and set about wrapping them around her wounds.

"I don't know," Lu said, grimacing. "Maybe. I can't—*ah.*"

"Here." Ben took her wrist and tightened a strip for her.

She let him, which surprised him almost as much as the brazen way she asked Gunnar, "How was it made permanent?"

Gunnar blinked. Lu's face flashed with empathy.

"I can't undo it if I don't know how your people gave it to you," she said.

Gunnar dropped to the floor in a huff. Silence held, no distant footsteps or grating walls.

"They slaughter the bear," Gunnar whispered.

Lu hardened under Ben's touch and met his eyes. Gunnar was still in a drug-warped fog. Did he know he was speaking? If he was clearheaded, he wouldn't tell them this—

Ben almost spoke, but Lu snatched his hand.

"They are rare, the bears. The embodiment of the Visjorn spirit. One of the few things Mecht clans agree on is that Visjorn bears are only to be killed for—this." Gunnar launched a flame into his palm. "Eye of the Sun commanders hunt one into the mountains. They slit its throat, gather the blood. They take it, and Eye of the Sun flower, and they—" He made a motion like stirring. "Warriors drink it. They cannot stand, cannot speak, even, for days after. Others—" Gunnar threw his head back so his golden hair fell away from his face. The knot in his throat bobbed on a swallow. "Some women volunteer to drink the mixture, their swollen bellies . . . It is an honor, to birth an Eye of the Sun warrior. They are stronger. They are near gods.

"My mother volunteered." Gunnar's voice had been soft before, but now it was snowflakes on a blanket of snow. "She is revered for having me. But she is not . . . right. The women, they survive, but barely. It is not a life. Not an *honor*."

His cheek glinted. He was weeping.

Ben choked down the urge to unravel.

"Pregnant women." Lu pierced Ben with a look. "Your father can never know that."

Could he already? Ben had no idea what other experiments Elazar had employed over the years. Or which ones he was still doing.

"Even if I can remove it from you," Lu started, "we need your abilities to get out. *I* need strength too. The secret is Visjorn blood?"

"Or the way they cook it," Ben said. "Or the way they prepare the flower. Or all of it, a perfect dance. There are too many variables—we should focus on another escape option."

"I tried to escape while you were gone." Lu motioned to her now-bandaged arm. "We need a weapon that will make us stronger than Elazar. To get out—and to win this war. Grace Loray put everything we had into the last revolution, and we still ended up back here, under Argrid. To stop them, to truly win, we need an undefeatable weapon."

"I won't make permanent magic while we're under Elazar's control," Ben said, "and I will never make it as a weapon. I will not become my father to stop him." *I still feel*, came the unwarranted thought. *I am not him—I will* never *be him—*

Lu looked ready to scream, but Gunnar spoke first.

"She's right," he said. "This is how wars are fought— with weapons, not with secrets."

"You told me the opposite on the *Astuto*: that this magic

is burning the Mechtlands. That making permanent magic will encourage greater threats. What changed?"

Gunnar's face was soft, his head bobbing. "Permanent magic is a powerful weapon. Creating it invites threats. But your father is already a threat. I did not know him before. We must create a weapon powerful enough to match him."

"But you heard Elazar in the villages." To Lu, Ben explained, "He spoke of a coming light that will bless those who surrender to him and destroy the ones who fight back. He has a plan that he believes will be enough of a sacrifice to make the Pious God grant him unchallenged power—which means people will *die*. What if permanent magic is the final piece of his plan?"

"We already know that permanent magic is the final piece to his plan," Lu shot back. "He wants to make his soldiers unstoppable as they force Grace Loray to submit. *There's* his coming light. But if I have permanent magic first? I will be unchallenged. Not him. This was his plan and ours when we were still on your father's ship. Why would you think it's changed?"

Ben shook his head, unable to process the level of pain in her eyes. Perhaps she was right. With everything that had happened, Ben had lost sight of the details. Elazar himself had told Ben his great plan in the Grace Neus Cathedral, to create unstoppable defensors.

Still, Ben couldn't soothe the itch that Elazar had not told him about every facet of his final triumph.

Lu tapped her fingers on her knee. "We can't get Visjorn blood without Elazar's knowledge. But we can work on other things once he gives us magic. Maybe it's temperature, like you said. Or method."

Ben jerked back, his fire wearing off, leaving him exhausted to his bones.

"We must try," Gunnar said. "To fight this way. What would you rather do?"

All Ben had was the image of Lu's bloodstained shirt. The memory of Gunnar's whimper after his beating. The cheers of the people whose loved ones Elazar had healed in the villages.

Hopelessness beat an empty laugh from Ben's chest.

Everyone except Ben wanted to use magic in this war. How could he be the only one who sensed how futile it would be? Using magic against Elazar was like tossing buckets of water into a flood—it would add more of the danger that would destroy them.

❖❖❖

Monxes brought Lu and Ben the crudest of laboratory supplies. A table, mortars, pestles, and vials of the most harmless plants: some for healing, some for strength, some for movement. They left a book as well—Lu's worn copy of *Botanical Wonders of the Grace Loray Colony*, the bullet hole in its cover an oddly calming link to her life outside this prison.

But she had no use for this book now, knowing how incomplete its information on Grace Loray's magic truly was. She knew about reducing plants to increase their potency from what Fatemah had done with Budwig Beans. To cure Shaking Sickness, which was caused by taking too much botanical magic, one needed to take the plants that countered what they had ingested—a realization Lu had come to on her own. Ben had explained on the *Astuto* what plants had gone into his healing potion. Gunnar had given them the piece about Visjorn blood, and the notion of specific heat, or the addition of nonplant ingredients, or length of cooking.

Tom couldn't have learned any of that, even with her slipup in mentioning the Tuncians. So he couldn't be that close to making permanent magic.

Could the secret lie in the cause and cure of Shaking Sickness? To take, at once, both a concentrated version of a plant and its counterpart with no delay between the absorption of one over the other. Aerated Blossom, a plant that gave levity and flight, counteracted Powersage, a strength-enhancing plant—could distilled versions of both in one tonic balance their effects and give extended, permanent strength and flight?

Monxes provided a pair of tongs similar to what Lu had used to pick the cell's lock. The curved metal glinting on the table was as if Milo were outside the bars, unlocking the door and ushering her out. He wanted her to try to escape again.

Ben and Gunnar were here, though. This time would be

different. They would get out, but they would have to be strategic—and they would need permanent magic.

Lu worked.

At some point, monxes returned with defensors. Maybe a day later, maybe longer, time was impossible to tell. They asked what progress had been made.

"None," Lu said. Before she could regret it, defensors chained Gunnar and whipped him forty-two times while the monxes prayed to the Pious God for understanding.

"Lu." Ben was next to her, his voice rough with tears, his matted hair falling around his face. Behind him, Gunnar moaned as he was let down from his chains.

"Some plants are already permanent, in a way," Lu whispered to a vial of Cleanse Root. She had used Healica to mend her own wounds, but they wouldn't be able to reach Gunnar, across the hall. "Permanent in that when you ingest a healing plant, your injury does not return. Or—" *With Menesia, your memories do not resurface.* Lu blocked the discussion Milo had had with her father. "What we want is similar, but to make it so plants continue to work. For them to lie dormant in the body until called upon. That's right, isn't it?"

Gunnar cried out and Ben's eyes snapped shut.

They were all stretched so thin, Lu thought she must be translucent.

Ben dropped onto the cot next to the table. "What do you want me to do?"

She and Ben tried to make Powersage and Aerated Blossom permanent. The difficulty lay in the application—Powersage gave increased strength when absorbed through the skin; Aerated Blossom gave a few seconds of flight when inhaled. They infused Powersage with Aerated Blossom smoke and cooked it over a burner on high, high heat until they had a single dose—but how to apply it? To rub it on the skin? To eat it?

Lu dreamed of Tom. Of him arguing with Kari in their sunlit apartment. Of him working on magic in his own laboratory and making discoveries Lu hadn't yet realized.

He never came to see her. Whether by Elazar's choice or his own, it didn't matter.

Milo and Elazar came. Ben choked out the excuse that he and Lu had ruined their latest batches of magic—but Lu had a vial of mixed Powersage and Aerated Blossom in her boot.

Elazar stood in the hall, Ben restrained by Jakes and Gunnar rattling on the bars of his cell, as Milo dosed her with Lazonade and cut her apart.

After Milo left, she sat on the cot, her head on Ben's shoulder, dreading and hoping for her numbness to subside. Ben ground down more Healica for her.

"Vex," Lu said into the stillness. Horror set her spinning. "I haven't . . . I haven't asked you what plants the Church might have given him."

Ben moaned in confusion.

Sensation crept into Lu's hands and she fought not to scream as her new wounds burned. "Shaking Sickness. The Church gave him Shaking Sickness. You would know what they used."

Ben shifted. "Paxben has Shaking Sickness?"

She frowned. He didn't know? She had to have told him. . . .

Ben drew her closer to him and handed her the prepared Healica. "We can talk about—Vex—later. Rest."

Panic split through Lu's fog. They couldn't rest. Milo would return, again and again; defensors would whip Gunnar, over and over.

She wanted to get out. She wanted to go home. She wanted to be alone on this island with only the people she loved. She wanted *peace*.

Lu reached to her boot, a shout cracking her lips. She grabbed the vial of Powersage and Aerated Blossom.

Ben didn't speak as Lu downed the vial. She cringed at the syrupy tartness, not at what it might do to her. Whether this potion worked didn't matter—when Lu was healed, she would pick the lock again. She would leave this cell and never come back.

One way or another.

9

VEX, HIS CREW, and Kari were going to break into the Port Camden prison with the Emerdian and Tuncian raider syndicates.

No matter how many times Vex repeated that, he couldn't take it seriously. But if the war went as expected, *all* the syndicates would be working together, and with the Council too. It was so inconceivable that Vex found himself constantly shaking his head.

While Cansu's raiders used Nayeli's Budwig Bean to coordinate the arrival of the Tuncian raider armada, Nate went over the prison layout. His syndicate had gotten schematics for the building over the years—Emerdian raiders were, after all, the ones most likely to get locked up there—so he showed them sketches of the prison's floors, explaining which halls could be moved and where the levers were hidden.

There were as many as seven levels, four deep in the prison's plateau, three aboveground; but with a twist of a lever, one section connected to another and seven levels became six. When the Emerdians and the Tuncians attacked the prison, their priority would be getting to the levers and knobs first, and putting a half dozen people in charge of fighting off any guards who tried to overtake them.

"The levers correspond to walls; the knobs to cells; large cranks move whole hallways," Nate explained one night to Kari and Vex. A fire raged in the peach-blush brick hearth, sweltering the room alongside the constant island heat. Having a fire whenever people were in a room was an Emerdian tradition, Vex had learned.

After four days cramped in Nate's rickety townhouse—*"This is just a beat-up old safe house. My real home is far more lavish—don't touch that! It's an antique!"*—Vex had learned more about the Emerdian Head and his raiders than he had ever wanted to know. They couldn't go into the city too often for fear of Argrid snatching them up, so they'd stayed cramped in this three-story hotbox, sleeping on the floor, arguing over the food Nate's raiders managed to find in the desolate streets, and generally getting in each other's way.

Nate gulped from a canteen and hissed at the acidity of—he'd told Vex three times now—*liquor that'll rip the skin off your throat.*

"That water too much for you, Nate?" Vex asked.

Nate ignored him and leaned over the table. He was the

only one standing—a sad attempt at snatching control when it was clear at every moment that Kari was in charge.

"There are four places in the prison with smaller control panels." Nate pointed at a map. "Only the guardhouse—here—has a panel with all the controls, but shit, it's a nightmare. Twenty different levers. Fifteen knobs. Five cranks." Nate folded his arms triumphantly. "Luckily, you have someone who understands the innermost workings of this complicated system."

"Oh?" Vex leaned back in his chair. "When does he get here?"

"You're dying of Shaking Sickness, yet you have the energy to insult me. I'm honored."

The heat had already made Vex's face red, but he swallowed hard. They'd spent too long in this small space together—Vex knew Nate had a minor Narcotium Creeper addiction and chewed leaves every night before bed; another of his raiders hummed in his sleep; one raider named Barnabas had a bag of nasty Emerdian licorice hidden under a floorboard, and he'd stuff a few pieces in his mouth when he thought no one was looking. As though candies that smelled like feet were in danger of being stolen.

If Vex'd noticed that, of course someone had noticed him shaking. It happened all the damn time now, anyway.

"Insulting you is effortless, Natey," Vex spat. "I hardly break a sweat."

"Why are you here?" Nate countered. "You aren't

contributing. Go wait for the Tuncians by the door like the good little unaligned Argridian rat you are."

"Really don't like how you keep saying Argridian rat."

"Really don't care, *Argridian rat*."

Vex scowled. He'd joined every meeting where Kari and Nate went over their plans, and all he'd done was make smart-ass comments. He could see Kari's growing exasperation, but damn it, he would've contributed if he could. But any suggestion he thought of, they'd already planned.

What would Ben do? He'd have added something useful about other allies or a single move that'd make the whole war easier. Vex had had lessons on diplomacy and war alongside Ben when they'd been younger, but he'd spent those classes drawing inappropriate sketches of the monxe tutors. Anytime Rodrigu had discussed strategy with him, Vex had been so fidgety he'd ended up with his legs slung over the back of the chair and his head on the floor.

Nate was right. Why *was* Vex here?

Kari stood, lifting her hands between them. "Nathaniel, we will send you in with the group bound for the guard tower. Is there a way to reset all the dead-end hallways, so we can move through the prison without hindrance? A failsafe, perhaps?"

Nate shook his head. "Engineers designed these prisons to make escapes impossible. We won't have much time before the soldiers stationed there raise the alarm and any Argridians in the city add reinforcements. Our best bet is splitting up, sending in as many groups as we can, and having our people go cell by cell to lead the prisoners out so they don't get lost."

"We could divide our numbers into four effective groups. How do the guards at the main control panel communicate with those in the prison?"

Communicate? Vex frowned, thinking.

"They don't," Nate said. "They establish a pattern for the day, the guards memorize it, and every guard knows where the smaller control panels are hidden in the prison itself."

"Then we will need to memorize a pattern. Which arrangement would access the most cells at once? We can shift halfway to reach any cells we might—"

"Budwig!"

Nate and Kari whipped to face Vex, who had shouted the word.

He cleared his throat, trying as hard as he could to look helpful. "Budwig," he repeated. "The Tuncians might have more sets of Budwig Beans when they get here. We can use them to communicate with the guard tower—have Nate open walls or shift hallways as we need them."

Kari smiled. "Good idea, Devereux."

Vex had to use his not considerable store of resolve to keep from looking at Nate and going, *You hear that? The Argridian rat had a good idea!*

Nate rolled his eyes as though Vex had said it anyway.

"Speaking of plants." He reached into his pocket and pulled out a vial holding a tangle of leafy green vines.

"Now's not the time for a Narcotium Creeper high, Nate," Vex said.

Nate's nose curled, but he ignored Vex. "Emerdian prisons are a treat, but this one is special. The architect took full advantage of Grace Loray's offerings and cooked a couple bricks with Bright Mint. There're a few enhanced bricks throughout the place, most on the lowest level, but damn it if they aren't potent. A feat of Emerdian engineering— spend too much time around those rocks without proper defense, and you'll lose your mind. Makes the prisoners near the bricks docile as kittens, but it'll be hell trying to get them out."

"The builders cooked Bright Mint *into* the bricks?" Vex gaped. "Is that possible? And wouldn't it make the prisoners smarter, enough to figure out how to escape?"

"You'd think that, wouldn't you?" Nate beamed, enjoying his countrymen's feat. "Emerdian bricks are made a certain way. A *special* way. Pushes the effects of Bright Mint straight past thinking better and into a full-on mental breakdown. That's what the Narcotium Creeper is for— it'll counter the Bright Mint for the affected prisoners, and if any of our group get woozy."

Vex recoiled. He'd heard that the Port Camden prison was disorienting, but he'd attributed it to entire goddamn hallways moving, not to *magic*.

But Kari nodded. "I am pleased that you will be providing Narcotium Creeper."

"Wait," Vex said to Kari's lack of surprise, "you knew about the Bright Mint?"

"The Council was aware," Kari said.

Vex watched Kari watch Nate. They'd both known about the Emerdian prison's extra twist of insanity? The way they were staring at each other—

It'd been a test. If either hadn't known about the Bright Mint, they could've left that group in the prison, stoned off their asses, while their people got out. Beneath planning a dangerous prison break, there'd been a level of political bullshit Vex hadn't known about.

He rubbed his temples. God, being a leader was exhausting.

The tension shattered when Nayeli barged into the room, her face sheened with exertion. Or maybe fear.

Vex's stomach dropped. If she was afraid—

But she shook her head as if to banish a bad thought. "First—the Tuncian steamboats are about three hours out. They'll be here by dusk."

Kari waved her thanks. "We will move as soon as they arrive."

"We will?" Vex croaked.

Nate grinned. "Scared, Bell?"

But Kari didn't let Vex respond. "Word of an influx of raiders and steamboats in the port will spread quickly.

Likely Argrid has already heard of their approach, and may have prepared. Our best chance is to act as soon as we are able. What is the other news?"

Nayeli's eyes touched Vex, then Kari. "Cansu's raiders say there've been rumors of Elazar's presence in villages around Port Camden, telling people that raiders are to blame for their suffering and Grace Loray has to unite against their evil. He arrests people like he snatched up the missing raiders, and he *heals* people, too—apparently it's the Pious God's power, but I believe that as much as I believe I'm a long-lost princess—"

She was rambling. A tremor shot to Vex's toes.

Nayeli gathered herself. "And . . . he has Ben with him. Elazar drags him around as proof that he'll make sacrifices to create a better world, too."

Vex wheezed, the room going dark. "Ben's still—" God, no, he didn't want to ask that question. "Elazar hasn't said when he's going to—"

"He's alive," Nayeli confirmed. "If they're so close, it means Ben's probably in the Port Camden prison after all."

"Elazar too," Vex said. He shoved up from the chair to prove to himself that he still could, but his legs ached, that last tremor affecting his muscles longer than normal.

"Ben?"

Vex looked at Nate, who was glaring at him with a new toxicity.

"Benat *Gallego*?" Nate continued. Vex cursed. "In the Port Camden prison? The *Crown Prince*? What the hell, Andreu?" He spun on Kari, his face going purple-red.

Kari put her hand up. "The prince turned traitor to his father and has been working against Elazar. His imprisonment and this treatment"—Kari motioned to Nayeli—"is proof of that. We were not certain where he was being held, or if his rescue would be a factor in this prison break. He will be a valuable asset in the coming war—whether or not you choose to join our fight afterward, the prince will be my responsibility."

Nate glowered, unconvinced. "Just get my people out and get these damn Argridian rats away from Port Camden," he grumbled, and strode out the door.

Vex didn't move until Nate's footsteps receded. He slumped forward.

Nayeli winced. "Sorry," she said.

Kari shook her head in dismissal. "Go prepare."

Nayeli started to leave, but Vex hesitated. "You didn't tell Nate that Ben's my cousin."

Kari's eyes were shielded. "Neither did you" was all she said.

Vex swallowed. Dread tasted like acid and iron and the cedarwood his father used to burn in his study's fireplace. Should he let everyone know his lineage? What good would it do?

"Tonight!" Nayeli bounced over to Vex, trying overly

hard to be cheerful. "Tonight, tonight! We'll get Cansu and Ben back tonight!"

"Yeah. Let's hope."

"No hoping." Nayeli poked him in the chest. "Certainty. We've lost too much already. We will get them back."

Vex almost said, *I hope you're right*, but he caught himself.

Nayeli hooked her arm through his and led him out of the room. Kari stayed at the table.

They had *all* lost too much to this war. But what about the people who couldn't get back what they'd lost? What would Kari gain from this? Not that saving Ben would fill Vex's chasm of missing Lu, but it would ease a different pain.

Vex let Nayeli pull him down to the basement, where the Emerdians had weapons and various plants. He didn't remind her, or anyone, that giving him a weapon was five kinds of stupid. As he walked down the stairs, he had to keep a death grip on the railing through a spasm. There was no way he could fight, but he'd be damned if he'd stay in this townhouse.

Dread could fill Vex up. Tremors could break his legs.

But he was going into that prison, and he was getting his cousin back.

The Port Camden prison sat in the northeast corner of the city, near the tanneries that billowed sour, gaseous clouds into the air. The stench was the least of Vex's worries as he crouched on the deck of a Tuncian steamboat, pistols across his waist and an ax on his back.

The exposed wood frameworks and ivory masonry of the city gave the buildings white teeth that gnashed in the moonlight. The threat of Argridian arrests had emptied the streets, so when Vex's boat and three others stopped at a cobbled road, they had an unobstructed view of a winding staircase at the north end. At the top of that staircase, a black square cut through the cloudless night sky—the Port Camden prison.

Next to Vex, Nayeli let out a long breath. On his other side, Edda settled her loaded guns next to the Narcotium Creeper tonic she'd been given, like everyone else.

Vex steadied himself, telling his body it wouldn't break down. He wouldn't have any shaking fits. He wouldn't fall, or drop his weapons, or mess up this plan in any way.

One of the dozen raiders on the boat disembarked. Another—Nate. A mix of Tuncians and Emerdians were landing farther west, coming from a different angle. To the east, more waited on the prison docks in the Scoria River, which connected Port Camden to Lake Regolith, with seven steamboats for the freed prisoners.

Once the escape boats were full, they would either head for Port Mesi-Teab or split up and leave Nate's two boats in Port Camden. It depended on whether Nate joined the war against Elazar. Even Vex, with his weak knowledge of politics, knew Nate was keeping that decision for bargaining power. Not like the freedom of Grace Loray depended on it or anything.

If they all decided to head for Port Mesi-Teab, each escape boat had a different route, to give them the best chance of not getting caught as they made the day-and-a-half-long journey—another contribution Vex had been able to make. He knew routes across this island that had made Kari and Nate gape at him in equal parts concern and confusion. Rivers that overflowed and connected one to another; streams that weren't on maps.

He was Devereux Bell, after all. He knew this island so well, a politician's daughter had broken him out of prison and hired him to find a missing Argridian diplomat.

Mapping those escape routes had felt like an homage to Lu. Like she was watching him chart the ways, smiling over his shoulder.

God, he missed her. He missed her in breaths that only filled halfway, in heartbeats that quivered. He had to actively remind himself that she was gone, or he'd cast an absent glance around a room for her and remember she wasn't there in a fistful of grim sorrow.

Now Nayeli leaped off the boat. Edda followed, and when she reached back to help Vex, he grabbed the railing and hurled himself off just to prove he could.

Only he couldn't. Landing on the cobblestones shot pain up both his legs, and a spell came on, a quiver in one ankle, a twitch in his thigh—

He started walking, hands in fists, damn it, he would *not* collapse.

Nayeli shot ahead, and Vex knew *Find Cansu, find Cansu* rolled through her mind the same way *Find Ben, find Ben* rolled through his.

Nate led their group up the road, noiseless but for the rattle of their weapons. A few of his raiders scrubbed pastes on their skin—Powersage, the plant that gave strength. The more extreme Emerdians had vials of Croxy, the berserker plant, reserved for the heat of battle; a select handful had small, rare Incris fruits, the plant that gave increased speed.

Everyone readied plants and weapons alike as they reached the staircase, the stones slick with moss and a recent rain. They began to climb, tension as thick as the humidity.

The stairs led to a narrow yard that ran along the prison's plateau. A handful of paces away, a wall loomed. Midnight choked the port; the prison sucked away all sensation. Vex could almost hear the shift of his own muscles as he followed Nate along the wall.

Their group stopped at a road that ran out from the west gate. Shadows heaved behind parked carts across the way. The other group, led by Kari.

Raiders from both sides of the road, including Nayeli, broke off and met at the gate. They shuffled in the dimness, a heartbeat passing, two, before they shot away at an all-out sprint, some moving so fast they had to have taken the speed-giving Incris.

Stealth had brought them this far. But it had to end.

Sparks of light flickered around the gate. A second more, and a dozen Variegated Holly leaves did what they did best: blew up.

Vex stifled a shout. Destroying the gate had been the plan, but knowing didn't counter the shock of going from hollowing silence to instant chaos.

Nayeli, Edda, Vex, and the rest of Nate's group dropped behind a short stone wall along the road as splinters shot through the air. The corresponding *BOOM!* set a ringing in Vex's ears, the vibration of the blast stopping his heart so he gasped, breathless, stunned.

He glanced over the wall. Dust from the explosion made the entrance hazy, but he had to imagine the gate was gone.

A bell started tolling from the prison. The shouting of orders echoed.

Nate and Kari were in charge of almost a hundred Emerdian raiders and twenty-two Tuncian raiders, divided between here and the escape boats. Getting a head count on enemy guards within the prison had been impossible, but Nate had guessed there could be as few as two dozen, or as many as *"Well, how big's Elazar's army?"*

That kind of math made Vex queasy.

Pistols blasted through the explosion's fog from the other side of the former gate—soldiers firing at anyone who would enter. Nate shoved himself to his feet with a war cry, brandishing a pistol in one hand and a sword in the other. His raiders joined him from either side of the road, the Tuncians too, everyone rallying with an invigorating scream that ushered Vex to his feet.

A group of Tuncians dove for the gate. Three shrieked, grabbing a leg, an arm, as pistols fired from within. Two of Nate's raiders dropped, the dust and night's cover hazing the air.

"How are we going to—" Nayeli started, but she squinted. "Shit, what's she doing?"

Kari stepped into the dead center of the road, a pistol in each hand and a murderous look on her face. Horror pinged off Vex's chest with every bullet that narrowly missed her.

Kari was going to take out the soldiers beyond the gate on her own.

�֍֎֍

A bell woke Lu from the restless sleep she had managed while Ben kept watch. One of them was always awake, should Milo or Elazar decide to pay a visit.

Lu sat up, muddled. Her first thought went to her wounds, healed thanks to another application of Healica.

"Lu." Ben was standing in the middle of their cell, his head cocked.

The bell tolled again. Distantly, defensors shouted: "Lockdown—we're under attack—"

Lu rubbed her forehead. She had started drinking the water at the insistence of the defensors, but these delusions seemed determined to—

Ben looked down at her. "Tell me you hear that."

She shot to her feet. "It's not . . . it's real?"

He grinned. Happiness was so foreign here that it sent Lu back a step.

"Gunnar," Ben gasped, relief gushing out of him. "Gunnar, wake up!"

Gunnar, curled with his back to the hall, was on his feet before Ben finished saying his name. He blinked at the ceiling, confused.

"Alarm?" he asked. He flinched, eyes unfocused. "Thaid fuilor—well—all is well—"

His delirium made Lu waver. Maybe the prison wasn't under attack.

But if something had happened that had the guards distracted, and Milo came by to see Lu tucked into her cell, not having taken advantage of the opportunity to run . . .

The thought of his smile, wicked and satisfied, filled Lu with determination.

No picks. Nothing delicate that would take time. They were leaving *now*.

She dropped onto the table. The distance from there to the cell door would give her the leverage to kick at the lock.

"Lu!" Ben jumped away. "You could—"

One firm jab of her heel and the lock cracked, the door flying open.

Ben gaped. "The Powersage? It worked?"

Lu eased off the table, stretching her fingers experimentally. Had it? What about the Aerated Blossom that had been in the potion? She felt no lighter, even bouncing on the balls of her feet. Had only some of the potion worked?

Shouting came. Defensors, running toward them.

"We're getting out of here," Lu stated.

Ben's eyes were drawn, his relief flickering at the reminder of the obstacles in their path. He nodded and yanked their cell door shut so it looked as though locked.

Seven defensors swarmed the hall, pistols out, swords flashing in the torchlight.

"Ben." Jakes grabbed the bars of their cell—and the door opened. He looked up, startled.

"Gunnar," Lu said in a tone like murder. "The lights."

He curled his fingers and the torches along the stone walls snuffed out.

The defensors' shock was rich and satisfying. Lu didn't wait for her eyes to adjust—she swiped the mortar with their remaining healing plant, Cleanse Root, off the table. Ben had prepared it should Lu need something strong, but the skin-mending Healica had been enough.

Gunnar would need Cleanse Root, though. Lu grabbed the pitcher with their antidote water as well, a few swallows that would help clear him of the prison's magic.

Lu barreled through the door, flinging Jakes back.

"There!" a defensor cried.

"No—that spot, the corner—"

Lu bounded across the hall, weaving through the confusion, a blur of shadow in a world of shadow. She grabbed the door to Gunnar's cell and pulled, hard. The lock broke with a pop.

Her veins tingled, her muscles surged—the Powersage? Was it a part of her now? Had she and Ben, against the impossible odds of their situation, made a magic plant permanent? She couldn't bear the answer with its ramifications and blessings, not now.

A day, maybe two, had passed since Gunnar's last whipping. The monxes had healed him enough to keep him alive, but he was in no state to escape, let alone fight as Lu needed him to.

She shoved the prepared Cleanse Root and water at him, expecting to have to force him to take it—but he snatched both and downed the contents.

In the darkness, he growled. "Grab Ben. Get low."

She dove back into the hall, taking out one of the defensors with the point of her elbow. The man's yelp drew awareness, but Lu dropped to her knees and rolled across the floor into her cell. She wrapped her arms around a set of legs and heaved—Ben.

He crashed to the ground. Beside him, a defensor stumbled blindly. "Ben—wait—"

Jakes drew closer, a looming swath of blackness against the dark. Lu shoved herself up, punched him in the temple, and dropped back down as his body fell.

Next to her, Ben swayed. "Did you—is he—"

"He'll live," she said, though she wasn't certain. Her strength was new and unfamiliar.

A defensor managed to light a torch. Or—no. The light came from Gunnar, who held a flame in his palm. The golden brilliance made all attention swivel to where he stood, out of his cell, a beast of flame and ash whose eyes said one thing: retribution.

10

VEX WATCHED IN horror—and awe; god, she was so like Lu—as Kari lifted both her guns, fired, and ran at the prison's gate.

"Give her cover!" Edda started shooting into the dust fog caused by the explosion. Other raiders obeyed as Kari gained speed, leaped through the remains of the gate, and was lost from sight in the prison's courtyard.

"Go!" Nate shouted, and the raiders descended on the prison in a mad dash.

Beyond the gate, the bullets stopped coming, agonizing screams splitting the air. Vex ducked through behind Nayeli. Where the raiders expected to dive into battle, they stopped at the edge of a courtyard, gaping at ten Argridian soldiers—now eight, now seven—who Kari was methodically taking down.

Three of Nate's raiders finished off an equal number of

Argridians while Kari used one soldier's body as a shield. She stole his sword and supplemented it with her knives, spinning as she slashed at the next-closest guard. He fell, and she ducked under another's sword to skewer the final one in the chest.

When ten bodies lay around them and the warning bell still tolled, Kari stopped, the blood on her skin gone black in the night. A darker spot on her side might have been her own wound, but she looked over the crowd.

"The groups bound for the lowest levels—remember your Narcotium Creeper if you grow disoriented. You have extra doses should you encounter any prisoners too far gone from the Bright Mint. Nate—to the guard station."

Nate nodded dumbly. Vex and Edda eyed each other.

Kari was a Senior Councilmember. A politician, a lady. But right now, she was Kari the Wave. She was the reason the revolution had ended in victory for Grace Loray. She was relentless, a warrior—and had lost more to this than Vex could comprehend.

Nate and six of his raiders broke off, three of them taking Croxy to drive them into a battle-blind rage while the other three put Budwig Beans in their ears. The Tuncians had only had that many plants with them, and each plant contained two beans that let people communicate. Nate and his people would change the hallways and doors throughout the prison as needed.

One of Nate's other raiders had a corresponding Budwig,

as did Nayeli and Vex. Nayeli had used her influence as a Tuncian representative to refuse to let anyone use Budwig unless she led a group. Vex could taste the anxiety coming off her. She needed to *do something*, and Vex had made her demand to let him lead the last group for the same reason.

Nate vanished into the prison. Nayeli, Vex, and the Emerdian fished out their Budwig Beans. Shouts came from within—more guards—but the narrow prison halls would bottleneck the fighting.

The rest of the raiders waited to split into groups that would search the prison. Nate had to get to the guard station first—two minutes, he'd told them. They'd have to hold off any Argridian defensors who came at them in the courtyard, but for the moment, they had a reprieve.

Vex stepped up to Kari. What had he said to Lu when she'd gotten that look in her eyes like she'd become a version of herself she hated?

"Send any prisoners you find out this way," Kari shouted at the raiders in the yard. "I will escort them to the river."

The raiders waiting in the escape boats would have fought the soldiers near the prison docks, but energy palpitated off Kari. She'd plow through any other defensors.

Vex put the Budwig Bean in his ear, his mouth cocked to the side as he looked at Nayeli and Edda. Nayeli was too focused on the looming walls of the prison, but Edda gave him a frown that said, *Not now*. No time for soft conversations or moments of pain.

He settled the Budwig Bean. Breathing grated in his ear, followed by *"Fucking hell and God above—"* A pause. *"Don't get righteous with me, Barnabas. I did not use the Pious God's name to curse."*

"Hello to you, too, Nate," Vex said.

Nate huffed. *"Get someone else. I don't want a damn rat in my head."*

Vex managed to restrain himself. "Oh, Natey, I was already in your head."

"I swear to God—yes, Barnabas, I mean the actual Pious God, so it was not a curse—"

A thud, a pistol fired.

Vex put his hand to his ear at the same time Nayeli and the Emerdian raider did to theirs. The rest in the courtyard leaned forward.

Shuffling, more thuds and cracks and a bark of pain, then a squeal of hinges.

And Nate's voice. *"We're in."*

Vex nodded at Kari.

"Three groups, go!" she shouted. "You—top levels. Nayeli—middle. Vex—"

But he was gone, surging with the current of raiders into the bleak stone halls of the prison. Edda followed him, as always, his murderous shadow.

Moonlight from behind and faint torches lit a circle of an atrium with three halls splitting off. Raiders struck lanterns to life, the cages bouncing against their hips.

Vex and Edda gave a nod of encouragement to Nayeli

before they took their respective paths. According to Nate, the lower levels branched off the rightmost hall, so Vex shot down it, followed by a dozen or so raiders, weapons ready.

The first hall was bare, no cells. Vex hit a corner, turned—dead end. He whipped back the other way, but a raider at the rear of his group shouted, "Dead end here!"

"Nate," Vex said, cupping a hand over his Budwig Bean. The bell echoed, a persistent *dong-dong-dong* that shook into Vex's chest. "One hall into the lower level. Left turn, dead end."

The wall in front of Vex jerked, releasing a cloud of dust into the damp air. A scent burst through—Vex sniffed, his mind spasming. The medicinal earthiness of dried plants and the spiced zest of Tuncian spices.

Why the hell was he smelling that here?

The raiders' lanterns pitched in the sandy clouds, hungry fingers of light snaking around the stones as they rolled into a recess in the wall. A new hall appeared.

"Thanks, darling," Vex said. "And—cells!"

The raiders cheered and shot around Vex, who yanked a lockpicking kit from his pocket and threw himself at the first cell. Edda set to work on the next cell, raiders up and down the hall doing the same. The smell was stronger—definitely Tuncian spices. And plants.

Unease matched the dried, dead stench on the air.

"Bell! Who is it?"

Vex finished with his lock and yanked the door open. The other raiders backed away from the cells, their faces varying mixes of furious and sick and blindsided. Argridians had been arresting raiders on Grace Loray. *Raiders,* people who looked suspicious or evil. But the people who shuffled out of the cells were not who anyone in Vex's group had expected to find.

"Damn it! What the hell is going on? Who is it?"

"Families," Vex said, his voice frail. "It's . . . kids."

�֍✖✖

Smoke wafted off Gunnar's skin. His bare chest gleamed, his clan mark carved and deadly. Through tangles of his blond hair, he looked at the nearest defensor, and Lu felt a shock of fear where she had only felt numb for days.

Gunnar spoke in his language, inhaled until his chest puffed, and exhaled fire.

The defensors screamed. One dropped, his body aflame as Gunnar swung his inferno across the stones. A knot of heat punched over Lu's head and choked in the smoke. One defensor crawled back up the hall; two more were already dead. Gunnar forced the flames, twisted his hands and stomped hard on the floor to surge fire out, up, hotter, *more.*

The iron of the cell bars started to melt. The stones glowed red.

A break appeared through the orange and gray. Gunnar's eyes flashed like blue flame from Ben to Jakes's unconscious body on the floor.

"Let's go!" he shouted, and stomped up the hall, making a tunnel of clarity in the blaze.

Lu hefted Ben to his feet. He gaped at the inferno chewing apart what had once been their cot, as she dragged him out of the cell.

They reached the end of the hall. The fire popped and charged, finding new fuel in the mortar between the bricks, the wooden lining along the ceiling.

Ben grabbed Gunnar's arm, stopping him in the doorway. "Gunnar—please!"

Gunnar clenched his fists and the flames snuffed out. Lu staggered, but the lull didn't linger—Gunnar shoved ahead and the three of them raced into black halls. Smoke followed in choking billows as though they were running from hell itself.

They took a turn, and Ben snatched Lu's arm. "Wait—"

Gunnar swung around, a flame in his hand shooting light into the hall. Ben gasped for breath and Lu couldn't tell whether the look on his face was pain or horror or disbelief.

The energy of the fight pumped through her veins. They had gotten out of those cells. They had gotten *out*.

"Benat," Gunnar tried. "Are you—"

"The defensors." Ben looked up at him, a war in his concern. "Should we go back for them? They could be dead."

"They were Argridians," Lu snapped. "This is what they deserve."

Ben's mouth dropped open, horror widening his eyes.

Lu watched him from a distance, ash embedded in her nose as she took a bracing breath. She should feel the same pain for the defensors who had only been following orders and might have burned to death—but all she felt was rage. At the soldiers. At Ben, for defending them, these cruel, stupid Argridians—

Her own thoughts alarmed her so purely that she gasped.

"I'm sorry. I'm so sorry, Ben, I—"

Ben's eyebrows dented and he started to speak, but she held up a hand.

"Please don't." Agony filled her chest. She welcomed it, to know she could still feel it. Empathy. *Pain.* "I'm sorry. This is war; I am a soldier."

The words slipped out, instinct, truth. Lu's soul hollowed.

I'll always be a soldier. No peace. No reprieve.

It's what I deserve.

"We should go," Gunnar said over the continuing alarm.

Ben pushed up the hall, his face severe until Lu lost it in the darkness.

She started to follow, but Gunnar stepped into her path. "You saved us," he said. "But that gives you no right to be heartless. We all have suffered."

We all haven't caused suffering. Lu nodded.

Gunnar shot off, taking his flame with him, leaving Lu in blackness and smoke.

She looked down at her hands. Her augmented strength felt . . . wrong. She felt like herself again, no tingle in her veins. Had it been magic, or had it been the rush of the fight?

Magic's absence brought both relief and a plummeting drop of defeat. The potion she'd made hadn't been permanent after all. Why hadn't it worked?

"Lu!"

Her own name jolted her to her bones until she recognized Ben's voice. Not Milo. Not Vex. Just Ben.

She hurried around a corner to find Ben and Gunnar watching her.

"What is—"

But she couldn't finish the question. At the far end of the straight stone hall, a man held a lantern. Every wound he had given her pulled a sob from her lips.

They were so close to freedom. Milo would not keep her here.

�֍֍֍

A mother with two children clinging to her; a father carrying a third. The prison's hall filled with bodies young and old, people who might've been out shopping at a market when Argrid decided they looked like raiders. Whatever the hell that meant.

They were, all of them, Tuncian. That family each had the four-dot tattoo that honored Tuncay's gods; those two women had the curly black hair and round faces of Tuncay.

"Families?" came Nate's voice. *"The hall you're in should have ten cells, and you're telling me they're filled with kids?"*

"Most of 'em," Vex said. "A few elderly. Families."

The raiders in Vex's group were as stunned as he was. Some retched in the corner while others drove into a frenzy, sprinting down the hall on piercing war shrieks.

Vex's stomach spasmed as prisoners crowded the hall, the musk of spices and plants stronger now. *What the hell—*

"Here!" one of Nate's raiders called at a cell.

Vex pushed over to it. The raider lifted his lantern into the cell, revealing crates and barrels and a table spread with—Vex could hear Lu's voice in his head—laboratory supplies.

Edda stepped into the room and stuck her hand into a barrel. She removed her hand, brown powder trickling between her fingers and perfuming the air with a hearty smokiness.

"Harmedeku," Edda said.

The Emerdian raider grunted, but Vex recognized the word.

"A Tuncian spice." Vex's eye went to the other barrels, the different-colored powders, the crates with vials of plants. Tuncian spices and Grace Lorayan magic?

"Bell! You to the next hall yet?"

"Not yet, Nate." No time to figure out what this meant. Vex shared a look with Edda and backed out of the cell.

A little girl tugged at her mother's skirt as they shuffled by. "Are we forgiven?"

The mother gripped the girl's shoulders. "We didn't do anything that needed forgiving. You hear me? The defensors lied. They *lied*. These people are here to free us, aren't they?"

She looked at Vex for confirmation.

Vex nodded, dazed.

The mother tucked the girl into her side. "The defensors lied," she repeated, softer, to herself. "Nothing we gotta atone for."

But she didn't look convinced. None of the prisoners did, and a few made the symbol of the Church against their chest. Some clung to books—Church scriptures. Hymnals.

Vex blanched. "You"—he pointed at the closest raiders—"get these people to Kari. The rest, keep going!"

He started to lead the way. His words were enough encouragement, and the group broke apart to obey—but Vex tripped and had to grab the bars of the cell across from him to keep from sprawling in the hallway.

Edda seized his upper arm. "You all right?"

Vex shook her off. Damn, this spell was a long one. Both of his legs shook so hard his knees cracked into the bars.

Stop it, stop it, stop it. He needed to run through this prison, find Ben and Cansu and any other prisoners before Argridian reinforcements showed up. He didn't have time to be weak.

He didn't have time to think about what Elazar did when he got his hands on kids. How a thirteen-year-old boy deserved to be strapped to a chair and force-fed magic until his body couldn't handle any more. How did Tuncian spices fit into any of this? Elazar loved to experiment with magic. Maybe—maybe—

The dimness shifted and blurred, Vex's heart leaping hard against his ribs. Argrid was doing it again. Purifying Grace Loray. Burning those who resisted too much.

"Vex," Edda tried. "What's wrong? You need to leave?"

"No." *Damn it.* "No, I'm fine."

The prisoners were gone by the time the shaking stopped. Vex lowered his weight onto his legs, but a twinge of agony shot up his calves.

"Bell? You there? Where are you now?"

Shit. "Hang on, Nate."

Vex took a step, winced. Edda's grip on his arm pinched tighter. He bit down on his tongue and walked one step, another—then he was running, Edda jogging alongside him.

Vex's mouth curved in a permanent grimace. "Another level down, Nate." He took a corner and found the rest of his group waiting by a dead end. "Right turn, hall's blocked."

A rumble, and stones swallowed the wall again, revealing another hall with more cells. Noise flared, the warning bell keeping time alongside prisoners here. They were singing.

Vex recognized it. A Church hymn, one about Grace Aracely, the Grace of penance.

The raiders started picking the locks as Vex leaned on

the stones, sweat pouring down his face. Was lung collapse a symptom of Shaking Sickness? He couldn't take a full breath.

Edda shot out her hand to him. "Vex, give me the Budwig. Go to the surface."

He glared at her. He couldn't argue without Nate hearing.

"Bell! You find Pierce? What's going on?"

Vex eyed the prisoners. More families, old, young—not only Tuncian now, though.

Vex shouted at the raiders, "Keep going! There's more, right? Nate?"

"Should be one more level with two—"

"Go!" Vex screamed.

Prisoners rushed past, more raiders peeling off to escort them to the surface. The hymn softened, some people choosing to stop while others carried the tune.

Vex kept shouting, at Edda, at his body. He had not survived this far to fall apart in a prison he hadn't even been arrested and thrown into.

He swung down a hall and jerked back, shock startling him. Two figures stood at the end, far enough away for the raiders behind Vex to cry in alarm and raise their pistols.

"Wait!" Vex said.

One person dove in front of another.

Ben.

He was a mess, bloody and dirty, but he was standing, and he was alive.

Relief tugged at the tension keeping Vex upright.

Ben shouted. It carried—not a word, a name. "Lu!"

Vex gaped. Why had Ben shouted that? He couldn't mean—

A heartbeat later, a third person appeared down the hall, and the exhaustion in her gaze made him tired by extension. Vex watched her shoulders rise and fall, rise and fall. He hadn't known a simple motion could make him so elated—

Vex's knees hit the stones. A tremor pitched him and he caught himself on the floor, joy bursting through his body in waves he, for once, welcomed.

Lu was alive.

11

LU'S LIMBS FLARED to readiness, legs set to run, arms set to fight. They were so close to escape. She would not let Milo—standing at the end of this hall, holding that lantern—bar their way.

"Lu." Ben reached for her. Why wasn't he panicking? Oh no—could he not see Milo? Was this another delusion of this hellish place, like that vision of her parents and Vex's voice?

Ben's fingers closed around her wrist. The bell tolled, matching the tempo of her heart.

Lu lurched back. "Let me go! He's there, Milo—please don't—"

People she didn't know filled the end of the hall, holding weapons and lanterns that chased the darkness. None of them were defensors. The man—he wasn't holding a lantern, he wasn't sneering at her—dropped to the floor with his hands out, his eye wide and his mouth open and the whole of his soul pooled in the look he gave her.

"Lu," he said. And again, smiling through tears, "Lu—"

Lu's body slackened. Ben released her, but his hands were out as though he would grab her should she run. She might, still—she gaped at the man saying her name.

"Vex?" she panted. She shook her head, and it broke her heart that she didn't trust herself or the soft, imploring way he called to her.

"He's here," Ben assured her. "He's really here."

Her shoulders caved. And she was running. Running as she had up the prison's halls, to escape one thing and reach another—imprisonment for freedom, terror for joy.

Vex was the reason for the warning bell. He was here.

Lu dropped to her knees before him. Vex lunged forward, scooping her up so their torsos collided and knocked the air from her lungs. The reassurance of that force made her sob, and the scent of him, sweat and ashy fire smoke and spice, sent her anxiety skittering.

She pressed closer, not close enough, wanting to claw into him and feel his heartbeat thunder alongside hers. His own passion ruptured in the way he clamped one of his hands around the back of her neck, the other digging into her hip, resolute and present, here and *real*.

"We have to go!" one of the people behind Vex shouted. "We don't have time!"

Gunnar and Ben brushed past them, and adrenaline

flooded Lu again. She grabbed Vex and hauled him up, but he buckled.

Edda was in front of them, tears glossy on her cheeks. "His Shaking Sickness—"

"Damn it, Edda, *I'm fine*," he snapped.

His Shaking Sickness had progressed in the time they'd been apart. Guilt rendered Lu silent. She looped Vex's arm around her neck and helped him up the hall with the mass of people clawing for the surface.

Edda fell in step beside them and pulled a vial from her vest. "What about you?"

She offered Lu the vial. Lu frowned, heart thudding at the idea of more magic.

"Narcotium Creeper," Edda explained. "To combat the Bright Mint in the stones."

"Bright Mint?" Lu almost lost her footing.

"You didn't know?" Vex eyed her. Lu swayed to see his face, to hear his voice, *his* voice. "The Emerdians cook it into the stones. It enhances the Bright Mint's effects. It didn't get to you?"

"Elazar gave us an antidote." Lu nodded at Ben. That was all she could muster.

The Emerdians had cooked Bright Mint into the stones of the prison, enhancing the effects, driving Gunnar mad.

The Mechts prepared Eye of the Sun with their sacred bear's blood.

Lu stowed this information as Vex twisted against her.

"There's one last hall!" he shouted at the crowd, and Lu didn't question how he knew. "Keep going—straight ahead—that door!"

Their group shoved through and a hall of cells stretched on. Arms wove through the bars; people begged for release. Raiders shot to pick the locks while others kicked through the iron.

People shoved out in cries of joy. "The Pious God has freed us!" an older woman wept. "He has saved us!"

The woman's declaration was so repulsive that Lu didn't notice the other prisoners until a small form hooked her waist.

"Thank you" came a high voice.

Children. Families. Innocents who Elazar had deemed raiders.

Vex brought his hand up to cup her chin. "Lu. Hey—Lu, look at me—"

Lu rocked back as the little boy rushed past. He was the right height, the proper build, with dark hair and vibrant eyes, and Lu heard the distant sound of her own voice saying, "Teo?"

"Teo isn't here," Vex told her. "He's in Port Mesi-Teab. He's safe, I promise."

These children weren't, though. Because of Argrid. Because of the cause Lu had unknowingly aided.

This was why she didn't deserve peace. This was why Grace Loray was suffering again, still—but she would fix it. Even if she never got that peace. She would make this island right.

The torchlight thrashed. Lu wobbled, Vex's weight too much for her. She dropped down the wall and he twisted, swinging around to kneel in front of her as children scrambled to escape and the world broke.

"Adeluna," Vex said. His voice was gentle, so unlike Milo that Lu grabbed his shoulders to make sure he was there, in front of her.

The tolling prison bell increased its cadence. They needed to leave.

Someone was saying that. *We need to leave.* One of the raiders, ushering people out. Vex waved them off. *Give her time—we'll be right behind you—*

Gunnar glanced to the side, then spun. "Where's Ben?"

Vex pushed to his feet. "What? Ben!"

Up the hall, torches showed someone slamming another person into a wall—

"Stop!" Gunnar took off, Vex and Lu clawing to keep up.

❧❧❧

The rush of the fight, the surge of prisoners into the hall, the heave of raiders acting as one body to help these people—Ben hadn't realized how much he needed this. Hope, action, *progress*. The last time he could remember feeling this consumed had been with his uncle at the University, with Inquisitors buzzing around him as they studied magic and advanced their understanding.

The delirium, the weeks of torture, had cooked his heart and soul down as he'd cooked plants with Lu—distilling, evaporating the extraneous, until all that remained was a shell of a boy who had spent most of his life alone.

The energy hummed in Ben's veins as he flew from cell to cell. He reached the last one in this hall, but hands within were already fast at work picking the lock.

A wisp of a man stomped out, flicking a braid of dirtied, white-blond hair over his shoulder. Three other people followed him, large, burly men with gnarled pale hair.

"It's about damn time," the man said in a shockingly deep voice for someone so slender. He arched his back, stretching. "Nathaniel sure took his sweet time coming—"

One of the burly figures nudged the man. "Pierce."

Pierce stopped. He looked at Ben and his narrow face pinched.

"Argridian," he spat. A blink, and his hand was around Ben's throat. "This a trick? You here to make us beg the Pious God for salvation? You here to make us belt out hymns? You disgust me, warping the doctrine like that, like *heathens*—"

Ben choked, waving his hands to keep balance. Instinct from his training with defensors flared countermoves into his limbs, but Pierce's words stayed him.

"I'm not—" Ben tried. "I wouldn't—"

"Stop!"

Ben and Pierce turned to see Lu, Gunnar, and Paxben

only paces from them. The clatter and shouting of the escape rushed all around.

Pierce surveyed Ben's group. "Devereux Bell? What the hell—"

Devereux Bell? Oh. Ben's vision spun, his mind tripping over Pierce's grip. *Paxben.*

"We're with your husband!" Vex tried. "We came with the Tuncian syndicate too, for Cansu Darzi, but we're getting you out—this is Argrid's doing—"

"That I agree with." Pierce retightened his grip on Ben's throat.

As Ben struggled to think through which move would cause the least damage to Pierce, Lu swooped in and ripped Pierce off him. Air rushed into Ben's lungs and he doubled forward, scrambling until his hand connected with someone.

He expected his cousin. But Gunnar slid one arm around Ben's waist, his eternal heat enveloping Ben in a cocoon of warmth.

Ben was pretty sure he could stand on his own just fine. But he didn't tell Gunnar that.

Lu shoved Pierce back. One of his men slammed his forearm into Lu's chest.

Vex ripped something out of his ear. "Stand down, Pierce! God, talk to your husband, all right? It's Budwig. He's got the other one. He's in the guardhouse."

Pierce grabbed the Budwig. "We'll see how much longer

he's my husband after letting Tuncians and Devereux Bell rescue me. I cannot believe this." He thrust the Budwig into his ear. "Nathaniel Gilroy Blaise, you incompetent, scheming—" A pause. *Devereux Bell? And you listened to him?* Pious God help me, I leave you alone with our syndicate and you make an alliance with the Tuncians and— Oh, don't you take that tone with me. It *is* our syndicate."

Pierce elbowed around the remaining raiders who crowded the hall. When he got to the end, he looked over his shoulder.

"Are you coming? Nathaniel claims to have an elaborate escape in the works."

Pierce took another step and slipped on mildew. He stomped the rest of the way into the darkness, grumbling about how he wasn't made for this kind of environment.

Lu and Vex started off behind Pierce, Gunnar helping Ben to walk. One of Pierce's raiders touched Ben's arm as they passed.

"Thank you," the man said. "We've been in a cell with him for two weeks. *Thank you.*"

Another of the raiders punched the first one. "He's the Head's husband!"

"Doesn't stop him from being a spoiled pain in the ass."

Gunnar dragged Ben out of the hall, the slightest grin tugging at his lips.

"Which part of this do you find funny?" Ben asked as they squeezed into the narrow passage. They were chest to chest, and Gunnar seemed to realize the awkwardness of holding Ben. He let go and dipped ahead.

"Pierce sounds like you," Gunnar said over his shoulder. "How you talked to your defensors on the ship, telling them to do this and get you that. I like that word. *Spoiled.*"

Ben squeaked offense. "I talked to them like that to make them *think* I was—that was a ruse—you knew it was a ruse! You were part of it!"

Gunnar looked back at Ben again with a taunting smile. Ben's chest ruptured, filling him with a heat as intense as when he had been in Gunnar's arms.

By the time they got free of the prison, *chaos* seemed far too simple a word to describe the courtyard. People sprinted in every direction, most following the direction of a raider on an overturned crate who bellowed the way to the escape boats. Other people ran for freedom beyond the gate and into the city, electing to risk their luck with the Argridian defensors again.

The prison's alarm still tolled, and out in the city, defensors shouted, booted feet thundering up the road—and an explosion came that Ben recognized.

He shouted, "Cannons!" a mere breath before part of the courtyard's wall erupted.

Stones on the outward-facing side of it shot into the air, a shower of dust and shards of rock. Everyone in the courtyard ducked at once, the silence after the blast punctured by screams. Where there had been chaos was now utter bedlam—bodies shoved and fought for escape, children wailed, raiders brandished pistols over their heads in search of an enemy.

In the madness, a slender Tuncian girl bolted forward and threw her arms around Lu. Ben had seen her on the deck of the *Astuto*—she was one of Vex's crew, like the tall Mecht woman who had caught up with them as they left the prison. Nayeli and Edda, Lu had told him.

Nayeli pulled back from Lu and looked at Vex.

"Did you find her?" Vex and Nayeli asked each other in tandem.

Nayeli's eyes widened. "*No one* found her?" She swung around. "Cansu! CANSU!"

Vex put a hand on her arm. "Maybe we didn't hit all the prison's levels."

Next to them, Pierce whipped around from searching the crowd, likely for his husband. "Are you questioning Nathaniel's methods?" He tapped the Budwig in his ear. "He says we searched every level. If we didn't find someone, they aren't here."

Nayeli dove at Pierce, her fingers in claws. Edda caught her around the waist.

"Cansu could be in this madness," Vex offered. "We'll get to the escape boats and go to Port Mesi-Teab—it's the first place the Tuncian Head would go."

People ran, cannons blasted, and Nayeli screeched horror and frustration and grief. Edda heaved her around and the two shot off into the courtyard along with the thinning stream of people, followed by Pierce and his raiders. Lu and Vex, his arm over her shoulders, limped across the trampled grass.

More cannons fired, more defensors were coming.

Ben took off, Gunnar hot behind him, ushering the last few stragglers out of the courtyard and to the twisting stone staircase that led to the prison's wharf.

Docks stretched into the water, most holding quiet prison transports. To the left, other docks held steamboats for escape: two huge paddlewheels and five smaller boats with single smokestacks. Three had launched off into the water, their decks alive with escapees.

"Blaise!" a raider cried from the deck of a paddlewheel. "Where to? Head Blaise!"

A voice came from the crowd, disembodied—but furious.

"Port Mesi-Teab! God help me, Port Mesi-Teab!"

A cheer went up from here, there, a boat farther down. A decision had been made, one Ben couldn't recognize, and he left it in the pile of things he would deal with later.

Ben and Gunnar leaped onto a paddlewheel with a wide deck of dented pale wood and a two-story section of rooms rising above the pilothouse. Ben looked over the railing and spotted Lu and Vex crouched on the deck of a different boat before a voice bellowed, "Off!"

The command echoed across the boats. A rev of engines, and the steamboats launched away from the docks, charging out into the river as the final prisoners leaped to the decks.

None too soon. Defensors arrived close enough to fire at the escapees, bullets clanging off hulls, people shouting in fear. Orders volleyed, and defensors boarded the prison boats—

"The pipe's broken!"

"This one, too!"

The raiders had disabled the prison transports. By the time the defensors found functioning craft, the escapees would be long gone.

Port Camden's night-shadowed silhouettes faded, and a hush fell over Ben's steamboat. He noted the gaunt, watchful faces across the deck—some prisoners, others raiders who had helped with the rescue, stricken by the sight of Port Camden shrinking into the night.

These people were likely Emerdian, then. Or had called Port Camden their home.

Someone started a lilting hymn about healing from sorrow. Others joined, and Ben winced. Were they singing for their own devotion, or had Elazar's imprisonment manipulated them? Had monxes sung over them as they had over Ben and Lu? Without the antidote for the prison's magic, hymns and prayers could have compounded, warping minds, stunting reason.

Ben started to remind these people that they were free and didn't have to bow to Elazar's influence. But tears streamed down the face of an elderly man, and Ben's eyes lifted to Gunnar, behind him, shadowed in the heavy night.

"You will confirm that you are the traitor he has made you," Gunnar had said in the first village Elazar had dragged them to.

What could the Crown Prince of Argrid do here, now?

Ben leaned against the railing, memorizing the shape of Port Camden's buildings against the swell of the jungle, the rush and rise of the escapees singing.

He couldn't help these people yet. He just wanted to remember this moment.

Narcotium creeper

Availability: extremely common

Location: grows up the sides of trees in
    Backswamp

Appearance: vine

Method: leaves are chewed and the
    juices are swallowed

Use: hallucinogen

12

THE STEAMBOAT'S WINDOWLESS washroom had a metal basin, a water pump, a waste bucket, and a stack of towels, some already used by the other prison escapees. The kick of relief when the door closed at Lu's back came with a tug of sorrow, that this dingy room, with its odor of tartness and mildew, felt more luxurious than any place she had ever been.

Lu plugged the basin and sloshed in two pumps of water. It was river water, gritty with sediment, but it was cool and smelled of Grace Loray—sunshine and freshness and plants. She splashed a handful on her face, letting it trickle over her chin and between her fingers.

This was the safest she had been in weeks. Yet the knot of horror in her chest remained, drawing tighter when she braced her hands on the basin's edge.

Silence had gripped the steamboat until they were away

from Port Camden. Now that they were almost to Lake Regolith and the Argridians had't pursued them, the dozen prison escapees had started moving, whispering, lining up for the washroom.

And Vex, one of the three raiders on this boat who had saved them, had done his part to help, passing out rations, water, blankets. He had tried to see Lu when he could, but—

She flinched, running her fingers through her greasy hair to work it into a new braid. She knew she couldn't avoid him much longer. But she had no words for him. Why was it that she had spent so long trying—and failing, as it turned out—to make permanent magic, but hadn't made more of the plants that would cure him? She hadn't told Ben that Vex was sick until recently. On top of everything, she was a murderer, a traitor—and he had even known that before he'd come to save her.

But he hadn't come to save *her*, had he? He'd come for Ben. Or Elazar's other prisoners.

Lu squeezed her eyes more tightly shut, using a half-soiled rag to scrub off the gunk of the prison. It was the best she could do here, but being moderately clean soothed her soul.

She slid out into the blue-gold softness of early morning. A man, next in the line that wrapped up the stern, shoved his way around her and slammed the washroom's door. Everyone on this boat, save for their rescuers, was caught between horror and the relief of freedom.

Lu curled her arms around herself and angled between

the line of waiting escapees and the railing, making for the bow. As she passed, an elderly woman turned to a man beside her.

"Is it true that raiders planned our escape?"

"No," the man said. "It was that councilmember. Saw her overseeing it."

"Kari Andreu?"

Lu faltered. The raiders had mentioned her mother in the chaos of the escape, but she hadn't seen her. After all Kari had done for Grace Loray, fighting for freedom and unity, Lu couldn't believe she had been involved in Tom's betrayal. Did Kari know of the things Tom had made Lu do? What would she think when she found out the unforgivable acts Lu had committed for Argrid?

Lu took another wobbling step, steadying herself on the starboard railing.

"The Council saved us?" The confusion in the old woman's voice was palpable.

"Nah—that councilmember sided with the raiders," the man said. "I'm not saying Argrid's right. But I don't know if I'm comfortable here. With criminals. With *them*."

"*They* saved your sorry ass" came a snapping reply. "Show some respect."

Lu jerked forward to see Vex, his gaze murderous.

The old woman huffed and twisted toward the pilothouse's wall.

Sunrise cut gold and pink columns through the jungle

canopy as Vex transferred his gaze to Lu. His face softened, and he motioned behind him to the more open deck. A tremor shook his hand, and he tried to hide it by pushing the sleeves of his black shirt to his elbows.

Lu pushed up the narrow walkway, angling around him. Her shoulder brushed his chest and she caught a startled breath from him—but the terror and guilt in her heart pushed her on.

A stack of crates sat in the middle of the deck. Escapees lounged around it, using it to create something like privacy as they slept and talked. Lu sat on an empty side, facing the passing shore with her arms around her knees.

Vex lowered himself to the deck next to her. "Are you hungry? There were rations—"

"No, I'm fine." Though she couldn't remember when last she had eaten. She glanced at him, and softness tapped on her mind. "Thank you, though," she added.

Vex half smiled, his mouth open as though another question waited beyond his lips. But he shook his head, clearing his throat. "Your mother is on the largest getaway boat, one of Nathaniel Blaise's paddlewheels. Uh—Blaise is the Emerdian raider Head. They helped us get you out." His voice came fast and forced, trying to fill the silence. "We'll meet up with them in Port Mesi-Teab. At least, that's the plan, unless it's changed. But I don't know why it would have. But—wait, that's where we're going, did you know that? To Port Mesi-Teab. Teo's there. He'll be damn excited to see you. Anyway, we'll join up with your mother there and make sure everyone's all right—"

He stopped. Lu didn't move, and he dropped his eye from her face to her lap, where his focus stayed as he licked his lips and asked, his voice fragile, "Are you? All right, I mean. What the hell am I saying—of course you're not all right. *Damn it.* God, Lu, I'm sorry. I—"

"*You're* sorry?" Lu gasped the words.

Vex looked up at her. "Well, yeah. I left you on Elazar's ship to begin with. I thought . . . I thought Milo killed you. I shouldn't have believed it. I should've torn this island apart to—"

"You aren't furious with me?"

Vex cracked a laugh. "Why in the Pious God's hell would I be furious with you?"

A million reasons slammed into Lu. She clenched her hands in her lap and before she could speak, Vex covered her fists with his palm, warm and soft.

"You're part of my crew," he told her. The urgency with which he spoke, passion vibrant on his face—it stunned her silent. "You're family. Whatever you have to deal with, whatever happened to you, you won't go through it alone."

"You know what I did during the war." Her voice shook. "And you know—I did those things for *Argrid*. For my father. I've hurt this island. You know what sort of monster I am—"

"I know what sort of *person* you are. You're strong and loyal and brave—"

"I killed people!" Lu fought to keep her voice low, not wanting to draw attention, wanting to be as small as possible. "My father made me a traitor to Grace Loray. I'm not—"

"—and reckless and maddening and breathtaking, and I've missed you every moment since I thought you were dead."

Lu stopped. Vex pried one of her fists apart to nestle his fingers beside hers.

She looked at their clasped hands, bearing down on her last shreds of resolve.

"I've missed you," Vex repeated. "Watching Milo stab you and leaving you on that ship—it was the worst thing that has ever happened to me. I didn't realize how much pain I was in until I saw you in that prison, and it all vanished." He bent closer, beseeching. "Being part of someone's family doesn't come and go based on behavior. Hell, if it were, Nay, Edda, and I never would've lasted. No matter what you do or have done or might think you're responsible for, we're in this together now. Forever."

A sob tore up from Lu's gut. She covered her eyes with her free hand and hunched over, weeping.

Vex's hand untangled from hers, but only so he could pull her into his chest. When he'd touched her before, he had been hesitant, as though he feared breaking her—but now, his arms clamped around her, a resolute hold on the boat's deck.

"We're going to be okay," he told her, his hair brushing her cheek. "Lu, I swear to you—we're going to be okay. We've both survived too much to be destroyed."

Lu wasn't sure she believed him, but the comfort he offered was seductive. She allowed herself to feel it, the curve of his body around her, the tremor of the taut muscles in his forearm.

She had missed him, too. She had missed what they might have been. She had missed how he saw her, all those words he said—*strong, loyal, brave, reckless, breathtaking*—and she had missed the way she thought she might be those things when she was around him.

Vex held her and whispered promises in her ear, and she memorized the warmth of his breath on her skin.

❈❈❈

Dirty faces and gaunt eyes crowded Ben's steamboat. An escape he owed to the Emerdian and Tuncian raider syndicates—as well as Kari Andreu. A councilmember, and Lu's mother.

The raiders were reluctant to tell Ben even that much. He and Gunnar helped in any way they could—escorting people who struggled to find seating, passing out canteens of fresh water, taking quick breaks for themselves in the cramped washroom. Ben was careful to speak in the Grace Lorayan dialect and mask his accent, but the raiders recognized him as Argridian regardless. Had they recognized him as the Crown Prince, too? Pierce had attacked him in the prison for being Argridian—what would they do to Benat Gallego?

Hours out of Port Camden, the raiders finally gave in to Ben's questions about their plan. But they spoke while swinging blades, twirling the steel with wickedness in their eyes.

They were heading for Tuncian syndicate territory— the raider group that had started, hundreds of years ago, with the purpose of defending Tuncian immigrants from Argrid's cleansing of the island. And deep in Port Mesi-Teab sat a sanctuary that hid people who otherwise might have been imprisoned, or who needed help.

"Port Mesi-Teab?" Ben asked.

"Our main city. I'm surprised the prince doesn't know that," one of the raiders said. Ben jolted. They had recognized him after all. "Though I guess the cleansing of Tuncian whores isn't considered worthy news to Argrid's upper reaches."

Ben's eyes widened at the word *whores*. The raider grinned and tapped a tattoo on his cheek, two vertical dots above two horizontal. "Four gods. Four *true* gods—Order, Chaos, Rebirth, and Death—who could destroy your one flimsy god of piety with a flick of their hands."

"Why *don't* they destroy him, then?" the other raider sneered.

The first raider stabbed his knife into the wall of the pilothouse. "They don't need to. The Pious God doesn't exist."

When he was younger, Ben would have argued. Monxes

had ingrained devotion and loyalty into him above anything else. *"Those whose souls are corrupt will spew falsehoods. The Devil lies, in whatever form."*

Now Ben's disagreement didn't come from devotion. It came from knowing the truth.

"You're wrong," he said, and the raiders faced him, eager for a fight. But Ben didn't speak maliciously. He was tired. "My father is the Pious God. If your gods can destroy him, tell them to do so."

Ben left, moving to join Gunnar on the edge of the cramped deck.

As morning crested, the scenery changed from open lake to dense jungle. On the horizon, a river branched around a towering fort with a curved ivory *V* on the outward-facing wall.

People around Ben whispered, "Fort Chastity."

He had known the Church had imprisoned people on Grace Loray during the war, either executing them or branding them with an *R* for "redeemed" and releasing them. But for the Church to target a group here in such a personal way . . . it was cruel.

It was Elazar.

The midday hour meant boats were out, though not many. Those other boats kept a steady pace, their crews staying tucked inside the pilothouse, not wanting Argridian defensors or Council soldiers to cry, *Magic! They're seeking magic!*

Everyone on the deck of Ben's steamboat shifted uncomfortably, realizing their inability to hide from patrols. And as they drew closer, angling down the branching river that ran along the southern part of the city, Ben saw docks around Fort Chastity buzzing with activity. Defensors unloaded cargo from steamboats in various sizes and shapes—all flying Argrid's navy flag with the white curved *V* cut through by crossed swords.

"What's happening there?" another escapee whispered behind Ben.

But the Tuncian raiders didn't respond. Ben looked back, seeking an answer, only to find their faces gray and twisted in confusion.

"Fort Chastity was empty when we left," one raider finally said. "The Council wasn't even there. Thought they'd all moved out to join up with Elazar."

Another raider shot Ben a glare. "What do your people need in Fort Chastity?"

Ben swallowed his helplessness, bitter and vile. "I don't know," he admitted.

Elazar had listed Port Mesi-Teab in his proclamation—that the coming light would start in Grace Loray's outlying cities, such as this one. Whatever the light was, defensors were preparing for it. And Ben still had no idea how to stop his father or what solace to offer his victims. Or even what Elazar was truly planning to do. He didn't have permanent magic yet, so why was he still moving forward with preparations for his coming light in Port Mesi-Teab? What had Ben missed?

The raiders huffed. Next to Ben, Gunnar shifted closer. Or maybe Ben just wished he had.

Beyond the fort, a city of stone and wood rippled in the distance: Port Mesi-Teab.

Over the years, Ben had visited two cities in Tuncay with Elazar's retinue for various social engagements. The empire was a sometimes-hostile unification of five different peoples. Tuncian stewards had told Ben that he would need to visit the outlying villages to truly experience the cultural differentiations between the five groups, but each major city had become a hub of integration. From the architecture—buildings with spiraling narrow towers cozied next to squat structures with ballooning onion-shaped roofs; to the cuisine—some storefronts proclaimed that eating only food grown from the earth pleased the God of Rebirth while others peddled freshly slaughtered goats, but all adhered to a love of spices.

Port Mesi-Teab was a testament to Tuncay's diverse peoples, fused with Grace Loray's climate and resources. The architecture showed more practicality than design, with only two twisting towers poking the sky. The rest of the buildings were multistoried and looming, built of the island's lumber in stages of additions—new, old, decrepit—and reminded Ben too much of the areas in Deza his father had forbidden him to go to for fear of kidnappers and thieves.

The Tuncian raiders turned the boat down one of the narrow, meandering rivers that cut into the port. The streets held an aura of silence and fear, with those who shuffled down the cobblestones huddling in protective groups. The only noise came from the patrols at every major intersection: a mix of defensors and Council soldiers around a bellowing monxe or priest.

"The light is coming!" these evangelists cried. "In a matter of days, the Eminence King's light will bathe this city! Prepare your souls; cleanse yourselves of—"

The raiders on Ben's boat glared at him. His body ran ice cold.

Elazar had chosen Port Mesi-Teab as the first port to receive his *light.* Coincidence, that it was also the port of the raiders who had overthrown the Port Camden prison?

Ben felt ill.

Getting the boat to the sanctuary required backtracking, gliding through shadows, sending scouts ahead, and heavy silence. The moment Ben's boat docked, barely avoiding Council soldiers ransacking a storefront, he and Gunnar were swept into the madness of escorting people into the sanctuary. They wove through the port, into a building, down a dark staircase, and emerged back outside in a burst of sunlight and campfire smoke and conversations in Tuncian dialects, Grace Lorayan, and now Emerdian. Various food smells blended together too, zesty spices and syrupy sugars and something acidic that might have been ale.

The sensations overwhelmed Ben in a welcome shock.

He didn't know what he had expected. But it hadn't been this.

Buildings loomed over three sides with the wall of the city on the fourth, all towering high to block the sanctuary from view. The campfires were few so as not to draw attention with smoke, and all conversation was soft. Families spilled out of shacks like produce bursting from a too-small crate; thin faces sipped bowls of water; a baby cried somewhere to Ben's left.

The delayed arrival schedule meant everyone showed up in shifts, and chaotic shifts at that—other boats had arrived before Ben's, by the look of it.

Gunnar nudged him. There, moving toward them in the crowd, were Nayeli and Edda.

Edda nodded toward the door Ben had come through. "Was Vex on your boat?"

"Or Cansu?" Nayeli added.

Ben's throat was dry. Did Vex's crew know who he really was? "No—I'm sorry."

Nayeli released a string of curses in several languages. "I'm going to see if she's shown up anywhere else yet," she grumbled and spun off.

But a woman came up one of the roads, anger written in the creases on her face, and Nayeli stopped with another curse. Long gray hair trailed behind the woman, and when she hit the clearing, she whipped her head from side to side, eyes lapping up everything.

There was movement in the crowd, and another woman emerged, wiping her hands on the already soiled fabric of her skirt.

"You must be Fatemah Nagi. I am Kari Andreu—"

Ben's eyebrows shot up. This was Kari. She looked like Lu—the same face shape and eyes, the same ferocity in her bearing.

"I know who you are," Fatemah snapped. "The Senior Councilmember who will save the island. Again." Fatemah switched to Thuti, the main language of Tuncay, as she glared at Nayeli. "Was she worth it?"

Did she mean for only Nayeli and the nearby Tuncians to understand her? Ben almost told her that he spoke Thuti, or at least enough to pass in diplomatic meetings.

"Was a Grace Lorayan councilmember worth losing Cansu?" Fatemah repeated. She shifted, the slightest movement, and her glare fell back farther, on Ben.

No. It had been a glare before. Now it was wrath embodied, fire and loathing.

"Was *this*," Fatemah started, back in Grace Lorayan again, waving at the weeping children and bodies packed together, "worth bringing the *Crown Prince of Argrid* into the place we created to remain safe from Argrid's reach?"

The people standing closest might've been acting like they couldn't hear them, but at Fatemah's words, they gasped.

"The Crown Prince is *here*?"

"How? He'll lead Elazar to us!"

"The councilmember did this. They've betrayed us again!"

Fatemah didn't try to soothe the panic. She stood there, staring at Ben, then at Kari.

"Lock 'em up!" someone shouted. "Don't trust Argridian rats! Don't trust the Council!"

Kari lifted her chin, hands raised to show her surrender.

"My name is Kari Andreu," she started. "We come to you seeking asylum. I am here first as a victim of Argrid, second as a councilmember. And Benat—" Kari looked at him, but he was already facing the crowd.

"My father imprisoned me," Ben said, raising his voice as high as he dared. "I have no loyalty to him. I swear to you, I will not betray this place or these people. I—"

"Your words mean nothing." Fatemah batted her hands in the air as though she could will the situation to comply. "I must take care of this mess you have made, bringing these people here. This is a *Tuncian* sanctuary. You have sullied our peace."

She turned and marched away. Kari hurried after her, Nayeli too, and the crowd moved again, trying to arrange themselves or settle in or avoid Ben.

He almost followed Kari and Fatemah. They were the leaders here; he was too, in his own way. He needed to assert himself in their favor, make sure they knew he was on their side.

The people on Ben's steamboat had kept away from him,

scowling at him only when they thought he couldn't see. Now the former prisoners trickling into the sanctuary whispered to each other and gave him tight glowers.

Ben fought the urge to shrink. What could he do to convince these people he was sincere?

Edda remained, standing between Ben, Gunnar, and the people firing glares at him. She actually snarled at someone, who cowered and shot off.

"You don't have to do that," Ben said.

Edda's eyes went to Gunnar and dropped to his chest. Though Lu's Cleanse Root had healed him, three criss-crossing bandages remained from the prison, but his chest was bare otherwise. His clan mark peeked through the wrappings, the curve of the sun's center here, a twisted sun ray there.

An odd expression passed over Edda's face. She said something Ben didn't understand, but by the way Gunnar's blue eyes widened, he did. He responded, seemingly awed. She shrugged off whatever it was.

"Fatemah always puts the needs of this sanctuary over anything else," Edda said to Ben in Grace Lorayan. "Don't take it personally. She fancies herself the queen of Port Mesi-Teab, though she'd never say it out loud. Anyone gives you trouble, find me."

She left, and Gunnar gaped at her retreating back.

"What did she say to you?" Ben asked.

A dimple sliced through the stubble on Gunnar's cheek.

"She speaks Pratua."

"What?"

"Pratua. My clan's language."

Shame hit Ben. He had never asked what language Gunnar spoke. He had thought of it only as *one of the many spoken in the Mechtlands* as Gunnar had whispered reassurances across the prison hallway.

"Four Mecht clans speak Pratua," Gunnar continued. "We were once one clan, before the wars. Edda—I heard of her. She—" His lips lifted in a shocked smile. "She murdered an Eye of the Sun commander. It was . . . like unusual, like strange—"

"Unprecedented?" Ben offered. "Impossible?"

"Impossible. Eye of the Sun commanders hold the clan's secrets to Eye of the Sun preparation. No one kills them. But she did. People rejoiced in my clan when it happened. We attacked her clan and won a great victory." Gunnar shook his head. "She is terrifying."

Ben panted. No argument there. "What is your clan?"

Such a simple question, but that simplicity felt vital. Ben wanted to ask more, to know Gunnar's people and history and where he had gotten that scar at the base of his right ear—

Gunnar's face was sardonic. He said a word that had Ben stammering.

"Anoch—enoch? Enochjof—jia? Enochjofjia?" Ben repeated.

Gunnar barked a laugh. "You should not speak Pratua."

"I did, in the prison. Thaid fuilor mauth."

Gunnar's eyes sparked. "Now that we are out, I can tell you. Your accent is terrible."

Ben scoffed. "I speak four other languages—"

"Argridian tongues are too delicate for Pratua."

"And what should I use my delicate tongue for instead?" Ben's eyes went wide. *Pious God in heaven.* Did he really just ask that?

Gunnar squinted. He was likely translating it to Pratua and back to make sure Ben had asked such a presumptuous question.

Gunnar grinned, halfway to laughing. "I am sure I can come up with something."

Ben blushed so hard his chest burned.

"Ben!"

The call brought relief—something else to focus on. But he heard it again, the voice coming as it had all the other times. An echo from a dream Ben never thought he'd have again.

He turned to see Paxben—Vex, now—standing on the dirt road of the sanctuary.

The image of his cousin, the whisper of Pax saying his name still in the air, struck Ben so hard he grinned.

The horrors he'd endured to get here had been utterly worthwhile.

13

VEX'S PULSE HAMMERED him speechless.

It didn't matter that he'd had to hobble from the boat to the sanctuary on Lu's arm. It didn't matter that he was standing now by sheer force of will, gritting his teeth and taking too-deep breaths to combat the splitting pain in his legs.

Ben was here, *free*.

Vex surged forward and tackled his cousin. Ben gave a startled oath before he gripped Vex with the same ferocity.

Since they'd been reunited weeks ago on the *Astuto*, either Vex had been a prisoner, or Ben, or both of them. This was the first time in more than six years that they'd stood together without threat of a pyre or secrets wedged between them.

Vex sagged against Ben, unsure of a time in his life when he'd been this relieved.

A sharp cry pulled Vex away.

Kari stood up the road, her face the rawest Vex had seen it. He turned to Lu, who had her head tipped, peeking up at her mother the same way she'd first looked at him on the steamboat.

The memory still cored Vex out. Lu had expected him to be upset with her. How could he—he would *never* be—

Neither would Kari.

She scooped Lu in a hug that re-formed her whole body, taking her from rigid leader to a parent who had never thought she would see her child again. "Adeluna," Kari sobbed, "my love—"

Lu didn't try to reason with Kari as she had with Vex. Maybe she'd intended to, but the moment Kari's arms were around her, a whimper broke out of Lu's mouth and she buried her face in her mother's neck, shoulders heaving as Kari rocked her.

A tremor started in Vex's hands. He couldn't stop smiling, a manic, idiotic grin, and he gripped Ben's arm, looking from him to Lu and back. People from Vex's boat passed into the sanctuary but gave them room.

His focus caught on someone who had been on the road behind Kari.

Teo stood beside Edda, holding the edge of her shirt.

Kari untangled herself from Lu. Everything in Vex's body went still.

The barest flicker of hope brightened Lu's face. "Teo?"

Teo's wide, dark eyes fixed on Lu. Vex hadn't told him Lu had died—or that he thought she'd died, at least. All Teo knew was that Lu hadn't come back.

Vex held his breath. *C'mon, kid . . .*

Lu reached for him.

Teo didn't move. "You left."

A pause. Vex watched Lu, saw her take a shaky breath.

"Yes," she said. "I'm sorry."

"You won't leave anymore?" Teo pressed. "You're here now. We're all here, and we're safe, and you won't leave again."

Vex's chest caved in. No one could make that sort of promise now.

The grayness in Lu's expression said she knew that. She slid forward, her arms still out. When she didn't respond, Teo took an equally large, definitive step back.

"Teo." Lu's voice was pinched and throaty. "Teo, let me—"

But he took off, shoving through the mass of people and vanishing into the sanctuary.

"Teo!" Lu shouted. The crack in her voice, the wobble of tears, made Vex heave forward.

Edda gave Lu a sympathetic look before she jogged after Teo.

Kari beat Vex to Lu. "Give him time. He has been through more than anyone his age should. He needs—"

Lu shook Kari off and turned away.

Vex's grip on Ben's arm tightened. To stop a tremor, and to hold himself there, and to make sure Ben was there, too.

"What happened to her?" Tears blurred Vex's vision, but he looked at Ben and saw the same exhaustion that weighed down Lu's shoulders. "What happened to you?"

Kari heard him ask, and she hesitated.

Memory passed over Ben's face like a shadow. Vex almost stopped him—it was too soon, they'd just gotten free—but Ben closed his eyes.

"Elazar tried to get us to make permanent magic for him," he said. "He had . . . incentives. Lu's father. General Ibarra. Beatings."

Vex thought he might be sick right there, all over the wall of a tenement.

Lu lifted her head to the sky, seemingly unaware of their whispered conversation.

Vex squinted at Ben. "You were out of the cell when we found you. How'd you escape?"

"Lu made the magic that Elazar wanted. She made a permanent magic potion with Powersage and Aerated Blossom." Ben's face grayed. "And took it herself. It was how we got out of the cell—she kicked through the door."

"It didn't work."

Kari, Ben, Vex, and Gunnar spun toward Lu. She still had her back to them, but she held up her hand now, examining her palm.

"The potion I made," she continued, eyes fixed on her skin. "It wasn't permanent. I might have lengthened the effects, but that's all."

She said it with noticeable disappointment.

Vex's heart cramped. He was scared for Lu, of course, and damn furious at Elazar for putting her in a situation where she'd try to ingest permanent magic—but there was something else. Something that sounded like Rodrigu's voice in a dim room long ago.

The fire in the hearth of his father's study had made the whole room sweltering. Paxben had sat in a velvet chair before it nonetheless, his shirt unbuttoned, his buckle shoes discarded, his legs bent underneath him. His father's steward had ushered in the usual group of Rodrigu's allies—a comodoro from Elazar's navy; a conde who owned the richest mines in northern Argrid; a duquesa who funded the poorhouses and hospitals in Deza's slums; and even a priest from the Grace Ismael, the small cathedral that overlooked Deza's port.

All people who wanted Rodrigu to serve as regent over the too-young prince and usher in an era of magic tolerance and acceptance.

Rodrigu insisted on Paxben being present for his meetings, hoping he would learn something. But Paxben had to pretend he was a spy to pay attention, hiding in the shadows. He still remembered stupid details—the duquesa always wore her hair in a jeweled redecilla, a hairnet with gaudy rubies the size of acorns; the priest was shifty and stood closest to the door, as though he might sprint out at the first startling noise.

Rodrigu was sitting behind his desk, asking after the war on Grace Loray, when the comodoro rose from his chair.

"We're here to see if you've reconsidered," the comodoro had said.

Rodrigu sighed to the papers spread before him. "You're asking me to carry on with one of my brother's goals—everything he touches is steeped in madness, which is why we have formed this resistance at all. My answer is as it has always been—*no*. I will not continue Elazar's experiments with permanent magic."

The comodoro looked at the duquesa, who gaped, horrified.

"You still say no?" Tears choked the duquesa's words. "You spend too much time in your gilded mansion. You do not walk the streets, watching people shrivel away, cast out after Elazar finishes using them as his playthings. You would deny them healing?"

"The experiments to make permanent magic have caused Shaking Sickness," Rodrigu had said. "The cure cannot lie in *more* permanent magic. You are asking me to create a deadly weapon in the faint hope that it could save lives—where is the wisdom in that?"

A desire to bring understanding and magic to Argrid had united Rodrigu's group, where the Church wanted to keep everyone in fear. But some of Rodrigu's conspirators had wanted him to take up Elazar's quest of making the effects of Grace Loray's plants permanent, even after they overthrew the king.

Rodrigu had been adamant. *"It's a deadly weapon,"* he had said any time the others pressed him. They would make magic legal for everyone to use, but he would not stretch its powers to dangerous limits. That had been the cause of dozens of late-night arguments that Vex had eavesdropped on, up until Elazar found out about the resistance and killed them.

Vex's leg throbbed. He couldn't absorb the idea of Lu making permanent magic, let alone taking it herself. Not after everything Milo had done to her, and everything she knew Vex had been through, too. Permanent magic *was* a weapon.

But Tom had made Lu kill people during the revolution—she was already a weapon.

What had all this done to her?

"Lu," Vex pleaded, and his voice cracked. He cleared his throat—she didn't need someone who would fall apart, but he wasn't sure he'd be able to give her that. Someone to lean on, when he could barely stand on his own. "Remember what I said on the boat? You aren't—"

She turned, but she wasn't looking at him, her focus on the sanctuary.

"Do you hear that?"

"Adeluna," Kari sighed. "We're trying to help—"

"It sounds like shouting," Lu said. Vex's heart broke a little more.

But he heard it, too. An uproar came from the middle of the sanctuary, a crashing like pottery or windows—

Kari and Lu took off. Gunnar ran too, and Ben started to follow, but Vex grabbed him.

"Can you"—Vex grimaced at the dirt—"help me get there?"

He couldn't make himself look at Ben, so he had no idea what his initial reaction was. Sympathy, probably.

Damn sympathy.

"Of course," came Ben's reply, and he hooked his arm around Vex's waist. The two of them started off, weaving through the people who crowded the roads but frowned at the noise.

Or maybe it was Ben they were scowling at. Vex couldn't tell—he was too focused on how each footfall shot questions into his heart. *Has it been too long? Even with Lu back, can anything stop the Shaking Sickness's progression?*

Vex refused to answer those questions. He ached, and damn it, he *hated* his body. With every flare of pain and every breath. *He hated it.*

He and Ben were the last of their group to reach the source of the shouting. In the middle of the sanctuary, the buildings sat in a crude square. Vex had seen markets here on past visits—lean-tos and stalls with vendors hawking bolts of linen, bananas, and salted fish.

But now, it was all the worst parts of a tavern brawl.

Dozens of people flailed around in manic fights. Fists flew. Bodies crashed through benches. Someone catapulted off a barrel onto the back of another person. The air filled with flying pots and buckets, anything that could inflict pain.

Vex was surprised that something like this hadn't happened already—cramming the Emerdians and the Tuncians together and expecting them to get along was a lot to ask of any two syndicates.

Kari was nowhere to be seen—no, wait, she was in the middle of the ruckus with Lu and . . . Fatemah?

"You brought this here!" Fatemah barked. "Now, *three* syndicates—"

Vex squinted. Three syndicates?

The Mechts had sided with Elazar. The Tuncians and Emerdians were here. Which left—

Vex hissed in panic. That girl socking another raider in the eye—she had a piercing in her right ear, a garish chunk of gold that made her earlobe droop.

Neither Emerdians nor Tuncians wore things like that.

Nayeli slid up on Vex's other side. Behind her, Edda came too.

Vex released Ben to seize Nayeli's arm. He pointed. "Does that look like—"

Nayeli followed his direction. "Oh *shit*."

Edda's reaction was far less shocked. She shrugged. "We would've reached out to them to unify the syndicates. Maybe they heard and sought asylum here too?"

Whatever the reason, the fight in front of them was between Tuncians, Emerdians, and the final and farthest removed of all the raider syndicates: the Grozdans.

On the Mainland, Grozda sat in the southeast, an inhospitable country of half mountains, half coastline. The sheer bleakness of Grozda's terrain had created a people of relentless courage, with their leader—called the Gloria—determined by trials of physical prowess every few years. Grozda was small but packed with warrior-citizens who sold themselves to anyone with enough coin. They were aggressive, fearless mercenaries.

And their counterpart syndicate on Grace Loray embodied that.

Vex's heart dropped into his stomach. He knew the plan was to unite the raider syndicates to push back against Elazar—but he hadn't thought past finding Ben. He needed to get better at big-picture planning so he could be more prepared for situations like this.

The girl he'd seen in the brawl, the one with the gold stud in her earlobe, leaped up onto what might've once been a market stall. She bellowed a phrase in Grozdan that meant *glory in the attack*—god, she still shouted that?—before kneeing a raider in the face.

Rosalia Rustici.

A dozen different memories flooded Vex, a wave of dread tinged with disgust.

He disliked the syndicates for various reasons. The Tuncians treated Nayeli like shit; the Emerdians put more value on *things* than on the people they were supposed to protect; the Mechts were mostly high on Narcotium Creeper—and had sided with Argrid, of course. But the mission prison on Grace Loray where Elazar's cronies had tossed Vex six years ago had been in the northeastern part of the island—smack in Grozdan syndicate territory.

When monxes had labeled Vex redeemed, branded him, and released him into the jungle, they'd freed Edda with him, and she'd taken pity on him. The two of them hid out together in various ramshackle towns until the war ended. In an alley near New Deza, Mecht raiders had outnumbered a fifteen-year-old runaway who'd tried to rob them—Vex and Edda had saved Nayeli, and the three of them became something like a family.

When they ended up back in Grozdan territory, it'd seemed like fate. They weren't in Tuncian territory, so no tension with Nayeli; they weren't in Mecht territory, so no tension with Edda, who'd left the Mechtlands to get away from her countrymen.

Sixteen-year-old Vex had told himself he wanted to join the Grozdan syndicate because he had fond memories of his first experience with Grace Loray outside the mission-prison.

Sixteen-year-old Vex had been a love-struck dumbass.

Someone fired a pistol into the air, silencing the area. Raiders froze mid punch; others dropped to the ground, instinctively ducking.

Fatemah stood in the center of the square, the smoking pistol in her hand. "You come to my sanctuary," she said, not quite shouting, but not speaking softly in any way, "and you force me to *fire a weapon* when we are trying to stay hidden. You *ruin* my home"—she gestured at the disaster of the fight—"and you take resources away from Tuncians who need it! Get out! Get out of my sanctuary! Get—"

"You aren't the Head here, Fatemah!"

Vex went rigid. Rosalia leaped off the stall and shoved her way through the raiders.

"Cansu sent for me. She promised she'd make it worth my time." Rosalia turned to the crowd. "Come out, Cansu! Make Port Mesi-Teab worthwhile!"

Uproarious laughter came from the Grozdan raiders. Vex frowned.

"She's talking like she's the Head," he whispered to Nayeli.

But Nayeli looked at Vex, desperation in her eyes. "Cansu sent for the Grozdans. She must've done it before we left to get Kari from New Deza. Gods, Vex, Cansu wants to unify—she wants this—"

Nayeli put a hand over her mouth and spun away. Vex wanted to go after her—of course Cansu would come to her senses about everything she and Nayeli had disagreed over after Cansu had been *captured*—but his legs were still unsteady.

Nayeli's movement away from the crowd drew some attention. Fatemah, Kari next to her, Lu—and Rosalia.

Rosalia hooked her eyes on Vex and beamed, all flashing teeth and sharp blue eyes and a deepness to her tan skin that was less blush, more intensity. Even when Vex had been, as Edda had said, *smitten* with Rosalia, her smile had seemed possessive. Cruel, almost.

"Cansu is not here," Fatemah snapped. Rosalia held Vex's gaze for another second, two, three, before she faced Fatemah. "I am acting Head in her absence. And I am telling you to go."

"If they are Grozdan representatives," Kari tried, "we need them. We have to unify *all*—"

"Like *hell* am I going to ally with the Grozdans!"

The shout—scream, more like—came from Nate, who barged out of the crowd, straightening his curved leather hat. Pierce ran alongside him, his hair ripped free from its ordinarily pristine braid and flailing around him in a white-blond flurry.

"You knew the plan in accompanying us here, Head Blaise," Kari said.

"We didn't have a whole helluva lot of choices. Stay in

Port Camden and get slaughtered by Elazar, or run with you. But if you want the Emerdian syndicate's help now to push out Argrid, you're gonna have to get rid of these brainless mountain hermits."

The only mountains on Grace Loray were volcanic peaks far north—Nate meant the mountains in actual Grozda. It was another slur.

"I told you, Andreu," Nate continued, "I told you I thought it was the Grozdans taking my people before Elazar showed up. Did a head count of all the Emerdians rescued from the prison. Some of my people are still unaccounted for. If Elazar didn't take 'em, who did?" Nate crooked his finger at Rosalia. "I'll string you up, Rustici, I swear—"

Rosalia looked confused for as long as it took her to blink. "*You're* the one who's been taking *my* raiders! My people have been going missing for weeks."

"I'd get more use filling my syndicate with swords propped up on bags of flour."

Rosalia whipped out a dagger as a few of her raiders swam free of the crowd to back her up. Nate fumbled at his hip for a pistol and Pierce grabbed his arm.

Elazar had damn well nearly taken over the island— again—and these dumbasses still wanted to fight each other.

"For the love of whatever particular god you call holy," Vex shouted, "can at least you *pretend* not to be raging murderous toddlers? It's enough that Fatemah let us in here."

Pierce ran his tongue along the inside of his cheek. "Look who grew up since he was last making a mess of Port Camden. Feel good about yourself, if that helps. You set us to rights."

Pierce rolled his eyes. Rosalia coughed a laugh into her hand. Vex glowered.

"Enough!" Kari stabbed a glare at the crowd. "All raider Heads and acting Heads, we will talk. No weapons. The rest of you will wait here. *Peacefully.*"

Rosalia barked laughter. "Who're you? Why should I—"

Kari gave her such an intense, penetrating *obey me* look that Rosalia shut up.

Vex started. Maybe Kari could teach him how to do that.

14

FATEMAH LED THE way to her office in one of the tenements that overlooked the sanctuary. Nate and Pierce took over the oak desk in the center, Nate on the chair and Pierce perched on the edge of the desk with his legs crossed.

Kari and Fatemah stood on either side of the desk, while Vex, Nayeli, and Lu hovered in the middle of the room. Ben and Gunnar slipped in behind Edda and retreated to the back corner.

Vex couldn't help it. He looked at the door.

"Of course she'd be last," grumbled Nayeli.

"The Grozdan Head?" Lu asked.

"Rocks were younger than the last Head," said Vex, "but I can't believe she took over."

"*I* still can't believe you slept with her," said Nayeli.

Vex was choking. Or suffocating. Or dying of Shaking Sickness here and now. He doubled over, unable to look at

Nayeli long enough to even glare at her.

"But don't worry," Nayeli said to Lu. "I'd be the first one to castrate him if he had any inclination to go back to her."

Vex instinctively pressed his knees together. "God, Nayeli—"

"What happened?" Lu's voice was flat.

"It's not—" Vex fumbled, still looking at the floor. "It was a long time ago—"

"Grozdans value glory over everything," Nayeli told Lu. "Which means they have to win at every gods damn thing they do. And raiders in the Grozdan syndicate feel like they gotta prove themselves more since they aren't *really* Grozdans—so people like Rosalia? She's heartless. Doesn't take help from anyone outside her own circle, even worse than Cansu with accepting the Council's authority—more because her territory doesn't need much outside help to curb their poverty. And Vex was all too happy to let Rosalia dominate him—until he wasn't. She had the Grozdan syndicate chase us out of Port Fausta."

Vex winced. He'd trotted after Rosalia for three months, doing whatever she asked of him. Lose at sparring, which he didn't mind because he wasn't good enough to win against her anyway; give credit for raids to her crew, which cut the percentage he got in half—that sucked a bit; flirt with people so Rosalia could deck them for *trying to take what was hers*. And his Grozdan wasn't very good at the time, so when she called him mezzochi, he'd taken it as a pet name.

She'd used it like that, leaning suggestively against tavern bars and stroking his temple.

"*Mio mezzochi,*" she'd say, and grin, and god, he still hated himself for how long it'd taken him to realize that she didn't see him as an equal—she saw him as an easy target.

Vex gagged down his shame. "I was a different person then. And it's difficult to have a healthy relationship with a member of a crime syndicate."

"Ain't that the truth," Nayeli muttered.

"But," Lu said, her voice still devoid of emotion, "*you're* a criminal."

Vex pushed himself up. Lu's eyebrows were lifted in curiosity—and amusement. The smallest flicker, there, in the corner of her eye. It settled Vex's chest.

"I'm a decent criminal," he said. "Rosalia cut off her crewmate's finger *on a dare.*"

Lu blanched and exhaled what was almost a laugh. "You're joking."

"Grozdans are an incomprehensible level of unbalanced."

"I'm surprised you and Rosalia weren't a fit, then."

Vex tried to look offended, but he was smiling too much. Lu had made a joke. At his expense, but he'd take whatever he could get.

"Thank you for waiting." Rosalia draped herself against the doorframe, her black curls falling around her arms. "Being a Head is *so* taxing, you understand. Well. Most of you."

Fatemah straightened. "Come in. Shut the door. We don't have time for nonsense."

Rosalia obeyed, the door clicking behind her. She leaned against it with a contented sigh. "Gloria bless me, this is what it feels like. To be one of the chosen few."

"The chosen few who will push Argrid out of Grace Loray," Kari amended. "It is why Cansu called you here, I believe. To join our cause."

"You have no right to speak on behalf of the Tuncian syndicate!" Fatemah snapped.

"But I do." Nayeli met Fatemah's expected glare. "And I agree with Kari. Cansu wanted the syndicates to unify to push out Elazar—that's why we're all here. Port Camden's taken. New Deza's long gone. I'm guessing defensors and Council soldiers overran Port Fausta too?"

Rosalia huffed but didn't deny that soldiers were swarming the Grozdan syndicate's main city. Vex's eye widened, and he looked back at Nayeli. Here Vex'd assumed Rosalia had come just to stir up trouble, but Nayeli had realized that Rosalia wouldn't have just strolled on down to Port Mesi-Teab herself unless she'd had no other choice. *Really desperately* had no other choice.

"So Port Mesi-Teab is the last free port on this island, and even it is struggling to combat Elazar's call to arrest anyone raider-like," Nayeli continued. "You can't deny it anymore, Fatemah. Grace Loray needs the Tuncian syndicate, and we need Grace Loray."

Fatemah's face flared red. "You forfeited your position here long ago."

"But I never stopped being your niece. I never stopped caring about Port Mesi-Teab."

Vex glowed with pride. In a different life, Nayeli had been Cansu's closest confidante, and being Fatemah's niece gave her standing too—but she'd left that behind when Cansu and Fatemah had told her they'd rather die fighting than submit to the Council's rule.

Vex shared a look with Edda, but his pride flickered in her bittersweet gaze.

No matter how this war ended, it would never be him, Nay, and Edda again. Would it?

"Fortifying the sanctuary as our base would protect the people here," Kari added.

"It will make them targets," said Fatemah. "How many will we lose in another conflict between Argrid and Grace Loray?"

"You're already losing people," Vex cut in. "When we were in the Port Camden prison, we found a wing of prisoners of Tuncian heritage and a room stuffed with Tuncian spices. Elazar's already targeted your people for—something," he finished weakly. Elazar's goal of making permanent magic wasn't a known fact yet, and it was better if the power-hungry, violent raider Heads didn't have that possibility in their arsenal.

But the room didn't notice Vex's slip, gaping at him in unveiled surprise.

He was getting real tired of people being shocked when his contribution to a conversation wasn't a sarcastic comment.

Lu was the only person not gaping. Her face set in that studious, thinking look of hers, her dark eyes flashing over him.

"Tuncian spices?" she echoed. "You found Tuncian spices in the Port Camden prison?"

Normally, her intense focus entranced Vex—but now it worried him. "Yeah. Why—"

He bit back the question. The room was still watching him, and Lu now, and he couldn't very well ask her if she knew why Elazar had had Tuncian spices without leading to a discussion on permanent magic. His mouth stayed open, caught, and Lu's eyes drifted to the floor.

"Fine," Fatemah relented, pulling the conversation away from them. Her voice was smaller than Vex had ever heard from her. It was terrifying—Fatemah never showed vulnerability. "You may use this sanctuary for your . . . war plotting."

Lu didn't react. Vex frowned.

"You all right?" he whispered to her, touching the fabric of her sleeve.

✥✥✥

The meeting was happening around Lu, her mind ebbing and spiraling.

Vex had said he'd found a room full of Tuncian spices in the Port Camden prison.

Lu remembered Teo's face. His look of betrayal when she'd seen him in the sanctuary—

Focus—Elazar had Tuncian spices? No—Tom had Tuncian spices.

Tuncian spices. In the Port Camden prison, surrounded by stones that Emerdian architects had infused with Bright Mint. A few levels above Gunnar, whom Elazar had kept alive for his connection to Ben—and his knowledge of Eye of the Sun.

Teo hated her. He hated her as much as these people hated each other, fraught with distrust and pain. Teo's mother had died of Shaking Sickness, and his sister, Annalisa, not a year later, of the same illness. Then Lu had been snatched away in a war of her own making.

Lu looked out the window, at the clouded sky blurred gray white.

Tuncian spices. Emerdian stonework. Mecht Eye of the Sun.

Was the secret to permanent magic in there? Had Tom figured it out on his own—impossibly, before Lu or Ben?

Emerdian stonework changed the effects of Bright Mint—the prison was proof of that. Mechts had used or done something unique to them that made Eye of the Sun permanent—Visjorn bear blood, Lu knew. But Tuncian spices? Why—

Lu had crouched in a shack with Fatemah and Cansu in this sanctuary over a bubbling pot of dissolved Budwig

Beans. The memory was what had led her to mention the Tuncians to Tom, the contradiction between Tom believing in her ability and Fatemah questioning her ability.

But there was more to her memory. The shack had smelled herbal, of bitter dried plants and magic hanging from the rafters—but it had smelled spiced too, a zest Lu had attributed to Fatemah herself. Kari always smelled of Tuncian spices. What else would it have been?

Had Tuncian spices been *in* the Budwig mixture? Had that enhanced the magic and let Cansu hear through every bean on the island?

Kari had talked of Tuncian spices throughout Lu's childhood. On special occasions, Tom had bought small bags of rich, buttery powders. Kari had kissed him, and laughed, and the three of them had feasted on Tuncian-spiced food "blessed by the gods."

At the edge of her mind, Lu heard Vex ask her something. She turned to him.

"The Budwig mixture," she whispered. She included Nayeli with a look. "That Cansu and Fatemah made. Do they put spices into it?"

Vex squinted, but it was Nayeli who said, "They put spices in everything. It's a Tuncian thing—certain spices bring good luck, some ward off evil, and so on. Why?"

Lu went dizzy. Tom had figured it out. How skilled in magic was he? He had lied to her. He had misled her. *Again.*

And now Elazar would bring his coming light to Port

Mesi-Teab. If Lu and Ben weren't instrumental to whatever that was, and if he still planned to carry it out, was Tom involved?

Fear wrapped unrelenting hands around Lu's throat and squeezed.

"Lu?" Vex touched her chin, trying to drag her attention up to him.

Lu had left Teo. And, worse, she had caused him that pain because of her own mistakes. She had seen the extent of her failure in Teo's wide, hate-filled eyes.

She would not fail anymore. She would not let Elazar win.

The room was still in tight discussion. Fatemah was trying to give a definitive list of requirements for all the "outsiders" staying in her sanctuary. Kari countered with calm reminders that the sanctuary was only a part of the larger conflict. Nate and Pierce begrudgingly deferred to both Fatemah and Kari, having no actual bargaining power beyond the few dozen raiders at their command. And Rosalia had her hands on her hips, defiance embodied.

"Fatemah doesn't want us here," Rosalia snapped, eyeing Kari as if judging whether she could take her down. "Why not retake Port Fausta and use my city?"

"We are fighting for *Grace Loray*," Kari clarified. "That is the goal: the entirety of the island, free from Argrid and ruled by raiders *and* the Council, as it always should have been. We have a base to fortify and prepare—that is the first step. The next step is to determine our best move against Elazar that will both rescue your people and break his hold on Grace Loray. An outright attack? An assassination attempt? We need to—"

A heavy presence tugged at Lu's side. Ben. He looked at Vex and dropped his voice.

"Tell her—on the way in, my boat heard criers in the city," Ben said in Grace Lorayan. "Saying that my father's light would come here in a matter of days. And defensors were unloading cargo into Fort Chastity—"

Ben's face paled, his lips in a thin line as Pierce shot off the desk.

"*Waaait* a goddamn second," he said, and pointed at Ben. "Argrid is currently ransacking our island. We've named this place our stronghold—fine. But the Crown Prince is listening in on everything we say."

※※※

Ben had considered not going to the meeting and instead hiding while Grace Loray fought for Grace Loray. But whatever the raider Heads, Kari, and the rest of them decided, it would affect Ben's country, too.

All eyes swung toward him.

"Kill him," Rosalia suggested. Ben winced. "Elazar should suffer the consequences if he's dumb enough to use his own son as a spy. There's no glory in that."

"Stop!"

The group turned to Lu. Ben's soul cramped in sympathy. They had barely arrived here after having fled Port

Camden for their lives. If he was exhausted, she had to be fighting for consciousness with each breath.

"I watched his father torture him," Lu continued. "I saw firsthand the cruelty Elazar showed his own son. Ben turned on his father and refused to be part of Elazar's madness."

"We're supposed to believe the prince had a miraculous change of conscience?" Pierce scoffed. "He's still an Argridian leader. We can forgive him for the acts committed when he was a wee princeling, but what about in recent years? He stood by while Argrid did a lot of awful shit. Why now, sweetness?" Pierce threw the question at Ben. "Why'd you turn on your father *now*?"

Fatemah, Pierce, and Rosalia waited. Nate lounged back in his chair, his eyes shooting up to Ben with a similar hatred.

A headache drove into Ben's neck. What Pierce accused him of was true. He had watched burnings in Deza, overseen debt and disease grip his country—and whiled away hours drinking and tangled in bed with Jakes to avoid confronting the impossible task of changing Argrid. Why had it taken him so long to wake up?

Because Ben hadn't been part of it before, not directly. But when Elazar had tasked him with working in magic, Ben had become complicit in hurting people. Elazar hadn't pushed him too far until he'd threatened to put blood on Ben's hands, not just Argrid's soil.

Disgusting, Ben thought. He had never realized what his

breaking point had been.

A brush of heat. Ben tipped his head to see Gunnar beside him, silent support.

"Elazar asked too much of him. Of us both," Lu answered for him. "He asked us to make permanent magic for him."

The bottom of Ben's stomach dropped out.

Rosalia, Nate, Pierce, and Fatemah spun on Lu.

"*Permanent* magic?" Pierce echoed. "You want to expand on that, love?"

The tension in Lu's shoulders eased. A gasp tumbled from Ben's lips.

Permanent magic had not been a factor to the raiders in this war until now.

"It's what Elazar wants," Lu said. "He wants to weaponize magic by making it permanent. Powersage, for endless strength; Cleanse Root, for healing; Incris, for speed—all of them. That's why he's taken so many people. To experiment on them. That's what this war is about—Elazar wants ultimate, unstoppable power."

Silence gripped the room. Pierce was the first to speak, his eyes narrowed.

"And he thinks you—and the princeling—can give him that?"

"None of the people we saved mentioned anything about Elazar's people experimenting on them," Kari interrupted, eyes on her daughter. "We would have seen or heard something—"

Rosalia whistled, ignoring her. "Shame and hell, with permanent magic, we'd get our people back and never have to worry about an enemy again."

"Permanent magic is not Elazar's ultimate plan," Kari tried. "That is *how* he will enact his ultimate plan. What will he use it for? Does he mean to purge all the raiders, as he has said? We need answers to these questions before we form our next steps."

"A purifying light," Ben said. "Elazar kept talking about a light bathing Grace Loray, starting in the outer ports and culminating in New Deza. Blessings to those who obey and punishment to anyone who fights. We thought the light might have been Elazar giving permanent magic to his most loyal defensors, but the fact that he is still moving forward with his plans without having permanent magic—he has something else in the works. Some of his priests announced it on our way in, and dozens of his defensors were at Fort Chastity. I think my father knows we retreated to Port Mesi-Teab, and whatever he has planned will happen here first."

"Whatever Elazar's gonna do doesn't matter now, does it?" Pierce surveyed Lu. Vex snarled, looking liable to murder him. "Not if we have a weapon like permanent magic. Can you really make it?"

Kari surged forward. "No. She can't."

Pierce gave Kari a sardonic look. "I'd like to hear for myself, Madam Councilmember."

"It doesn't matter if permanent magic can be made," Fatemah said. "You will not commit such cruelty in my sanctuary. That is what it will be—*cruelty*, experimenting on people, manipulating our island's magic. And"—she hesitated, disgust curling her lip as she glanced at Ben— "we have heard the proclamations too, from Elazar's people, of a light coming. Rumors say his *blessings* will start in a few days. If it has nothing to do with permanent magic, Elazar could be planning more arrests, more burnings, interrogations, the sorts of things that nearly destroyed Grace Loray years ago. We must act before Elazar gets the chance."

"How?" Pierce planted one hand on his hip. "Say Elazar is planning to attack Port Mesi-Teab. We could march on him first and—what? Politely ask him to leave? With our couple dozen Emerdian raiders, however many Rosalia's got left, and the Tuncians, who don't have their Head? All that, against the whole of Argrid's military *and* the Council's soldiers?"

"We had small numbers during the revolution," Kari countered. "We utilized our island's terrain and defeated Elazar's forces with guerrilla attacks. We can defeat him now the same way. I move that our next steps be to scout for Elazar's location and assassinate him. Killing the figurehead of this war in a single, decisive act will make it far easier to reclaim the island and demand return of your missing people."

Ben's heart tripped. *Assassinate him.* He knew, in the fog

of his mind, that this war would end only with Elazar dead. But the idea felt uncomfortable.

Pierce's lips twitched. "And I move that we fortify this sanctuary. We batten down and let Elazar throw his worst at us. We already know his ultimate weapon is here." He jabbed his thumb at Lu. "We go on the defensive until we get permanent magic—then we march on him, and we take out not just him, but every goddamn defensor stinking up this island. It'll be *far easier*"—Pierce's voice turned mocking—"to get our missing people when *all* of their captors are dead."

"How long will that take?" Kari's voice pinched. "What if you never get permanent magic? You are basing our next steps on a weapon that doesn't exist."

Pierce ignored her, staring at Lu, who eyed everyone in the room.

Ben started to pull attention back onto himself—he could make permanent magic, too; let the raider Heads torment him—but Lu turned to Kari.

"I can make permanent magic," Lu said. "And with it, we will destroy Elazar."

❈❈❈

Rosalia applauded. The noise sounded dull in Lu's ears.

"Permanent magic doesn't help us with an immediate plan of action," Kari said, her face frail. "It could be months before you perfect any potion."

"I'm close," Lu said. "I know I am. Days, at most."

"We need to focus on steps to take against Elazar *now*." Kari was trying so hard to convince Lu without derailing their war plots—leader, mother; general, parent. "We will fortify our position in this sanctuary, as Pierce mentioned. We will build our defenses. But we cannot sit behind those defenses hoping for permanent magic."

Fatemah stepped up. "I second your earlier motion to scout for Elazar's location and assassinate him. We will not turn this into a magic war. We go after Elazar as we are, or you all will leave my home."

"It isn't just your home."

Nayeli's face was grim. "As long as Cansu's missing," she continued, "we'll do everything we can to get her back. Including permanent magic. I'm with Lu."

"We cannot win this war divided," Kari said, her voice cold. "We must find a compromise. Many of you believe in permanent magic; many of us believe in acting as soon as possible and keeping magic out of this war. But we must find a way to—"

"Tell you what, Councilmember." Pierce sniffed. "If you figure out where Elazar's hiding and scrape together an assassination attempt before Lu here makes her potion, we'll join in. But if *we* get permanent magic first, then we stage our attack with that weapon and wipe out as many of his defensors as we can. How's that for compromise?"

Kari's face paled. Her hesitation made Lu's chest buck with terror. That was all she could feel: fear, hatred, *need*.

The need to obliterate Argrid the same way it had obliterated her.

That need blinded Lu as Vex shuffled next to her.

"No," he whispered.

Lu deflated. "What?"

"No. Not with . . . not with magic. My father didn't want—"

"Since when do you do things because of your father?" Nayeli snapped. "Cansu is gone, Vex! Argrid captured her because *you* left her in the castle. You owe her."

Vex shivered, a tremor that made him dip his chin to his chest.

Pain lit like an ember in Lu's heart. She stoked it higher, willing herself to feel it beyond the numbness, beyond the *need*.

He disagreed with her. Vex, who had been tortured with magic in the Church's prisons. Vex, who knew her history with magic as well, and for a moment she saw the situation from his view: Lu wanted to create more of what had hurt both of them.

But it was different. They would be the ones in control. They would be the victors.

Nayeli, her eyes red, grabbed Lu's hand. "C'mon. I'll get you someplace to work. Let them scout for Elazar. We'll get permanent magic and end this whole mess."

Nayeli dragged her out of the room. Pierce and Nate trailed them; Rosalia lingered for half a breath longer, enough to throw a parting wink at Vex.

Pierce sidled up next to Lu in the hall. "What do you need? We can get you anything."

Rosalia, not about to be outdone by anyone, offered the same.

"Plants. Laboratory supplies," Lu said. The more she listed, the lighter she felt. This was right. This was active. "Tuncian spices, the steps to make Emerdian stones, Visjorn bear blood—"

Pierce gave a scowl. "Why do you need Emerdian stones?" he asked at the same time Rosalia grumbled, "Nothing Grozdan?"

Nayeli ignored them. "Visjorn bear blood? How're we gonna get Mechtlands shit on Grace Loray?"

"Leave it to me." Rosalia's smile was eager.

"And—" Lu paused. Darkness welled over her, thick and brutal. "I need to find my father."

Pierce frowned. "Huh? Why?"

"Does it matter?" Lu snapped. "Kari and Fatemah will send scouts searching for Elazar—you can send scouts searching for my father. Tomás Andreu."

Pierce drew back, calculation marring his fine features. "All right, girlie. He won't be able to take a whiz in a river without us knowing about it."

"Adeluna!" Kari's voice echoed behind them. "Please—"

Lu went rigid. The group stopped around her, and she pulled out of Nayeli's hand. "Give me a moment."

Nayeli nodded. "We'll wait for you outside," she said, and corralled Rosalia, Pierce, and Nate down the hall.

Lu turned toward her mother. Her skin prickled with worry that Kari would hug her again and Lu would be powerless not to disintegrate in her arms.

Kari pressed her lips together. A pause, and she motioned behind Lu, at the hall now empty of raiders. "Your father? That's what this is about to you?"

Lu jolted back a step, fury and fight coursing through her in a reflexive wave.

"You don't think I want revenge, too?" Kari pleaded. "After everything he did—to *you*—but there is a bigger war right now, sweetheart. And making this magic won't—"

"I'm done fighting this war," Lu cut in. Each word tore through her like a scream, but all that came out was a whisper, soft and agonized. "All my life, I've only ever fought this war. I will make permanent magic because it will undo the horrors I helped commit and it will save this island. But I'm done being a soldier."

Lu turned from the argument that would come.

"You're right."

She froze, muscles turning to stone.

"You're right," Kari said again, louder. "It was wrong of us to put this war on you when you were a child, and it was wrong of me to ask the same of you now. I'm sorry, Adeluna."

Shock twisted Lu, and she met her mother's tear-filled eyes.

"You don't have to fight," Kari said, a hopeful smile lifting her lips. "You don't have to do anything at all in this war. You can be done, sweetheart."

Kari opened her arms to Lu, an offering of rest and unity.

But in this instant, Kari took everything from Lu's childhood and turned it upside down. She confirmed that every pain Lu had borne, every moment of silent suffering, every task and secret, had been based on incorrect intentions.

Everything Lu had ever done had been wrong—as a traitor to Grace Loray when she obeyed Tom; and as a misguided rebel child when she had obeyed Kari.

She had wanted her parents to fix what they had made her, but now that Kari's apology hung in the air, Lu felt like she was drowning. She was a spiral of doubt and horror, a life built on a foundation of slipping mud.

Lu took a step back. Kari's smile fell, her open arms drooping.

"I'm sorry, Mama," Lu whispered, tears tracking down her cheeks. "I'm sorry."

She didn't intend to run, but her body forced her into a sprint when Kari shouted her name, the sounds soaked in tears.

15

THE ROOM EMPTIED, leaving Ben alone with Fatemah, Edda, Vex, and Gunnar.

Ben weighed the path he had chosen. He could have sided with Lu and worked to give dangerous magic to criminals. Instead, he had stayed in this room with those who would still plot the assassination of his father, but without waiting for a war-changing weapon.

When this war was won, when the mantle of Argrid's rule passed to him, he would spend the rest of his life working to make up for the atrocities he was about to assist.

Paxben—*Vex*—took one hobbling step forward. His focus was on the door, the path Lu had taken. Kari could be heard shouting Lu's name.

Ben put his hand on Vex's forearm.

Vex gave a weak smile. "I'll come back." He saw Fatemah

and his shoulders drooped. "Or—I don't have to go—"

"Yes, you do." Ben pushed him a little. "Go find Lu. I handled Argridian court politics; I can handle raiders."

Fatemah dropped into her now-vacant desk chair. For a moment, her attention was elsewhere as she shuffled through one of the bottom drawers.

Vex's smile turned real, bright and invigorating like the Paxben from Ben's memories. "Court politics. I haven't thought of that drama in years. Do the nobles still try to outdo each other at that festival? Damn, which one was it—the one with all that awful-smelling garland?"

Ben grinned. Vex meant the Día de Dar, the holiday of Grace Neus, the Grace who had been sainted for embodying the Pious God's pillar of altruism. Every year, the Church held a festival where nobles set up booths throughout the city, giving away food and drink and clothes, anything the poor might need. Pungent garlands of oleander, orange, and lavender decorated each booth, a sad attempt by the nobles to combat the body odor of so many people.

The nobles had turned the holiday into a contest. They all wanted to give away the most, the best, the grandest.

"Yes," Ben said. "A duque gave away his mansion last year."

Vex snorted.

"My father put him up in an apartment to keep the man from being impoverished himself."

Vex's snorts sharpened. Ben laughed too, swept away by an image from the recesses of his mind: laughing like this with Paxben, the memory blurry and weakened by time.

Edda cleared her throat. Gunnar looked past them.

Fatemah was watching them.

"Are our attempts to save lives from your king humorous to you?" she snapped.

The blood drained from Ben's face. He'd been talking with Vex in Argridian. It had been so natural, to speak to his cousin in their language again.

Vex winced. "Sorry, Fatemah."

But Ben pushed him toward the door. Vex needed to find Lu. He needed to mend whatever he could while there was still hope to fix them.

Ben's eyes went to Fatemah as Vex and Edda left.

"Fatemah," he beseeched her. "I don't mean to—"

"I speak Argridian." Fatemah looked back down at the paper she had removed from her desk. "Do not think you can plot secretly."

Ben's body went cold. She had understood what he had said to Vex. But they had spoken only of Argridian traditions. They hadn't called each other *cousin*, nothing that would incriminate Vex as someone to hate as much as the raiders hated Ben.

"I wasn't—" Ben caught himself. No excuses. He didn't want to appear insolent. "I—"

Kari slid back into the room. Her posture was defeated

now, exhaustion darkening her face and a few strands of thick black hair breaking free of her bun. She scratched her forehead, eyes closing, gathering herself.

"That is the compromise, then," she started, eyes still shut. "If we locate Elazar first, the Emerdian and Grozdan syndicates will join us in assassinating him. But if they create permanent magic first, we must join with them in attacking Elazar's army enhanced with magic."

"Then let us find Elazar." Fatemah stood, a wide parchment in one hand. "I'll have my people use our Budwig Beans to listen for his location, his goals, how many defensors are moving on Port Mesi-Teab. And when we all rescue my missing Tuncians, as well as the Emerdians and Grozdans, Nate and Rosalia will beg the Tuncian syndicate's forgiveness."

Kari shrugged. "In the meantime, we will extend the sanctuary's perimeter and solidify Port Mesi-Teab. Head Blaise and Rustici appeared to agree with that venture now, at least."

"They will," Fatemah stated. Her focus turned to Ben. "Or they will leave."

He stiffened. "I want to earn your trust."

Fatemah's face was a slate of stone. She stepped around her desk and thrust the parchment at Ben. "Then earn it. This is a map of Fort Chastity."

Ben took the paper and stared down at a rough sketch of five levels. Some places were labeled: a wide inner hall, guard stations, weapons storage; exits here, there—

He looked up at Fatemah, careful to keep his face impassive.

Her voice took on a note of maliciousness. "Rumors have spread through the city of a gathering at Fort Chastity happening in a few nights. We need to know what it is— and as Kari said, we need information. If your father"—the words came on a low growl—"plans to usher in his coming light, perhaps this is it. Get into the fort. Find out what the defensors are doing."

Ben gaped. "You trust me with this?"

"No. My people will accompany you. But you will know your defensors' inner rotations, how to avoid them, how to work around Argridian setups—and you will gather information *only*. No attack yet. Get my raiders in, get the information we want, and bring them all back alive, and maybe then, Prince, maybe then we will trust you."

Kari tipped her head at Fatemah. "You do not have Budwigs in the fort? Could you—"

Fatemah's lips crinkled. "The ones we hid there have been . . . removed."

She said nothing else. The implication sank into Ben.

Cansu was still missing, along with other Tuncian raiders—who would have known the Budwigs' hiding spots in the fort. If the magic was gone now . . .

Elazar had gotten at least one of the raiders to tell him about the hidden Budwig Beans.

Ben pressed the map to his chest. "I am honored to do this with your people, Fatemah."

"Good. Take some time to prepare."

She marched from the room. With a pause and a heavy exhale, Kari left as well.

Tension alone had kept Ben upright this far—now that it was gone, he collapsed on the edge of the desk.

Gunnar's hand dropped onto his shoulder.

Ben couldn't remember the last time anyone had touched him with such gentleness. Even with Jakes, they had been surrounded by courtiers who disapproved of a noble consorting with a guard, so they'd had to keep any caresses private. And Elazar—cruelty laced his every touch.

It was yet another shock to Ben that, with everything he'd been through, he wasn't repulsed by Gunnar's hand on him. As though every touch from Gunnar wiped away a bad memory and replaced it with something new.

"We should listen to her," Gunnar said. "Prepare. Rest. We will need it."

Ben cocked a look up at Gunnar. "You're coming with me? You—" Realization sent his eyebrows lifting. "You agree with Lu, though. About making permanent magic. Why did you stay here? I chose not to side with her, but that doesn't mean—"

"Did you want me to go with her?"

"Are you asking my permission?" Ben shot up from the desk. "You aren't my prisoner anymore. This war has already cost you too much. I don't want it to hurt you more than it has—you don't have to choose either side. You can go home. Maybe the Tuncians can get you an escort to the coast, or a boat."

Gunnar shook his head, once, quick and short. "I'm not leaving, Benat," he stated.

Ben's heart was a mess of beats tripping over themselves. "You aren't?"

Gunnar turned to the window, the sanctuary beyond. The ramshackle buildings and refugees and volatile raiders. "I left because I could not help the Mechtlands. But I can help here. I can help *you*. I want to help you."

Why? Ben almost asked. But Gunnar took his hand, and Ben forgot how to speak.

Gunnar covered their clasped hands with his other one and nodded at Ben's free hand. "Yours."

Ben shakily laid his fingers over their conjoined knot.

Pious God, he feels like scalding stones.

"Visjorn lofta blo," Gunnar said. "It means . . . closest might be *united on the blood of the bear*. To make a promise on the Visjorn is the most sacred of pacts; to break it will bring violence on you. It is how we join a union, in the Mechtlands."

"You speak of the Visjorn like my father speaks of the Pious God," Ben said.

Gunnar's face flashed with anger. "The two are not—"

"No, I'm sorry." Ben fumbled. "I meant the similarities. The Visjorn bear-spirit. The Pious God. The Tuncians' four gods. And the Grozdans worship—glory? I think." Ben shook his head. "My father seeks to exploit that devotion. Magic or not, whatever he has planned, that's what he wants. Reverence. How do you fight a war when the enemy wants not land or wealth, but hearts and souls?"

The anger receded from Gunnar's face, leaving a gentle glow of—awe? Ben faltered even more, wavering on the edge of something warm and welcoming and undoing.

"That is why I will help Lu only if you want it," Gunnar whispered. "I have served commanders. No leader has asked questions like that, has *cared* like you do. I am not Argridian, but I will serve you, and I will go with you to Fort Chastity."

Gunnar pulled the tangle of their hands to his chest, holding them above his heart.

Ben floated out of his body, tethered only by Gunnar's hands. Selfish delight swelled in his chest—but hearing Gunnar's oath, Ben thought of his father. Of Argrid's defensors. Of oaths like that spoken to kings, priests, no doubt syndicate Heads too. People giving their lives for belief and letting the rightness of their cause justify any terrible acts they committed.

Like weaponizing Grace Loray's magic to enhance the strength of unstable criminals. Like ingratiating themselves into the Argridian king's household, seducing his son, and plotting regicide.

As Argrid's next king, Ben would inspire such commitment. He would have an army of people who would march to their deaths if he asked them.

Permanent magic wasn't the most dangerous weapon to bring to war. Devotion was.

And Elazar had already mastered it.

"I accept your oath," Ben started, his voice a whisper, "but not your service. If we make this pact, you will help me in this war, and when it is over and I am king, I will help you bring peace to the Mechtlands."

It was the first time Ben had ever said that aloud—that he would be king after this. And not only king, but Eminence too, and that terrified him more, that he'd step into the role of leader for a religion he wasn't sure he still believed.

The responsibility punched him in the chest, how much he didn't want it.

How much he *did*.

Ben steeled himself, holding on to the growing question in Gunnar's eyes. "We are equals. It is a trade of service. You are not bound to me by anything else."

Gunnar's confusion lifted in a small smile. "Equals. I like that." He squeezed Ben's hand. "Visjorn lofta blo," he repeated, earnestness in his deep blue eyes.

Ben smiled back. "Visjorn lofta blo."

※※※

Lu and Nayeli were nowhere in sight by the time Vex got to the door of the tenement. His legs screamed with pain and he slumped against the doorway, watching people move between the shacks.

Vex's heart was broken, shattered into sharp little pieces in his chest.

Lu was scared. She was powerless. She wanted it to *stop*, and he knew that because he felt the same way. Only—god, he'd disagreed with her. *And* Nayeli. For the first time in his life, he'd made a decision about something that mattered, and it felt like he'd stuffed a fistful of stones into his lungs.

Edda, in the entryway behind him, didn't speak for a long moment. When she cleared her throat, he braced himself. She hated when he and Nayeli fought. It was usually about stupid stuff that they worked out by punching each other. In the rare instances when the bickering turned serious, Edda'd plunk them down and set them right. It was her job to keep their crew safe, and a divided crew wasn't good for anyone.

But were they even a crew anymore? Nayeli'd snatched up her role as Tuncian representative. Vex'd let his father's voice make up his own opinion about permanent magic.

Maybe Nayeli was right. Why did he care what Rodrigu thought? He'd never—

"You were a kid," Edda cut over his thoughts like she was listening to his inner turmoil.

Vex shuddered. "Don't."

"You don't owe Argrid anything. You were a *kid*, Vex, a kid who watched his father burn to death, who got dumped into a prison, who got tortured. You don't—"

"Goddamn it, I said *don't!*"

Vex shoved away from the doorframe. A tremor hit him,

and he made it one step before he slammed backward, his spine thudding into the wall.

Edda dove to help him, but he flapped his hands at her, unable to speak. He burrowed his fists in his eye sockets and his eye patch slipped, the scar rough on his knuckles.

That scar was one more thing he hated about his body. Maybe the thing he hated most.

"I ignored all this—all I am—for six years," Vex croaked to Edda. "I owe my father. I owe Ben. I owe Argrid. I was a kid when it all happened, but I stopped being a kid *because* it happened. So I owe my country and my family for what I haven't done, all this time. Don't I?"

He looked up at Edda, hoping she had an answer. God, she had to have an answer. She knew everything. She was the most constant force in Vex's life. His real mother had died not long after he was born, so he didn't have any memories of her, and he figured Edda was as close as he'd ever get to . . . not quite a mother, but something like that.

Her face flushed pink. "I swore I'd keep you safe," she told him. "When we got out of that mission-prison. You were like those kids my husband roped into becoming Eye of the Sun warriors—broken way too young, holding burdens no one so small should have to bear. So I made myself a promise that I'd atone for what I did to my husband by helping you."

She chuckled and a single tear shot down her cheek. Vex couldn't breathe.

"But I've done a shit job of it. I knew your past would come creeping up on you one day. And what have I done to stop it? I don't think you owe your father. What he dragged you into was damn selfish of him, and I watched war in the Mechtlands destroy too many kids like that. You owe it to yourself to let all that go and run as far from this shit as you can, run until you're safe. I think you should do whatever you have to do to be *happy*, Paxben."

Vex froze. She'd called him that only a handful of times in the years since he declared that he wasn't Paxben anymore. He was Devereux Bell, a new person, and she should call him *Vex*, because god, wouldn't that piss off his uncle?

But he'd never been new. He'd always been Paxben Artur Gallego, the rambunctious nephew of the Argridian king, the royal menace who stole sweets from the kitchens and snuck dye into the wash to stain all the monxe robes a hideous green-brown. He'd always been who he was, this broken child who now hated his body most of all because it was *alive*. Because it hadn't died that day alongside his father.

Vex had spent too long being a shadow of what he thought would be easy.

"I think I'd be happy," Vex started, "if I atoned for my past. If I stopped running."

Edda bowed her head. A long moment, and she met his eyes, her tears gone but redness remaining. "All right," she said. "Where should we start?"

"You're not gonna argue? You think I'm making the right decision?"

"There aren't any right decisions in a war." Edda shrugged. "Let's see how it feels fighting for something bigger than the *Rapid Meander* for a change."

Footsteps sounded on the stairs. Kari came down, followed by Fatemah.

Vex pushed his way out the door, making room for the group as they emerged into the sanctuary. "What do you need done? What's the plan? I want to—"

"More Argridians trying to help," Fatemah grumbled.

Vex drew back, confused.

Kari gave a sympathetic smile. "We will find Elazar. Once we do, the Emerdian and Grozdan syndicates will abandon their quest for permanent magic and join us in assassinating him. Until then, you could volunteer for a defensive position to expand the perimeter, or help with housing and food—"

Kari ran off a list of tasks. Edda volunteered for a defensive post, no surprise.

Vex stayed quiet. For all his certainty that he wanted to help, he wasn't paying attention to them—his focus was on Teo, coming up the road.

Teo passed a group of disheveled, vacant-eyed kids on the doorstep of a shack, kicking a rock between his boots. He stopped to ask them something—probably to play a game. The oldest kid, no more than thirteen, straightened, his face brightening.

"Vex."

He jolted. Edda grabbed his forearm to steady him.

"Volunteer to do something," she pressed.

"I—" His body would be a mess in any sort of fight. He could pass out food. Arrange bedding. Easy enough, right?

Teo picked up his rock and mimed some game to the kids. The oldest had stood up, trying to get the others into it—but they were cut off by a woman who stuck her head out of the shack's door and thrust a mangy broom in the air.

"Argridian rat!" she screeched. The four kids ducked. Teo, red-faced, froze in horror.

"Hey!" Vex wobbled forward. "The hell is your problem?"

The woman snapped to face him, deepening her frown. She lifted her broom, her kids scattering into the road, and Teo, his eyes wide, shot toward Vex.

"This used to be a place of peace," she said. "Now it crawls with *scum*—"

Edda grabbed Vex's arm. Between them, Teo clung to her shirt.

"We are here to help you." Kari stepped around them. "We are not here to cause harm."

"I'll cause her harm," Vex snarled.

"That won't help," Edda countered.

Vex spun on Edda as Kari and Fatemah went to the woman. "She threatened Teo!"

"I'm all right, Vex," Teo said softly. Vex shivered and managed a smile down at the kid.

Edda's grip on his arm went tight. "Kari'll handle the politics. But you getting into it with some scared Tuncian woman ain't gonna be good for anyone. You wanted to *help*, right?"

Kari and Fatemah talked with the woman now, the three of them leaning over the steps.

Vex grinned faintly at himself. "Think Kari's got a job for someone to stand around making sarcastic, unhelpful comments?"

He thought Edda'd berate him for *that* sarcastic, unhelpful comment, but she said, "Laughter is useful."

Teo still stood between Vex and Edda, the fist-sized rock in his hand.

Vex shivered again, clamping his arms over his chest. He looked down at that rock, up to those scared kids now hovering in the street.

Vex shrugged off Edda. "Hey, Teo—let me see that?"

Teo handed over the rock with a questioning look.

Knees cracking, Vex took a step, winced, took another, gritting his teeth as he put enough space between him and anyone still standing around.

The kids on the road perked up. God, did he still remember how to do this?

Vex tossed the rock into the air and caught it on his toes. He waved his arms for balance and a tremor made his foot twitch. But he held, sweat beading across his forehead.

Forget remembering how to do this. He wouldn't be able to, even if it came back to him.

The kids on the street stepped closer. A few more peeked around corners ahead.

Vex popped the stone into the air and spun, catching it on his other ankle. Pain flared up his legs, echoed into his torso. He kicked it up again. One more time, he spun, caught it on his first foot, and landed that foot back on the ground.

The kids were smiling. Jostling each other, searching the ground for stones.

Teo tugged on Vex's sleeve. "Can you teach me how to do that?"

"Yeah, kid." Vex kicked the rock to Teo—and buckled to the ground. "Put it on your toes," Vex said, hoping he didn't sound like he was in too much pain. The other kids moved closer, watching him instruct Teo. "Yep, just like that. Now—careful, you gotta keep your balance—kick it up. Not so high!"

Teo launched the stone skyward. It plummeted back down, eliciting yelps of laughter from the kids who'd gathered.

"Like this?"

"Watch me! I think I got it!"

A handful of kids kicked rocks into the air, giggling at the inevitable rain of stones when their friends overshot.

Vex sat there, elbows on his knees, fighting wave after

wave of tremors. His eye went beyond the kids, to Kari, Fatemah, and the angry woman, who were all watching the game. Kari and Fatemah smiled, and the woman—she still looked distrustful, but she didn't come raging into the group to chase off the Argridian kid.

"Huh." Edda lowered into a crouch next to Vex. "Diplomatic."

Vex rolled his eye. "I got 'em focused on something fun. It won't stop the war."

"If I remember, though, doing this almost got you killed once."

Vex squinted up. The sun cut through the cloud cover, shining a sliver of light across Ben. Beside him, quiet and sullen and the very definition of *brooding*, stood Gunnar.

It'd been years since Vex'd figured out that the statues of the Graces in Elazar's palace office had removable heads. And when Elazar had found him popping the head of Grace Biel, the Grace of the pillar of chastity, from foot to foot to ankle to knee and ankle again—

Ben had sat on the carpet in front of Vex the whole time. And after Ben'd gotten out a few rounds of *"We shouldn't be in here—my father doesn't like me to be in here without him—he says those statues are holy, Paxben, we shouldn't—"* he'd laughed until he couldn't breathe when Paxben had started kicking the statue head around.

Vex was so close to making a joke about it, but behind the humor on Ben's face, it was clear half his mind—more than half, likely; most of it—was on this war. Just like Lu, off making permanent magic to create an army of supplemented raiders. And Kari and Fatemah, who would go on to secure Port Mesi-Teab and send out people to assassinate Elazar. All these people, doing things and making plans that would bring real, true safety to the world.

Like Rodrigu had tried to do.

Vex rubbed a hand across the back of his neck. He couldn't help but smile when Teo kicked a rock twice in a row and pumped his arms into the air with a cheer.

"What did Fatemah give you to do?" He angled the question up to Ben.

"Help a group scout Fort Chastity."

Vex nodded. His eye cut to Edda. "We can do that."

Edda gave him a considering look. "You'll need Lu to cure you first."

That truth dug into Vex's chest. He could tell Lu what they were doing. Maybe he could convince her to come along, even. To abandon her dangerous weapon.

Ben sat next to Vex. "Shaking Sickness. When did Elazar—"

Vex dropped his hand over Ben's knee. "Doesn't matter. Your father's tried his hardest to kill me, but I gotta say, he's really bad at it."

Ben gave a brittle chuckle. He hooked his hand around Vex's, and they sat in silence beside Edda, Gunnar a shadow behind them, watching kids play a game from their childhood.

16

THE SHACK NAYELI found for Lu was overflowing with supplies. Here, Lu had watched Fatemah and Cansu cook down the Budwig Beans to search for Milo. Now it was filled with Tuncian spices; begrudgingly given details about how Emerdian stones were made, process and temperature and ingredients, from Pierce; and various plants. Nate, Pierce, and Rosalia were still looking for Visjorn bear blood, if they would be able to find any on Grace Loray at all.

And they were still looking for Tom.

Lu sorted her supplies, willing her mind to stay focused. Were there other ways to prepare magic, other ingredients that changed the plants' uses? Argridian, Grozdan—the options were innumerable, but she had enough to start experimenting.

She set aside Narcotium Creeper, Bright Mint, and Drooping Fern. Back on the *Rapid Meander*, when Vex had taken the potion to help him remember what plants had given him Shaking Sickness, he had thought of two: Aerated Blossom and Croxy. Lu had given him what she hoped was the cure for Aerated Blossom back then. Now she made a concentrated dose of Narcotium Creeper, to counter the Croxy.

That was the way to cure Shaking Sickness—how Lu had inadvertently healed herself as a child: by offsetting whatever plants had been taken in excess. But what else had the Church given Vex? The mystery was why Lu made another Bright Mint and Drooping Fern paste, the same one that had helped loosen Vex's mind before. He mightn't need it, though—he could ask Ben what the Church had given him. But if Ben didn't know?

As night fell after the meeting, Lu knew the voices outside the shack were those of Vex and Kari, demanding to speak with her. She gave Nayeli the vials to pass on, explained how Vex should take them, and told her not to let anyone through.

Lu didn't relax until the voices faded. Even then, her body felt on edge, braced for attack.

How quickly could she work? How long would she need to test any concoctions? What had Tom already created— and how could she counter it?

The echoes of knife cuts ached on Lu's skin. Her mind beat itself ragged remembering the way Vex had looked at her in the office and said, *"Not like this."* She listened hard at every noise that passed her door, hoping Teo would come, if only to yell at her.

Vex didn't want her to make this potion. Teo wanted her to promise him that she wouldn't leave. Kari disagreed with her.

But Lu could keep them all safe. This *would* keep them all safe.

Nayeli occasionally came with news. The raiders were setting up lines of defense and patrols to fortify the sanctuary. They arranged barricades of furniture, wood, odds and ends; they worked together to make it known to Argrid that here were those plotting against Elazar, a hive that would break open and unleash fury on his bid for Grace Loray.

That was where the cooperation ended. Kari and Fatemah sought to locate Elazar; Ben and Vex prepared for a mission to determine what the coming light would be. At the same time, Nate and Rosalia let their raiders do whatever they liked when they weren't expanding Port Mesi-Teab's perimeter. Half-drunk raiders lounged in tents or picked fights with each other across the sanctuary.

"People are crying to expel the other syndicates," Nayeli grumbled the third morning after the meeting in Fatemah's office.

Lu sat on the floor and watched coals flicker orange and yellow in the shack's central firepit. The fresh clothes Nayeli had found for her bunched when she leaned forward, the loose white shirt bagging around the navy-blue vest and dark breeches.

"But at least your mother and Fatemah have a plan," Nayeli continued. "I swear, the only plan Nate, Pierce, and Rosalia have is to take permanent magic and go on a rampage. Which would be *swell*, seeing as how Elazar's been spreading a general distrust of raiders. The families here are terrified of them. Nate's pissed that anyone'd be against them, 'cause he thinks it means they're *for* Elazar, and he wants to outright kill any dissenters. Kari, of course, ain't about to let that happen, so now we got some people under our protection who think we're becoming too raider-focused and not— Hey, you listening?"

Lu used tongs to adjust a metal grate over the coals. On it, a pot of Tuncian spices, Powersage, and Aerated Blossom had been brewing since dawn while she kept the temperature as close to the Emerdian brick instructions as possible. Despite their promises, neither Rosalia nor Pierce had found Visjorn bear blood yet, but maybe this combination would be effective.

Lu didn't look up. "Hmm? Yes. You mentioned—"

She gaped at Nayeli, at a loss for what to say or what they had even been talking about.

Nayeli's face softened. She folded her long legs under herself as she knelt next to Lu. "If you've started having doubts about making permanent magic—"

"I haven't," Lu said.

Nayeli cradled her hands in her lap. After a long while, she spoke, her voice small. "Vex and I had a bet. Who could get Rosalia to fall for them first. I'm glad now that I didn't win, seeing what a shitty person she turned out to be, but I don't usually lose that bet. One time, there was another girl, at a tavern in New Deza. I'd had a huge fight with Cansu, and I was . . ." She gave a halfhearted chuckle. "Vex spent the whole time talking to that girl about *me*. How great I was. *'Because there are other people in the world than Cansu,'* he told me later. That idiot."

Tears rimmed Nayeli's eyes. Lu forced herself to draw air into a body gone rigid.

"We'll find Cansu," Lu promised her.

"That isn't why I told you that." Nayeli stilled. "I've never disagreed with Vex like this. Every time I see Rosalia, every time I talk to Nate and Pierce, I want to projectile vomit. All they really care about is getting their syndicates through this unscathed—they'd sell us all out if it meant they'd be the victors. Are we doing the right thing by working with them?"

"There is no right thing in a war. There is only what you can live with."

Nayeli turned her teary eyes to Lu. Lu's numb heart cracked to see so much emotion from her. "And after the war, will you be able to live with this?"

After the war. Lu had been thinking in day-by-day increments—the farthest ahead she had gotten was imagining

Elazar's defeat. But beyond that? What would happen when she stood before Vex in a free Grace Loray and she had even more atrocities tethered to her soul than now? Would he look at her with the fear he had shown in Fatemah's office? Would he ever be able to touch her, knowing how many lives had ended because of the weapons she made? Would she one day be an anecdote from his past, like Rosalia?

It didn't matter. None of the victory was Lu's to enjoy—she knew that. Her purpose was in bringing peace to Grace Loray, whatever it required of her.

Nayeli rested her head on Lu's shoulder. Lu closed her eyes.

The door of the shack banged open, followed by a triumphant "Who's the greatest?"

Nayeli sat up and gave Lu an exhausted look. "Go lick the poison off Digestive Death leaves, Rosalia."

"Only if you lick something for me first."

In an instant Nayeli was on her feet, a knife out. Lu scrambled up and grabbed Nayeli's wrist.

"Don't you want to know *why* I'm the greatest?" Rosalia pressed. "Another group of my raiders just got in—with news that they saw a whole heap of people disembarking at Fort Chastity. Rumors are that two of 'em are General Ibarra and Tomás Andreu."

Lu's grip on Nayeli's wrist slackened. "He's here?"

Rosalia beamed.

The world contracted. To no one in particular, Lu said,

"We're going to Fort Chastity."

"What?" Nayeli and Rosalia asked simultaneously. They glared at each other.

"You finished the potion?" Rosalia asked.

Lu looked at her. "No. But Tom is the one person in Elazar's employ who might be able to make permanent magic for him. If Elazar is moving forward with his plans, it could be because Tom has been successful. We need to know—and we need to stop him."

A murderous smile unfurled on Rosalia's face. "Why didn't you say that from the start?"

Nayeli huffed. "Not *kill him*. Tom is Lu's father. We'll just—steal his stores of magic to delay his progress?"

She waited for Lu's confirmation.

Kill him. Tom is Lu's father. Had that been what Lu meant? She needed to stop Tom. She didn't know far she would have to go to do that.

"We'll steal his magic. Or destroy it," Lu said. "Whatever we have to do to end this."

Nayeli gaped.

Rosalia hooted with laughter. "Gloria, this councilmember's daughter is more raider than anyone on Vex's sorry excuse for a crew. Seems he hasn't had a chance to turn her soft yet."

"No," Nayeli said. "You think that because you couldn't make him *hard* at all."

Rosalia howled again. Lu gawked at Nayeli.

"Do you want to bring that up?" Rosalia tipped her head to the side. "I thought our darling Lu here was mezzochi's next conquest."

Nayeli cursed in Thuti, a spectacular list of things she would do to Rosalia with her knife. Rosalia held her hands up but grinned—it was clear she'd been intending to hit this nerve.

Lu squinted. "Mezzochi?"

"You don't speak Grozdan?" Rosalia's grin went malicious. "Once Vex's taken you to bed, ask him what it means. Gloria, I wish I could see the look on his face!"

Nayeli spat at Rosalia's feet. The blood drained out of Lu's extremities. Some part of her said she should feel jealous, as was Rosalia's intention. But the image she suggested—being in bed with Vex—was such a far-off concept that Lu had no idea how to respond.

Lu spun to the firepit. "I need to finish what I'm working on," she told Rosalia over her shoulder. "But I want to leave as soon as possible."

"With pleasure." Rosalia's voice came with the lilt of a venomous smile. The door to the shack opened and closed behind her.

"Lu," Nayeli said the moment they were alone again. "You don't want to think this through more? Rosalia—even Nate and Pierce—they'd kill Tom without a second thought. Maybe you should lay out some goals? Tell them where the line is?"

The tonic over the coals had cooked down enough; Lu could add a few more ingredients and let it sit while they—

Nayeli grabbed her arm. Lu swung into it, pressing close in a swell of rage.

"I have underestimated my father all my life," Lu said. "I can't lay out rules about what we should or shouldn't do, because I know *nothing* about what he is capable of. If we have to—" Her voice caught. "We have to stop him. I can't say what that means."

A sheen of sweat glistened across Nayeli's cheeks, and her lips parted with a long, soft exhale. "This isn't some nameless defensor. This is your *father*. And what if Elazar is in Fort Chastity too? Shouldn't we coordinate this with Kari and Fatemah? Shit, Lu." Nayeli ripped back and tore her fingers through her wild curls. "Look what you're doing. You're making *me* the gods-damned voice of caution."

"Don't caution me, then. Act." Lu's lungs were leaden, her horror twisting into excruciating determination. "This isn't about the bigger war. This is one mission. One task. Then I'll come back here and make permanent magic, and we'll save the island. But for now—" She stepped closer, vibrating with self-hatred and fear. "Help me do this reckless thing."

※·※·※

Three nights after the meeting in the tenement office, the sun was starting to set, and Vex saw Fort Chastity through the narrow gaps between Port Mesi-Teab's buildings.

Kari and Fatemah's scouts had heard that Elazar's coming light would happen that night, in Fort Chastity. On the deck of this Tuncian steamboat, Ben, Gunnar, and Edda huddled in the shadow of the pilothouse. But when Vex perked up, straightening under the thick weave of his cloak, the rest of them twisted to look. And hardened.

"Two minutes," said a voice from the pilothouse—Mani, the only person Vex had ever seen beat Cansu in a sword ring, was one of the two raiders Fatemah had sent off with them to infiltrate Fort Chastity. Not on the *Rapid Meander*, again. *"Tuncian mission; Tuncian craft,"* Mani had said, and forced them onto this tiny dollop of a boat. The other raider, Zey, was coming up from monitoring the engine, the trapdoor closing without a sound behind him.

Despite this crappy little boat, Vex was running a mission with Ben across from him, Edda next to him. It was almost perfect.

He looked at Ben and tried a smile. It burst onto his face stronger than he'd thought—they were sailing into a dangerous mission, after all—but Ben relented with a smile back, shaking his head on a muffled laugh like he understood the reason for Vex's joy.

Getting Ben back had clicked a piece of Vex's soul into place. But Nayeli and Lu not being there chipped off an equally large piece.

Vex's smile flickered.

Edda nudged him and he fell against a stack of crates

covered in a battered tarp. A corner dug into Vex's side, and Edda jutted her chin. Zey was frowning at him for smiling like a damn fool, like they weren't sailing into enemy territory, like there wasn't a war going on.

Vex shifted, trying to dislodge the crate from his hip.

Zey's frown deepened. Vex shrugged.

Their little craft gave a throaty rumble as it took another turn onto a wider, more populated river. In this area of the city, the utilitarian buildings took over—government houses and barracks and infirmaries. The sad, unadorned structures were silent now, wrapped up tight in the evening stillness. Violet and orange dying light set the boats on this river glowing, chugging sleepily for the residential areas, workers heading home.

"There are a lot of boats around us," Ben noted, a half question.

Zey, whose only joy in life seemed to come from scowling, glared at him. But his eyes lifted. He assessed the river, and that pause grabbed everyone else.

Around them, a dozen boats chugged in the same direction: toward Fort Chastity, at the end of this river. The crews varied from families to smudged-faced workers. No soldiers.

"Is that normal for this time of day?" Ben whispered.

Zey's scowl deepened, thick lines forming between his brows and around his lips. "No."

Ben's face showed the unease everyone felt. "They heard

about tonight's gathering."

"They're innocents," Vex said. Like when they'd been in the Port Camden prison. Families, normal citizens—not people who should've been caught up in a war.

Zey stormed into the pilothouse and started talking quick and low with Mani.

Ahead, the river broke in an oblong pool with a handful of moss-covered docks jutting out from the road. Stone walls rimmed either side, racing up the shore to encompass a wide stone plaza, great flat steps—and the forbidding black-gray stone of Fort Chastity.

"This was supposed to be for information, right?" Vex asked.

Edda grunted a confirmation next to him, her eyes on the growing thickness of the boats around them. "No attacking. No fighting. We get in without causing any trouble."

"I don't think that'll be a problem."

She glanced at him, then followed his gaping stare to the fort's plaza.

Dozens of people crowded the stones. Hundreds, maybe. All shuffling in from side streets, or disembarking from boats, or seemingly crawling out of the road itself.

Everyone Vex could see was a normal citizen of Port Mesi-Teab. Families, mothers and fathers herding dark-haired children for the towering—and open—main doors. Elderly people shuffled on canes, their tunics fluttering in the evening breeze.

Defensors weren't forcing these people into the fort. Elazar wasn't standing over them, threatening everyone to enter or else. Why were they all here?

Mani docked the boat in one of the remaining spaces. Zey leaped off to tie them.

"What," Edda started, her voice low and angry, "in the *hell*."

Mani stomped out of the pilothouse and joined Zey on the dock.

Nausea surged into Vex's stomach, ripe and bitter. "Let's get in there," he said. "Now."

Ben stood, pulling the cloak tighter around his body. Even with the sun going down, the air was still humid and hot. The cloaks were for disguise, not warmth.

Gunnar followed him up, Edda too. The same shock and worry linked them—they'd expected to infiltrate a secret gathering at Fort Chastity with stealth, sneak in once it got dark, and maneuver through an almost empty fortress. Not . . . *walk in* with an eager crowd.

Vex wobbled upright, his legs creaking from sitting for so long. Lu had refused to talk to him since the meeting— which he couldn't linger on, not now, goddamn it—but Nayeli'd passed on some cure Lu had made and a potion to help him remember other plants the Church had given him. Nothing had come to mind, though, and he'd taken the cure, but he didn't feel any better. He wasn't shaking less, and his legs still ached.

Too late. The words played in his head on repeat. *Too late, too late—*

Behind him, the tarp-covered crates shifted with a startling thud. Mani whipped back and gave Vex a look that told him, *Don't draw attention to us, you dumbass.*

Vex spun to catch the teetering crates, wincing at a pain in his ankle—

The tarp lifted from within. A face peeked out.

"Are we there? Is Elazar here?"

The air left Vex's lungs in a rush that was half gag, half choking wheeze—and, all right, a little bit of a laugh too. "Teo?"

Vex grabbed the boy's arms and yanked him free of the crates. Teo stumbled out, wide eyes darting from Vex to Edda to the bustling fort beyond the docks.

Heat rose off Edda, worry and anger twice as potent, to compensate for all the worry and anger Lu would've felt if she were here. "*Teo Casales!*" Edda hissed. "What are you doing?"

Teo faced her, hands curling into small fists. Vex's brow stayed lifted and he tried with every speck of seriousness in him to stop the slow smile spreading across his face.

Sneaky little wonder of an urchin.

"I'm helping stop this war," Teo told Edda, redness rising to his already Argridian-red cheeks. "I won't lose anyone else. I'm going to *stop it.*"

Well. That sucked the smile right off Vex's face.

He dropped to his knees. "Hey, kid—you didn't lose Lu. She's back, isn't she?"

Tears sheened Teo's eyes, but he sniffed and puckered his lips and gave Vex such a furious, bold, *dogged* look that Vex rocked backward.

"I want it to stop," Teo growled.

"I got some rope," Mani offered from the deck. "We can tie him up in the engine room."

Vex and Edda made identical noises of protest.

Mani held up his hands. "Fine. What do we do with him, then? We aren't going back without going in. Neither Zey or I is staying here with him."

"Gunnar—could you?" Ben asked.

Vex had learned Gunnar's Grace Lorayan was weak, but he must've understood enough. His eyes popped open in a panic that was equal parts *I won't let you go in there without me* and *I don't know anything about kids* as he stammered.

"I'll run," Teo threatened. "If you leave me here with anyone, I don't care. I'll *run*, and I'll get in there—" He pointed at the fort. "And I'll stop Elazar. You know I will."

"All right, all right, calm down for a second." Vex rubbed the middle of his forehead.

They were running out of time. The crowd leading up to the fort was starting to thin, the remaining stragglers slipping up the stone steps and into whatever the hell waited beyond.

But. Most of the people who'd gone in had been families.

Lu was going to kill him. Then create a plant potion to revive him. Then kill him again.

Vex bent down, eye to eye with Teo, wincing the whole while. "Teo, our purpose in coming here wasn't to confront Elazar. We need information, all right? That's how we win, sometimes. We gotta be patient, and feel stuff out, and *then* we make our move. So when we go in there—we're just looking."

"Devereux," Edda said in warning.

"Can you promise me you won't run off?" Vex pointed at Teo. "You gotta promise me, kid, that you won't leave my side, you won't try to find Elazar, you won't do anything but get information. I swear that this is the best thing you can do to stop the war. Can you do that?"

Teo considered. His eyes went past Vex, to Edda, Ben, Gunnar, the Tuncian raiders.

He inhaled, deep and long. "Yes," he said.

Vex pushed back up to his feet, biting back a shudder, and held out his hand. Teo took it.

Edda rolled her eyes and jumped off the boat before reaching back for Teo. When she lifted him under his arms, she held his face right above hers and glared up into his eyes.

"You're a smart kid," she told him. "And I know you know that hiding on this boat was a damn fool thing to do."

She plopped him onto the dock. He wavered, looking up at her with glassy eyes.

Goddamn it, Edda, go and break the kid's heart—

"But," Edda continued, thumping Teo on the head, "you're also a helluva lot braver than most of the raiders back in the sanctuary. So c'mon, Raider Teo."

She snatched his hand and dragged him onward. Teo glanced back at Vex with a smile.

"His insolence reminds me of someone," Ben whispered.

Vex chuckled. "I was never as selfless as him."

Ben went silent. Vex snuck a look at him.

"Yes, you were," Ben said in Argridian.

A weight pushed Vex's heart down into his stomach, low, throbbing heaves in his gut.

"Let's *go*," Mani demanded. He and Zey shot off, catching up with Edda and Teo.

Ben touched Vex's arm as he disembarked. Vex clambered down and marched up the dock next to his cousin and Gunnar, letting that brief levity of an idea overpower the ricocheting pain in his legs.

Had he been selfless? Something about Ben thinking so made it seem like Vex'd been . . . Rodrigu. Like he'd embodied more of his father than he thought.

17

BEN AND GUNNAR shuffled in the middle of the group as they made for the fort's open doors. Mani and Zey took up the rear; at the front, Vex hid his eye patch under his cloak's hood, Teo pinned between him and Edda. All of them watched the people who pressed inside Fort Chastity.

The circular entryway showed five doors that Ben knew led deeper into the fort, thanks to the map tucked into his shirt. One stood open, the crowd funneling through. Here were the first signs of Elazar's presence: a defensor stood on either side of the open door, hands behind their backs, eyes pierced ahead. To the right, on an overturned crate, a priest held his hands out over the crowd.

"The light has come to Port Mesi-Teab!" the priest bellowed.

"Elazar's light," Vex hissed back at Ben. "It's happening *now*?"

Mani cursed. "Zey—use the Budwig. Send a message to Fatemah. Shit, we aren't ready for an attack yet."

"I don't think it's an attack," Edda whispered. "You see any armies?"

Zey put a hand over his ear and mouth, whispering quick and low into the Budwig Bean that reached back to the sanctuary. But Mani frowned, and Ben shared a look with Gunnar.

There had been no armies in the villages Elazar had paraded Ben to, either. Just Elazar, a handful of defensors, and righteous certainty.

"She says we go in," Zey huffed. "Stick to the plan. Keep an eye out for Cansu or any of the missing raiders. Leave if things get dangerous."

Ben pulled his chin to his chest, hoping his cloak's hood kept the soldiers from recognizing him. But the defensors didn't flinch; the priest didn't pause in his shouting.

Ben's group moved from the entryway into the fort's central room, a large open space with a mezzanine framing the upper reaches and the ceiling open to the pink-blue evening sky. A place for public executions or announcements, with a platform at the far end.

Here, the crowd stopped. People packed the room so thickly that Ben and his group could take only a few steps inside, the door close to their backs. Which was preferable, despite their unease at seeing so many of Port Mesi-Teab's innocents gathered here.

Everyone was quiet, exchanging whispered words as they eyed the empty stage. Torches lit the area as the sun slipped away.

"Defensors above," Ben whispered back at Mani and Zey. He jutted his chin upward, to hidden forms in the mezzanine's shadows. "If my father keeps his normal security for public functions, there will be one standing every seven paces, armed with two pistols and a sword. The ground floor will have the same."

Mani nodded. Zey held a distrustful gaze on Ben before sweeping his eyes over the mezzanine and shifting his grip under his cloak, flashing the pistols strapped to his own waist.

"You're the prince," came Teo's soft voice.

Vex shushed down at him. Mani and Zey went rigid.

But no one outside their group had heard him.

Ben's heart lodged in his throat, but he managed a smile at Teo. "Yes."

Teo didn't smile back. His eyes hardened. "He's your father."

It was an accusation. Vex gave Ben an apologetic look, but Ben stayed focused on Teo.

"I know," Ben whispered. "Who is your father?"

Teo's eyes narrowed. "Mama said he died."

Ben shrugged. "Sometimes we are like our fathers. Sometimes not. I promise you, I am nothing like mine."

Teo looked unconvinced. But a deliberate stomping cut

off further conversation, whipping every head toward the platform.

A man stood in the center of the elevated wooden planks. Ben squinted.

His breath twisted in his lungs, a squeeze of memories and hatred.

Vex growled. Gunnar angled closer to Ben.

"Citizens of Port Mesi-Teab." General Ibarra raised his hands for attention. "Thank you for heeding the Pious God's call to gather here tonight. I know you came at the risk of great harm by those who fight to drown this island in sin and magic, but I assure you, we took every precaution to keep this gathering hidden from impure, evil souls."

Behind Ben, Mani snorted. Edda rolled her eyes.

Ben swallowed any reaction, his body washing with a calming sense of separation. He didn't have the right to be repulsed by Ibarra's twisted words. It wasn't his luxury.

"Now," Ibarra continued, "let us welcome the Pious God's representative on this earth—the Eminence King of Argrid."

Ibarra stepped aside as soft applause rippled across the room. Edda was the first in their group to clap, and she glared at the rest of them until they complied.

"Blend in," she growled.

Ben managed one clap. Two. His hands hardened, his heart unresponsive and icy, as at the far end of the room, his father took the stage.

"People of Port Mesi-Teab," Elazar started. Others

came up the side steps behind him, defensors dragging a manacled prisoner with a bag over their head. The prisoner bucked wildly.

Ben's stomach sank. He met Vex's eye, dropped a look to Teo. Would his father kill someone here, before this crowd of families and children?

Edda was already twisting to hide Teo's face against her when Elazar continued.

"You have heard, by now, of the light that the Pious God will bring to Grace Loray," he said. "A light that will bestow blessings on those who are obedient, and will eradicate the evil from your island. I bring to you, good people of Port Mesi-Teab, the first look at what this light will do to those who insist on sullying your country."

Elazar waved at the defensors. One yanked the bag off the prisoner's head.

The prisoner wavered, blinking in the torchlight. Even from the back of the room, Ben could see she had been ill-treated: bruises purpled her skin, dried blood matted her short hair to the side of her head.

She pierced Elazar with a look of passionate hatred. "You manic son of a bitch!" she shouted, loud enough to carry across the room.

Gasps rippled out. Mani and Zey were loudest.

Vex whipped back to look at them, desperation paling his face.

"Cansu," he said. To Edda, again, aching, "*Cansu.*"

The press of the crowd heading for the single open door in the fort's entryway had been the perfect cover to let Lu, Nayeli, Rosalia, and Nate slip through one of the closed side doors.

"Vex and Edda are in that crowd," Nayeli said as Lu shot down a dark stone hallway after Rosalia.

Lu didn't pause as she said, "They have their mission. We have ours."

Nayeli didn't respond. Lu knew half of her was here with Lu; half was with Vex and Edda.

Lu felt it, too. She felt a lot of things, all of them suffocating, but she kept walking, pistols rattling against the sword at her waist.

A map of the fort said that the storage area was on the lowest level. If they didn't find Tom's supplies there, they would search this fort, ceiling to cellar, until they located his plants, his equipment, whatever potions he had made—and destroyed them. Nate hoped they'd be able to steal a good amount of magic. Rosalia hoped for bloodshed.

Lu couldn't get her mind to function. Each step she took peeled more of herself away, until she was less a living girl, more an embodiment of years-held fury. This was who Tom had wanted her to be, wasn't it? A weapon. A murderer.

The hall took a turn. Rosalia, at the head, swung down it—and quickly flew back as defensors beyond cried in alarm.

She grinned. "Two defensors at the top of a stairwell."

Nate checked his pistols, his manic smile peeking out from beneath the brim of his curved leather hat. "Guarding something?"

"Should be the— *Shit!*"

Rosalia's words cut off in a startled shriek as Lu brushed past her and chucked a small satchel down the hall. The explosion was small enough not to rattle the stones, sending a feeble, echoing *pop* back at them.

The defensors went silent.

Nayeli sank her fingers into Lu's arm. "Rhodospine?" She had recognized the noise. Each Rhodospine pod released a barrage of piercing spikes—a deadly, violent thorn grenade, far more dangerous than its cousin plant, the Rhodofume smoke screen.

Lu nodded, unfazed. Rosalia cackled and shot back around the corner. Her cackling faded to a long, impressed whistle.

"Well, they're dead," she announced.

Nate chuckled, brushing past Lu and Nayeli. Lu made to follow, but Nayeli seized her arm, two bright red spots touching her cheeks.

The emotion—or absence of emotion—in Lu's eyes must have been clear, because Nayeli didn't say anything. She released Lu and held her hands up in surrender.

The defensors were, indeed, dead. Slumped against either wall, their bodies contorted in macabre dances, skin and uniforms riddled with the Rhodospine spikes.

Lu's eyes trailed over the blood leaking from their wounds, the glazed surprise to their vacant expressions. Her eyes moved to the stairwell. At the bottom was the lowest level of the fort; the storage room. Tom?

Rosalia was busy searching one of the bodies for anything of value. Nate had the other, and as Lu walked past them, she stopped to make sure Nayeli, at least, had her.

A step behind, Nayeli's face was pale, her eyes on Lu's boots.

Lu ignored any feeling of sympathy. She took the stairs, dropping down, down, down.

Two more defensors waited at the bottom. This time, a satchel of Variegated Holly with Hemlight—one to cause an explosion when lit; one to do the lighting.

The aftermath left two dead soldiers at the base of the stairs—right in front of a wide storage room. Boxes and crates filled the space in something like organization, netting holding barrels to the ceiling and the air thick with the smell of decay, dust, and earthy plants.

Rosalia and Nate stumbled down the stairwell as Nayeli pulled various plants out of her own pouches. More explosives, again Hemlight and Variegated Holly.

"What do we destroy?" Nayeli asked, moving for the closest crate.

"Let's see what it is first," Nate countered. "We'll take as much as we can carry."

"I would prefer you didn't," came a voice.

Rosalia, Nate, and Nayeli spun. But Lu smiled. She wasn't sure where it blossomed from, this odd, uneven tilting of her lips.

Across the room, taking slow steps toward them through the maze of waist-high crates, came Tom.

Lu had her pistol out. Her thumb hit the hammer, cocking it, and she looked at her father down the barrel.

Her heart didn't beat. Her mind didn't spin. She was blood and rage and she hadn't come here to destroy Tom's plants or stop his progress on permanent magic. She had come here to stop *him*, to feel something, to steal herself back from him.

Tom stopped. His face rippled with understanding, followed by agony. "You've remembered, then," he whispered.

Lu's pistol bobbed. Remembered? Remembered what?

"Lu?" Rosalia said. "This him?"

"I begged the king, for all my years of loyal service, not to put you in that cell, Lulu-bean," Tom said. "It was why you woke up in that room with me. And if you had listened, you would still be unaware of your memories."

"Memories?" Lu re-aimed, refocused. "You're stalling."

She swept the room, seeing no other defensors, hearing no raised alarms. But the explosions she had set off must have alerted someone.

Tom took another step closer. His agony cracked into uncertainty, eyes narrowing. "It was why I didn't visit you in the prison. I thought you would need time to reconcile your new memories. The Bright Mint in the prison. The defensors gave you small doses of Narcotium Creeper to counter it, but I feared—" He stopped when the confusion didn't leave Lu's face.

Bright Mint was in the Port Camden prison's walls. A green, bushy plant used to enhance mental clarity— countered by Narcotium Creeper, a plant that caused delirium. It was not unsurprising that the plant used to enhance thought could cause insanity in high doses—and that the plant known for causing hallucinations would balance it out. It was poetic, almost.

Lu's mind raced. Bright Mint could be countered by Narcotium Creeper, as Tom had said. But Bright Mint also had connections to another mind-altering plant: Menesia.

Argridians had given Menesia—the memory-erasing plant—to the Mecht raiders in the Port Camden prison's laboratory. But anyone who forgot things using Menesia could undo the magic with Bright Mint.

Lu's world went to shadows, back to light. "You thought I remembered something," she rasped. "You've given me Menesia."

Tom wheezed in relief. "The Narcotium Creeper was enough to keep the prison's Bright Mint from undoing the Menesia? Thank the Pious God. Lulu-bean, he watches out for you—"

Menesia. What had he figured out about Menesia? What had he made her forget?

And what other piece did he have in play?

Nayeli grabbed Lu's hand, yanking her up the stairwell, back toward the ramifications of where Lu's revenge had driven her.

✤✤✤

Ben faltered. "The Tuncian syndicate Head?"

Zey whispered into the Budwig Bean again, his throat pinched. Mani, red-faced, had a knife in one hand, a pistol cocked in the other.

On the platform, Elazar lifted his arms, reciting a prayer from a hymn on cleansing. The defensors held Cansu behind him, her hands manacled. Her dark, livid eyes never left Elazar, as though she could incinerate him with the heat of her fury.

Mani surged forward a step. Zey ripped a plant out of a pouch on his waist: Rhodofume, used for smoke screens.

Gunnar gaped at Ben. "They can do nothing. Not here. Benat—"

Ben spun on Mani, pressing close. He spotted the nearest defensors at the edge of the room, hidden in shadows along the wall, but armed and watchful.

"Stand down," Ben begged Mani, Zey. He turned to Vex. "Tell them. They can't do anything here."

Vex, at least, didn't make a move to draw a weapon. But his face was a mess of pain.

"It's *Cansu*," he pleaded, and though Ben didn't know her, didn't feel the connection, he felt the weight. Responsibility and family.

"Teo," Ben whispered, his eyes dipping to the boy.

"Vex, get him back to the boat," Edda ordered. "We'll meet you there. Mani, Zey—"

But they were already off, cutting two separate, careful paths through the crowd. Edda growled a curse and slipped away, taking a step, pausing, then another, then shifting left. No one else in the crowd was moving; if they walked too quickly, defensors would swoop in.

Defensors would swoop in either way, once they got to the stage. How would they free Cansu? What would they do to get her out of Elazar's grasp?

Elazar finished his prayer. "This woman has been a menace to your city for years." He motioned to Cansu, who spat at him. He didn't flinch. "She has demanded your tithes, your loyalty, your resources—for what? Feigned protection, weak support? No, good people—this raider has let the Devil claim her soul, and by extension, she has locked your city into a state of destitution. But tonight, the Pious God will cleanse the evil from her soul—instantly."

The defensors forced Cansu to her knees. She dropped, chains rattling, and for the first time, her eyes left Elazar to hit the crowd.

Mani and Zey were halfway across the room. Edda was even farther back.

"They won't reach her in time," Vex wheezed.

Ben snatched Gunnar's arm, clinging to his biceps, but what could they do? A distraction, maybe. Whatever attention they drew to themselves, they would draw to Teo.

Elazar began to sing. Not a prayer this time; a deep, guttural hymn. Ben knew it—"The Feast of Grace Biel." A song about the celebration that the Pious God held once Grace Biel died and entered heaven, to reward him for living the most chaste life of all his children.

Cansu, her eyes still on the crowd, stopped fighting. Her shoulders drooped, her face softened, a storm of rage giving way to a vacant stare.

"What is he doing?" The question left Ben's mouth in a quiet rush.

Gunnar moved closer, his arm around Ben's waist, holding him up as Elazar's voice filled the hall and rose beyond the open ceiling, swelling into the starry night sky.

Cansu seemed to go with it. Every bit of tension in her body unwound, her arms in her lap, her face serene.

The hymn ended. His face red from exertion, Elazar turned to Cansu. "The Pious God bids you banish the evil from your soul. Unlock her chains, defensors, so she may rise, made anew by the Pious God."

Mani reached the front of the crowd and dove onto the stage. Zey, down from him, hurled a Rhodofume pod that coated the platform in a thin veil of smoke.

The crowd erupted. Screams crashed through the air,

people shuffling as they turned for the door.

Vex yanked Teo into him, face buried in Vex's stomach. The defensors onstage drew weapons. A single pistol fired, the flash and burn of a bullet that careened into the sky.

But Elazar didn't call for attack. "Friends," he said, "raiders have found our gathering, but you have no need to fear. The Pious God will protect us—using the very ones who stand against him."

The defensors on the edge of the room moved into the light. They directed the crowd's attention to the stage with careful guidance, though many had guns drawn in their hands.

The screaming ceased. The crowd stilled.

On the stage, Cansu was standing now. Her eyes stayed on the crowd, no reaction to seeing Mani a pace away from her, or Zey next to him.

Elazar turned to her. "Kill them," he said.

Ben's chest incinerated. Vex buckled, pressing Teo closer.

Edda appeared next to Vex. Clearly, she had read the situation, her face white with panic. "We need to leave," she said. "*Now.*"

On the stage, Cansu looked at Mani. Her face showed no recognition at all.

She closed the space between them and took the weapons from his outstretched hands. He let her, stricken by shock and confusion and the hovering trust that this was his leader—

Cansu turned the pistol on him and fired.

Mani crumpled to the stage. Zey cried out, but Cansu drove the knife into his gut.

Startled yelps dotted the room. Someone was weeping.

As Zey's body crumpled to the stage, Cansu came into view again. She dropped the gun and knife and stepped back, showing neither reaction nor remorse.

"Sin is strong," Elazar announced. "But the Pious God is stronger. This is the second of the four once-great stream raider Heads who the Pious God has purified. The first, Ingvar Pilkvist of the Mecht syndicate, surrendered himself to cleansing. Most raiders will be like Cansu Darzi: resistant to the Pious God, drowning in magic. But the light has come, and it will subdue even the greatest evil to obedience. You need not fear anymore. I will save your country."

Ben had forgotten Ibarra was there, but he moved at Elazar's beckoning.

"General," Elazar said, "here is a tool the Pious God wishes you add to your great command as we bring the light to Grace Loray."

Ibarra smirked. "Thank you, Eminence."

Ben's fingers dug into Gunnar's arm until they went numb.

His father had used Menesia in the past to wipe memories of experiments. Ingvar might have surrendered to Elazar willingly, but Ben had seen him in the villages—the man was under Menesia's influence to make him pliant.

But whatever Elazar had done to Cansu was deeper than simply forgetting. He had made her murder her own people.

"Benat." Gunnar's breath brushed Ben's jaw. Sometime in the madness, he had come to hold Ben, one arm gripping his shoulder, the other across his waist.

Ben followed Gunnar's look to the defensor closest to them—who was staring back, head tilted in a curious frown.

"Run!" Edda shouted as the defensor's eyes widened in recognition.

"The prince!"

The room came alive again. The defensors along the edges, on the mezzanine, all swung toward the cry. That movement sent the crowd into a frenzy, screams and tangled prayers shooting up into the night sky.

Gunnar whirled Ben around and shoved him toward the door. Edda did the same to Vex, who grabbed Teo by the arm and ran.

The defensors stationed outside the room had weapons ready, but Gunnar washed them back with a wall of angry flame. They screamed, and a path cleared. The wide main doors of the fort still sat open.

Ben flew across the entryway behind Gunnar. He glanced back to see Edda, Vex, and Teo close behind. The entirety of the crowd was behind them, families and elderly and desperate citizens squeezing through the single door of the fort's central room.

The plaza before the fort was empty. No army waited to intercept Ben; no defensors had looped around with ready pistols and vicious orders. The oddity of that socked Ben in the chest as he leaped down the steps, scrambling after Gunnar, who kept flames alive in each fist.

The dark night obscured the expanse of stone. But as they angled for their dock, a form materialized, a single person who stumbled across the ground.

Gunnar slammed to a stop, one arm arching back to pin against Ben's chest. Around them, the crowd ran for their own boats, crying out that raiders had attacked, Pious God, they will kill us—

The teetering form twisted, eyes locking on Ben.

"Jakes?" Ben frowned, breathless.

Pain twisted Jakes's face. A jagged cut lanced across his cheek; sweat and dirt made a paste over his neck, his once-pristine uniform wrinkled and torn.

He looked how Ben had after weeks in the Port Camden prison.

"Ben—" Jakes's voice caught. "Message—from—"

He faltered, dipping forward and slamming to his knees at Ben's feet.

Gunnar grabbed Ben's arm and yanked him on, making once again for the dock. Ben pushed his heels into the ground.

"We can't leave him—" The plea left Ben's throat before he could consider it.

Jakes had betrayed Ben, yes, but he was still Argridian as much as the defensors Ben had worried for in the prison's burning hall. He was still one of the people Ben was responsible to protect.

Shaking, Jakes reached out a blood-covered hand and seized Ben's leg. His face paled, his other hand gripping his side. Blood glinted in Gunnar's firelight, fresh scarlet streams of it leaking through a wound in Jakes's stomach.

Ben's own blood turned to ice.

"Message—*listen*, Ben," Jakes begged, his voice cracking on the narrowness of fading consciousness.

Edda met them in her rush to leave. She saw the wounded, battered defensor as Ben bent down.

Around them, the crowd ran. Somewhere, a priest had started praying again, trying to infuse calm in the people screaming, sprinting, scrambling to get *away*.

Jakes transferred his hand to Ben's shoulder. His grip was weak, fingers slipping on Ben's borrowed raider clothes. "Your father," Jakes hissed, one hand still pressed to his side. A fresh spurt of blood trickled down the stained cloth of his breeches. "He knew you would come. Knew someone would—come." Another wince. "If they couldn't get you—told me to tell them—tell *Adeluna*—to surrender. All of you, all raiders, surrender, for the boy." Jakes fisted his hand in Ben's shirt on a renewed burst of desperation. "They're going to follow you to where he is. They're going to take him. A—Teo? They said—"

Jakes's eyes rolled back in his head. His body went slack, crumpling to the side.

Ben gaped at him. Elazar had tortured Jakes? *Why?*

The agony that came dragged a dozen other sensations with it. A stab of betrayal at everything Jakes had done; fury that Jakes could still foster such strain in Ben's heart; and a vulnerable wretchedness when he looked up into Gunnar's rage.

"What did he say?" Edda demanded. "What the hell was he talking about?"

All of you, all raiders, surrender, for the boy.

Ben grabbed Jakes's arm. He didn't stir, but his chest rose and fell in sharp breaths.

Ben turned to Edda. He couldn't ask Gunnar for this. "Help me—he's alive. We can get more information out of him. We can—"

Vex broke out of the running horde. Tears streaked down his face, his eye wide in panic.

"He's gone," he gasped at Edda. "Teo. Defensors took him. *He's gone.*"

18

THE NEXT MINUTES were a dream.

Lu swayed as Nate plowed their steamboat through the night-drenched waterways. Screams chased them, tangled cries from people fleeing the gathering at Fort Chastity.

In the very heart of a clandestine Argridian assembly, Lu had done nothing. She had no information, nothing to hold as proof that this mission had been worthwhile. At least they had destroyed Tom's stores of plants—thanks to Nayeli. Did he have more, though? Why had Elazar called so many innocents to Fort Chastity? What had stoked them to such panic?

And what had Tom meant by all his talk of Menesia?

Too many questions. Too much pain. Not enough action.

Lu rocked with the steamboat, bleary and blank. She couldn't put a name to her state: a cloud had fallen over her, and though she drew in shuddering breaths, she felt as though underwater. The living embodiment of a breath held.

The farther they sailed from Fort Chastity, the more Lu expected the screams to dissipate. But old cries flowed into new, coming from ahead—the sanctuary.

Nate docked the boat, and Nayeli was the first to race off. Rosalia and Nate closed in behind, while Lu moved sluggishly, stumbling across the dock and past the barricade.

Voices rose. As Lu wove through one of the tenements guarding the main bulk of the sanctuary, screams became accusations.

"How *dare* you!"

Torches and lanterns flickered on a dozen refugees in the center of the main outer road. A mix of raiders surrounded them, some confused, others jostling one another and mocking the obvious turmoil. But a single group stood apart—a knot of Grozdan raiders.

Rosalia was already with them. A canvas bag sat on the ground at their feet, and she was talking with her people, shaking her head, chuckling at something in her hand.

The refugees were not amused. One shot forward.

"We never agreed to this!" he bellowed. "It's thievery—but what else should we expect from the likes of you?"

Lu hung back, scanning the crowd. There—Kari pushed through behind a fuming Fatemah; Nayeli, next to them, looked drawn and exhausted.

"Where have you been?" Fatemah demanded of Rosalia.

"Is this how you run your syndicate—vanishing without a word, leaving your raiders to ransack innocent homes?"

"Ransack?" Rosalia scoffed. "They didn't rob anyone. It's a *tithe*, woman."

Fatemah's face went purple with fury, but her voice came low and controlled, the growl before attack. "You will return what your raiders stole from those under our protection. The people of Port Mesi-Teab who desire Tuncian protection pay a fee—but it is their choice. This is war. You cannot demand tribute from those who have no say about our—"

Nate and Pierce shoved out of the shadows, into the little clearing that had formed in the road. Raiders and refugees alike watched on.

"We're well aware of this being a war, Fatemah," Pierce said. "But we'll be damned if we return to Port Camden empty-handed after this. We can't be running a charity. Protection takes resources, time, funds, and we got a list of some rare shit we need for our ultimate move against Elazar."

Realization stabbed Lu.

Rosalia took a half step closer to Lu, enough to get her attention, and chucked a bauble into the air. Lu caught it, a chain coiling in her palm around a small trinket.

It was a glass sphere the size of Lu's thumb. A murky maroon substance swirled behind an etching of a bear's face, curved teeth bared in a vicious snarl.

Rosalia was too far away for conversation, but when Lu met her eyes again, she gave a wicked smile and mouthed, *Visjorn bear blood.*

Lu's eyes widened. They'd found Visjorn bear blood.

Lu had tasked Pierce, Nate, and Rosalia with gathering items for permanent magic. This was how they had gotten her supplies so far? By robbing these people?

The refugees were terrified. A man stood at the front, his shoulders heaving; a woman and her child huddled against each other.

This necklace had to be sacred to whomever Rosalia's people had stolen it from, a Tuncian or Emerdian with Mecht ancestry. But Lu tucked it into her pocket, hoping the refugees would forget this trinket, her heart a tangle of eagerness and regret.

"What you are doing is not normal syndicate function," Kari tried now, stepping between Fatemah and the others. Ever the peacekeeper. "It is extortion. And we cannot—"

"Oh shut up, Councilmember!" Pierce's cry rang off the surrounding buildings. The Emerdian raiders shot fists into the air. "You're the reason that this is *normal syndicate function.* Your lot stole the magic trade with the Mainland from our syndicates. *Extortion* is the only way we keep our syndicates running, and like hell will I sit here while these people"—Pierce pointed at the refugees, who flinched—"owe us. They owe us, like it or not. When we get Grace Loray back from Elazar, how did you think we'll run things?"

"With agreement," Kari said. "With proper involvement and all voices heard. With—"

"With *the Council*? You think we'll bow back down and let you idiots plow Grace Loray into the depths of the ocean? No, sweetheart—*this* is the future now, like it or not. Your way didn't work. Our way—"

"It doesn't matter!"

Lu whirled. The voice yanked the crowd with her, all whipping to the entrance of a tenement and the mangled, bloodied people who stumbled out into the road.

Edda hobbled—holding on to Vex, oddly, a gash through her cheek and across her leg. Tear trails left bright streaks on Vex's face, and as he helped Edda sit on a crate, his eye leaped up to Lu's.

The sense of fogged wrongness contracted.

Behind Edda and Vex, Gunnar came with a body sprawled over his shoulder. He dumped the person into the road, an unconscious moan breaking the man's lips.

Lu staggered. Jakes.

"It doesn't matter," the voice said again, carrying out of the tenement's door. Ben followed it, emanating a level of fury Lu had not yet seen on him. Hands in fists, eyes aflame, he marched forward and stopped over Jakes. "You're arguing about a future that *won't exist*—we saw Elazar's light tonight. He showed hundreds of Port Mesi-Teab's citizens what he can do when he used Menesia to make Cansu Darzi submit to him."

"What?" Fatemah went still. "No. Menesia only erases memories—it does not allow someone to *control* another person. You are lying!"

Lu stepped forward a pace, her heart dragging her into the middle of the clearing. "I don't think he is," she spoke up. Fatemah's lips flattened into a line. "One of Elazar's servants said he discovered something that Argridians can do to Menesia. They have figured out a way to manipulate it—not permanent magic, like the Mechts do, but it must be this. They have a way to make Menesia let them control another's actions."

Fatemah went still. Nayeli wavered back, back again, stopping when she hit Kari, who grabbed her arms and said something low and quiet to her.

Vex was next to Lu, looking at the ground. At the dirt beneath his boots.

Her heart swelled. Pressure building. *Wrong, something is wrong.*

"Lu," Vex whispered. "He's—damn it, we *tried*—we went back. We fought. But they got him. They took—"

"You mean to say"—Fatemah's voice was ice and death—"that not only did you leave Cansu there, but she now does Elazar's bidding?"

Ben turned to Fatemah. "We failed. Your people—Mani, Zey—they died trying. And—" He paused and Lu went forward another step, hearing both Ben, distantly, and Vex, even farther:

"Elazar is holding a child as ransom," Ben told Fatemah, the crowd, "for our surrender. He has two raider Heads now, bowing to him. His coming light is a dangerous sort of mind control, separate from permanent magic, and I don't care what in the Pious God's hell you all disagree on regarding Grace Loray's future—there won't *be* a future, for either of our countries, if you don't stop and—"

"Teo." Vex's voice was soft. "Defensors got Teo. They were planning to follow us back to where he was and take him, but he was there. They took him."

Lu's vision blackened. The pressure in her heart ruptured, spilling horror into her soul.

"There is another piece at play," Tom had said. *"You won't want me to use it."*

Lu put a hand to her mouth. Without Milo's ministrations, how best to control her? By ripping away someone she loved. By taking the remaining source of innocence in her war-torn world.

Her father had taken Teo to force her to submission.

"Lu?" Vex stepped closer. They were in the center of the clearing, Kari and Fatemah arguing a few paces away, Nayeli at the edge, Ben standing over Jakes's body, and dozens of eyes, raiders' and refugees', watching, judging, fearing.

Lu looked at Vex. She hadn't realized she was so close to crying, but a tear fell, hot and heavy, on her cheek. "Why was he there? *How?*"

Vex shook his head and reached for her, but she recoiled.

"Lu—god, I'm sorry. He hid in the boat. I should've taken him right back, but we had to go in. We had to find out what Elazar was doing, and I—I'm such an idiot, such a— *damn it*, Lu, I—"

"You took him"—Lu's voice ached—"into Elazar's gathering?"

Vex tore his hands through his hair, sobbed, and the world broke.

Edda pushed out of the crowd, hobbling on her injured leg, pain contorting her face. "It ain't his fault," she tried, but Lu spun on her, shock drowning under a gush of rage.

"*You*," she spat. "You let him do this? You both—after everything, I thought the one thing I didn't have to worry about anymore was your responsibility with Teo. How could you—*how could you do this*—"

Vex reached for her again. She slapped him away, and shame sent him reeling back, hands up, surrender and apology and a hundred things she had no strength to acknowledge.

Teo was gone. He was a prisoner of Elazar—of Milo. As she had once been, not much older than him, tied to a chair in a safe house.

Her mission to Fort Chastity had sent slivered cracks through her drive to end this war, letting in the faintest rays of reconsidering other paths. Now, those cracks smoothed over, an unbreakable varnish of fury and dread.

Tom and Elazar had wanted her to return to them, to

make permanent magic for them. They were so certain of her weaknesses and thought they could play her by kidnapping Teo.

No more hesitation. No more weighing morality.

She would obliterate them.

Ben was tired. He was sore, beaten and bruised and aching. Behind him, waves of Gunnar's heat raged, the same that had drenched their boat in sweat and stifling breath.

He was furious that Ben had brought Jakes.

Ben was furious that all this had happened, every moment, and that he had to stand here, listening to Kari try to soothe Fatemah, only to have Fatemah whip on him with an unrepentant barrage of hatred.

Jakes made a moan of coming to. Fatemah's eyes dropped to him.

"You brought a defensor here," she stated. Her hatred sharpened, found its mark.

The crowd of refugees gasped. The raiders bellowed in shock and objection.

"As a prisoner," Ben stated. "He knows my father's plans. He has—"

"The Argridian prince left with two of my raiders"— Fatemah licked her lips, her teary eyes leaping back up to his—"and returned without them—and with a defensor instead."

Fingers gripped Ben's wrist at the same moment he felt

the intensity of what he had done. He glanced to the side, saw Gunnar, backing him up, even with their disagreement.

He had no time to think further. Fatemah waved a hand, and one of her raiders slid a sword out of a holster on his back. Ben had seen similar weapons during his few visits to Tuncay—a brutal, jagged blade that weighed as much as some full-grown men.

Other raiders reacted. Emerdians armed themselves; the group of Grozdans, behind Rosalia, did the same. The refugees screamed.

Ben held up his hands. "I don't want to fight—"

Fatemah ignored him. "We gave you liberties—but we owe you nothing. Even those of Argridian descent here owe you *nothing.* You are deposed, exiled, worthless in—"

"Fatemah, stop!"

Vex staggered forward. Behind him, Edda rocked in the torchlight; Lu, her arms folded, glowered from the shadows. Ben's heart squeezed with sorrow on her behalf, for Teo—but Vex's fury raged bright and high.

Ben couldn't remember ever seeing Paxben upset. Not like this, shoulders hunched and eye bent and lips pulled back in dire focus through the blotchy redness on his face.

He looked like Rodrigu.

"I won't let you talk to him like that," Vex told Fatemah.

Fatemah laughed in furious amusement. "*You* won't let me?"

Vex went rigid. He looked at Ben, the rage on his face flickering away to worry.

Ben wavered. Gunnar's hand went to the small of his back, holding him still.

"What is going on, Devereux?" Fatemah asked, her tone a threat. "Why do you, an unaligned Grace Lorayan raider, defend the Crown Prince of Argrid?"

Vex closed his eye as if unable to watch the coming storm. "He's my cousin," he whispered, three small words that sucked in all the surrounding noise until there was only that admission.

Fatemah was the first to recover. "You are the nephew of Elazar?"

"Fatemah." Vex shivered but faced her. "Fatemah, you know me. You've known me for years. You haven't always liked me, I admit, but *you know me*—"

"You are Argridian. I always knew that. You've been spying on us, haven't you? All this time. I allow you into my home, and you've been one of *them*."

"No—"

"The prince; this defensor; Cansu, unsaved. Mani and Zey, *dead*. Now—this betrayal. Raiders!"

Fatemah's supporters surged out. The refugees, cowering, let out startled chirps of fear.

Ben tried to throw himself in front of Vex, but Gunnar whipped around and planted a hand across Ben's hip. Edda was already in front of Vex anyway, glowering, while Nayeli heaved closer to her aunt.

"Fatemah, stop!" Nayeli said. "You know this isn't—"

"Emerdians!" Nate cried. "If you don't lock him up, Fatemah, I will. Goddamn *spy*."

"I'm not a spy!" Vex's voice broke. "Let me explain—"

"Lock them up!" Fatemah waved her raiders to action. "All of them! I won't tolerate this anymore—this is my home, and I will have *order* here! Lock up all Argridians!"

A dozen things happened in the span of a breath.

Gunnar shoved Ben back, over Jakes's stirring body, as if they could run.

The Tuncians made for Vex, who gaped but didn't try to fight back.

The refugees, whom Fatemah had dragged here to reclaim the items stolen from them, screamed, shoving to leave the area. Ben caught confused cries: "The raiders will kill us—"

A single man at the front of the refugee group didn't move. His wide eyes and heaving breaths spoke to fear, but he stayed rooted, his hands in his pockets.

"This isn't the way!" Kari tried. "We are losing this war. We cannot turn on each other!"

Nayeli ripped bundles of Hemlight out of her holster and blocked a Tuncian raider with her forearm. "Don't make me hurt you. Any of you. You know I can."

"Surrender," Edda said, to Vex, to the raiders. "Stand down! Nayeli—stand down!"

"STOP!"

The plea came from the refugee man still in the middle of the road, exhaustion and terror wiping his face into a snarling mask that horrified Ben to his soul.

"Gunnar." Ben dug his fingers into Gunnar's shoulder. "Gunnar—"

"Raiders, Argrid, Council—you're all the same! Claiming you fight for us. Claiming you want peace. Lies!" The man pointed at everyone, one hand still in his pocket. "You all keep fighting, drawing the war out for yourselves while we die for you! If you love Grace Loray, you'll surrender. Elazar's right. You're evil, and so is he, and all of you need to *stop!*"

The man yanked out his hand. A bundle of plants sat in his fist, a tangle of greenery the size of his fist. Ben squinted, trying to place what it was in the darkness.

In the man's other hand, he struck a match to life on his boot.

Nayeli gasped. "Variegated Holly. Oh gods—*stop him*—"

Variegated Holly. The most explosive of Grace Loray's incendiary plants. One leaf could blow apart a stone wall.

This much of it would decimate the whole street.

"Surrender!" the man bellowed. "SURRENDER!"

Gunnar moved. Ben screamed, stumbling after him, while the remaining refugees barreled out of the area; raiders shrieked and clawed away into the darkness.

The man touched the lit match to the bundle as Gunnar

tackled him. The two hit the ground, the now-lit wad of Variegated Holly rolling across the dirt street. The leaves sparked in the unsteady torchlight, caught; they had a second or two before the plant combusted—

The bundle stopped at Vex's feet. Ben's whole world narrowed as Vex bent, grabbed it, singeing his fingers, and on a cry, he chucked it *up*, high into the air.

But he faltered, limbs quivering.

When it exploded, it didn't harmlessly puncture the sky. It struck a nearby tenement, blowing a hole through the top two floors of apartments with a percussive *BOOM!*

Screams ruptured from the sanctuary, from the building. Ben stared at the destruction, his heart gone still and brittle, hands over his mouth as, somewhere distant, Fatemah wailed.

"Murderers! You bring destruction here—you did this! Arrest them, lock them away—"

Rough hands grabbed Ben. He didn't fight, even when Tuncian raiders yanked Gunnar off the refugee man, who scrambled away, tears streaking down his face. Raiders grabbed Vex, too, as Edda hauled Nayeli away.

"Stand down, we're outnumbered—Nayeli, *stand down*—"

Nate and Pierce were gone. Rosalia huddled next to one of her raiders on the side of the road. Kari shouted orders, sending people into the building to help any survivors.

Survivors. Ben went limp in the hands of the Tuncian raiders.

The only person not moving in the bedlam was Lu. She stared up at the tenement, tears glistening in her eyes as she lowered her gaze to Vex, being dragged away.

"Fatemah!" Lu shouted. "You're just as much to blame as anyone!"

The declaration filled Ben's chest. Their war. What did it even mean? *This?* Fighting Elazar, the raider syndicates, the people of this island? Who were they fighting for, who was on their side, *what was the point?*

Lu's face was murderous with the unbreakable determination of someone who didn't care about the answers to those questions. Ben couldn't process the horror of Teo being gone, but he had enough control of his mind to see beyond it. Lu was like Fatemah, Nate, Pierce, Rosalia—she would fight for blood. She would fight for revenge.

"This is our war!" Lu screamed. *"Our war!"*

19

THE TUNCIANS HAD converted the ground floor of a tenement into cells, replacing the hall-facing walls with floor-to-ceiling iron bars. They shoved Vex into one with Jakes; Ben and Gunnar got their own across the way. Fatemah had enough grip on her sanity to realize that Jakes could be useful—one raider chucked a satchel of healing plants at Vex's feet before he left.

Vex stared at it. On the floor, Jakes moaned, unconscious and dying, and Vex had—almost—agreed with Gunnar's desire to leave him for dead at the steps of Fort Chastity. But when they'd gone back to search for Teo, fighting off defensors and nearly getting killed themselves, Jakes had become their only option for answers.

Vex riffled through the satchel. A bundle of Healica— he'd have to grind it up for it to be useful at healing the gash in Jakes's side. Beneath it rested a small vial of liquid.

By the orange hue and the fact that the Tuncians wouldn't have given prisoners anything dangerous, Vex assumed it was liquefied Healica, for drinking and healing internal wounds. Good enough.

"How do we fix this?" Ben asked in low, brittle Argridian.

The Healica sloshed into Jakes's mouth, a bit trickling down his face and wetting the floor. But his throat swallowed and Vex dropped back onto the wood planks with a huff.

He had no response for Ben. He'd been asking himself that question since Teo's hand had been ripped out of his.

A sob burned Vex's throat. He beat it down, scrubbing his forehead. He didn't deserve that release. He deserved the accusation in Lu's eyes. The blame in her voice—"*I thought the one thing I didn't have to worry about anymore was your responsibility with Teo.*"

Vex hadn't processed what it'd mean to bring Teo into Fort Chastity. He hadn't *planned*, or *prepared*, or done anything but be the same useless fuckup he always was.

A noise in the hall made Vex look up. Edda and Nayeli appeared between the cells.

Vex held his breath. Lu wasn't with them.

Edda kept her eyes on Vex. "The Variegated Holly hit mostly empty rooms."

Vex didn't move. "Mostly?"

"Two people have been found so far. They should recover."

Ben moved to the back of his cell. Gunnar turned to him, whispering low and calm.

"You saw Cansu?" Nayeli asked.

Vex rocked forward, propping himself on his knees to brace against a painful, jarring shudder. He nodded, unable to look at Nayeli.

"And you didn't—" Her voice caught. "Why was she there?"

"Elazar did something to her." Vex's voice was small. "Drugged her. Same thing he must've done to Ingvar, to get her to submit to him."

"You saw that happen?" She didn't wait for him to answer. "And you didn't stop it."

The pain on her face filled Vex's whole body with toxic guilt.

"Gods, Vex," she hissed. "What the hell is wrong with you? What'd you expect to happen when you chose to go into Elazar's gathering? Don't you ever think?"

Vex shoved to his feet, needing to expel his self-hatred. "No, I don't think. I do whatever I want and to hell with everyone else. I'm a good-for-nothing, unaligned heretic and—"

Nayeli squinted. "An unaligned *heretic*?"

"A raider." Vex's face heated. "A useless, unaligned raider. And I—"

"You two—*enough*." Edda grabbed Nayeli's shoulder. "Nay, we're all scared out of our minds for Cansu. We did everything we could in a room packed with defensors. You know we wouldn't have left her there if we'd had any choice."

Nayeli looked at the floor.

"And you." Edda swung on Vex. "*A heretic*," she parroted.

Vex shoved back, but tripped on Jakes and slammed to his knees. The impact sent a sting of pain up his thighs, his torso, and Vex slumped there, his face contorted.

"Is that what you think of yourself?" came Nayeli's voice.

Vex closed his eye.

"What voice do you have in your head all the time, huh, Nay?" Edda asked. "Fatemah's? I'm willing to bet Vex has his dad, or Elazar even, shouting at him all hours of the day."

"Dumbass," Nayeli scoffed.

Vex smiled. It rose to a chuckle, and when he opened his eye, Ben was watching him from the back of his cell, Gunnar next to him. Jakes breathed steadier off to his right.

"I know you love us, Nay." Edda nudged her. "But your heart ain't in this crew. It's always been right here with Fatemah and Cansu. We were a way to bide your time till your heart healed."

"You weren't a way to bide my time," Nayeli whispered. She looked up. "You weren't—this *meant* something—I may yell at you a lot, but you're both—"

A weight thudded into Vex's stomach. He felt wetness on his face. He was crying, surges of tears, all brought on by Edda, weeping, and Nay, weeping, and—*goddamn them.*

"We love you too," Vex said.

"I was trying *not* to say it, Vex." Nayeli scrubbed her eyes and looked at him. Her face softened. "I'll talk to Fatemah. I'll get her to let you out, or at least listen to your story and why you didn't tell her who you are. I don't know what I can do for your cousin, though."

A too-familiar wash of dread made Vex shiver. "Just—" He hesitated. "Make sure the people in the tenement are all right. And see how we can . . . how we can get Teo back."

Vex looked at Ben, who nodded.

"We'll give Fatemah time to calm down," Ben said. "If she is willing, I will speak with her. But I understand my presence here is—difficult."

Nayeli shrugged without looking at him, her gaze still on Vex's. "I'll talk to Lu too."

His body went rigid. Even if there weren't bars closing him in, he wouldn't be able to run to Lu. He wouldn't be able to sweep her into his arms and make everything better. He was broken, and falling apart, and she hated him now.

God, *that* was what would kill him, the jagged teeth of his failure.

"Thanks," he told Nayeli, but he knew it was pointless.

She nodded. Edda planted her hand on Nayeli's shoulder.

Vex flicked his eye from Edda to Nay and back, and let this reunion nestle into the tangle of emotions inside him. He might be a useless unaligned raider—*heretic*—but as long as he had Edda and Nayeli, he wouldn't choose any other fate.

❖❖❖

The Visjorn bear blood necklace was easy enough to break. Lu put it in a mortar and gently, *gently*, cracked the glass, letting the precious blood drip into the stone bowl. It was such a small amount—would it be enough? How much did the Mecht clan leaders use in their potions? She couldn't bring herself to ask Gunnar, not now, when going to him would mean facing Vex in the cells where the Tuncians had locked them away.

She sorted her Tuncian spices. She picked which magic plants to use. She went over the steps to make Emerdian stonework, the temperature and molding, the time and pressure.

How, all this time, have so many cultures used our magic and not realized it was happening in Port Mesi-Teab, in Port Camden, in the Mechtlands? How has no one pieced this together before now?

Rosalia came, and Lu asked if there was anything Grozdans combined with Grace Loray's magic that was unique to them. Rosalia couldn't think of anything, but that didn't mean something wasn't out there, being used even now. Would Elazar and Tom find it first?

They had done something with Menesia to make it control Cansu after Elazar sang a hymn. That paralleled how the Mechts used Eye of the Sun, and the Tuncians used Budwig Beans, and Emerdians used Bright Mint. Tom had

302

put that together, experimenting with different concentrations of Menesia—as he had done on her.

Lu's hand hovered over a vial of Bright Mint. She could make a condensed dose of it, take it, and see what memories Tom had erased from her mind.

She stayed herself and got back to work.

Kari came. Nayeli wasn't there to bar her entry, and she stood next to the table as Lu laid out the most potent of the Tuncian spices.

"We have had news," Kari was saying. "Elazar has left Port Mesi-Teab. He appears headed northeast, for Port Fausta, to continue 'spreading his coming light.'"

Rosalia was in the sanctuary, though. Whoever Elazar would get to bow to him as a symbol of Port Fausta's surrender, it wouldn't be the Grozdan syndicate Head.

"Tom is gone as well?" Lu asked.

Kari hesitated. "Yes."

Whenever she left to fight Elazar, Tom would be there. And Teo. That likelihood circled Lu's plans, a hawk with a crooked beak and bloodthirsty talons.

Lu refused to let it debilitate her. Confronting her father would invigorate her, and when she stood before him this time, she would not hesitate. She would not let him break her.

Kari's voice quickened. "Now that we know Elazar's plan, we will follow him to Port Fausta and assassinate him. Heads Blaise and Rustici have agreed to join us, and Head

Rustici will contribute knowledge of Port Fausta. But, sweetheart, you don't need to be involved—"

Lu flinched away. "Harmedeku," she said, touching a jar of spice. "Nigrika. And—" She couldn't remember the name of this one, but it was rich and chocolaty and a single whiff had made her eyes water—from its potency, and from memory.

Kari had cooked with this spice. A breakfast treat on Lu's birthday—pork that had marinated in it for days, with sticky, fresh honey and tart grapefruit, cooled by yogurt and eaten with stone-cooked Tuncian pastries from Kari's mother's recipe—

"Mootabel."

Lu looked up.

Kari stared at the jar. "Mootabel," she repeated. "The spice. They say it comes from the god of Rebirth, Eshepri. That eating it can make you anew." She lifted her eyes to Lu's. "You can't still want this, Adeluna. Permanent magic."

Lu gripped the jar of Mootabel. New starts—that was why Tuncians associated it with birthdays. "He's already working on magic," she whispered. "If he figures out how to make it permanent while he still has Teo—no. I will do this. I have to do this. For Teo, for Grace Loray, to make this island safe."

Kari's eyes glistened. "You've never felt safe, have you?"

Lu didn't respond.

Kari's eyes drifted back to the table. She lifted the jar of Harmedeku. "This one is used in offerings to the god of Death, Fapsanti. She is the wife of Eshepri, so it is often paired with Mootabel. Nigrika—this is associated with lesser blessings. Has Nayeli gotten you Hadiza, or Tale? Those are the spices of the other two gods, and could be—"

A thin yet sturdy thread of tension wound around them, but Lu shoved it to the edge of the room, scooping up Kari's help and her presence with greedy hands.

Years ago, they had sat in ramshackle hideaways together, Kari explaining the finer points of stealth and spying to Lu. This was no different, and as Lu asked about the amounts of spices often used, she saw an echo of her younger self, staring up at Kari with wonder.

This was her mother. This resilient, controlled woman, who could analyze any situation and adapt it to her own ends. Who could bring an entire country to its knees. Who could wage war and rip victory away with bloody hands and never once lose her poise.

Tom had made Lu a traitor. But this was her mother, imperfect and indestructible, and maybe, since Lu had come from her, she could be those things, too.

Equal spoonfuls of Tuncian spices—Harmedeku, Mootabel, Hadiza, and Tale, the four added to concoctions to demand the gods' blessings. They perfumed the air with zest and smokiness. Adding spices in those amounts to

Budwig had let Cansu listen through every similar plant on the island.

The steps to make Emerdian stonework. Cooking at the highest temperature the little fire could reach for four and a half hours, then five more hours on low, orange-gray coals. This preparation had taken Bright Mint's effects from mental stimulation to insanity.

Mecht Visjorn bear blood. Such a small amount—Lu added all of it and prayed to whatever god would hear her. Mixing it with Eye of the Sun let the Mechts have permanent fire control.

Should Lu sing an Argridian hymn over it? No. She wouldn't add Menesia to this potion. She wanted no part in controlling others if that was what Argridian hymns did.

Then she added plants. Powersage. Aerated Blossom. Cleanse Root. Incris. Lazonade. Croxy. Plants for strength, flight, healing, power, movement—their counter plants too, all broken down and combined.

For two days after the explosion, Lu hadn't left the laboratory shack. She hadn't gone to see Vex and Ben; she barely knew anything that was happening outside these walls, aside from Kari's visit and her news that Elazar—with Tom and Teo—was heading for Port Fausta.

But after all her work, her careful monitoring of the various ingredients and preparation steps, Lu came away with a large enough amount of potion to fill five vials with permanent magic. Well—possibly permanent. There was one way to find out.

Lu stood over the table, digging through her soul for the resolve to take one of the vials.

The shack door opened. A spurt of panic welled up. She didn't want to relinquish control of this magic—it would be passed out on *her* terms. Lu swiped at the vials, trying to hide them. She managed to get only two into her pocket before Nayeli and Rosalia appeared.

Why? If this potion worked, they would need all five vials, every weapon possible to destroy Elazar.

Lu took a fortifying breath. If it worked, she would reveal the two remaining vials. All five had the same potion within them, and Lu didn't have enough ingredients remaining to make more. No need to waste all the vials if the magic within was—or wasn't—permanent.

"That councilmember has us moving out to Port Fausta later today. Have you finished?" Rosalia leaned around the table. "Those vials. Gloria! You did it!"

Lu slammed her hand over them as Rosalia reached around her.

Rosalia wasn't deterred. "What'll they do? Strength? Flight? Speed?"

"Lu—have you tested it?" Nayeli analyzed Lu with new purpose. She was wondering if Lu had taken permanent magic. If she had . . . abilities, now.

Lu shook her head.

Nayeli growled—but looked relieved. "Fatemah was right about that, at least—who are we going to test it on? It's a bit . . . cruel. Isn't it?"

"I can find some volunteers," Rosalia said. "Grozdans aren't afraid of *cruelty*."

"We're well aware of Grozdans and their lack of standards," Nayeli snapped. "But by *cruel* I mean *runs the risk of giving someone Shaking Sickness*."

Lu stared, hearing aloud what she had been trying not to admit to herself. She saw Vex, grabbing the Variegated Holly bomb. Shaking as he threw it. His grimace of pain and fear.

These potions—that she had made, that she was responsible for—could give someone Shaking Sickness. Or worse. Was she any better than Elazar if she made someone else test it?

"Well," Rosalia giggled, "it's a good thing we have a disposable Argridian piece of shit."

Lu's blood sank to her toes. "You will not touch Ben," she stated. "Or Vex."

Rosalia's grin soured. "Not them. That other one—the defensor."

Lu had heard that the Tuncians had given Jakes magic to heal his wounds. He had awoken this morning and confirmed that Elazar's plan was to host a gathering in Port Fausta before heading to Port Camden and, finally, New Deza.

Nayeli's face screwed up. "You think he'll volunteer? He's a defensor of the Church—"

"Who said anything about volunteering?" Rosalia kept her eyes on Lu as she spoke.

Nayeli blanched. "You want to *torture* this poor kid?"

Lu huffed. "*Poor kid?* He guarded us in the Port Camden prison. He stood by while defensors whipped Gunnar, while Milo tortured *me.*"

"So he deserves to be tortured too?"

Hesitation yanked on Lu's chest. "That's . . . that's not what I said."

"What are you saying, then?" Nayeli asked. "Because that's what this will be. We're forcing magic on him. It's *torture*, and you know it."

"Don't you want Cansu back?" Rosalia cocked her head at Nayeli. "She'd be heartbroken to hear you weren't doing everything possible to save her."

"Shut up."

"That defensor is Argridian. He's an enemy." Rosalia stomped for the door. "I'll get Nate and Pierce to grab him. Elazar's almost to my city. *My city.* I don't have time for morals."

Lu was leaning against the table by the time Nate and Pierce hauled Jakes into the shack.

She had watched revolutionaries die from Argridian bullet wounds, or hung from the walls of ports, or burned on stakes. She had spied for her parents, killed for Tom, because Argridians were enemies. They were heartless, and evil, and that made them inhuman.

So it was all right that Lu had killed them. It was all right that she would experiment on this one, Jakes, because he was an enemy. Just like Tom had taught her.

If this potion worked, it would make her strong enough to defeat Elazar and save Grace Loray. It would let her save Teo.

Nate shoved Jakes into the middle of the room. Manacles clamped his arms behind his back, and he stumbled to keep from falling into the smoking fire.

When he looked up, his eyes locked on Lu. "What is happening?" he asked in stunted Grace Lorayan, his accent thick. He knew he was outnumbered, even if he didn't know the why or the how, and his throat worked on a hard swallow.

Nate kicked the backs of Jakes's legs, sending him to his knees. "Fatemah's raiders have been questioning him all morning. Most of his information is stuff we already know. The Tuncians handed him over—seems they were happy to find a use for him."

Jakes hung his head.

Nayeli pinned Lu with a look. "Go ahead. Give him the magic." There was a dare in her voice, not to do it.

Lu pushed back from the table and picked up one of the vials. Her hand shook.

She had no idea what it would do. What abilities it would give him, if any.

A low, rhythmic noise emanated from Jakes. Humming?

Lu frowned. Nate grabbed Jakes's chin and jerked his head back, readying his mouth to open.

The humming cut off. Jakes's eyes went to the vial in Lu's fingers.

Understanding made his eyebrows raise. "It's all right," he told her, sweat beading on his forehead. "I understand why you have to do this. I want it, too, believe it or not."

Lu held her frown. "If you think you can take permanent magic back to Elazar—"

"I won't." He inhaled, and Nate jerked his grip on Jakes's neck tighter. "Elazar turned on me after the Port Camden prison escape because I told him I let you go. I couldn't . . . he isn't the future. I will go where either you or Ben are. You two will end this war. You two are the future."

Nayeli stepped up beside Lu. "What? Wait—no, still confused. *What?*"

"Didn't you swear loyalty to Elazar?" Lu pressed. "You are a defensor of the Church."

"I swore loyalty to Argrid." Jakes nodded at the vial in her hand. "Do what you must."

He closed his eyes with a deep breath.

Nate glanced at Pierce with a baffled squint. Jakes must have stopped fighting him. Sure enough, Nate backed away, and Jakes stayed on his knees, eyes closed, head tipped up.

Rosalia looked just as perplexed. But it was a murderous, dark confusion, a reflection of her impatience in Fort

Chastity. How she had unflinchingly shot Tom.

Jakes started humming again. Lu wanted to question him more, to figure out why he was accepting this experiment—this torture—

She recognized the song.

"All this," she started, "and you hum a revolution song?"

Jakes's eyes split open. "What?"

"Rebels made it up during the war." Lu hummed a few bars. Teo had sung it to himself more times than she could count. It had been a popular song among revolutionaries, a bawdy tune sung during dark nights. Teo loved it because his mother had sung it as a lullaby to him. A memento of a time Teo didn't know.

He knew it now, though. He was living it.

"It isn't a revolution song." Jakes's face hardened.

Something about his tone—disgust, maybe—made pride swell in Lu's chest. She started to sing. *"Dirt and sand, all across the land; the currents are ours, you see."*

Jakes hesitated, but started alongside her—in Argridian. *"Prayer is ours, devotion too; so we do not fear the flames—"*

They united on *"No god, no soldier, no emperor, no king—"*

And gaped at each other.

Jakes's face grayed. "How . . . how do you know that?"

"I told you," Lu said, easing into a raging river. "Revolutionaries made it up."

"No. My sister wrote that. In Argrid, when I was a child."

Lu looked at Nayeli, as though she would have an

explanation. But Nayeli's eyes were wide. "It became popular among the rebels," Lu said. "Perhaps it spread to Argrid, and the people there changed it?"

Rosalia groaned. "This is all fascinating—give him the potion!"

Lu glared at her, fury heating her face. Rosalia faltered back a step.

"*No.*" Jakes's insistence pulled Lu back to him. "My sister wrote that song. She wrote it *for Argrid*. For the people there who wanted more than Elazar's tyrannical rule. She sang it to me, and her daughter, when we were scared, when the Church did horrible things around us, when we couldn't escape the hell it was to grow up in Argrid. And when Elazar killed her and my niece with Shaking Sickness in Deza, when priests burned my parents in front of the cathedral my family had gone to for years, I had only that song. It's all I have left of her. Revolutionaries on Grace Loray do not get to change Bianca's song just because—"

Lu grabbed for Nayeli, clutching her for balance. "What did you say?"

"I said, the revolutionaries—"

"No. Bianca. Your sister's name was Bianca?"

Jakes's eyes narrowed. "Why?"

Bianca and her daughter, dead from Shaking Sickness. Bianca, who wrote that song.

Lu's palm was sweaty around the vial, her heart thudding. "Bianca. And Annalisa."

Jakes teetered back, his cheeks blotchy. "How do you know those names?"

It was impossible—it was *mad*—

"Elazar didn't kill them in Deza," Lu whispered. "I watched them die here. On Grace Loray."

"No," Jakes protested weakly. "No, Elazar killed my sister and niece in Deza when I was thirteen. They've been dead for seven years. How could you— *What is this?* You got this information somehow, didn't you? You're trying . . . you're trying to . . ."

He bent double, his manacles clanking against his back. Tendrils of hair twisted around his face as he spoke fast and low to himself in Argridian.

There was a knock on the door and the handle rattled. Nate must have thrown the lock.

Rosalia cursed and stomped over to deal with it, but Lu knew nothing outside of this defensor at her feet. Bianca's brother. Annalisa and Teo's uncle.

"Bianca and Annalisa fled Argrid," Lu told him. She didn't owe him this. But she did, somehow, her heart unable to start again until she spoke. "They came to Grace Loray with other refugees. I was young—ten, eleven. Bianca became one of my parents' supporters. She helped them fight Elazar here. Annalisa was . . . a light."

Jakes looked up at her, his eyebrows rising.

"Bianca died two years ago, of Shaking Sickness," Lu told him. "And Annalisa too—"

She couldn't force the words out. So many more needed to come: *Annalisa died a few months ago. Has it only been a few months? But Teo is healthy. Teo is—*

Teo had been born on Grace Loray. Jakes had a nephew he didn't know about.

Lu almost told him, but the emblem on Jakes's uniform stayed her. Argrid's ivory curved *V*, the crossed swords, bloodstains and dirt smeared across them. She remembered this defensor standing outside her cell, complicit in Gunnar's whippings, in Milo's torture of her.

Jakes had proven he would sacrifice anything, anyone, to achieve his goals.

Lu would not let him factor Teo into his machinations.

Nate and Pierce joined Rosalia at the door, talking to whoever had come.

Jakes's eyes moved from Lu to the orange embers in the firepit. "We were part of the resistance in Argrid, and defensors caught them with other conspirators. Elazar experimented on them. Physicians told my mother that Bianca and Annalisa died, that my sister had been pregnant, and there were complications—" He cleared his throat, yanking his voice level. Glints of hope showed in his dark eyes. "But they went to Grace Loray? The resistance was only able to send a handful of refugees out of Argrid. Elazar watched everything—" Jakes sucked in a breath. "Elazar. Diaño. He did this. He sent them to Grace Loray. Bianca would have contacted me if they had lived. Elazar did this to her. *Why?*"

Lu lifted a trembling hand to her mouth. She looked at Nayeli, silent and watchful, but no help lay there. No help lay anywhere.

"My father found Bianca and Annalisa," Lu gasped. "He said he came across a refugee boat on the coast. That the rest of the refugees had perished in the crossing. But he was working with Elazar. The whole revolution, he was a spy for Argrid."

Lu's mind spiraled, wild and panicked.

Elazar had sent Bianca and Annalisa to Grace Loray.

Tom had found them. He had used them for something.

Nausea throbbed in Lu's stomach, up her throat, in the core of her being. What more had her father done? And Teo. No, *no*—Bianca hadn't been pregnant when she arrived in Grace Loray, had she? Teo was younger than that, Lu thought.

But Tom had made the defensors take Teo. Not Vex, who meant just as much to Lu. Not Ben or Edda. *Teo.*

Lu shot upright, her rage powerful and blinding.

Jakes shoved closer, his manacled hands hindering him. "My only desire has been to fulfill my family's goal of stopping Elazar from destroying our country. They died before they could see it through. I know you won't believe me, but everything I've done, getting close to Elazar, earning his trust—I've been trying to stop him with his own magic. Magic is a gift from the Pious God, something that should be free for all people to use. Elazar bastardizes it for his own benefit." He bowed, supplicating on the floor of Lu's makeshift laboratory. "I swear fealty to you, to permanent magic, to anything you ask, so long as you let me help end Elazar."

The impossibility of this outcome processed in startling jolts. Jakes, the defensor Ben knew so well, the one who had overseen their tortures in Port Camden—he wanted to bring down Elazar. He had been part of the resistance in Argrid, the same group led by Vex's father. Vex hadn't recognized Jakes, though. Had he? And Ben hadn't called him Jakes Casales, matching Bianca's last name—he'd called him Jakes Rayen.

Lu steadied herself on the edge of the table. The three vials of magic clinked against each other.

Rosalia swung from the door. "A messenger said Elazar is half a day from Port Fausta. Fatemah and Kari are getting ready to assassinate him. *Test the potion.*"

Nate and Pierce turned, backing up Rosalia, the three of them in rare agreement as they eyed Jakes and the vial in Lu's palm.

Teo's uncle. He was Teo's *family.*

Lu held her breath. Uncorked the vial. And gulped down the contents herself.

"Lu!" Nayeli grabbed her shoulder too late.

Lu coughed, the tonic bitter and thick. The potion burned her belly, a sensation of fire creeping higher, higher still, spreading out to her limbs and down to her toes and up to the tips of her hair. She doubled over, trying to contain the inferno within her, pushing it down into the crevice of her heart. Let it lie there, forever a part of her, unstoppable and brilliant.

She was fire, and ash, and strength and magic and *power*.

For a moment, everyone in the shack stared at her.

Pierce broke the silence with a heavy sigh. "Well, she isn't dead."

"Good enough for me." Rosalia grabbed one of the other vials.

Sweat burst down Lu's back and she stumbled forward, fingers out in panic to stop Rosalia. She blinked—and found herself face-to-face with the wall of the shack.

She had taken only a step. How—

"Shame and hell!" Rosalia cheered. "Incris? This is gonna give us permanent speed?"

Each vial had the same combination of plants, as many as Lu had been able to cook down and blend together. She hadn't known what the potions would do, whether all the plants within would take permanent root or a few or none. Had only Incris affected her?

Lu looked down at her body, her mind spinning end over end. She didn't feel any different, aside from a flutter in her chest of anxiety, fear. She took another step, for a moment giving in to that tingle of fear, and watched as the room rushed past.

She came up on Nayeli and grabbed her arms to steady herself.

Nayeli's eyes were wide and wondering and scared. "Shit, Lu—are you all right?"

Yes. No. She had no idea.

Nate guffawed and snatched a vial too. "Drink up!"

Pierce eyed Lu with sudden concern. "If this kills him, I'll kill *you.*"

Nate downed the potion. Rosalia said a phrase in Grozdan before chugging her vial.

Coughing, desperate, gasping breaths, and both Nate and Rosalia giggled maniacally.

"Did it work?" Pierce asked.

Nate took a step forward. He didn't shoot across the room like Lu had, and her heart squeezed. She wanted it to work? She didn't? She couldn't solidify her flipping emotions.

Nate glowered and stomped toward her—*hard.* His foot cracked the floorboards.

"Powersage," Lu whispered. She stomped, but nothing broke under her.

Rosalia stomped as well. She took a step, but didn't rush through the air like Lu—her foot lifted, hovered, and she dropped to the floor on her backside.

"Aerated Blossom. Aerated Blossom!" Rosalia dissolved in giggles, shoving to her feet and hovering a beat, landing, jumping up, hovering, landing again.

Lu, Nate, and Rosalia had each taken the same potion, but the plants seemed to work at random. Were the effects permanent, though? Time would tell. And battle. And winning this war, annihilating Elazar, saving Teo.

Any fear or hesitation went tumbling to the edges of Lu's mind. This was what she had wanted, to look at her allies and herself and know they were stronger than Elazar. To march into battle and know they would defeat him.

To rescue Teo before Tom could destroy him, too.

"We're going to Port Fausta," Rosalia announced, but her eyes glinted with manic intent at Nayeli. "We're gonna kill Elazar. We're gonna kill his defensors. We're gonna end them *all*."

Nayeli's jaw set. How could she still hesitate? How could she not be elated?

Pierce grabbed Jakes's manacles. "Back to the cell with you."

Jakes stumbled, crying out that he could help, but Pierce hauled him out of the shack. Lu let him go, too unstoppable, too *much*—

"Lu," Nayeli said, shaking her to get her attention. "How do you feel?"

"I feel wonderful," Lu said. A lie—she felt monstrous.

But monsters were fighting this war. She had become what she needed to be to win.

20

THE RAIDERS KEPT Jakes away for an hour, maybe less. When they came stumbling back and shoved him into the cell with Vex, they sneered at Ben and swept away without a word.

But behind them, in the space of a breath, Lu and Nayeli followed.

Vex shot up from the floor and launched himself at the cell bars. "Lu—talk to me. Lu—"

"It's too late," Jakes said. His eyes were on Ben. "She did it. She took it herself."

Ben wheezed. "Permanent magic?"

Jakes nodded, smiling.

The breath left Ben's chest. Jakes was *happy* that Lu had created permanent magic? And that Lu had taken it herself?

"Did you—" Vex started to ask, but gulped down the question. "Lu. Are you all right?"

Lu's eyes lifted to Vex, but she didn't respond. She turned to Ben. "Elazar is almost to Port Fausta. We're leaving to meet him there, scout his gathering, and attack. We'll get Teo. We'll get Cansu. We'll free everyone. And I—"

She moved closer to where Ben stood against his bars and reached through to press her hand to his chest. He felt something against her palm—a vial. Permanent magic?

"You remember what we did in the prison," she pushed on, the words causing her pain. "You have to make cures for Vex. You have to keep going."

Ben took the vial from her. Was it not permanent magic? By the earnest way she looked at him, it was clear she didn't want the others to know she was giving this to him.

"There's one more. In the shack," she told him. She hesitated. "Jakes. Can he be trusted?"

Ben's response was instant. "No."

Lu turned, moving fast—faster than should have been possible—out of the hall.

Vex jerked after her. "Lu!"

Nayeli remained. "Edda's staying here to help guard the sanctuary." She didn't acknowledge anyone other than Vex. "We'll come back. I'll bring Lu back."

She left.

Tonight. The raiders would leave to attack Elazar tonight.

No—it couldn't be that simple. They couldn't destroy him in one easy battle.

But Lu had permanent magic. That could change . . . everything.

Ben knew his realization was clear on his face when Jakes bowed his head. "King Benat Elazar Asentzio Gallego," he said, all mockery gone.

The world rocked, one violent shift. When his father died, Ben would take the title-name of Elazar. It was tainted now. Desecrated.

Ben turned away, blood rushing to his head, his grip tightening on the vial of Lu's magic. He shoved it into his pocket. Had she meant for him to drink it? Or had she given it to him because she knew he *wouldn't* drink it?

"The walls are wood," Gunnar noted. He birthed a flame in his palm. "I can burn our way through—"

"Don't. Please."

The flame went out. "This is your fight," Gunnar said, as though Ben might not know. "You do not deserve to be in here while your country wars out there."

"I need these people to trust me." Ben cleared his throat, trying to be resolute, but he couldn't hear his own conviction over the screaming in his mind. "If I can't get the people of Grace Loray to trust me, how can I ever win over Argrid? I have the same problem there that I do here—this isn't a war of weapons, it's a war of hearts. Even if my father is overthrown tonight, he will still win this war, because he was so effective at playing this game and has planted belief so thoroughly. I don't even know where to start."

Jakes looked at him. "You lie," he said in Argridian. "It's the only way to survive. I thought you knew that—you lied for years, too."

"What happened to you?" Ben twisted, facing Jakes for the first time, an anxious quiver vibrating him head to toe. "You're a defensor of the Church. Your piety was what kept me going most days, trying to be worthy of you. What are you doing? Tell me the truth. You owe me that."

Exhaustion left purple bruises around Jakes's eyes. "I don't owe you anything. Your unreliability has been—"

Ben barked a laugh. "*My* unreliability?"

"Until you fought me on the deck of the *Astuto*, I had no idea you were capable of turning against your father," Jakes hissed. "And your imprisonment? I thought you were clinging to your rebellion to punish Elazar for what he did to your cousin. I kept waiting for you to break, and when you did—you were so cold. You didn't surrender like I thought you would, begging your father's forgiveness. You stood up to him. I felt like I was seeing you for the first time. Clearly I was not the only one who lied during our relationship."

That socked Ben in the chest. "Your lie betrayed me to a dangerous madman."

"Spying on you for Elazar wasn't what I meant. I've been playing this game longer than you can imagine. You have no idea what it takes to fight Elazar—and win."

"Fight him?" Ben staggered and bumped into someone—Gunnar. When had he moved?

Ben stayed there, his spine pressed against Gunnar, gaping at Jakes.

"You are a defensor of the Church," Ben repeated. "What are you talking about?"

Jakes looked up, tears on the edges of his eyelids. Next to him, Vex was motionless, his brow furrowed.

"I became a defensor to get close to Elazar," Jakes said. "To take control of permanent magic once he gets it and kill him with it."

He said it with a shrug and a tired blink.

The whole of the world could have broken and swallowed everyone outside this room, and Ben wouldn't have moved.

"Permanent magic is the only thing strong enough to bring him to justice," Jakes continued. "You know how he ingratiates himself in the minds and hearts of Argridians. Defeating him isn't sticking a blade in his heart—that would make him a martyr. My family realized what it would take to defeat Elazar, but he killed them before they could do anything."

"My father." Vex's voice was soft and childlike. "Are you part of his resistance?"

The muscles in Jakes's shoulders bundled, something dark and furious passing over his eyes. "There is no resistance. There is only me, living out the promise I made to my family." He turned back to Ben. "You wanted the truth? This is who I am. I'm still devout, I still serve the Pious

God. I never—" He winced. "I never meant to fall in love with you. It almost ruined everything, and I knew you'd hate me. But I promised my family. I watched them *die*."

Just when Ben thought all lies had been revealed. Worse was that this piece had been in front of him all along—Jakes had talked about his family, hummed that song his sister had written every day.

Jakes had been adamant that Ben continue working. When it had been a cure for Shaking Sickness; when it became permanent magic—Jakes had always been there, pushing Ben on, and Ben had blamed it on Jakes's loyalties to Elazar, to the Church.

Ben hadn't thought his chest could be emptier, but another shovelful of his soul lifted out. "You watched your family die," he echoed.

Rodrigu. Paxben. Uncles and his grandparents and his mother, sister—why hadn't Ben been driven to Jakes's extremes? He had lost as much. More, even. And Lu—grief had unraveled her inhibitions, too.

So many people would lose themselves in the battles if it meant winning the war.

Looking at Jakes now, Ben expected some satisfaction, pieces clicking together and filling in gaps. But he felt . . . nothing. Except maybe sadness.

"Trust me, Ben," Jakes said, softer now. Almost imploring. "This is how you fight this war. You lie, you say whatever you have to say to get these Grace Lorayans to accept you. And you do the same to Argrid. The truth will get you killed."

"Despicable," Gunnar grumbled.

"Necessity," Jakes countered. "You tell your truth, it gets used against you. The raiders? They want you to be supportive of permanent magic. Argrid? Wants you to be against magic. So you lie to one of them. And you survive."

"Sounds like a quick way to get everyone to turn on you," Vex added. His posture slumped, arms twitching as he leaned against the bars. "What if they find you out? They'll hate you. But that's who we are, isn't it, as Argridians? The source of the world's problems. Our existence messes everything up."

"My people are barbarians," came Gunnar's calm voice. "Is that all I am? A barbarian warmonger, covered in blood, wild?"

Jakes huffed. "Yes. But you use that in your favor when you need to. You take the lies and the opinions and the beliefs and you make them your armor."

Gunnar ignored Jakes, grabbing Ben's eyes. "You can't be that kind of king," he said, so low Ben wasn't sure Jakes or Vex could hear him. "You have been true to yourself. After the battle, the world will be new. The rules will change. Keep holding to your truth."

"Even if it kills me?" Ben asked.

Gunnar's lips quirked in a sad smile. "Would you rather die any other way?"

Fatemah and Kari might have disagreed with using permanent magic, but there was little they could do to stop Nate, Pierce, and Rosalia from mobilizing their raiders. A haphazard group of Tuncians, Emerdians, and Grozdans prepared to leave, with a few dozen remaining from each syndicate to guard the sanctuary under Fatemah's watch.

"With Cansu gone, the responsibility is mine," she had said with a pointed look at Nayeli.

Kari would lead the Tuncian raiders against Elazar. As far as Lu knew, their plan was still to assassinate him, while Nate, Pierce, and Rosalia planned an all-out attack against Elazar's Port Fausta gathering. Likely Kari would use the battle between the raiders and defensors as distraction, slip the best Tuncian fighters through Elazar's lines, and end him—if Emerdian or Grozdan raiders didn't get to him first.

But Lu didn't know the specifics. She didn't want to.

Kari called her name over the docked steamboats, but Lu shot into the crowd. She was able to take a few steps at a normal pace, and it wasn't until she leaned into her desire to be *away* that she launched forward at a breakneck pace.

She had taken Incris twice during the war. It was a rarer plant, so when the revolutionaries found some, they had put it in their spies' arsenals to be used as a last resort. Lu had taken Incris once to escape a fortified Argridian storehouse in New Deza, and once to combat the Lazonade that Milo had forced on her the night the war ended. Incris was the counter plant to the numbing Lazonade.

Having Incris inside her now, potentially a permanent part of her, Lu expected to feel poetic righteousness. Of course it would be Incris, a lasting rebuke to what had happened to her during the war. Of course it would be speed, allowing her to rush away from Kari and her own crippling thoughts, barreling straight into the tangled growth in her chest that wanted to lash out at Argrid, and Elazar, and Tom, and rip Teo back to safety.

She didn't care what Kari's plan was—because all Lu wanted out of this, her singular, selfish need, was blood. She wanted Milo to be in Port Fausta so she could run a sword through his stomach. She wanted to watch Elazar's composure crumble as he realized he had lost, and to hear the pop of a gunshot as a bullet lodged in his chest. She wanted Tom to be—

As Lu slowed her Incris enough to slip onto a steamboat, she thought his name again. Twice.

She knew what she wanted with everything else. But Tom? What would she do when she stood face-to-face with him? Would she be able to find it within her to kill him—*should* she? Would Kari stay Lu's hand, beg for her traitor husband's life to the child he had betrayed?

Lu re-counted the weapons she'd taken from Rosalia's people. Pistols, knives, a few vials of plants used in fights—

Hemlight for small explosions; the cousin plants of Rhodofume, for smoke screens, and Rhodospine, for thorn grenades.

Plotting murder. Checking weapons. How was this any different from the last revolution?

Tension ate at Lu's stomach.

The Grozdans, Emerdians, and Tuncians organized into dozens of steamboats. Everyone around them knew what Lu had done. Raiders rejoiced, guffawing when Nate lifted the bow of a boat clear out of the water or Rosalia flew up to the top of a pilothouse. But Fatemah, Kari, the Tuncian raiders—they watched with darkened expressions.

Refugees, watching from high windows in tenements, slammed their shutters. They were terrified. These mothers, fathers, the elderly, the innocents—what frightened them most? Rosalia and Nate parading their magic, or the preparation for war?

Lu and Nayeli sat on a cramped Grozdan boat. Fatemah was on the shore, arms folded, talking to Kari, who stood on the deck of a Tuncian steamboat.

Kari felt Lu watching and turned, her lips parting. Lu closed her eyes.

I'll be better this time, Mama.

Nayeli took Lu's hand as the boat's engine growled, surging them through Port Mesi-Teab and out into the twisting waterways of their island.

❊❊❊

They reached Port Fausta at sunset.

This city was one of the most well maintained on Grace Loray, its roads smooth, with clear rivers snaking into it and bridges made of well-worn stone. The buildings mimicked the architecture on Grozda, everything coated in pale gray or tan stone with dozens of arching walkways and airy mezzanines. Chimneys poked the sky from domed rooftops, the curved shingles and graceful slopes too soft to come from a people so aggressive.

While most Mainland countries had switched to negotiating official trade agreements with the Grace Lorayan Republic after the revolution, Grozda was one of the few countries that had kept a trade set up with its raider syndicate counterpart. They bought heaps of magic from the Grozdan syndicate—Aerated Blossom and Healica, things of use in mountainous terrain.

The money stayed in the Grozdan syndicate, and the benefits did as well.

Lu had been to Port Fausta one other time since the revolution's end. But now she huddled on the deck with Nayeli and other raiders, seeing this city after all that had happened, the awareness that had lifted her eyes.

The Council's trade agreements had pulled funds away from other syndicates, yet the Council hadn't taken steps to redistribute the services, protection, order, and regulation that the syndicates provided. When the war ended this time, things would be different. Whoever took power would *understand* Grace Loray's needs.

Lu's boat was in a tight cluster of three. The rest had split off into small groups, all coming at Port Fausta from varying directions. Rosalia had spread word via Budwig Beans that the most likely place for an Argridian gathering would be Port Fausta's main square, a wide area centered in the port where the city held daily markets, announcements, and executions.

That was their destination. They would dock. Sneak ashore. Eliminate any defensors they came across.

And unleash hell.

The setting sun cut scalding orange rays between Port Fausta's buildings as Lu's boat made one final turn. Ahead, vessels displaying the Argridian flag crowded docks. Seven, Lu counted, mostly medium steamboats and a few narrow longboats, possibly holding crews of six to ten people. There could be more boats docked elsewhere, more defensors already stationed here.

Lu tightened her grip on her pistol. Beside her, Nayeli pulled two clusters of Hemlight from satchels on her hips.

"Remember our goals," came a voice from the pilothouse—Rosalia. "Kill Elazar. Grab a defensor or two to find out where our missing people are. Other than that"—her voice twisted into her usual giddiness—"have fun."

The raiders grunted their agreement across the deck; a few made soft chirps of excitement.

Fun? Lu raised her eyebrows at Nayeli, who gave a sympathetic sigh.

Around their boat, the two others flowed at the same pace, one Grozdan, one Tuncian, waves shushing against the bows and bodies crouched, waiting.

Lu didn't know where Kari had ended up, if her mother would join the fight or be one of those chosen to assassinate Elazar himself. Regret spiked in Lu's chest, metallic and demanding, but she turned away to watch as the city center's docks drew closer.

Two Argridian defensors stood at the end of the closest dock.

"Hold," one called, "in the name of—"

A gunshot. One of the defensors tumbled into the water with a splash.

Lu jolted, catching herself with a palm flat on the deck. But this was war, wasn't it? This was what she had wanted. Blood. Death. To watch defensors suffer as she had suffered.

"Gods," Nayeli whispered.

The other soldier sprinted up the planks, shouting, "Attack! Raiders!"

Rosalia was all wicked grins and flashing eyes. She holstered her smoking pistol as her boat bumped the dock. "You heard the man! Attack!"

21

DOZENS OF GROZDAN and Tuncian raiders flooded the docks. Some didn't even wait for their boats to land—they dove into the river, sloshing to the shore with swords and pistols ready.

Lu didn't move. The raiders emptied the deck of her boat, one remaining to watch the vessel until their departure.

Nayeli's grip on the Hemlight pinched tighter. "What's our plan?"

Lu frowned at her. "Our plan?"

"Yeah. Are we gonna just listen to Rosalia? Grab some random defensor and hope they know where Cansu is? Tell me you've come up with something better."

Lu's mouth dropped open. She hadn't come up with anything better. Her skin crawled with the remnants of her bloodlust, half of her still clinging to it, half of her terrified.

She wanted to use her newfound speed. She wanted to

race into the battle, expel the horror Argrid had heaped on her for years.

She wanted to hide on this boat and wait for Kari to come find her.

A cry came from the square. A child screamed.

"We should—" Lu swallowed. "I don't—"

Gunshots peppered the air in a sickening volley. Lu couldn't get her mind to think past it—this was what she had wanted. Why couldn't she move?

"Damn it, Lu!" Nayeli launched up and leaped onto the dock. Lu followed, her heart fluttering at a hum in her chest. Her grip slipped on her pistol and she righted herself. She needed to focus. To survive. To keep some semblance of control on this war.

The city center was a wide square of gray stone rimmed by sweeping, graceful buildings. Citizens had packed it as tightly as they had at the assembly in Fort Chastity, and they ran and screamed now, ducking into buildings or hiding behind market stalls.

A platform stood at the far end in front of a squat stone building. A weather-beaten carving sat on top, telling why this structure's design contrasted: it was a mission. An Argridian Church outpost that the citizens of Port Fausta had not torn down after the revolution, likely for the same reason the Tuncians had left Fort Chastity: a reminder of Argrid's truth.

The thought spiked Lu's fury again.

Defensors formed a tight knot as they fled the platform for the mission's open doors. Elazar. They were covering him. And likely Tom, Milo—

She could reach that group before any of the defensors so much as breathed. But could she break their lines and get to Elazar? She needed an opening.

"There!" Lu shouted. "Elazar—there!"

Across the square, a face whipped toward Lu's cry. Kari. She was with a group of Tuncians, and at Lu's prodding, she sent them racing toward Elazar's protective guard.

From the north, an Emerdian group broke through the streets. Nate, supplemented by Powersage, bellowed a war cry, ripped a shutter off a building, and hurled it at a defensor. The corner impaled the man's chest, eliciting shrieks from cowering families.

The Emerdians dove into the fight, slicing and firing and tearing at the defensors with no care for the innocents among them. Rosalia was the same, leaping high, hovering, getting off better-aimed shots and *giggling* as citizens, her citizens, looked on in horror.

One, a little boy, clung to his mother's skirts, tears streaming down his face.

"What are they doing?" Lu asked no one in particular. "It's Elazar! *Get him!*"

Nayeli, next to her, shook her head. "We shouldn't have trusted them. They don't care about this war. They care about themselves."

Elazar and his knot of defensors vanished into the mission, the doors slamming tight. They would have the upper hand in defense now.

Nate ripped apart a market stall and dragged a man and woman out of their hiding place.

"Help!" the man screamed. "Help—defensors! Pious God, help us—"

Pierce cocked a pistol. "The Pious God can't help you, Argridian sympathizer." He aimed at the people his husband restrained. "Elazar's got our raiders stashed away. Where are they?"

"Stop!" The Incris propelled Lu across the space. Pierce didn't have time to fight her—she knocked the pistol from his grip. He swung on her, Nate jolting forward and releasing the man and woman, who scrambled away.

Lu, gasping, looked from Nate to Pierce as the screams and fighting intensified. Somewhere, Kari shouted at raiders to break into the mission; innocents cried for the Pious God, begging him to save them from the *evil raiders*; defensors fought and pistols fired and Lu swore she could feel Elazar in the mission, smiling.

The raiders were confirming everything Elazar claimed about them.

For all his insanity, Elazar knew this island well. This was the battle Nate, Pierce, and Rosalia would have fought regardless of their magic abilities. They would have been a mess of violence and disorganization; they would have tossed goals aside and given in to pride and bloodlust. Elazar had planned for it.

And Lu had given a powerful weapon to criminals.

Guilt had been on her shoulders for more than half her life. Guilt from being unable to stop the war, from killing people, from contributing to the horror that warped their world. It had been her fuel every waking moment, compelling her to mend the wounds she had inflicted.

She had caused so many horrors. It was her fault—so she would fix everything.

But in that moment, Lu realized it *wasn't* her fault. People like Elazar, Milo, and Tom, even Rosalia, Nate, and Pierce—they were the ones who would do horrible things no matter what. Whether Lu agreed to help them or not, the awful acts they planned would occur. She was a tool, but she wasn't at fault.

The world was bigger than her. One girl could not break it. But she could improve it.

Admitting that unraveled the layers of tension Lu had built, a delicate weave she had constructed to keep herself emotionless and determined. She didn't want to be emotionless, she didn't want to be a monster or a murderer or a soldier or any of the things she was. That childlike desire overshadowed everything else in a rush of undeniable need.

"Stop," she repeated, unwilling to let go of Pierce's arm, even as he bucked. "Look around! These villagers are afraid of you! This is wrong—"

"*Argrid* is wrong." Rosalia shot up on Lu's other side. "Argrid is the enemy. This? This is the way we'll stop them. If you're not with us, you're in the way."

"And we don't need you, sweetheart," Pierce snapped. "Not anymore. Tuncian spices, Emerdian brickwork, Visjorn bear blood—I'm sure we can find someone else who can figure out the formula for permanent magic again, now that we know it's possible."

"Elazar," Lu said. "He went into the mission. That is where you should go."

"We don't have time for this." Nate shoved Lu back from Pierce. His supplemented strength slammed her into Nayeli, hard enough to knock the breath from her lungs.

A gun clicked. "Do not threaten my daughter," Kari said.

Lu spun to see Kari, gun aimed. But her relief lasted for only one full inhale.

A fog of chokingly thick smoke crashed over the area. Lu lost sight of the raider Heads, Nayeli, her mother. Everything was gray and blurred, stinging her eyes and burning her nose.

"Magic!" someone cried. "The raiders—they're using Rhodofume!"

Rhodofume, pods that released a smoke screen.

People coughed and shouted, bodies jostled in the gray-yellow cloud, and through it, Lu heard a staggered *pop, pop, pop*. More Rhodofume pods; more smoke, more and more.

Lu almost used her speed to break free of the smoke, but

what would she run into? A building? A sword? It was all she could do to inhale. She staggered, turned—

A hand clamped her arm. Her chest simultaneously soothed with relief—Kari?—and vibrated in a steady hum of unease.

A face leaned through the smoke, a scarf looping across the person's mouth and nose.

His eyes were clear. And Lu knew him.

She yanked down, hard, at the same moment she bolted away. The combination of her speed and movement broke Milo's hold on her, and she ran with every bit of Incris in her.

He would not get her, not again—

She smacked into something. Some*one*. A cry, desperate hands moving through the fog until a touch on her cheek, a face through the stinging grayness.

"Adeluna?" Kari coughed into her arm. "Adeluna— what—"

A bellowing laugh broke over the stunted cries. All gunshots stopped; swords ceased to clash. The battle had paused—an effective, blinding trick by Argrid.

Lu grabbed her mother's shoulders, horror racing through her as the laugh came again.

"Adeluna Andreu," Milo called. He was close, too close. "Are you using magic plants in this battle? Or have you been busy in our time apart, fulfilling the Pious God's will for you to create permanent magic?"

Kari shoved Lu behind her, bracing herself as a shield in the dense grayness. "General Ibarra," she shouted, "stand down. Tell your king to—"

"I hardly think you are in any position to make demands, Councilmember Andreu. Or, no, it's Senior Councilmember Andreu, isn't it? So difficult remembering whether you or your husband is the one in charge."

Kari's hands tightened on Lu's wrists. A long, aching moment, and when her voice came again, it was as piercing as ever. "If Tomás is here, I will speak with him."

"Your husband won't be joining us. A shame, but he had to prove his loyalty elsewhere." Milo chuckled. His voice stayed the same distance away but circled them.

Tom wasn't here? Was Teo? Oily dread slipped between Lu's fingers.

A flash came from Lu's right. The spark of Hemlight lit the fog enough for Lu to see Nayeli and Rosalia, the two of them flopping back-to-back in defense as Rhodofume pods continued to break around them.

"I admit," Milo continued, "I am surprised it took you so long to learn the extent of your husband's betrayal. That while he was bedding you, he was also in bed with Argrid."

"Adeluna," Kari whispered over her shoulder. "He's stalling. Get to the mission."

Lu hardened even more. "What? No—I'm not leaving you!"

A smile touched what little of Kari's face Lu could see. "I can handle General Ibarra. Wait until his voice is in front of me. You have Hemlight, don't you? Use it as Nayeli did—light a way, use your Incris to run to the mission. Stop Elazar. That is the goal."

"Your husband reported every action of yours to our king," Milo said. "But do you know everything he did? Every order he obeyed?"

"Adeluna," Kari chastised.

Lu scrambled for Hemlight in her pouches. She found a bundle, then turned, putting her back to her mother's.

Deep in Lu's heart, she had wanted this since she was twelve years old. For her parents to stand against Milo for her, fight this battle for her, protect her.

Tom wouldn't. He would put both hands on her back and push her closer to Milo—but Kari would throw herself in front of Lu, a shield of loyalty and honor.

"Do you know everything he let happen to your daughter that night the war ended?" The sneer in Milo's voice was debilitating. Lu's body went cold. "Your husband told us how to find the safe house, how many people would be stationed there—and that, if we did not uncover the war secrets we sought, we would find a child. My defensors were quite at a loss as to what to do with such a pretty little girl."

The Rhodofume's fog crept into Lu's mind. It weighted her limbs, blurred her thoughts.

She had never told Kari what Milo had done to her. She wasn't even sure Kari knew that Milo had been there. The truth was unbearable, and Lu had known the horror that she would see on her parents' faces would be too potent to withstand.

Behind her, Kari was as solid and motionless as stone. She made a noise Lu had never heard from her—a sob, a cry, a growl all in one.

Lu gasped, the smoke filling her lungs with grit.

"But you both are to blame." Milo didn't stop. Wouldn't, not until everyone was broken at his feet—until Kari the Wave was just as destroyed as Lu. "Your husband didn't tell me that it was his child, merely that she was observant and would give up the secrets she had learned from the revolutionaries. But Pious God above, she did not break. I know now—it was because of you, wasn't it, Kari?"

Lu swayed. The Hemlight dropped from her fingers.

At her back, Kari's shoulders heaved. "Adeluna," came her rasping voice. She sounded in pain. "Go. You wanted . . . you wanted to be here. Go get Elazar."

Milo's voice was directly ahead of Kari now. "You made her too strong for her own good. So you see, both you and your husband are to blame for what I had to do to your daughter that night. She still has scars from me—I know. I've seen them."

Kari screamed as though her soul had been cleaved out of her chest.

Her mother was unbreakable, a commander, an impassable wall. And that night in the safe house, Lu had imagined Kari in this situation, tortured by an enemy, and had known Kari would never yield. The very idea of her mother breaking was unfathomable.

But in that scream, Lu could hear Kari's heart fracturing.

Milo had hurt her, too. Milo had made her mother wail like that.

Kari took a step forward and Lu spun with her, knowing that even if she didn't have Incris in her body, she still would have moved faster than candlelight. She knocked her mother to the ground, and Kari fell with a cry in the disorienting fog, but Lu was gone, footfall after footfall, breaths hoarse in her ears.

Tears tumbled down Lu's cheeks, a sob stinging her throat as much as the Rhodofume fog. She ran. She ran hard and straight, a knife out in one hand.

It happened in a blink. To Lu, the seconds stretched out, her speed slowing the fogged world around her to the single point where she had last heard Milo's voice.

He appeared through the Rhodofume. And she was upon him.

Her knife was in his stomach.

Milo jolted with surprise. The scarf around his face slipped, showing his grimace as he looked down at the hilt of her dagger in his gut.

"Bitch," Milo rasped. He grabbed her arm. "You bitch."

They had been here before. Lu had survived.

Milo would not.

She had wanted blood from this fight. Blood she got.

Lu twisted the knife in. Up. His blood poured over her hand, his fingers losing traction on her wrist. Every gush fed the darkness in Lu's soul, the part of her that wanted to cry out in joy at this man's life oozing between her fingers.

Milo choked. Blood spurted down his chin.

Around them, the Rhodofume fog was dissipating. Lu felt other presences nearby—Kari, a hand on her back; Nayeli, calling out to her—but this moment created its own fog.

Tom had spoken of fate to her once before, fate that she had killed for him.

This was fate. That she had used permanent magic to kill Milo.

His grip on her wrist tightened again. She sucked in a breath, her first sense of fear—her first sense of anything, truly, she was hollow and empty and a soldier—

"Kill me. Doesn't . . . matter," he sneered. "Still—have—Port Mesi-Teab."

Lu lost all feeling in her body. She yanked back, freeing her dagger, and Milo sank to the ground at her feet.

Beyond him, the defensors were in retreat. Had the Emerdian, Grozdan, and Tuncian raiders truly overpowered them? Battered raiders chased the defensors down the twisting streets and alleys; the defensors who had been on the rooftops, hurling Rhodofume pods, were the only ones left to look down and see.

"They killed the general!" they cried. "The raiders murdered our general!"

The defensors' accusations stoked the remaining Port Fausta citizens. Weeping grew, savage screams for safety, and Lu reveled in it.

Let them weep, part of her thought. *Let them know what I am capable of.*

But Lu looked down at her scarlet fingers, hearing the words Milo had left in her mind. *Port Mesi-Teab.*

"Port Mesi-Teab?" Nayeli echoed, somewhere to Lu's right.

"We don't know he meant anything by that," Kari tried. She put a hand on Lu's back. "Adeluna—are you all right? Do you—"

"Why'd he mention Port Mesi-Teab at all?" demanded Nayeli. "He got Cansu to submit to him—what if she told him stuff about the sanctuary? Its secrets?"

"He was desperate." Kari came to stand in front of Lu, between her and Milo's body.

Milo was dead. Dead at Lu's feet. Dead by Lu's hand.

"Adeluna. Look at me."

Lu lifted her eyes. When they met Kari's, she braced herself to unravel, but all that came was a statement, old and weathered and as achingly empty as her soul.

"I don't want to do this anymore," Lu whispered.

Milo was dead. She had killed him. She had murdered again. She was a soldier *again*. The Incris in her body, if it truly was permanent, had made her even more lethal, a better version of what Tom had helped her become: an assassin-spy, blood on her hands, her heart in tatters. Which war was this? Whose blood was that? This was her life, a cycle of hatred and fighting.

Kari's lips flattened into a line, the pinch of holding back tears, or a scream, or an argument. All she said was an echo of her promise outside Fatemah's office. "You don't have to, sweetheart. You can be done."

Rosalia came running across the square. "Elazar escaped! He waited until we'd put in a good fight, lost half a dozen raiders, and he slipped out the back door of the mission."

"He left?" Nayeli whipped on her. "Why'd he wait at all then?"

Lu staggered, seeing a scene from a lifetime ago, when she had been twelve, the night the revolution ended. Two little girls huddled in a revolution safe house, a handful of people watching over them, because who even knew where they were? The rest of the revolutionaries gone, off on a mission to take an Argridian storehouse.

That tip had been a lie to empty the safe house. Argrid had attacked.

Tom had arranged all of it.

"We need to leave," Lu said. She was sick, aching deep in her soul. "We have to get back to Port Mesi-Teab. *Now.*"

22

SILENCE CHOKED THE sanctuary after the raiders moved out. It sounded more intense than the shouting, as though every passing second was building to an explosion. With so many of the raiders gone, would the refugees retaliate like the man with the Variegated Holly bomb?

Not that Vex could bring himself to care. Whatever disaster Fatemah would have to deal with, let her drown in it. He'd put up with her mistreatment of Nayeli, her views on who deserved help and who didn't, for way too long. He should've stood up to her years ago.

Vex grimaced. Guilt, not Shaking Sickness, would kill him. Was this how Lu felt? Why she'd apologized to him after they'd saved her from the prison?

She'd come back. Nayeli too. They'd saunter into the sanctuary with Cansu and Teo, and Vex'd grovel until they forgave him. Things would go back to normal. They had to.

Except now Lu had taken what was apparently permanent magic. How would that change her? Could Vex bring her back from whatever it had made her?

Ben paced the length of his cell. Gunnar sat on the floor, watching him. Jakes stayed on the opposite side of the cell from Vex as though shoved away from him by some invisible force.

Vex curled in on himself, sulking, chin to his knees. Every time a tremor grabbed him, he sank his teeth into his tongue.

Whether Ben could heal him didn't matter. If Lu didn't come back . . . not a whole lot else would matter to Vex. He wouldn't survive losing her twice.

He winced. He couldn't think like that. The island was at war; Lu and Nayeli were gone, fighting that very war; people were suffering, dying, imprisoned and burned—and then there was Vex. The useless raider with Shaking Sickness who cared only about the people closest to him.

He was worse than a coward. He barely even existed.

A shout echoed through the barred window in Vex and Jakes's cell. The four of them pulled to attention as the raider guarding them at the end of the hall vanished outside.

Jakes crossed to the window, frowning.

"Too soon for them to return," Gunnar noted.

Vex slammed his head back against the wall. "Great. The refugees are rising up?"

Jakes grabbed the window's bars. A pause, and his mouth dropped open.

The shouting outside broke on a noise Vex knew too well—a gunshot. Another.

Screams, then. Howls of terror.

"The refugees aren't attacking." Jakes didn't move away from the window. "They're shouting at Argrid. At defensors."

***

Ben's arms dropped, immobile, at his sides.

"Defensors?" Vex was the one who questioned Jakes. "What? No way—the Tuncians keep this place locked down. Argrid couldn't have—"

But they had expanded the perimeter. They had stretched their raiders thin between patrol and the battle. Elazar would have heard of them stationed here, a haven of raiders.

And he had Cansu submissive to him now.

Gunnar shot up. "Elazar lured everyone away."

Ben nodded, numb. "A trap."

How had he not foreseen that?

Vex pushed to his feet. Ben watched him falter, clinging to the wall with a desperate, aching look from Gunnar to Ben.

"I can speak to them," Ben said.

Gunnar's face flared red. "Benat—"

"Help me get out of here. I need to get to whoever is leading the charge. I can—"

A wave of gunshots broke over a high-pitched shriek.

The door to this hall of cells banged open, and a cry came from their guard.

Ben didn't have long to reflect on the senseless death—two defensors stormed the hall, weapons out, taking stock of the place and the prisoners.

One smiled. "Príncipe Herexe," he said to Ben, mocking.

Gunnar dove in front of Ben, flames alive on his arms. Ben put his hands up, sweat dripping down his spine in response to the heat and the panic and the look of feverish delight on that defensor's face.

"Defensors!" Jakes yanked on his bars. "Defensors—free me. These heathens took me prisoner. I have secrets about them that the Eminence King will want to know."

Ben shouldn't have been surprised, but a part of him seized. Was Jakes lying? Did it matter?

The defensors—they must have gotten the keys from the dead guard—unlocked Jakes and Vex's cell. Vex stayed against the wall, but he was a prisoner of the raiders, too, and the defensors didn't recognize him—they ignored him.

"What about the prince?" one defensor asked. He cocked a pistol at his thigh but didn't take aim, and Gunnar's fire rose hotter.

"He is useless." Jakes stayed the defensor's wrist. "The raiders were considering killing him. They will now, especially after this attack. The Eminence King will benefit from raiders executing his son."

Ben's heart gave one aching thud when the defensor

grinned at him. It was not untrue, and if Argrid was attacking, then yes, Fatemah would kill him.

"True. Praise the Pious God," the defensor said, and handed Jakes the loaded pistol.

He left with his comrade. Jakes lingered until their footsteps faded.

Before Ben could shout any of the blame he wanted to, Jakes pressed against the bars.

But he faced Gunnar. "Keep him here," he said. "If Ben shows himself out there, whoever is leading this attack will kill him. Elazar knows he doesn't need him anymore—he needs Adeluna. Ben is too much a figurehead. His very existence is a threat to Elazar now. Keep him *here*."

Ben balked. "Like hell! Jakes—"

"I'm not the monster you think I am, Ben." Jakes gave a sad smile. "I'm sorry I couldn't prove that to you. But when you are king, I hope you can forgive me for everything I did to get you the throne."

Jakes sprinted away.

"Jakes!" Ben rattled the bars. "JAKES!"

His voice broke in the lack of response. Gunshots came from the sanctuary, screaming and desperate pleading for help.

Ben spun on Gunnar. "Get us out."

Gunnar didn't move.

Ben wavered. "Gunnar. Please—"

"He's right." It came from Vex, who stood in the hall

now, facing the open door and the escalating fight beyond.

"Vex, don't go out there." Ben's words came too fast, high-pitched and terrified. "Wait for me—Gunnar, get me out of here!"

Gunnar stared at the floor, his eyes closing.

"I'll come get you when it's over," Vex told Ben. There was something absent in his eye, a vacancy that terrified Ben to his soul.

Over the years, Ben had captured so many heretics who had looked at him like that. Like they were reconciled to their death.

"Paxben." Ben's voice cracked. "Irmán."

Vex half ran, half tripped up the hall, his body shaking so hard Ben wondered if he wouldn't collapse. But he vanished from sight.

"Paxben!" Ben screamed. "Gunnar—you can't listen to them. You're helping *me*, aren't you?"

Gunnar shot a glare at him, his blue eyes piercing through bloodshot veins. "If you go out there, they will kill you."

Gunshots intensified, defensors hooted victory, people screamed and hurt because of Ben's countrymen.

"You wanted to break me out earlier, to go with Lu and fight Elazar," Ben said. "How is this different?"

"Jakes—coward that he is, he is also right. Whoever is leading this attack is not Elazar. Whoever it is, they will see you, and they will kill you. Your role will be in facing your father, if it comes to that."

Reality settled the more Gunnar spoke, warm like his fire, searing with each word.

He wouldn't break the door open for Ben. Vex was gone, the rest of the sanctuary was under attack—and Ben would be trapped in this cell.

"Too many times in my life, I've been unable to stop people I loved from dying," Ben said, one breath away from disintegrating. "Don't do this to me again."

"I left the Mechtlands because I was tired of people *I* cared about getting hurt," Gunnar snapped. "Don't do this to *me*. I won't watch your own people kill you."

"If you care about me"—Ben's body lightened, dizzying, and he fought past it with a shake of his head—"you will see that this *is* my life. Danger. War. Leading."

"Yes. *Leading*. Argrid needs you to lead. You are too important to lose on a suicide mission." Gunnar leaned against the wall, arms folded.

Ben bit the inside of his cheek, his heart rupturing in a flurry of shards. "This oath between us—Visjorn lofta blo—I thought it made us equals. I didn't think it would let you make decisions for me."

Gunnar wouldn't look at him.

Ben stepped back and tried to break the lock himself. It was thick, well made, and he kicked it three times before he fell to the floor with a cry.

The vial of permanent magic Lu had given him dug against his hip. He touched it, desperation blinding him to the consequences for one full breath. Would it make him strong enough to break out? Would it make him powerful enough to stop the battle outside?

Argrid hated him. How would they react to a king imbued with permanent magic? Would their future aversion to him be worth stopping this one battle?

It wouldn't stop just this battle, though. It would stop the whole of the war. Ben could march up to his father and defeat him with whatever powers this magic gave him.

Knowing that, knowing the possibility in this vial, Elazar wouldn't hesitate to drink it.

Which made Ben rip his hand away from his pocket.

Arms on his knees, he looked at Gunnar, wanting to hurl the vial at him and scream, *Look what you are making me consider!*

"I don't know if I'll be able to forgive you for this," Ben said.

"As long as you are alive to hate me," Gunnar replied, and they fell silent.

�֍✖֍

Vex trailed Jakes and the defensors through the hall. He had to sidestep the Tuncian raider who'd been guarding them, slumped over the doorstep, blood rippling out of his unmoving body.

After a dry heave, Vex steeled himself. What was his plan? To fight? Lot of help he'd be, barely able to stand on his own—

He got outside. It didn't look like they were under attack from here. The roads around this building were empty, no defensors, no raiders. Vex hobbled on, pulled by the shouting and crash of fighting, the pop of pistols sounding innocent from far away. It could've been a child bouncing a ball, or cooking pots banging, or—

Someone darted around a corner. Vex froze—but it was Edda, a pistol in each hand, her face streaked with sweat.

"Vex!" she shouted. "What the hell are you doing out of your cell? You were safe there!"

Vex winced. Safe and useless. "I want to help. What's happening?"

She relented. "Defensors, everywhere," she said, nodding at the buildings. "Coming in through the tenements. Someone told them how to get here."

Vex's body went cold. The look on Edda's face said what he thought: Cansu.

"Can you fight?" Edda twisted a pistol toward him.

Vex swayed and took it. Hell yes, he would fight. Screw his body. Screw this *pain.*

Vex hobbled forward. Edda fell in beside him, keeping pace with Vex's slow steps. They turned a corner that took them to the sanctuary's outer perimeter—and found chaos.

Argridian defensors streamed into the sanctuary, doors thrown wide and bodies shoving through in the ivory-and-blue uniforms that made Vex's heart sink. The people in the sanctuary ran and screamed, but there was no escape—incoming soldiers blocked every exit.

Vex's first thought was *They want something.* Lu or Ben-Elazar had sent his soldiers here to reclaim his prisoners. But in the few seconds Vex stood against Edda, watching the defensors shoot and stab and take down innocents—not just raiders, but people who cowered in cottages and screamed as soldiers dragged them out—he realized what this was.

A massacre.

Edda spun around, barring her arm across Vex. "Get back! We need higher—"

Vex turned. Four buildings behind them, defensors ran onto the road. Edda cursed and yanked him to the side, behind an overturned cart. Vex dropped to the dusty road, clinging to his pistol, arms shaking.

Back up the street, toward the bulk of fighting where defensors poured into the sanctuary, refugees screamed. Alongside it came Fatemah's voice: "You destroy my home—you monsters!"

Defensors forced her to her knees in the middle of the road.

"Commander Andreu," one defensor said, "she is the leader of these raider vermin. What example should we make of her?"

A man approached Fatemah, the defensors. Tall, with the russet skin and sharp features of Argrid.

Vex's stomach shriveled up. Commander Andreu. Lu's father?

He gripped the pistol tighter. "Edda—oh god—"

Tomás Andreu nodded. He crooked two fingers and someone stepped up beside him: Ingvar Pilkvist, the Head of the Mecht syndicate.

"Monsters!" Fatemah wailed again. She started screaming in Thuti, yelling and yelling—

Ingvar pointed a gun at her and pulled the trigger.

Fatemah's body sank to the ground.

Her death—execution—consumed Vex's senses so much that he didn't notice the smaller figure behind Tom until it rocked back and *screamed*.

Tom didn't react. He turned. "Stop fighting it. I know it's in you—stop fighting what the Pious God wants for you."

Vex wilted. Shriveled up and died right there.

Teo.

Teo. He'd seen Fatemah get shot. He was here, in the middle of a massacre, tears streaking his face and his mouth open in a violent, helpless sob.

Vex shoved to his feet, every nerve vibrating like a strummed string. "Teo!"

Tom whipped his head toward the call. Ingvar, too; and the defensors; and Teo. Teo looked and saw Vex, Edda—he sobbed again.

But he didn't run to them. He didn't even try.

"Get them!" Tom ordered.

The defensors obeyed, swarming around them in a circle of raised weapons. The overturned cart was at their back. Trapped.

Edda shot to her feet. Teo screeched, and Vex fought to lurch for him.

"Damn it, Vex!" Edda snapped. "We can't—"

The cock of a pistol. Vex went rigid, muscle by shaking muscle.

Ingvar wasn't pointing a gun at Edda or Vex. He was aiming at Teo.

Tom hissed. "Pilkvist, *stand down*—"

But Ingvar didn't react. Next to Ingvar, Tom growled and faced Vex.

"My orders are to rid this place of its infestation—even you, our king's nephew. I may kill you, or I may leave you maimed. The choice is yours."

"Go to hell," Vex barked.

Tom lifted his eyes to the sanctuary, surveying the tenements as he might a complicated art piece. "Do you know how we found this place? The people of this city told us— of their own free will. They came to the Argridian soldiers and spoke of raiders forcing them to live under their rule. Your own people have turned on you. That, believe me, is the definition of hell: betrayal." Tom's focus lowered to Vex. "It will comfort you to know that I take no pleasure in this bloody work, but my king demands it. Now, where is my daughter?"

In the silence after his question, each pop of a gunshot beat into Vex's soul. People were dying around him. People he'd known for years.

"Lu will stop you."

Vex whipped his head back down to Teo, who glared at Tom and Ingvar. God, brave kid.

"Lu'll hurt you for what you're doing," he said.

Tom snapped at Ingvar, who lowered his pistol. Vex gawked until he realized why—more defensors were coming in, circling them. Edda's pistol was out of ammunition. They had only Vex's.

Edda, Vex—they were all going to die. Like Fatemah.

Why was Teo even here? What the hell was Tom getting out of him?

One defensor rushed forward and handed something to Tom. "We found this in a shack nearby. One of our own tried to keep it for himself—said it couldn't fall into Elazar's hands."

Tom took it, staring at a vial, the mixture within.

A scuffle broke out among the ranks of the defensors. Jakes, pinned by two of his comrades, tried to break free, to get to Tom.

"This is Adeluna's potion?" Tom asked.

"Give that to me!" Jakes demanded. His eyes were wide, his breathing unsteady. "Now."

Tom's lips formed a tight line. "My daughter isn't here. I know her—she would have shown herself by now. But she was here." He pocketed the vial. "The Eminence King will be pleased, defensor. You should be as well."

"No." Jakes trembled. "No, don't give it to him, do not give it to him—"

A defensor slammed the hilt of a knife into the back of Jakes's head. Jakes dropped, limp, to the ground. Teo chirped and jolted but held strong, tears tumbling down his cheeks.

Tom closed his eyes and rubbed the skin over his nose, gathering himself, before he looked down at Teo with a smile, gentle and fatherly, and Vex understood why Lu had believed this man her whole life. "You know why I brought you here. The Pious God has blessed you—and you are ready, I know you are. Give in. The strength is inside you. Teo, give in."

What the hell? "Don't talk to him," Vex spat, the hair on the back of his neck rising. "You don't have any right to—"

Teo shook his head, sobbed again. "No. No, I can't." He whipped a look at Tom that wasn't glare or hatred or defiance—it was regret. "I'm sorry."

Vex blanched. Tom wanted to get something out of Teo—by bringing him to a battle?

Tom sighed again. He put his hand on Teo's head and nodded at Ingvar. "End this."

Ingvar stepped toward Edda and Vex, his face glistening with sweat.

Teo wailed at the same moment Edda grabbed Vex's unused pistol and leaped upright.

Blood trickled down her face from a cut along her eyebrow. "You will leave," she stated, aiming at Ingvar. "Without the boy."

Ingvar looked at her. Vex had seen eyes like that only on a dead man.

Cansu is like this now, wherever she is. Empty.

"Tell my daughter if she wants Teo"—Tom spoke to the ground—"she will come to me. She will surrender to Elazar. Pilkvist, defensors—"

Edda shouted. Her finger tensed on the trigger, and Vex blinked, knowing she'd pull it, knowing Ingvar would drop and—then what? Dozens of defensors still stood around them.

But Ingvar moved. He was an arm's length from Edda—Vex knew, because it was the exact distance for a disarming technique Edda had tried to teach him. Grab the barrel of the gun, twist, break the attacker's index finger, and spin the pistol back on them. Vex had been hopeless at learning it, but he'd seen Edda do it flawlessly time and again.

She knew that move. She'd know to defend it.

Ingvar grabbed the barrel and snapped the gun to the side. Edda went with it, twisting to avoid her finger breaking—but it put her against Ingvar.

Who had his own gun out, against his hip, cocked and ready.

The gun fired. The vibration created a sinkhole in Vex's chest.

Defensors moved, shoving Vex back. He flailed, but there were too many hands—he bucked, swung his elbow into one defensor's face with a satisfying crunch.

A shudder ran through Edda. She dropped to her knees.

Vex's mouth opened on a long, croaking plea. "EDDA!"

Teo screamed. "No! No!"

A defensor hefted Teo over his shoulder and marched up the road behind Tom. Ingvar followed, no emotion, no reaction at all.

Edda pitched to the side and hit the road with a heavy thump. Vex kicked the dirt, but he was shaking again, every part of him, goddamn it, *goddamn it*.

A circle of wine-dark red spilled out of her, across the ground. She wasn't moving. Not to breathe. Not to wince or look back at Vex with that frustrated scowl she wore so well.

They'd been talking moments ago. *Seconds* ago. They'd been sailing all over Grace Loray. They'd been two broken hearts released by the Church, trying to survive, and Vex wouldn't have, he wouldn't have made it a month on this island without her.

Vex pressed his foot for leverage against the soldiers holding him. He got halfway up, fueled by fury and horror and Teo's cries.

Defensors kicked Edda as they marched over her body. Her body.

"Teo!" Vex screamed again. "Te—"

A thud echoed through his head. All Vex knew was the ground rising to meet his cheek, and darkness creating a warm, velvet cloak around him. Teo's screams faded and the cries of the sanctuary dissolved into blackness.

Digestive Death

Availability: moderately common

Location: peat deposits

Appearance: magenta leaves of the
Digestive plant

Method: come into contact with the oils
of the leaves in any way

Use: fatality in less than a minute

23

LU AND THE raider army left the center of Port Fausta in ruins. Two buildings were ablaze, the rest missing windows, doors, walls bashed in. People wept, families huddling together and casting furious looks at the raiders. Elazar's defensors—any who had survived—were gone. Only bodies remained, raiders and Argridian soldiers alike, sprawled in grotesque poses across the stones.

This had been a mistake. All of it. A bloody, costly mistake, and Lu relived every poor decision as she paced the bow of Rosalia's steamboat, a low, dull ache throbbing in her head.

She wanted to run back to Port Mesi-Teab. To use her Incris and traverse the island in a single step. But, equally, she shuddered at the knowledge that it was inside her. Only time would tell if the magic she had made was permanent, but at the very least, she had lengthened the effects—and it still felt like she'd lost this war.

Milo was dead thanks to permanent magic she had created.

She had to think that, over and over, to hold the truth in her mind. *Milo is dead.*

It didn't feel real. It didn't feel like a victory. It didn't feel like anything.

Nayeli sat on the railing, her eyes on the deck, and for the first time since they had met, Lu saw herself in her. The delirious, hysterical girl was gone, and all that remained was a shell, vacant eyes on the teak planks and hunched shoulders caving her body inward.

They came at Port Mesi-Teab from the east. Fort Chastity punctured the horizon, the roofs of buildings peeking into the twilight. Smoke spiraled up from chimneys—

Lu stopped in the middle of the deck. Around her, Rosalia's crew halted their activities, everyone going silent. There was far too much smoke, billowing funnels of it as they entered the waterways of the city.

People filled the streets, weeping, shouting for help. No—not help. Lu clamped her arms over her chest, listening to angry fathers and red-faced mothers screaming obscenities as their steamboat came into view.

"You destroyed our home!"

"Get out—get out, now!"

The same accusations that defensors had shouted at her

as she stood with Milo's blood on her hands. Martyrdom, blame, hatred.

Lu glanced at the raiders on Rosalia's boat. Why would anyone be mad at them? They had opened Port Mesi-Teab as a haven. They had fought against Elazar.

"You criminals!"

"Argrid was trying to save us from *you*! They'll be back—and you will pay!"

Lu staggered at the hatred that poured over them. The sobbing, the destruction from what had surely been an Argridian invasion—how had Elazar spun this attack? Had his defensors cried salvation as they stormed the streets, promising they were here to save the lost souls of the raiders? Had the defensors feigned a peaceful approach and turned to defense only after raiders struck the first blow?

Rosalia's steamboat bumped against the shore closest to the sanctuary. Lu leaped off, Nayeli behind her, panic shooting through Lu the moment her feet hit the dirt road. The speed-giving Incris coursed through her, and she ran.

The hidden entrances in the tenements were open. The raiders who had been standing guard were gone. The twisting halls were bare, the stomping of their feet echoing as Lu and Nayeli and a hodgepodge of raiders chased through the buildings.

Lu stumbled into the sanctuary, the sky burnished rose gold by the setting sun.

Bodies lay all around. Alive, dead, injured—it was difficult to tell, and Lu teetered forward, the world spinning.

Nayeli grabbed her arm—to steady Lu, to steady herself as she shouted, "Vex! Edda! Fatemah!"

More names pushed at Lu's throat. *Ben. Gunnar*—

Nayeli gave a startled cry and shot forward. Emerdian, Grozdan, and Tuncian raiders streamed into the sanctuary, shouting for their own people. But it was Nayeli who drew Lu's attention.

Vex sat on the side of a road, elbows on his knees, head bowed between his hands. Ben crouched next to him, his hand on Vex's bent shoulders; Gunnar paced ahead of them, cut back, stomped away, paced back again.

Nayeli dropped to the ground beside him. Vex didn't move but for the rise and fall of his shoulders. Ben was the one who looked at her, whispered something that made him drop his eyes.

Nayeli screamed. She shoved herself to her feet, hands in her hair, her body doubling over in her agony.

Lu stumbled forward, one step, another. She got close enough that Vex noticed her, and he jerked back to look up at her, his face showing a wash of horror, relief, and sorrow all at once.

Hands touched Lu's shoulders from behind. "Adeluna—"

Lu spun to face Kari. Tears stained her mother's cheeks, dirt and blood caked over her shirt and breeches.

"What—" Lu started to ask as Nayeli heaved a sob, or a growl, or just *pain*.

"Some refugees told the defensors how to get in."

The voice came from behind her. Brittle, broken.

Lu couldn't look at Vex. Her body refused to turn back.

"Everything Elazar did to Cansu—and it wasn't her." He sniffed. "Edda's dead. Fatemah, too. And—" He stopped. "Your father was here."

Lu choked, the back of her hand to her mouth.

"He wants you." Vex coughed on a sob and Lu finally found it in herself to look back down at him. "He had Teo. Here. He wanted to get you to surrender."

A hundred questions. A dozen accusations. But Lu couldn't speak.

Vex looked up, his face red and blotchy, his eye tear-glazed. His sorrow pinched in a frown of confusion. "He wanted something out of Teo too. I don't know. I don't— and Edda—"

Vex's eye cut to the side and he sobbed again. Lu followed his gaze to Edda. Brave, loyal Edda, lying in the shadows of a hut across the way.

Nayeli saw her, too. She fell to her knees, weeping.

All the world had gone to glass, crystalline and fragile. Lu didn't dare move to break it.

"He took one of your potions," came another voice. Lu didn't have the spare energy to be threatened by Jakes, standing free in the middle of the road. He rubbed the back of his head, wincing in pain.

Gunnar's shoulders tensed. "You have no right to be out here now—"

"Wait." Lu held up her hand and looked at Jakes. "What did you say? He took—"

Tom had gotten the vial of permanent magic she had left in the laboratory shack. She hadn't expected an attack, not here. She hadn't hidden it very well.

Elazar had both Teo and permanent magic now.

Lu buckled, falling to her hands and knees on the dirt road. Kari knelt beside her and placed a hand on her back. It did nothing to stanch the grief.

"Lu—I'm so sorry," Vex rasped. He leaned forward, an arm's length from her. "I'm so sorry. He was right here, and I let him go *again*. If I'd been stronger—god, Lu, I'm sorry—"

Vex's voice broke on a sob.

If Lu had worked harder on a cure for him instead of wasting time on permanent magic. If she'd stayed here instead of going after Elazar. If she had gone into the mission like Kari said instead of charging Milo and killing him.

If she'd done more or been more or *tried more*—

Lu shot forward and clamped her arms around Vex. He cried out in shock and relief and something like desperation—but he locked his arms around her in return, burying his face into her shoulder.

Lu had been afraid many times throughout her life. There was no name for what she felt now. Stronger than fear, more crippling than anger, she felt beyond herself, watching the monster of this loss rise and rise over her—

When its shadow darkened everything within her, Lu expected to dissolve. She expected to shove away from Vex and retreat back into that laboratory and do anything possible to make a weapon even stronger than permanent magic. She expected to claw for any defense possible.

Instead, she clung tighter to Vex.

"It isn't your fault," she told him. Told herself. "It isn't your fault."

❧❧❧

Two days after Argridian forces surrendered in the revolution on Grace Loray, Elazar had paraded through the streets of Deza, outfitted in the emerald, daffodil yellow, and dull gray robes of Grace Neus, the Grace of altruism. Ben had trailed behind him, watching the train of Elazar's robes brush dirt off the road.

Around them, Deza was in ruins.

No battle had ever touched Argridian soil, but the war had drained this country. They had never needed to divert funds to the military before. Money for city upkeep, maintenance, cleanliness, security—Argrid had sent every galle to Grace Loray, and what did they have to show for it?

Cobblestones were missing from the streets, gaping potholes that made for wrecked carriages and the abandoned

373

carcasses of horses with broken legs. Every city block had a designated place to burn diseased clothes, furniture, and bodies. Crude planks of wood barred closed storefronts. The air was rank with sweat, ash, and the sickly-sweet tartness of foul breath releasing illness into the pollution.

Elazar had turned his hands palm up to the sky. He walked and prayed, belting requests to the Pious God as he traipsed down road after road in Deza.

"Help us . . . forgive us . . . we are your servants . . . find us here . . ."

People had emerged from the ruins of this once-great city, pale, gaunt limbs slinking out of the shadows. They had terrified Ben, and he fought with every choking breath not to beg to return to the palace. Surely these bony, starved creatures weren't the proud Argridians who had once bartered in prolific international trade. Surely those sunken eyes, those chapped lips, did not belong to citizens who had stood outside the palace, blazing with pride, chanting *"Purify Grace Loray!"* each time the war took a dire turn.

Elazar prayed more loudly, begging the Pious God to forgive Argrid. Argrid had desecrated Grace Loray. They had murdered hundreds of people and refused to relent until every last Argridian resource had been ripped away.

"Forgive us for failing you, Our Righteous God," Elazar had bellowed instead. "Forgive us for losing Grace Loray. Forgive us for not fighting hard enough."

People staggered closer to Elazar's parade. Ben remembered the stark, sudden shift on their faces, a widening of those sunken eyes, a parting of those chapped lips.

This was the reason for their suffering. They had failed the Pious God, and he had punished them. They deserved this anguish—it made sense.

If they did better, if they fixed their failures, the Pious God would bless them.

The people lifted their hands. They wept.

"Forgive us for our failure," Elazar shouted. "Forgive us."

�֎֎֎

Ben realized, as he pushed to his feet in the Port Mesi-Teab sanctuary, that he had never been in a war. The fight to escape the prison had been a mad scramble for freedom with a clearly defined goal: *Get out. Leave this place.* And Deza after the revolution might have felt like being in a war zone, but the causes had been internal, the suffering self-inflicted.

But here. Standing on this dirt road in the sanctuary, a boot-print collage trailing in every direction, blood and ash and gunpowder painting sunbursts on the walls, people tending wounded with a distant look in their eyes, like they hadn't woken up from a dream—it all said *invasion*. It all said *an enemy was here*. It all said *we did not choose this*.

Ben took a step away from Vex and Lu, who still sat on the ground, holding each other. In a square ahead, Nayeli and a dozen other Tuncians wept, occasionally screaming to the sky.

Other people dragged blankets over bodies and knelt next to them, staring into the abyss of exhaustion and blankness. Kari talked with a few raiders, likely getting the details of what had happened, how Argrid had gotten in, who had betrayed the sanctuary.

A handful of people moved through the wreckage, sweeping shattered glass into piles, straightening overturned tables. Jakes was one of them, helping a man carry a body to the side of the road. The fact that he was still here, and had been knocked unconscious by defensors, had seemed to smooth any worry about Jakes's loyalties. A foolish mistake, but Ben was too exhausted to care, just like these people, who worked and straightened and cleaned.

Ben moved toward a nearby pile of rubble—it must have once been crates of produce. Now the piles of broken wood and smashed fruit spread across the road.

Ben bent, retrieving pieces of wood. The gnarled edges snagged his hands.

"Here, let me." Gunnar reached for the debris.

Ben recoiled.

"Benat," Gunnar said, low and tinged with hurt.

A correction waited on Ben's tongue. *Prince Benat.* It had always been his easiest buffer when Jakes angered him. *I am your prince. I am royalty. How dare you take liberties.*

But Gunnar wasn't his subject. The two of them were in this fight against Elazar together, an equal trade of services that Ben would repay by helping Gunnar bring peace to the Mechtlands later.

Ben had no shield against Gunnar. Silence was the only thing keeping a cap on the torrent of agony in his chest, a storm that he wasn't sure he had the strength to weather.

These people. This sanctuary.

He could have saved it. He could have stopped this. If he had just taken the vial of permanent magic, still in his pocket; if Gunnar had broken him out; if Jakes hadn't realized that Ben would get killed if he left that cell.

Could Ben truly have gotten Tomás Andreu to leave the sanctuary in peace before defensors killed him? No. But right now, Ben hated that both Gunnar and Jakes had been rational in a moment of chaos, while he himself had been so *irrational*.

Ben kicked the remaining rubble of the crates aside, his nose burning with the stench of smoke and death.

"I'm sorry," Gunnar whispered. Ben felt those blue eyes crest over him once, twice.

The dull thud of wood drew his attention down the road. There, a man righted a barrel and leaped onto it, his cheeks tearstained, his clothes darkened with blood likely not his own.

The man pointed at the sanctuary. No one in particular; either he didn't know Ben, Kari, and the raider Heads were nearby, or he didn't care.

"Elazar's defensors fled in retreat!" the man cried. Ben winced at the grief in his voice. "He tried to cleanse this place, to save us. Who would have thought a day would come when Argrid was trying to save us? But it has come, and we did nothing to help ourselves! We are still here, trapped under foul raider cruelty, forced to mourn loved ones who are dead by their hand! If we want peace, we have to take it. We cannot expect Argrid to save us alone."

Ben braced himself. Around him, other refugees gathered, stumbling away from the corpses of loved ones caught in the battle, the destruction of this place they had called home, or at least safe. They gathered at the feet of the man, staring up at him through teary eyes.

"Raiders did this!" the man screamed, raw and cleaving. "The raiders are criminals and murders, heathens of the worst sort. Elazar was right. He was—"

A knot of rage formed in Ben's stomach. *No.* Not again. It was happening here, too, this manic devotion Elazar inspired in people. Argrid had been under his influence for decades, and seeing it there still broke Ben's heart—but on Grace Loray? The one country in this world that had every cause to loathe Elazar? They were rallying *for* him now?

Ben's hands closed into fists. His rage welled higher, pressing against his throat. "No," he said through clenched teeth, and he took a step forward.

Gunnar was there, an arm across his chest. Ben redirected his rage. If Gunnar told him not to confront this man—if he held Ben back, *again*—

But Gunnar's face softened. "He was right," he said. "Elazar, in the village when he paraded us. Everything he said, he was right then, too. If I was as these people, on the brink of another war in my country, searching for blame and hope—"

"You believe my father?" Grayness wavered at the edges of Ben's vision.

Gunnar shook his head. "No. But I see how they do. Elazar speaks to their fears."

A question came in the pause. *And what have I spoken to?*

Gunnar's arm was still across Ben's chest, not restraining now—more like holding Ben upright.

A movement to Ben's right made his head snap around. Nate stomped up the road, face red and snarling, a gun already in one hand.

Ben lurched around Gunnar. "And what of the people Elazar burned?"

His words in Grace Lorayan brought silence over the gathering crowd. Even Nate stopped, his glare transferring from the man to Ben.

One panicked breath, and Ben kept his eyes on the man as though no one else was here.

When he opened his mouth again, he wasn't sure what he would say. Half of him still wanted to scream at this man—he had to be one of the betrayers who had led Argrid here. A wave of accusation flooded Ben's throat. *You're wrong! How can you not see? Everything you say is disgusting!*

But this man would shout the same right back, wouldn't he? *You're wrong, Prince Benat! How can you not see?*

This man, all these refugees, were so certain of their rightness that some of them had welcomed an army into this sanctuary. An army that had, less than a decade ago, burned people on this island.

Gunnar was right. Elazar had spoken to these people's fears and woven a tapestry of promises that gave them everything they wanted. But all Ben had done was blame them, and cower from them, and wait for them to see the error in their choices because *of course* they would see it, the wrongness was obvious.

It wasn't obvious, not to them. These people had treated Ben as an enemy from the moment he stepped into this sanctuary—and Ben had treated them as enemies for just as long.

"What of the people Elazar burned?" Ben repeated. He didn't move closer, didn't recoil, wasn't sure he was still connected to his body at all. "What about the people still missing? What about the magic Elazar has forbidden, the livelihoods he's taken from Grace Loray?"

"All necessary," the man snapped back. Some of the grief was gone from his tone, following Ben's own: an honest search for answers. "Evil has made this island sick. Its roots are deep—"

"Evil," Ben echoed. "What is evil?"

"Raiders!" The man punched a fist into the air. "We

know now—raiders! They brought these calamities upon us! They—"

"There are no raiders in Argrid," Ben cut in. "And my country has struggled with poverty and disease for years. Who do we have to blame?"

The man's mouth fell open.

Somewhere in the crowd, another voice spoke: "It was punishment, wasn't it? Elazar said the Pious God punished Argrid for not getting rid of raiders during the war!"

Renewed by this, the man punched the air again, but Ben didn't let him speak.

"If you purge this island of raiders," Ben started, "the Pious God will reward you?"

A chorus of agreement, as though Ben had stated some plan.

"Raiders bring poverty, disease, and danger to Grace Loray because they are evil." Ben had to shout to calm the intensity. It settled, but he held his voice high over the crowd. "The Pious God is purity and joy, the opposite of evil. Yet he punished Argrid with poverty and disease. You believe he will bless you for purging the raiders. If the Pious God is pure, why does he produce the same results as evil? How do you know he will deign to bless you—because Elazar promises you that he knows the Pious God's will? If Elazar knows the Pious God's will, why did he fail so spectacularly during the revolution?"

Silence. Nate, still among the people, wasn't watching

Ben anymore—he was looking at the crowd. Farther back, Kari, Rosalia, Lu, and Vex, even Jakes all watched with various mixes of confusion and wonder, hesitation and fear.

Beyond the crowd's lingering—permanent—states of grief and anger, a change came. A brightness behind their eyes spoke of realization, however small, however fragile. Something in what Ben said had startled them into awareness.

A few turned to their neighbors, whispering cautiously.

Ben felt himself move through the crowd. People parted for him, and in a breath, he was at the base of the man's barrel platform, looking up at this stranger.

And then Ben was kneeling.

"I apologize for Argrid," he said. He projected his voice beyond this man, for the whole of the crowd. For Grace Loray. For Argrid. "In my time on this island, I have seen how deeply Grace Loray believes. In the Pious God, yes; but also in the Tuncians' gods, Kek, Keket, Eshepri, and Fapsanti; the Visjorn spirit of the Mechts; the Grozdans' belief in glory. One thing I can thank my father for is teaching me the importance of belief, and you, Grace Loray, have such beautiful conviction. But Elazar manipulated you. I am sorry we made you so afraid."

The man on the barrel gasped, tears on his cheeks.

He stepped off the barrel, and Ben lost him in the press of people.

A hand scooped under his arm. Ben rose unsteadily to

his feet and turned to Lu, her eyes glazed. She gave him a timid smile.

At her side, Vex eyed the dirt. Lu squeezed Ben's arm.

"Thank you," she said, the gratitude weighted by years of pain.

Ben shrugged. Around them, the crowd was slowly breaking apart, many people talking to each other, most looking at Ben with strange wonder.

"I didn't think it would help," Lu whispered, putting words to the crowd's confusion, "hearing an apology. Hearing someone admit what Argrid did. But—thank you."

Ben's eyes flicked to the back of the crowd. Gunnar, watching him, shoulder resting on a building. "I was just honest," Ben said. He looked back at Lu. "Argrid hurt this island, and my father is capitalizing on it. I'm tired of arguing about blame or division—Argrid did terrible things. I will take responsibility for them. We will get better."

Lu withdrew her hand. She looked to the sky, a single tear sliding down her cheek.

"I'm tired of division, too," Vex said. "This doesn't work. You"—he waved at Lu—"making permanent magic by yourself. And you"—he waved at Ben—"trying to bear this whole war yourself. I really don't care what you two want to do next. I'll support you. *Both* of you, goddamn it. I'm done letting Elazar drive me away from the people I love."

Vex looked directly at Ben as he said that.

Ben had been newly thirteen, Paxben twelve for a few more weeks, the two of them lounging in the preparation room off the Grace Neus Cathedral's altar. Well, Paxben was lounging, his long limbs sprawled on a velvet couch; Ben recited his lines moments before he would swear his oath to the Inquisitors, to learn the ways of judging crimes by Church doctrine.

"I just realized something," Paxben had said, tipping his head over the arm of the couch to look at Ben upside down. "One day I'll have to swear an oath to you, won't I?"

Was there tension in Paxben's voice? Ben had stopped pacing and shrugged. "If you want to serve me when I'm king." He paused. "You will want to serve me, won't you?"

There had been talk of unrest lately. Traitors in Elazar's own household.

Paxben had smiled and rolled off the couch. He arranged himself on his knees before Ben and looked up, his face smooth and serious.

"I swear fealty to you, King Benat Gallego. Whenever that happens. I'm yours."

Ben closed the space between him and Vex now, clamping one arm around his back. Tears washed through him from a hundred sources, grief and worry and pain and relief.

A light hand fell on Ben's arm. Lu. She touched Vex too, and he huffed.

"Adeluna Andreu," Vex said, and opened his free side to her. She slid in, no hesitation in how she welcomed this awkward tangle of arms and shoulders and tears. Ben shared a look of amazement with Vex over her head, but Vex just smiled and bowed his face into Lu's hair.

Nothing had truly changed. The sanctuary was still in ruins. The raiders and their Heads were still volatile and disjointed. But somehow, standing there, holding his cousin and this girl who had come to matter so much to him, Ben felt as though things had shifted in their favor.

Or maybe he just felt himself relax for the first time in years.

"Touching," snapped a voice to Ben's left. He stiffened, feeling Vex and Lu do the same, and was the first to turn to face Rosalia in the middle of the now-empty road.

The stains of red on her face were either from tears or fury. Likely both. She scowled at Ben, light catching the tears in her eyes.

"Apologize all you want," she spat. "But I'm done. My syndicate, too. We're leaving."

24

VEX HAD FELT a lot of things about Rosalia in the time he'd known her—but at this moment, he could honestly say he only hated her.

Ben pulled away from this weird cluster they were standing in, but Vex didn't. Which left him holding on to Lu, who hesitated one second more, and Vex savored every moment of her body being anywhere near his. But, too soon, she turned to face Rosalia, and Vex wobbled in the absence of both of them.

For the first time since—god, since he'd jumped off the *Astuto* without Lu—Vex felt not so damn alone.

A tremor walked up his left leg, digging into his hip with such determination that he leaned over, fighting not to wince at the pain.

He'd have to tell Lu he wasn't cured yet. He'd have to

ask her to make more counter tonics for him.

Guilt shot through him, just as strong as the tremor, and he almost pushed aside any desire to bother her with trivial matters like saving his life. But he heard Edda in his head. Saw that look in her eyes when things had gotten too emotional.

All she'd wanted was redemption. Like Vex, like Nayeli— only her redemption *was* Vex, in the same way he'd needed his redemption to be making her proud of him.

Edda'd died right in front of him.

Vex sniffed, scrubbing his fist against his cheek before he shifted to glare all this hatred at Rosalia. And Nate, now, stomping up beside her with his injured husband leaning on him.

Great. All three people Vex could unabashedly hate.

"What are you talking about, Head Rustici?" Kari stepped into the group, putting her body between Ben, Lu, and Vex on one side, and the raider Heads on the other.

Rosalia ground her jaw. "Exactly what I said. The Grozdan syndicate is leaving. You can keep fighting this war on your own—we're done."

"You don't get to ignore this," Nayeli countered. Where'd she come from? But she stepped up beside Vex, hands on her hips, tears streaking trails down her cheeks. He teetered.

She'd lost Edda, too. And Fatemah. And Cansu was still gone.

God, how was Nayeli still standing?

"And who're you to be talking?" Pierce snapped, adjusting his weight on Nate.

Nayeli rounded on him. "The Tuncian Head is still missing. The acting Head is dead. I've taken her place, until Cansu returns."

She spoke without hesitation or regret or pain. She was the Tuncian Head now.

Pierce scoffed and ran his free hand down his face. "I don't much care, honestly. Shoot me, but I agree with Rosalia. We've lost too damn much. Only a dozen of the raiders we left here are still—" He swallowed hard. When he started again, he spoke to the dirt. "The Emerdian syndicate is going back to Port Camden, and we're gonna figure out how to retake our city ourselves—like we should've done to begin with. This was all a waste, thinking we could unify, thinking we'd have strong enough weapons. She"—he pointed across the group at Lu. Vex straightened by instinct, angling closer to her—"already changed her mind. Damn pride getting in the way. If she doesn't make more permanent magic, we don't have a hope or prayer to any god of winning this war."

Kari looked at Lu with the same shock Vex knew was on his own face.

Lu had changed her mind about making permanent magic? But she'd still taken a vial of it, and Rosalia and Nate had, too, from what Vex'd heard. This was a start, though.

He got as close to a smile as he could. Lu returned it, her face relaxing.

"You won't keep working on permanent magic?"

The broken words came from the side of the road. Tattered uniform rolled to his elbows, Jakes held a rag in one hand, fear racing through his eyes.

Lu looked as though she might say something, but tears welled in her eyes, and she dropped her gaze to the road.

"You can't stop!" Jakes's expression was, remarkably, just as brittle as his voice. "Now more than ever—you *have* to be stronger than Elazar. His defensors took one of your vials! He'll come again, but undefeatable now."

"And death will come too." Lu cut her arm around the disaster of the sanctuary. "I won't foster more of this."

"You could save everyone," Jakes snapped. Vex eyed the raider Heads, Kari, Ben—would they lock Jakes up again? But Rosalia, Nate, and Pierce all held, maybe feeling their same grievances in this defensor. "You could stop Elazar. That boy his commander took at Fort Chastity? You could save him. You're being selfish."

Kari swung in front of Jakes, her hand lifted. "Don't you *dare* presume to—"

"That boy"—Lu spoke over her mother, her glare on Jakes dark—"*that boy* is Bianca's son."

⚜⚜⚜

Five simple words. *That boy is Bianca's son.*

Lu didn't know why she told Jakes now. She wanted to silence him; she wanted him to realize what this war truly cost.

But each word dragged forward one of Lu's memories and connected it with another, cobbling together a picture out of realizations, hunches, and fears.

Tom had gotten Lu's vial of permanent magic—but he wouldn't have known about it. Getting that vial would have been a surprise in addition to his true purpose here. Why *had* Tom come to the sanctuary, not gone to Port Fausta with Elazar and Milo?

Tom had brought Teo with him. To a battle.

"He wanted something out of Teo too," Vex had said.

Tom had made defensors grab Teo in Fort Chastity. Not Vex or Ben or Edda. *Teo.*

Tom had intercepted Bianca and Annalisa for Elazar. Bianca, who had died of Shaking Sickness. Bianca, who had given birth to Teo *while she had Shaking Sickness.*

"In the Port Camden prison." Lu looked at Gunnar, who seemed startled to have her attention on him. His wonder turned to confusion from the stunted, secret words that she had never intended to repeat for the danger in them: "Pregnant women. You said Eye of the Sun was given to *pregnant women.*"

Lu pressed a hand into her chest, unable to breathe.

Teo was a product of Elazar's experiments.

Tom had known—it was why Elazar had sent Bianca and Annalisa to Grace Loray. Had Bianca already been pregnant when she arrived on this shore? Could Teo's father be . . . *Elazar*?

No—Teo was too young. Wasn't he? Lu had heard from Bianca only that Teo's father was a soldier who had died during the revolution. But where did the lies end? Were other children of Elazar's experiments out there? Who was Teo's father? Worse, a question Lu could barely think, let alone ask aloud: did Teo have permanent magic?

No. Unless Elazar's people had figured out the proper mix of magic plants and Visjorn blood, the result wouldn't have been the same as when Mechts gave it to their people. Or Tuncian spices, Emerdian brickwork, and more—Elazar hadn't known of those things until recently. Teo couldn't have magic in his blood. He *couldn't*.

Of all the people around Lu, Jakes was the only one connecting the same pieces. His face went utterly white. "Bianca's child survived? Pious God—"

"Who's Bianca?" Vex asked.

A divot punctured Kari's brow. "Teo's mother."

"She was part of Elazar's experiments," Lu filled in, breathless.

Ben gagged. "My father experimented on *Teo*? No—"

"He thinks Teo has permanent magic," Lu said. "That was why Tom brought him here, to the attack. To test him."

It was madness. Throwing an innocent child into a battle to turn him into a weapon—

Bile seared Lu's throat and she closed her eyes. But there lay only memories, everything Tom had trained her to do, the blood on her hands, the secrets and lies—

This was it, wasn't it? This was what he had given her Menesia to forget. The dreamlike scene that had plagued her in the Port Camden prison, of Kari accusing Tom of destroying everything, of breaking someone's trust—Kari and Lu had found out about his involvement with Teo, hadn't they? That he had stolen Bianca's and Annalisa's memories too, and was a spy for Elazar, watching over Teo should he show any signs of magic?

Obliterate him, Lu's rage said. *Find him. End him like I ended Milo.*

But that demand was an echo now, a fiery cry that burned itself out.

No more blood. No more fighting, no more war, *no more.*

She wanted Teo back. She wanted Argrid off her island. She wanted peace.

"Elazar has everything now." Jakes's voice grated. "You can't—you can't do nothing. Why are you giving up?"

"I'm not giving up," Lu told him. "I'm just refusing to fight this war on Elazar's terms. I will not let Teo get swept into an even deadlier war. This has to end without more magic!"

"The goddamn Argridian defensor is on our side," Pierce

boomed. "Everyone wants to fight the war this way—*except you*." He pointed at Lu, Kari, Ben. "That's why we're leaving. Let your wrongness strangle you."

He turned, tugging Nate with him. Rosalia made to leave as well.

Kari shot a step after them. "And what is *your* plan, if ours is wrong?"

"The Grozdan Gloria has always supported us. If I ask, she'll send us aid." Rosalia turned back. She hovered a handbreadth over the ground, her Aerated Blossom powers undiminished. "I don't care about the rest of you. Attack, don't attack, die, live. This isn't Grozda's war, and if we can't get more permanent magic out of it, there's nothing here for us."

"Yeah," Nate snapped. "The people on this island hate us, anyway. *They're* the ones who told Argrid how to get into the sanctuary. I ain't gonna waste my time fighting for—"

"This city is *destroyed!*" Kari's shout silenced him and the whole area. "Port Fausta is destroyed. You say this island is yours, that it belongs to raiders, yet you have no respect for it because you demand that the people respect you first, or the Council respect you first, or Argrid respect you first. You always wait for others to move first. Take control! You cannot help only the people loyal to you."

Rosalia floated closer, intimidating. "The people on this island deserve to suffer. They deserve to know what it's like, to be hunted and hated and treated as less than human. You bet your ass I help only those loyal to me. The Council wasn't any different. Argrid, too."

She included Ben with a glance. Lu stepped between them, into the stream of hatred.

"You're right," Kari said, her voice lower but no less intense. "The Council had flaws. But when this war ends, what kind of world do you imagine if you become the oppressor? You want to terrorize people, and ostracize them, and be the one they hate? You feel you deserve to inflict pain because pain has been inflicted on you?"

Rosalia's shoulders rose, but her feet met the dirt road again. Lu's brows lifted.

"The Council had flaws," Kari repeated. "But keeping ourselves in these separate groups contributed to its flaws. When this war ends, Grace Loray cannot continue as it was before. The system that needs to be in place must be one of *unity*—all of you must be represented. We cannot fight this war or lead this island separately. That includes the raider syndicates as well as any who *aren't* raiders, as well as any who are more Argridian than Grace Lorayan, or who worship the Pious God, or who hold to a different deity. We are either together or ruined."

She paused. In that opening of silence, no one spoke up. No one argued. Even Jakes, fuming at the outskirts, only turned and marched up the road, hands in fists at his sides.

Lu watched him go as if watching her own rage walk away. Elazar still had her permanent magic vial as well as

Teo—but a lightness filled Lu's chest, something delicate and velvet. Something like . . . hope.

However they confronted Elazar next would be right, better, and wouldn't leave greasy disgust on Lu's soul.

Kari took a step back. "We have all been through an enormous horror. Think on what I have said and rest here tonight. Tomorrow morning, you make whatever decision you feel is best for your people. But I will be here, and with whoever remains, we will figure out a way to end this war and move toward a future benefiting us all."

Kari turned—and swept Lu up in a hug.

Lu stiffened, took a breath, and settled. A moment of comfort, a brace of *You are not alone. I love you.*

"How are you going to get Teo back?" Vex asked from Lu's side.

The question withered these rare gentle feelings.

Kari pulled back to brush the hair from Lu's forehead. "Tomorrow," she said. "We will discuss these things tomorrow. Tom knows how much Teo means to us. He will not harm him."

"Won't he?" Lu whispered, a single tear tumbling down her cheek.

Kari's smile was heartbreaking. She took Lu's head between her hands and gave her a resolute shake. "I have to believe that pieces of the man I know remain in your father. I know you don't trust him, but trust *me*. We will get Teo back."

She gave Lu a final hug and a kiss on her forehead, and left.

Lu started to follow Kari. Nayeli'd run off; Ben was talking with Gunnar up the road. Nate, Pierce, Rosalia—they were gone, too.

Vex's chest hollowed. Where did he fit—with his cousin in Argrid; or on Grace Loray?

Or with Jakes, who had vanished from the road and taken his opinions with him?

His answer had always been with Edda and Nayeli, on the *Rapid Meander*, in their own little haven. That life was gone, ripped from Vex before he'd had a chance to say good-bye. It squeezed a howl from his throat, and he bowed his head to cover it.

Now that that life was dead, where should he stand?

Lu was only a pace away. Vex shot after her and draped his fingers around her wrist.

She turned—but didn't smack him away or shout in his face. He scrambled for something innocuous to say, a joke or a flippant remark to cement this peace between them.

"Can we work on the cure again?" Vex gawked that *that* question had come out of his mouth. "I mean, I know there's a lot of other stuff going on, but I just thought, maybe—"

Lu freed her hand. His heart squeezed until she lifted that hand and put it on his chest.

Vex gaped as her thumb slipped under the gap in his shirt.

The muscles in Lu's throat constricted. "Of course. I'll see what I can salvage."

Vex winced. *Salvage.* The attack had likely destroyed most of the sanctuary's plants.

But he nodded, struck by her hand over his heart, and how warm she felt.

"Thanks," he said. And then, because he needed to see her smile, "Princesa."

Lu's gaze shot up to his. She rolled her eyes at him and smiled, a slight crook to her lips before she walked away.

Vex realized that he hadn't trembled since she'd touched him.

25

THE RAIDER HEADS couldn't agree on most things, but they agreed to have a vigil at midnight for everyone lost in the attack.

Most of the refugees had left by now, retreating to homes and buildings across the city, or maybe out onto the island to take their chances in another town. The rest of Port Mesi-Teab still spewed hatred whenever raiders emerged from the sanctuary, blaming the raiders for the attack and the lives lost.

Vex hated them. But he remembered that Rosalia and Nate hated them, too, and being similar to those two made him ignore his own anger.

Raiders had cleared the rubble and debris out of the sanctuary's largest square. A pile of scraps filled the middle: pieces of canvas, blankets, torn-up sacks, all things that had covered the dead until their bodies had been moved to a boat, to be taken out for a sea burial.

Vex stood at the edge of the circle. People pressed in from the side streets; some sat on top of buildings. He spotted Rosalia across from him on the feeble-looking planks of a hut's roof. Emerdian raiders surrounded Nate and Pierce. To Vex's right, Kari folded her arms over her torso, orange lantern light wreathing her in flame and shadow. Lu wasn't here—Vex had seen her slip into a hut somewhere behind him, and honestly, he'd almost not come to this, too.

Nayeli was not far from Vex, standing with a group of Tuncian raiders. He wanted to go to her. They'd lost Edda and Fatemah. They needed to—he didn't know. Mourn together? Something. But seeing her with the Tuncian raiders . . .

Vex didn't move. She was where she needed to be—even if it felt like he'd lost her, too.

A wash of heat came seconds ahead of Gunnar, who shouldered his way in next to Vex with Ben.

The lanterns made the cloths look like they were breathing in the undulating light.

"Your friend," Gunnar whispered, "Edda? I am sorry you lost her. She was good-hearted."

Vex smiled a sad smile that shot tears into his eye. "Did you meet her? She left the Mechtlands because she . . . um . . . disagreed with the whole Eye of the Sun thing."

Gunnar gave a half smile. "Yes, I met her."

Ben frowned down at his boots, hands in his pockets.

He didn't react to this exchange or look up at the gathered crowd. Was he praying? To *whom*?

They fell silent. Everyone around the square wavered in that place of grief, whispering to each other, going quiet, sniffing back tears. This vigil was a chance to mourn. Kari had said it would be cathartic. But the longer Vex stood there, his eye shifting from person to sobbing person, the more his chest filled with a crushing weight. They were just supposed to stand here, wallowing in what they'd lost? God, this was miserable—

On the roof across from him, Rosalia started to chant.

She leaned forward, hands to her chest, belting words in Grozdan that Vex could only describe as lamenting. It sounded a lot like Grozdan war cries—he'd heard enough of those from his time with her—but there was a desperate twist to her wails, and the words he caught were things about the afterlife and being heralded and glorious, glorious, over and over.

Her incantation ended, and silence reigned long enough for Vex to manage a breath.

One of Nate and Pierce's raiders started to speak. Vex didn't know Emerdian well enough to translate anything, but he caught the words *Pious God* and knew it was a prayer.

As the raider belted out words every bit as mournful as Rosalia's, a Tuncian raider started to thump softly on an overturned crate.

Vex had heard that before—here, actually. A Tuncian

funeral rite—drums to alert the gods to a soul's departure from earth.

The crowd stood frozen, caught in the lingering wails of the Grozdan funeral chant, the continuing Emerdian prayer and Tuncian drumbeats—

Gunnar pushed ahead of Vex and Ben. He took one step outside the circle, lifted his hands, and shot a stream of fire at the pile of rags. It caught, a small smoldering flame at the very top that stayed just there, neither raging nor dying. Gunnar must have been controlling it.

Vex heard gasps of grief. The crushing weight in his chest became unbearable, and with every pounding beat from the Tuncian drummer—growing stronger now, the raider losing himself in the thudding rhythm—Vex fumbled to think. All he could see was a small, cold cell on a ship leaving Deza, and a little boy curled in the corner, the wound throbbing where his eye had been. The ship had rocked and he'd been sick in the waste bucket, but he'd whispered a song to himself. A song he'd heard at Argridian funerals over the years, a hymn he'd always hated for how it made him cry.

He didn't like crying. He didn't like thinking about death. But he'd sung that song in the ship's cell, choking on the stench of bile and salt, because he knew no one would sing it for his father—and no one would sing it for him.

"Look to the depths," Vex started under his breath now, his eye closing. *"Look to the sky. Look—"* He faltered. *"Look to the—"*

A hand slipped into his. He gripped it, grounding himself here, with Ben.

Grozda had been represented. Emerdon. Tuncay. The Mechtlands.

"*Look to the Graces,*" Ben picked up, "*humble and high.*"

The people here probably hated them for it. Vex didn't know if the Tuncian drummer meant to drown them out. But Ben kept singing, and Vex linked his voice with his cousin's, the two of them pushing louder, louder.

"*Find me in the sun,*" they sang. "*Find me in the shade. This end, this triumph, this final gain—*"

Edda would've been proud of him. To stand there, in front of the raiders of Grace Loray, and belt out an Argridian piece of his soul.

The song ended in lines about the Pious God's mercy, his welcoming embrace, how he would make the transition to the afterlife smooth and safe. When was the last time Vex had remembered anything *good* about the Pious God? Elazar had warped every part of him, but the Pious God that Rodrigu had worshipped had been the one in this song—kind and compassionate.

Ben and Vex finished the hymn, and the Tuncian drummer ended, too. Silence rolled in, heavy in the rush and heave of people gasping around him.

Vex couldn't open his eye to see how many people were glaring at him and Ben. Everyone who'd died had been killed by an Argridian defensor—how dare anyone sully their memorial with an Argridian song?

Vex squeezed Ben's hand. "We should go," he whispered.

Ben returned his squeeze. "I think she wants you."

That made Vex open his eye. Ben was looking behind them, through the crowd.

Vex followed his gaze to see Lu, standing at the very back of the swaying people, her face fading in and out of the shadows.

By the time Vex got through the crowd, his whole body was trembling like a tuning fork gone to humming, but it had nothing to do with his Shaking Sickness.

Lu didn't move, her arms clasped before her, her eyes on him.

"Where were you?" Vex asked, his cheeks stiff from dried tears.

The back of the crowd was only a few paces away. The darkness of midnight blurred all around, flickering lanterns casting shadows.

She shrugged. "I couldn't—" She stopped. "I was working on another cure for you. It's done. I can give it to you."

Vex stared at the ground. Another cure. Would it work?

And what then? What would he do once he didn't have Shaking Sickness as an excuse?

He looked at Lu. There was something else in her eyes, something pleading for him to let her do this. To focus on something small and easy in a world of funeral songs and war.

Vex nodded. "All right."

❖❖❖

Lu might not have gone to the gathering, but she had heard it. Bent over the small fire in the hut, she had listened to the wailing, the drumming, the chanting—and Vex, singing with Ben.

That hymn still saturated her heart. All of it, really, every expression of melancholy from that square had been different yet similar, and Lu hoped Nate, Pierce, and Rosalia felt the same welling of unity that she did.

But beyond that, part of Lu had heard Vex's singing and come undone. She hadn't known he could sound like that, his voice shaky from nerves but still strong and rich, sculpted for grand Argridian cathedrals that would rebound the noise and build it higher, louder. It was what had pulled her out of the hut instead of crouching in the darkness, each crooning word sliding hands against her back until she had found herself standing behind him in awe.

Why did you go? she asked herself now. *The war may have changed. But you have not.*

Lu had found Drooping Fern in the ruins of the sanctuary. She wouldn't give Vex another tonic to induce his memories about what the Church had given him, but Drooping Fern was the counter plant to Awacia, the plant used to keep people awake. The Church had loved giving

404

Awacia to its victims, to torture them with sleeplessness, so Lu had made a concentrated dose of Drooping Fern to counter it.

The hut Nayeli had let Lu use as a laboratory was mostly intact, aside from one bashed-in window—and the now-broken chest of drawers where Lu had stored one of the two remaining vials of permanent magic. Ben likely still had the other one; she, Rosalia, and Nate were living embodiments of the final three.

Did Elazar have the one Tom had taken? What magic had implanted itself in him? Or was he holding off on taking that potion, instead letting Tom subject Teo to more tests, trying to break magic out of his blood and bones? Was Teo locked in a sticky, cramped cell in New Deza?

That Milo was no longer a threat to Teo offered meager relief. The lack of release in knowing he was dead continued to shock Lu. For so many years, she had thought that she would be able to breathe again over his body. That at the very least, knowledge of his death would free her from the memories he had left, the scars he had inflicted, the pain he had caused.

But his death felt all too similar to the realization she had had about herself, how horrible things would happen regardless of whether she committed them. Milo was a tool, as she had been. He was, in his own way, meaningless.

The only thing that could be done was to prevent more atrocities from happening. To do that, Teo needed her to act, so she put her questions and worries in a box deep in her mind. Every twitch of pain, every flex of strength it took to keep that box shut—she would use it all when she came face-to-face with Argrid.

Lu led Vex inside the shack and closed the door, blocking out the drumbeats. Someone was singing again, faster now—everyone was strung too tight from grief. They needed to expel it, the holes in their hearts begging them to *stop*, just for an hour of healing.

Coals glowed in the center of the shack, the only light source, making the small room shadowed and unsteady. Lu moved to the table and picked up the vial she had made for him. She heard a soft thud and turned to see Vex slumped on his knees next to the firepit, staring into the coals, pinpricks of orange reflected in his dark eye.

"I saw the flame Gunnar lit," Lu whispered. She couldn't make herself talk louder. "Edda would have liked that, I think."

Vex flicked his gaze up to her. He grinned, but it was frail. "She'd have been a sobbing mess for all of it. She hid it most of the time, but damn, that woman was the most sentimental person I've ever met. Thought she'd lose her mind when Teo became part of our crew—"

He stopped. His eye closed.

Lu's heart bucked and she folded to her knees next to him, the vial in her hand.

"I don't blame you," she said.

Vex didn't look at her.

"I need you to know that," she continued. "I need you to know that everything I said to you . . . I do trust you. It wasn't about you. It was *me*, and I'm sorry."

"I'm sorry too. I—" His face stayed impassive for one full breath before the corner of his mouth lifted in a small smile that sent a flurry of sparks into her gut. He opened his eye, finally. "I apologized. Again. To your apology. Can we . . . can we just stop apologizing to each other?"

Lu smiled too. It broke apart the darkness, a sliver of light in the strain.

Vex's smile faded, and Lu was suddenly, overwhelmingly aware of how close she was to him. The air between them was heady with sweat and mint, the tang of plants from her own clothes and Tuncian spices that were embedded in the very fiber of this shack.

"I know most of our interactions since Port Camden have been apologizing," Vex said. He tried for humor, but there was something tense to it, like he'd noticed how close they were, too. "Guess we'll have to find some other way to interact. I mean, *whoa*, that sounded—ahem—ignore me. I should leave now."

He took the vial from her open palm and started to stand.

"Why?" she asked.

Her question eased him back down. The orange coals caught the sheen on his face, highlighting the smooth expanse of his cheeks, the lines across his lips, the single bead of sweat sluicing down the contours of his throat as he worked a swallow.

His body was bowed toward her, knees bent. "You want me to stay?"

Lu sipped in a breath. Held it.

Why did you go to him? she asked herself again. *You don't deserve him. Milo was right.*

She hadn't told Vex yet that she had killed Milo. The confession gathered on her tongue, but she held down the mention of him, not wanting him to intrude here.

"Yes." Lu could barely hear her own plea. "Stay."

Vex thumbed the vial. His eye never left hers, one cheek caught between his teeth. "I don't . . . ah. I'm really not good at—*this.*" He waved to encompass something unseen and warm and as close as the air brushing Lu's skin. "Horrendous, in fact—god, you've met my whole history with women, so I need you to be *explicitly* clear about what it is you want—"

Lu started. "Rosalia."

Vex choked. "Well, that's . . . disappointing."

"That's not what I—no." Lu shifted upright. "She called you something. What was it?"

Lu knew as soon as it left her mouth that it was the wrong thing to ask. The sweet calm took a jagged turn in the tension on Vex's face, his body rocking back.

"No." Lu shook her head. "I'm sorry. Don't answer that—"

"Mezzochi."

Lu froze.

"It's Grozdan," Vex continued. He tipped his head out of the firelight. "For half blind."

Revulsion seized Lu's throat. Rosalia had tossed that word out as though it was something humorous. Even Vex shrugged, tried to smile, but his head was still angled away. The scarred part of his face, away from the light—away from Lu.

"I didn't know what it meant until a few weeks into our . . . whatever it was," Vex said, forced ease gripping his voice again. "Which is why I don't trust myself to act on anything unless you tell me, in very clear terms, what you want to get out of this. I'm marvelously bad at reading what's real, and what's a joke, and what I—"

His words cut off in a startled gasp when Lu grabbed the collar of his shirt. His face whipped around to meet hers, shock trading for wonder as she lifted her other hand to cup his neck, the vial forgotten on the ground beside them.

"I want—" Lu's mouth stayed open, trying to form the *clear terms* that Vex asked for. But nothing followed those two words, and they became their own plea:

I want. Since that moment on the Schilly-Leto waterfall,

when Vex had revealed his fear of heights. Knowing something so vulnerable about him—he could never be a threat. That depressing revelation had freed her to see him in a new, soft light. *I want.* Every act of bravery to protect her or Teo, even when she knew he was terrified. *I want.* His arms open to her in the Port Camden prison, his solidity and defiance and loyalty.

Vex was gentle and safe and she hadn't wanted to be so close to anyone since her body had felt violated and not her own, and she hadn't been able to endure the thought of someone else touching it when she barely felt like she had any right to it herself.

Again, she saw Teo, bound to a chair, Elazar and Tom standing over him—

Her breath fled. She was far from healed herself. She still wasn't certain how to go about every day with memories that were always on the edge of undoing her. But something about healing *Vex*, inside, outside, in every way, seemed so much more possible.

"You," Lu finished. "I want you."

Vex gaped at her in innocent wonder as she lifted both her hands to his face. His skin was slick from humidity and exertion. Closer, the scent of him intensified, cinnamon soap and bonfire from standing near Gunnar. She slid her thumbs under the straps of his eye patch and pulled it up, off, casting it to the floor next to the vial.

She put her hands on either side of his head and pulled

him down to her, pressing her lips there, and there, covering his mutilated eye with unspoken promises: that even though she was unworthy of him, of the desire that rose through her belly and heated her chest, she wanted him to have it. That even though the war was far from over, they were here.

Vex breathed against her and hooked his fingers around her wrists. She felt one small tremor in his right arm, the beat of his pulse in his fingertips.

Lu paused, lips over his scar. Had she done wrong? Maybe this had been too much—

Vex dragged his head up, up, to brush his lips against hers.

It was hesitant. Lu's mind fogged and details came to her in waves—the softness of his lips as they parted on hers, the contrasting roughness of his tongue against the inside of her mouth, the gentle twitch of his thumb on her arm.

She returned his kiss with a surge of pressure, and a wall fell. Vex grabbed her waist and released a deep, velvety mewl that opened a space in Lu's heart, had her reeling.

Rising drumbeats outside overlaid distant singing voices. The firepit in the hut hissed with dying coals, and as the last of the embers faded from orange to black, Lu and Vex fell to the floor, two broken things wordlessly making themselves whole.

26

VEX HAD NO idea what time it was. The sky through the cracked window was a hazy gray, so it must be early? Late? Were the funeral mourners still gathered? Their drumbeats had faded a bit ago.

Honestly, he didn't care if the sanctuary had up and emptied.

Lu stirred against him. Vex shifted with her, curling his body tighter, closer. She settled, and the even cadence of her breathing kept him calm by extension, her arms slumped over the thick quilt they'd found in the corner. It was scratchy and stiff but better than nothing, and right then, Vex wouldn't have moved if the blanket had been made of burrs and thorns.

He couldn't remember Lu ever being this calm. The tension in her shoulders was gone and her brow was smooth. He tightened his arm across her waist, that shift of skin against skin spinning him back to the feel of her lips on his face, the smoothness of her bare back, and the way she'd tasted, honeyed and perfect.

Vex didn't deserve her. He didn't deserve this stillness, when out beyond these walls, the whole of the island hated them. Teo was god knew where. Kari and the raider Heads would be preparing to confront Elazar. If the confrontation was another battle, would Elazar hold Teo in the middle of it, gun to his head, demanding surrender? If it was an attempt at peace talks, Vex could see his uncle's cruel smile. Elazar would have no peace, especially if he had Lu's vial of permanent magic by now. Or, worse—could Teo have magic in him, like Lu had said?

Did Kari think they could defeat Elazar without giving up Lu, or this island, or both? Vex could tell her she was wrong. But who the hell was he to tell a renowned war veteran how a battle would go? And when she asked him the inevitable question—*"What should we do?"*—he'd just shuffle his feet and slump away.

Lu made a soft hum in her sleep.

What should we do? The question splintered in Vex's mind. *What can I do?*

Vex closed his eye and buried his face in Lu's hair. It'd fallen out of the knot she kept it in, the black curls spilling across the mat they lay on. Silky strands rubbed his face, the area usually covered by an eye patch.

He kept waiting for that gut-punching urge to put it

back on, but every time he thought about it, he felt her lips on the scar.

Face buried in her curls, Vex inhaled. *Sunlight. Wood smoke. Salt. The wind that comes from the sea and slams into the air trapped in the jungle trees.*

A glint of rising sunlight caught something on the ground next to them. The vial of Drooping Fern Lu had made, the cure for him. The last cure for him, maybe. After it, he would be whole again. But who would be whole? Paxben Gallego or Devereux Bell?

Vex reached for the vial. Lu startled and gave him a bleary, questioning look.

"Sorry—I didn't mean to wake you." He grabbed the vial and tucked his hand back under the blanket, around her waist. "Go to sleep."

Lu closed her hand over his fist and the vial of Drooping Fern. "You haven't taken it?"

He smiled into her neck. "Haven't had a whole lot of time since you gave it to me."

She chuckled, the noise vibrating into his chest.

"I think I should go after Teo," Vex said.

Lu tensed, and Vex closed his eye. "What?"

"Elazar won't expect it," he said, talking faster than his brain was forming a plan. "If we come at him with a whole army—or just for peace talks, but still a whole army—he wants that, he wants a fight. But one raider? One search party?"

Lu shifted to sit up. The loss of her against him flooded him with cold, and he leaned on one elbow, chill bumps prickling across his bare skin.

The prickling sensation intensified at the way the blanket tucked under her arms, exposing the notches of her spine, the places his fingers had fit so perfectly last night.

A long moment of her dark eyes flashing through his. "All right. I'll come with you."

"I won't let you surrender for Teo's release," Vex told her. He didn't care if he sounded harsh. "It'll come to that, if you're there. Elazar will have your father and Ibarra, and I can't—"

His voice broke. He linked his fingers around her creased elbow, running his thumb against the soft skin on the back of her arm.

I can't lose you again.

Lu was silent a long while. Then, softly, "I killed Milo."

"What?"

She looked away from him. "The magic I took gave me Incris powers. They're still in me." Her voice dipped, but she cleared her throat. "I know you don't agree with permanent magic. I don't either, anymore. But I used it to kill Milo—I can help you get Teo too. I could end this whole thing, I think. Elazar and Tom. I could kill them like I did Milo."

Her voice sounded scared, small, and Vex ached for her.

"Would killing them really end this?" he asked. "After

everything that's happened—the refugees letting Argrid into the sanctuary; that man arguing with Ben—I don't know this war is that simple. I don't think it's ever been that simple."

Lu finally looked at him again. Vex inhaled.

Another long pause, and Lu seemed to decide something with a small nod.

"If you go after Teo," she began, "where will you start?"

Shit, he didn't know. New Deza, maybe? But there'd likely be defensors on guard—

Wait. "That defensor. Jakes," Vex said. "Last I saw him, he was helping raiders make repairs. He'd know the rotation of Elazar's soldiers, maybe where Tom might've taken Teo."

Ben would know all this stuff, too. But Ben needed to stay with the main group for whatever final confrontation happened with Elazar. This, a quick mission to snatch Teo back from the monsters who stole him?

This was a job for a raider. For Devereux Bell.

Lu turned away. "He might help you, actually. He's Teo's uncle."

Vex huffed. Oh—wait. That moment when Lu had silenced Jakes by saying, *"That boy is Bianca's son"*—that was how she'd chosen to tell him he had a nephew?

Vex grinned. He had to admit he adored how heartless she could be.

Lu shook her head, biting her cheek. "I don't know that

he is trustworthy. But . . . maybe Teo will change things for him."

"I can do this," he told her. "I'll bring Budwig so I can talk to you. You've healed me, too, after this." He lifted the vial, uncorked it, and sucked down the contents.

It tasted like licking the side of a riverbed.

He grimaced. "See? All healed now. You'll be at Kari's side, helping with magic. Not permanent magic," he amended when she opened her mouth to argue. "But magic, still. We'll need it. And Ben will be the bridge between Grace Loray and Argrid. This is what I can do for the war—I can get Teo back. I can remove him from the equation."

"*Remove him from the equation,*" Lu echoed. She smirked. "You don't talk like that."

"No. You do. You've been a terrible influence on me, Miss Andreu. I was once so innocent. Now look at me— volunteering for a role in a war. God"—he rolled his eye skyward—"my reputation will be in shambles."

"Most unfortunate," she said, and bit her lip. It was an absentminded habit, but it exploded in Vex's gut as a flurry of effervescent bubbles. "From outlaw to war hero. How will you recover?"

Vex sat up to be level with her. He trailed his fingers shoulder to shoulder, delighting in the small exhale of pleasure he got from her.

"I won't," he said, and the humor left his voice. He skimmed his fingers lower, cupping her hip and pulling her closer. "I plan on never recovering from what you've done to me."

He kissed her, knowing she would want to respond to that, to argue about all the ways she had affected him poorly. It baffled him that she thought herself unworthy of him, and he refused to hear her talk like that. He just kissed her, and kissed her, and kissed her.

I told your mother I thought I loved you. That was a lie.

I know I love you. I've known I loved you all along.

The sun was coming up when Vex found Jakes sitting against the outside of a tenement building, eating breakfast.

Vex's legs still ached, and each step felt like knives dug into his bones. He hadn't had the instant relief he'd felt with the other cures, as though his body finally got something it'd been missing for so long. He'd expected this cure to be *the* cure.

Maybe it would just take time. He had to press through— like he had to press through every step, in public, when he wasn't wearing his eye patch.

Putting it back on hadn't felt right after everything with Lu. But Vex wavered a bit now without it, watching everyone he passed who was able to see his scar.

Vex stopped next to Jakes. Jakes looked up at him, his recoil obvious and jarring.

Vex sank his hands into his pockets. "I have a proposition for you." *Asshole.*

Jakes dropped his breakfast plate on the ground. "What could Paxben Gallego want with me?" he asked in Argridian.

Vex's eyebrows shot up. He'd forgotten this defensor knew who he was.

He rethought his whole insane plan in the single breath before he said, also in Argridian, "The boy that Elazar has. Teo. I'm going after him."

Jakes didn't look up. "How does that involve me?"

"What the hell do you mean? He's your nephew. Elazar might be experimenting on him. I'm going to get him. Thought you might want in on it."

"Elazar doesn't return captives. Especially ones who are of use to him."

Vex bristled. "He's. Your. Nephew."

Jakes finally looked up at him. His eyes were bloodshot and his upper lip curled back. "Should I dissolve in a blubbering mess? Elazar has Lu's vial. And the boy. Lu refuses to make more magic. Whatever you think you can do—" Jakes snorted, brittle. "It's over."

"Like hell. You're still alive, aren't you? *Teo* is still alive. It isn't over till we're all dead." God, saying that was a knife in the chest. Vex braced himself.

Jakes's knees popped up, and he stared down at his hands in the cradle of his lap. Vex thought he might not respond until his shoulders caved.

"Tomás Andreu led this attack, and he's the one who orchestrated taking . . . Teo," Jakes started. He said Teo's name as though it was a foreign word, something his tongue hadn't been trained to handle. "But Elazar was beginning to question Andreu's commitment. Andreu will be trying to prove his loyalty. He'll be wherever Elazar is."

"And where is that?"

Jakes thought. "Elazar brought his light to Port Mesi-Teab and Port Fausta. Port Camden will be next—but he's likely already there. Your best chance is New Deza. His final stop."

"What's Elazar planning to happen there?"

Jakes looked up at him, annoyed. "I already told your leaders that I don't know. He kept me out of his final plans. It has something to do with the raiders he took, and his coming light—whatever it is, it will purify this island."

Vex hesitated. Kari and the raider Heads knew this much about Elazar's plans—that he was traveling from city to city, ending in New Deza. And Vex would have a Budwig Bean. If he saw anything important, he'd get news to Kari.

Resolution trickled into Vex's body, building and building as he stood there, on the precipice of action. "All right." He kicked Jakes's boot. "Get up. You're coming with me."

"What's the plan?"

"Get to New Deza. Do something courageous and likely stupid."

Jakes didn't stand. But his eyes flicked away, and his whole body shot upright, alert.

Vex turned to see Ben across the road, talking with a group of raiders.

"Fine."

Vex whipped back to Jakes, who was standing now, fuming.

"I'll come with you," Jakes snapped. "When are we leaving? Now? Good."

He marched away, toward the nearest exit to the docks.

Vex eyed Ben again. Behind him, Gunnar slumped out of the shadows of a cottage, watching Ben—the same way Jakes had watched him.

Oh. Vex knew Ben and Gunnar had become something of an item, but Jakes, too?

He trailed Jakes. As he walked, Vex's attention stayed on Ben one beat longer, until Ben lifted his head and looked at him.

Vex stopped. There was too much space between them, and Vex didn't have the fortitude for a sappy good-bye. He'd come back soon. Before Ben had to march to war against his father.

Getting Teo back would help Lu, but it wouldn't really do a damn thing to help Ben.

Ben cocked his head. Vex gave a bright smile. *Nothing's wrong. Carry on.*

Lu would explain why he'd had to leave. And maybe, by the time he returned, Vex would have figured out some way to help his cousin, too.

The *Rapid Meander* was still docked where Vex had left it weeks ago, tucked alongside one of the eastern tenements. It had enough supplies and moderate fuel, was in good enough condition—and was supplemented by weapons borrowed from the raiders.

Vex stood next to it, holding the tarp that'd covered it, unable to deny the swell of giddiness at the sight of his boat. The whole world had changed, but the *Meander* was still his. And here he was, Devereux Bell, about to cast off on a foolish, shaky mission.

Vex folded the tarp, trying to work it into the perfect little square that fit just so in one of the storage hatches.

"You never could fold that right."

Jakes, who'd been shoving a crate of rations on board, cursed in Argridian.

Nayeli was standing behind Vex on the dock, her arms folded, her brows lifted in an unspoken question of *What the hell are you doing?*

Vex dropped the tarp and swung on her. "We're going to get Teo. Kari doesn't need you here. You can come—" He stopped. "Only she does need you. You're the acting Tuncian Head."

Nayeli sniffed. She didn't give him that private smile and wink and skip off, letting him do whatever insane thing he wanted to do. She didn't ask how she could help.

"You're going to let us go, aren't you?" Vex took a step

closer. "You're not going to—"

"Your eye patch," she whispered.

Vex touched his scar. His stomach roiled. "Oh. Yeah."

Nayeli nodded as if he'd said something astute.

The silence between them was heavy. In it, Vex heard all the things they hadn't talked about. Edda's death. How Nayeli felt losing Fatemah. What it was like being the acting Tuncian Head, and how she was not going crazy thinking of Cansu every moment of every day.

Vex clamped his arms around her. "I've been a shit friend."

Nayeli grabbed onto him. "You always are."

"Hey."

"I have been, too. Edda was right." She paused, and Vex tightened his grip on her. "She always was. That idiot."

Vex smiled. "She was awful."

Nayeli pulled back from him. "And amazing."

She extended her hand to him and uncurled her fingers. A Budwig Bean sat in her palm.

"Lu told me to bring this to you," Nayeli said. "I have the other one, and I'll check in occasionally to yell at you about what a dumbass idea this was. But also . . . to make sure you're all right." She grunted and scrubbed at her teary eyes. "Shit, all this has turned me into a mushy fool. Take the bean so I can leave with some of my dignity."

Vex slid the bean into his pocket. "Same to you. Let me know you're all right, I mean."

And maybe I'll find Cansu, too. Maybe I'll find all the missing raiders, and stab Elazar, and solve all the problems of this war for everyone I love.

Was this how Rodrigu had felt? Was this why he'd led the resistance against Elazar in Argrid and risked everything?

The thought smacked Vex upside the head. He couldn't deal with the weight of his father's legacy right now, so he hopped up onto the *Rapid Meander's* deck. As he hit the planks, his legs sung out with pain, his knees cracking. He grabbed the railing and stood there, breathing through a spasm.

Too late, his mind whispered. *Lu gave you the last cure you needed. But it was too late. You're dying, and there's nothing anyone can do.*

Vex ignored himself and hobbled into the pilothouse. The table still sat in the corner, the knobs and levers on the wall gleamed. And the helm was waiting for him.

The smooth wood of the wheel clicked into his palms. He swore he felt the boat sigh.

"I've missed you, too," he whispered.

Jakes turned from the deck. "What'd you say?"

Vex shook his head. He looked through the window to see Nayeli, still on the dock, her hair snapping wild in the wind.

A quick lesson on shoveling coal, and he left Jakes belowdecks to work the engine. Vex twisted a knob on the wall and felt the boat hum to life. As the *Meander* shot away from the dock, a breeze slammed through the open pilot-house window, stealing Vex's breath.

Damn, it was invigorating. This boat. The purr of the engine. The feel of the wind and the smell of the river and the *rightness* of this action.

He was Devereux Bell, notorious stream raider. He knew this island better than anyone. He was an outlaw, a pest to everyone who tried to keep order.

And he'd take great pleasure in watching his uncle's plans splinter around him.

❊❊❊

"In the time since the attack on Port Mesi-Teab, our scouts have reported that Elazar retreated to Port Camden," said Kari. "He performed an abridged version of the gathering in Fort Chastity—this time, with an Emerdian raider bowing to him."

"One of my captured people," Nate muttered.

"Yes." Kari paused, an intake of breath that had Lu's nerves peaking. "Elazar also padded his speech with graphic details of the raider attack on Port Fausta, as well as a moment of silence for his fallen general, Milo Ibarra. He claimed raiders captured General Ibarra, tortured him, and murdered him, and that the raider attack on Port Fausta was a *senseless bloodbath.*"

A grunt—Pierce. "Damn, that man is good at twisting things to his benefit. It's almost like he wanted his general to die."

Lu flinched. Had Elazar wanted Milo to die? She couldn't find any solace in either a yes or a no. His death was . . . a void.

"But Elazar is readying to leave Port Camden," Kari continued, "and likely already has embarked. His final destination, as we know from his proclamations, is New Deza, where he will enact the final stage of his plan. He has an assortment of steamboats around him full of Mecht raiders, and other scouts have reported movement across the island—all Argridian or Mecht steamboats, headed toward New Deza."

"What exactly does that mean?" Pierce asked. "We still don't know a goddamn thing about his final goal—just that it'll end with him purifying the island."

"He has modified Menesia somehow," Ben said. "We saw that with Cansu. Perhaps he has devised a way to make it airborne instead of ingested? To spread it to everyone?"

"Gloria kill me now," Rosalia cursed.

Pierce grunted. "That's easy enough to counter. Just gotta have some Bright Mint on us."

Lu had squished into the narrow window seat in Fatemah's office. Her interactions with Fatemah had been brief and abrupt, but her loss had left an enormous hole in this sanctuary, as though its strongest wall had crumbled around it.

"That is the beginning of a plan," said Kari. "We approach New Deza armed with Bright Mint. We do not know what

Elazar will do, but we need to either have him agree to withdraw his presence from this island—unlikely—or find a way to force him off."

"Kill him," Rosalia spat. "Nate can tear his way through the defensors now. I can fly up over him. Lu already proved she's lethal with her Incris."

Lu cringed. Thankfully, Kari spoke up.

"Such acts would only confirm the lies Elazar has spread. This island has fallen under his false report that raiders are a danger, and that the Council—and Argrid—supports him. The attack on the sanctuary proves that Elazar has turned this island against us, and even if we manage to kill him now, I fear it will only make him a martyr. His cause and beliefs will linger. How can we undo his falsehoods?"

"Lu?"

She didn't turn to Nayeli as the raiders and Kari continued to discuss—*argue*—plans. But morning had dawned, and Rosalia, Nate, and Pierce hadn't fled as they'd threatened.

Others had left, though. Most of the refugees. Vex.

"Hey," Nayeli whispered, poking Lu's side. "You shouldn't sulk right now."

"I'm not sulking."

Nayeli poked her again. "Liar."

"*Nayeli*—I'm not sulking."

Kari was trying to figure out how many boats they had, whether they could approach New Deza under a banner of truce—too many would seem hostile, but perhaps they

427

needed a show of strength. Should they even try to negotiate peace? But what else could they do to prove that Elazar had lied to Grace Loray, and that he was the true threat? They needed the people of this island to turn against Argrid and trust their Grace Lorayan leaders again—otherwise Kari and the raider Heads would have to spend the foreseeable future fighting to keep their citizens from overthrowing them in fear.

Lu's eyes went to Rosalia—who was glaring at her. She hadn't looked at Lu with anything other than murder in her eyes since Lu had decided to stop trying to make magic permanent.

Lu turned away, staring out the window. Beyond the warped glass, Port Mesi-Teab was a ripple of sharp buildings and teetering slums, with far fewer twists of steamboat fog than usual. Lu imagined, beyond the edge where the horizon turned green with tangled jungle, Vex and Jakes on the *Rapid Meander*, sailing hard for New Deza.

If Tom had Teo there, Vex and Jakes would need a distraction to free him. What would draw all attention but not be a direct attack? What would ensure Elazar's full focus on them?

A word welled in Lu's mouth. She twisted in the window seat, leaning half off it, on Nayeli. As though Nayeli had any more strength to give than Lu herself.

Across the room, Ben was propped against the wall, his arms folded. Gunnar stood next to him, not as close as usual—the two of them had been unsteady since the attack.

Lu didn't speak until Ben met her eyes, a questioning furrow to his brow.

"Surrender," Lu said.

The whole of the room turned to her.

"Excuse me?" Pierce demanded.

"Ben and I will surrender," Lu amended. "Elazar has wanted it all along, hasn't he? He'll stop anything for it, including whatever he has planned. Tell him we will come to him under a banner of surrender."

Shock choked the room.

Ben straightened. "I agree."

"What?" Gunnar spun on Ben, fury incarnate.

Vex would have objected too. Even now, Lu imagined if Nayeli had the shared Budwig anywhere nearby, he would be raging against her plan.

"It wouldn't be true surrender," Lu told the room. Told herself. "But if Elazar thinks it is, he will prepare for it. Me and Ben, willingly kneeling at his feet? It is a sight he will want this island to see. It will confirm everything he has promised about himself, his power."

"His errant son, returned at last," Ben picked up for her, and Lu sagged against the window frame, grateful. "He will gather crowds, if he hasn't already for whatever he himself has planned. He will relish our supplication."

Gunnar growled, speaking in a patchy mix of Grace Lorayan and Argridian. "You will give yourselves to him.

He will suspect a lie. There is too much risk. Benat—"

Ben shook his head and pulled away, cheeks red. "Of course he'll suspect a trick. Which he will also want crowds to see—if we say we come in surrender, and lie? It will also confirm what he has said about us. Either way, this will guarantee we have an audience, and that Elazar allows us—me—time to speak. I can talk to Grace Loray. I can talk to my father."

Rosalia started to object, but Kari made a hum of agreement.

"As you did with the townsman earlier," she said. "You talked him down. Rationally, calmly—and openly. It is all this island wants, to be heard and gratified. If you present yourself to Elazar in such a way, before crowds, he will be unable to make you a villain. And if the raider syndicates come at your back, supporting you without arms—it will also undo Elazar's lies."

Ben nodded, eyes solemn. In that moment, Lu saw beyond the man who had comforted her in the prison cell after Milo's torture, the man who had kept her from losing herself during those disintegrating weeks. She saw a king.

"Will that be enough?" Pierce asked. "Just . . . talking? The people of this island will hear you apologize and go, 'Oh yeah, we've been fools to believe Elazar—all hail the raiders'?"

"Lu has permanent magic too," Ben said. "If Elazar has taken the vial of permanent magic and tries to present magic as the Pious God's blessing, Lu can disprove that by revealing her own powers. We will force him to show his true self to this island. And this time, if a fight comes, we will prove that Elazar instigated it."

Kari nodded. "We will not lift a blade until his defensors attack."

"What if Elazar uses our missing people as hostages?" Pierce kept on. "He already took that kid. And where will we *be* if we're supposed to surrender? How're we gonna fight?"

"Magic," said Rosalia.

"Permanent magic is not an option," Kari said. "We must consider other means—"

"Magic should still be an option, though," Lu declared.

Nayeli, still next to Lu, lifted her hands and stepped back as if to say, *You're on your own.*

"We cannot deny parts of this island," Lu said. The whole of the room turned to her. "We will win this war as Grace Loray, and that includes magic. Many of our plants are already weapons—Rhodofume, Hemlight, Variegated Holly. Others can be adapted to be useful in battle— Drooping Fern, Budwig Beans. We can go to this meeting armed in other ways."

"You didn't mention the ones we can ingest," Pierce said. "Powersage. That berserker plant, Croxy."

"As long as they are taken willingly. But I will not alter them. No one should."

Rosalia groaned, but Pierce put a hand on her arm and gave Lu a pointed look.

"Just because you decided to stop making permanent magic doesn't mean it won't happen again," he said. "Maybe not now. Maybe not before the war's end. But it *is* possible. It'll happen—so why shouldn't we get ahead of it? Make it, so we can control it."

Lu stiffened. "There is no controlling this. If—when—permanent magic is made, I will no longer be part of it. I'll prepare Grace Loray's plants for use in battle, but I won't continue permanent magic experiments."

Silence fell. Pierce waved his hand, conceding.

"We will send word to Elazar." Kari looked first at Lu, then at Ben. "That the two of you will surrender."

Gunnar, who had been silent since his outburst, shoved out of the room. The slam of the door against the wall signaled some kind of dismissal, and the rest of the room stirred, rose.

Ben disappeared behind Gunnar before Lu could speak to him. What was there to say, though? The plan was straightforward enough. They would surrender to Elazar. They would kneel before the man who had decimated thousands of lives and lied to two separate countries.

And in that surrender, they would force him to reveal his truths. Those truths would be his undoing.

Pierce and Nate left, but Rosalia lingered, her eyes flicking from Kari to Lu.

"We win this war," Rosalia said. "It doesn't mean I trust you."

"I don't expect you to," Kari replied. "As long as you accept that I do not trust you, either. Wariness will keep us in check as we proceed into a unified future."

Rosalia bit her lips together. She smacked her fist over her heart and said, in Grozdan, that phrase Lu had heard from her and her crew—*glory in the attack.*

Hearing her speak Grozdan spiked Lu's hatred of her. She was part of the reason Vex had, for so long, clung to the shame of his scar.

But Vex hadn't put his eye patch back on after last night. Lu had sensed his trepidation, but she'd kissed him again, willing the feel of her lips to act more as a shield than any eye patch.

Rosalia left. Nayeli let out a loud exhale and dropped against the wall.

But she shot upright. "Oh. I guess I have to go get the Tuncians ready, too."

Lu gave a half smile. "Head Nayeli."

Nayeli sobered. "*Acting* Head."

"Acting Head." Lu turned, legs dangling off the window seat. "Have you spoken with Vex?"

"He's still traveling. I'll tell him about our plans, though."

Lu nodded, her focus drifting to the floor in the heaviness that lay between now and the war being a memory.

The door shut behind Nayeli, and Lu lifted her gaze to her mother, realizing they hadn't been alone together since . . . when had they last had a moment to themselves?

On the other side of Fatemah's desk, Kari stared at the wall, her eyes glassy. "I suspected it was him," she said suddenly, and Lu frowned.

"Who?"

"Ibarra."

Coldness swept over Lu's body.

"I suspected he was the one in charge the final night of the revolution," Kari clarified, no emotion in her voice but for the smoothness of her tone. "The defensors in that battalion scattered. Only a few were caught, and they didn't divulge names. But I should have acted on my suspicions."

"The Argridians surrendered the next day," Lu whispered. "You couldn't have done anything. We finally had peace."

"You did not." Kari snapped her eyes up, and Lu jerked back from the anger she saw. "You suffered, you still suffer, and that was my fault for leaving you in that cottage. My fault for standing in front of Ibarra and accepting his surrender when I even *suspected* he was the one who—" She raised a hand to her lips. "Who hurt you. My child. I let him *live*—and you had to be the one. The one to kill him."

Kari raised her hand to cover her eyes. Lu couldn't move, frozen on the window seat, her lungs swollen. She had never expected Kari to take the blame. *Tom* should have taken it.

"You weren't part of it," Lu said. "What happened that night. I never blamed you."

The implication was clear. Kari dropped her hand. "Your father wasn't the only one who destroyed your childhood."

Lu looked away. Hearing him called her *father* sent a jagged bolt of anger through her gut.

"I've tried to tell myself that he was the one who suggested we use you as a spy," Kari whispered. A tear slipped down her cheek. "I've tried to put all the blame on him, as though I was helpless those years. I wasn't, though. Do not idolize me, Adeluna. I'm as much at fault as he is. I let you become a spy. I let you join this war. I put you in harm's way. And I'm so—" She cleared her throat. "I'm so sorry."

Lu felt tears well, matching her mother's. Kari stood only a few paces away, but she felt out of reach, fading farther and farther beyond an ocean of regret and pain.

"All the people I saw die," Lu started, "the families I watched split apart—I never thought it would be ours. I never thought we would lose each other in this war. But Tom is gone no matter how this ends, and I've lost you too, haven't I? We can't come out of this intact. How can we move forward as a family without him, after everything that has happened—"

Kari surged around the table and drew Lu into a hug. She held her there, hand on the back of Lu's head, her lips on Lu's ear. That embrace was the very place Lu thought of when she imagined warmth and security, and she gripped her mother's shoulders, holding on through the hot wash of tears.

"We will endure his betrayal together," Kari told her. "*Together*. Do not retreat into yourself, and I promise to do the same. This war will not take me from you. I swear, sweetheart; you have me. You will always have me."

27

BEN CHASED GUNNAR though the halls of the tenement. Like a moron.

Gunnar disagreed with Ben and Lu's plan to surrender to Elazar? He had *wanted* Ben to confront Elazar. But he wanted Ben to confront Elazar in battle, sword to his throat, not weaponless and in false surrender.

Ben was tired of Gunnar's personal beliefs acting as an impassable wall of what Ben should or shouldn't do.

"Stop!" he shouted. The word vented his frustration, steam shooting up his throat.

Gunnar whipped into a nearby room. It was even smaller than the office. A moth-eaten blanket covered a narrow cot in the corner; an empty plate on a table held moldy crumbs and a thick layer of dust. No one was there, and it looked abandoned—all the better.

Ben shot in after him and slammed the door. "What in

the Pious God's hell is wrong with you?" he demanded. His anger felt purer in Argridian, more freeing than constantly having to speak Grace Lorayan.

"You cannot just *go to him*," Gunnar snapped. "Benat, have you lost your mind?"

"It isn't a true surrender. We have to force his hand."

"No." Gunnar shook his head. "Not like this. Not—"

"I'm going to face Elazar," Ben stated. "It was the reason you kept me locked in that cell! Why have you changed your mind? Because the situation isn't exactly to your liking?"

"No situation would be to my liking," Gunnar said.

"Excuse me?"

The midday sun shoved through the dingy curtains over the small window, throwing speckles of orange on Gunnar's face. He cast his eyes to the side, his stance slackening so he looked timid; that timidness crept over Ben's spine, a distracting itch.

Obstinate to vulnerable. Protective to apologetic.

Holding Ben back in the Tuncian raider cell, then encouraging him to speak to the protesting refugee. He felt as though Gunnar had two hands on him, pushing him, pulling him.

"You have no right," Ben said, low. "No right to distract me like this. I thought you were going to *help me*."

Gunnar looked at him, sheepish. "I am helping you. I just—" He struggled, face pinching. "You are—"

"What?" Ben insisted, hands curling. "What am I?"

Gunnar slammed his fists to his temples. "Stop. I cannot—I can't *think* with you."

"You owe me an explanation," Ben spat. "As your prince, I—"

Ben stopped. Gunnar ripped his fists away from his head, his eyes flaring open.

"I am not your soldier," he said slowly. "You do not command me."

He looked liable to shove Ben aside and stomp from the room. And he could do just that—Ben had no sway over him. They could go into the coming battle with this back-and-forth rift widening until it swallowed them whole.

Ben didn't want that. He wanted the connection he and Gunnar had had in the prison, how they could look at each other and know some thought or plea. How they would whisper to each other, that one phrase, Thaid fuilor mauth, and it said a hundred things. He needed that, going into this battle.

Vex was gone. Lu had told Ben why, but it still stung that his cousin wouldn't be there for the final attack. This army of raiders hated Ben. Lu would be with Kari.

Ben would be alone.

Terror drove a jagged rod through his chest. He needed Gunnar. He needed him more than he could put words to.

"No," Ben said. "You aren't my soldier. You aren't bound to me by loyalty or blood. You're here because of that oath we took. What did it even really mean? Do you regret

439

swearing yourself to me—is that why your advice wavers? Are you only still with me because you fear the Visjorn's wrath?"

Or are you here because you want to be?

Gunnar's face washed with predatory anger in the way his neck tensed. "Do not mock the Visjorn," he said. A pause, and his anger softened—was he blushing? "Or my commitment to you. Since we were in the prison, when I think of you hurt, when I remember what it was to see fear on your face, I come unhinged. There is no situation safe enough. No plan I would hear and think, *That is all right, Benat will be in only moderate danger.* Any danger is too much. If your father touches you—"

Gunnar's skin seemed to glow, the scalding red-orange of a heated iron brand, and the temperature of the room flared high.

Ben felt as if he was on a cliff, staring into an abyss of shock. Gunnar's words were painfully intimate, enhanced by the visceral rage in his eyes and a spreading redness across his cheeks.

"You—" Ben stammered, feeling immensely stupid. "You care about me."

Gunnar's jaw worked. He didn't dignify Ben with a response.

"If I released you from the oath we took," Ben kept on, "you wouldn't leave?"

That earned a screwed-up look of confusion. "A Visjorn

oath cannot be released or broken. But of course I would not leave you."

"Why?"

Gunnar's brows lifted. "Really?"

A door opened in Ben's soul, one he hadn't realized had kept him so afraid. "Yes. Really. I need to know what would make you stay with me, if duty didn't hold you, if honor didn't trap you, if it was just you and me and no war or responsibilities—what would you do?"

Jakes had used him. Elazar had manipulated him. Rodrigu and Paxben had been forcibly taken.

Ben had never processed how damaged he was, to have been so achingly alone, or abused by the only ones who deigned to stay.

Gunnar hesitated for one shaky breath. On a snarl, muffled deep in his throat, he stalked across the room, took Ben's head in his hands, and kissed him.

It happened so quickly, the press of Gunnar's mouth to his, the sudden immersion in the scent of ash and warmth, that Ben went stiff, fingers spread at his sides.

Gunnar drew back. Ben's eyes couldn't get wider, his heartbeat tripped.

"No oaths," Gunnar told him, rubbing the pad of his thumb across Ben's cheekbone. He paused, seeming to realize something, and his grip on Ben's face stiffened. "But that does not mean we are not equals."

Ben's tongue was swollen and heavy with a rich flavor.

He knew how Gunnar tasted. Like wood burning, like the delicate twist of a flame swelling into the midnight sky.

He was silent too long.

Gunnar ripped back, his face red—with disappointment, with anger. "That is not enough? Would you prefer I swear fealty to you, submit to you, bow and scrape to you? I thought—" He scowled, tearing a hand through his hair. "It doesn't matter what I thought."

He started to make for the door. Everything caught up to Ben in a jarring ripple of panic.

Gunnar thought Ben *wanted* people to be beneath him. To be subservient to him as prince.

Ben snatched at Gunnar's biceps. The look Gunnar gave him was both daring and fuming. In their time together, Ben had learned how much effort it took to make Gunnar do something he didn't want to do. Which was why Ben had feared Gunnar would leave—he knew there was nothing he could do to get Gunnar to stay if he decided against it. Not that Ben would have forced him; but knowing the unstoppable power that Gunnar could unleash when he didn't want something made it all the sweeter when he stopped now, waiting.

"I never wanted you to make promises," Ben said. He was all rapid pulse. "I never wanted oaths. I've never had anything *but* those things, and every one of them has broken at my feet. When I face my father, I want you there with me. That's the only way I can do it. If you are there, not as my soldier, but just as—as *mine.*"

Ben pulled back from Gunnar, unable to do a damn thing to hide how much he was shaking. Slowly, muscle by muscle, he lowered to his knees and lifted his eyes to Gunnar.

"I didn't mean to bring my station between us," he whispered. He couldn't force his voice any higher, could barely breathe at all. "I'm sorry. I don't know how to be *this*, without titles and loyalty. Just . . . just tell me what you want. Tell me what to do."

He had never said that to someone before. Not Jakes, not his father. It should have felt foreign and awkward, this plea to be instructed, but somehow, it felt natural.

Gunnar looked entirely at a loss. His eyes flickered, and Ben grew increasingly aware of being on his knees. He'd meant it as a show of respect, equality, but—

Ben swallowed, throat working hard, and he had to drop his eyes to the floor before dizziness sent him sprawling.

A hand cupped his jaw. Gunnar's fingers played at the sandy stubble along Ben's neck. Heat built, and when Ben found it within himself to lift his gaze up again, silence warped the look they shared, meaning and intent and craving.

"You want me to tell you what to do," Gunnar echoed.

A delicious tingle shot through Ben and he bit his lip. Gunnar tracked the motion.

"Yes," Ben told him.

A smile. Dimples punctured Gunnar's cheeks. "Kiss me," he said.

Ben shot to his feet, his rough mouth smothering Gunnar's. Gunnar met his ferocity and forced him back, sending the two of them stumbling until Ben slammed into the wall. Sunlight flickered through the curtains, giving life to the uptick in temperature from Gunnar.

The musk of sweat and fire made Ben breathless. Gunnar grabbed his legs and lifted to wear him like a belt, Ben anchoring himself on Gunnar's neck, a war of bruising kisses and fingernails raking across shoulders.

Gunnar hefted his hips forward, pinning Ben to the wall so he could lift his arms over his head and peel off his shirt. It was an onslaught—the rock of Gunnar's hips between Ben's open legs; the press of hardness against his own; Gunnar's bare chest and exposed clan mark flooding Ben with heat, more heat, he was drowning in the intensity. Sensation trickled down Ben's spine and balled in his gut, driving him, unwinding him.

Gunnar was far less gentle with Ben's shirt—a rip, and it came off in pieces. Ben sank his teeth into Gunnar's bottom lip, and the Mecht purred as he moved his hand between their bodies. Ben yelped when Gunnar's fingers closed around him.

He growled in Pratua, flinched, translated, "This, now—"

A sharp pull of restraint yanked him to a stop before the

plunge into chaos and stars. Gunnar eased back, finding Ben's eyes through the sweat and fever.

"Not just this," Gunnar told him.

Ben sobered, gasping for breath. This moment might be all they could get before their group left to confront Elazar. What awaited them on the other side of this war?

That wasn't what Gunnar meant, but it shifted things into perspective—yes, just this. Just Ben, just Gunnar.

Ben tangled his fingers in Gunnar's hair and responded with another kiss, slowing the rhythm from that of a starving man frantic for food to one savoring an exquisite delicacy. Their mouths drifted just apart, milking a sigh from Gunnar.

Gunnar opened his eyes, the blueness alive with pleasure. "A girl in the Mechtlands—before I left—she said this was how Argridians were. Gentle, sweet."

Ben rolled back, hit by the desire to ask about Gunnar's former partners and a stronger, animalistic need to know—"How is it in the Mechtlands? Like this?"

He dug his nails into Gunnar's shoulder again.

The look between them was scorching, the taunting lift of Gunnar's eyebrow, the curl of Ben's bottom lip between his teeth.

"Yes," Gunnar hummed. "But this time, teach me how it is in Argrid."

Ben smiled, and taught him.

⁂

In no time at all, Vex was yanking on the levers to slow the *Meander* as New Deza came into view. Other boats dotted the lake around them—some family vessels, traders sailing into or out of New Deza. But most were either Argridian steamboats with the curved *V* cut through with crossed swords on flags rippling over pilothouses, or Mecht, flying the same flag.

Vex white-knuckled the helm as his eye cut over the approaching docks. "You wouldn't happen to know which docks Argrid is patrolling more now, would you?"

Leaning on the map table after having stuffed the engine with coal, Jakes grunted. "No."

"Some help you've been so far."

Jakes stayed silent long enough that Vex looked back at him. His arms were planted on the table's edge so his shoulders bunched to his ears, and after a moment, he huffed a sigh.

"What do you know about the boy?" Jakes asked, slipping into Argridian.

Vex steadied the boat around a passing vessel. "He's a good kid," he said, reverting to his native language too. "Smart. Loving. He'll—"

"Not that," Jakes snapped. "I meant—do you know how old he is?"

"Uh—six? I think."

Jakes kicked the floor. Vex kept flipping his attention between Jakes and the approaching port, but in those glances, he watched an entire war pass over Jakes's face.

"Why?" Vex asked.

"Who was his father?"

Vex shrugged. "No idea. Lu probably knows. I only met the kid a few months ago."

He looked out the window and angled the *Meander* for a dock in the middle of the wharf. It was a gamble, but every move was.

When he turned back to Jakes, Vex jumped. Jakes was glaring at him. Hot as flames.

"You didn't know Elazar sent Bianca here. You don't know anything, do you? And you didn't even try to convince Adeluna to continue attempting permanent magic. Why did I expect anything more from you? You're Rodrigu's son. Cowardice runs in your blood."

Vex gaped. He'd never in his life heard anyone call Rodrigu a coward.

They came on the docks. Rage welled in Vex's stomach. "Why would I have known who Elazar sent to Grace Loray? The hell would I have—"

"You knew my sister."

Vex frowned, steering the *Meander* down the narrow dock lane. "What? I told you I haven't known Teo that long."

"Teo, maybe not. But you knew my sister. Bianca. And her daughter, Annalisa."

There, that space ahead was free, and Vex didn't see any defensors on the dock. What he did see, up the wharf, were decorations. People scurried about, hanging banners in indigo and gold, the colors of Grace Loray's pillar of purity.

Vex tamped down his growl of disgust and twisted the helm to the left.

Wait—a memory scratched at Vex's mind. Why did he know those names?

Jakes must have seen the confusion on Vex's face. The map table groaned as he pushed off it, coming to stand next to Vex, near the helm. "You don't remember them. Of course you don't. I shouldn't be surprised—your father cared little for my family, too."

The *Meander* stopped in line with the other vessels on this dock. Vex needed to leap onto the wood and tie it off, but he was stuck at the helm, one slow tremor walking up his left leg.

Vex saw a knife, glinting in the torchlight of the Grace Neus' holding cells.

Rodrigu had been in a cell across from him. His father had been so relentless, even there. Spewing sureties. *"Things will get better, Pax, don't you worry, we'll get out of here—"*

"He's a child! Asentzio—the Pious God wouldn't let you harm a child!"

"He isn't a child," Elazar's voice said in Vex's memory. *"He's a heretic. And I know there are others hiding in my court."*

Two monxes held him down as another came at him with the knife. Elazar wasn't the one to do it. He instructed the monxe on what to cut, though—*"Slower, press the blade harder.*

Yes, just like that. What did you say, brother? What name was that?"

Rodrigu had screamed four names below Grace Neus Cathedral. Over and over, his voice had broken apart while Elazar had the monxe gouge an X into Paxben's eye.

Bartolomeu Montero. The comodoro from Elazar's navy. He was arrested before monxes were even done bandaging Paxben. His pyre burned the same day Rodrigu's did.

Alexandre Nuñez. The priest who ran the Grace Ismael Cathedral. When Paxben had been stuffed into a cell on a ship bound for Grace Loray, defensors had told him that if he was quiet, he could hear Alexandre screaming from a pyre a few streets away.

Estevo Ochoa. The wealthy conde who owned a prolific mine in northern Argrid. Months after Vex left Argrid, he heard that Estevo and his family had been murdered in their sleep.

Raya Cuesta. The last name Rodrigu had screamed, the duquesa who had overseen charity to the poor.

Paxben had known all of them. Raya had brought him a birthday present, a gilded dagger with his initials carved on the handle because her son had gotten one just like it and loved it.

Raya and her husband were thrown beneath the Grace Neus Cathedral as Paxben and Rodrigu were led out to their pyres. Defensors returned Paxben to his cell afterward, of course; his death had been staged. And in the bowels of Grace Neus, while he waited for Elazar to decide what to do with him, he listened to Raya lie.

"We are loyal to the king. My husband and I were not part of any resistance! We serve the Pious God and the Eminence King. No—no, I have no other family. No one was involved!"

"Bianca Cuesta," Vex said aloud now. He wanted to see Jakes's reaction. He *needed* to see Jakes's reaction. "That was the daughter of Duquesa Raya Cuesta. My father's ally. And—"

He struggled. Raya had had a son, too, a little older than Vex, and Rodrigu had mentioned once that they might get along. *"Paxben, you should meet him—he is new to Deza, and from what Raya tells me, Jakome is quite shy—"*

"Jakome. Jakome Cuesta." Vex's hands fell off the helm, his soul flickering out as he stared at the planes of Jakes's face. He felt naked now with his scar bare, and every look from Jakes felt like Elazar's fingers pressing on the corner of his eye, marking him.

Jakes smiled. There was no emotion in it as the *Meander* bumped into the dock, rocking with the current. "At least you remember me. I'm flattered."

Vex's mind hummed—he had another memory, fuzzier, further, of Raya weeping in the foyer of Rodrigu's mansion when she first joined his resistance. Something about her daughter and granddaughter dying. Paxben had watched from the stairway railing as Rodrigu ushered Raya into his study, promising her they would get justice for Bianca and little Anna—

They hadn't died, though. They'd been on Grace Loray, as Bianca and Annalisa Casales. Menesia. Elazar had to have given them Menesia.

Vex staggered, legs aching. "Why?"

"I couldn't parade myself around Deza with the name of convicted conspirators," Jakes said, assuming his question had been more direct. "So I made my mother's name my last name. You aren't the only one who became someone else to escape his past—though, in my case, I didn't change so much to *escape* as I did to *embrace*. Your father"—Jakes rounded on Vex, and he showed emotion now, emotion that had Vex slamming back into the wall—"your coward of a father gave them up. And I'd almost be able to appreciate the irony in him betraying the people who betrayed *him* if I hadn't had to watch them burn."

Vex had never found out how Elazar had discovered that Rodrigu was heading a coup against him. He'd always assumed defensors had uncovered a paper trail or rumors.

"Your mother," Vex said, a breath, "betrayed—"

"Your father promised us a new Argrid," Jakes stated. "But he refused to do what needed to be done to destroy Elazar, so yes, my mother took action. Elazar already distrusted his brother. She put one letter on Elazar's desk, one correspondence between Rodrigu and the Grace Lorayan rebels, and that was all it took. My parents were going to lead the rebellion after him. My parents were going to change *everything*."

"Your mother told Elazar—*she's* the reason for—"

"Elazar killed my sister and niece—and I find out, years later, that it was so much worse than that. He *used* them." Jakes slammed his fist into the wall beside Vex's head, making him jump. "And—and *Teo*. You have no idea where he came from? Defensors told my family that when Bianca died, she was pregnant. That she suffered complications—but Elazar experimented on her. On Annalisa, too, and I know—*I know* he defiled them. He, or one of his soldiers. Someone forced that child on her. And Teo is—Teo *can't be*—"

Jakes sobbed with such force that Vex almost felt sorry for him.

Vex stayed against the wall by the helm, his breathing shallow. His eye went to the table at the rear of the pilot-house. He'd left Nayeli's Budwig Bean in the top drawer. What could she do to help him now, though?

"Elazar has a vial of permanent magic." Jakes's voice was low, the tone of resolve fraying. "If he has already taken it, we've lost. *That* is my goal, my family's goal, to stop him."

Vex wilted. "You're—you're gonna go after Elazar *yourself?* Now? What about Teo?"

Jakes's jaw shifted. "If the boy has magic in him—no. He doesn't. Lu's magic has already proven itself. That is what will stop this war."

Vex snarled, shoulders tensing. "Rationalize all you want. Teo's the sweetest, most loving kid on this island.

Maybe this whole damn world. And the fact that you're trying to make yourself feel all right about putting Elazar's downfall over his security? *You're* the coward."

"I've given everything for this war!" Jakes screamed a hand's width back so Vex felt the full brunt of his pain and fury. "Elazar has ripped everyone I love out of my arms, and I will get that vial from him. I will stop him."

Jakes reared back as if to punch the wall again, but his stance shifted, and Vex saw the strike coming for him. He braced himself on the helm and kicked Jakes in the chest.

Agony flared up Vex's legs. Bones shifted and muscles frayed and he screamed as Jakes slammed into the opposite wall with a startled *oof.*

Vex dropped to the floor, his face contorted in pain.

Jakes gathered himself faster than Vex. "Find . . . find that *boy*," he spat, the weight of not saying Teo's name landing unsteady and weak. "Waste your time running useless missions. But *I'm* going to stop Elazar. *I'm* going to protect our country, you disgusting traitor."

He shoved himself to his feet, raced across the deck, leaped off onto New Deza's wharf.

Vex scrambled to the table and yanked open the drawer. The pouch with the Budwig Bean was still inside—he snatched it and planted the bean into his ear. "Nay? Nayeli?"

Silence. It would've been a miracle if she'd had the other bean in her ear at that moment.

Vex slackened, the current rocking the untethered

Meander. Jakes would go after Elazar—and what? He wanted permanent magic more than anything rational.

Jakes Rayen. Jakome Casales. Ben's former . . . whatever. Teo's uncle. Raya's son.

Whoever he was. Whichever side of this he was on. Not Elazar's side, but not the raiders' side, either. His own manic side.

Vex looked out the door, at the port. He couldn't spot in which direction Jakes had run off, the crowds pressing back and forth under the fluttering decorations. He felt like eyes watched from every angle, ears listened from every empty rooftop.

Let defensors catch Jakes in New Deza—it was as much as he deserved.

But that was the reason Vex had brought Jakes along at all. He knew the defensors, the pattern of their patrols. He likely still had friends he could trust not to turn him in. Would he trade secrets to Elazar for feigned security? *"Your nephew is in the port. He wants the boy."*

Vex had to move fast. Fast and carefully.

He grabbed a cloak from the pilothouse and tugged it on, covering his eye, before he swung off the *Rapid Meander.* Hopefully no defensor knew his boat enough to recognize it, but he latched it to the dock and left it with a reassuring pat.

His hands shook. Goddamn Jakes—goddamn Raya Cuesta—*goddamn it all.*

Teo. Focus on getting Teo back.

Vex trekked off into the city. He should've scanned roof-tops for soldiers, but his mind refused to think of anything other than every memory he had of Jakes and Raya.

He didn't have much. He'd been a kid. He hadn't paid attention to most things.

Regret came in a wave. If he'd paid more attention. If he'd *tried*, at all, instead of——

Vex caught himself when his plea to Lu slammed into his mind.

"Can we stop apologizing to each other?"

Regret wouldn't bring Rodrigu back. But Vex could stop Jakes. He could save Teo.

The New Deza castle shot into view on a plateau that overlooked Lake Regolith. If Elazar was in this city, if Tom had Teo with him, the castle was the likeliest—most forti-fied—place they'd be.

Hands in fists, Vex dredged up every bit of resolve he could find. He could get into the New Deza castle. He'd done it with Nayeli, Cansu, and Edda only a few weeks ago. He'd listen for any news, sneak down to the cells. Step by step.

The main gate was shut and soldiers paced on the top of the wall. The smaller side gate on the east of the yard was Vex's best chance of getting in unnoticed. It was how he and Lu had escaped with Teo in the first place, but its road had no cover all the way up to the gate itself.

Vex started walking up the road. It was what Lu'd done to get out of the castle's stable yard—she'd just strolled right up, like she belonged there.

He reached the gate. One door was closed; the other sat open enough to allow servants and other employees to slip through.

Vex held his breath and wiggled into the opening. The stable yard looked the same as last he'd been here. Three barns defined the area, while off to the right, the castle gardens could be seen, and to the left, the front gate. The castle itself towered beyond, and—

Vex's eye snapped back to the castle yard. People crowded there, shoulder to shoulder, not making a sound, not moving. Barely even breathing.

The gate behind him banged shut on the system of gears that commanded it. Vex whipped his head up, seeing defensors in the guardhouse now, their scowls deep and taunting.

Vex turned, slowly, facing the group of people again. He recognized them. Those, Emerdian raiders—those, Tuncian—Grozdan—

One stepped out of the group, her short, jagged hair wafting around her face.

Cansu. She aimed a pistol at Vex. "In the name of the Pious God, surrender. Heretic."

28

THE TONE OF the war had changed.

Refugees remained in the sanctuary by their own choice. No families were forced to stay. No raiders were required to prepare for the journey to New Deza. The prevailing attitude was one of tired acceptance, a resignation as thick as smoke.

The raiders would fight for the Grace Loray they wanted. If people disagreed with their leadership, let them leave to join Elazar, or run off to initiate their own plans. They would fight this war on a foundation of unity, and willingness was essential.

So Lu knew, as she watched Rosalia hand out small weapons to her raiders, that every Grozdan here *wanted* a new future. As Nate and Pierce's raiders brought Lu baskets of plants to prepare for the coming fight, she knew each of them had changed, linked to the Grozdan raiders and the

Tuncian raiders and even Kari and Ben, through the tightening bond of kinship. To feel the delicate beginnings of true peace was staggering.

All it had taken was another war with Argrid.

Kari's messenger sent word to Elazar, telling him of Ben and Lu's intended surrender. She chose the place and time: the docks in New Deza, facing an easy escape onto the lake; five days from the sanctuary attack, at dusk. Only three steamboats would approach the port, twenty raiders total. Kari doubted Elazar would truly stage Ben and Lu's surrender on the docks—it was far more likely that defensors would escort them somewhere undisclosed. For that reason, Kari would reserve the bulk of their forces to deploy around New Deza—Rosalia would come in from the north, Nate from the south; Nayeli the west. Pierce's men would be on steamboats in the middle of the lake, four raiders and himself all with Budwigs, waiting to swoop in if—when—things turned to a fight.

Lu kept herself busy those final days. She tied Aerated Blossom pods to strings that could loop around fighters' wrists. She captured Drooping Fern smoke in reeds, sealed until the user blew hard on one end and released the knockout gas. Hemlight went into pouches with other explosives to create crude grenades; healing plants nestled inside vials to be tucked into boots; Powersage's orange leaves became a paste to be used just before the battle, for added strength.

Most importantly: Bright Mint leaves went into snug

jars, as many as she could find. Everyone approaching New Deza would need this counter plant, should Elazar's final plan somehow involve widely spread Menesia.

Lu filled Fatemah's hut with Grace Loray's magic, transforming it in the simple, common ways she had learned over her years of study. Were Fatemah here, Lu thought she might be content to know what her former laboratory was now being used for. Not permanent magic—just magic, this island in its purest form. It felt like a fitting tribute to her.

Nayeli spoke to Vex with the Budwig once, when he was still hours out from New Deza. Otherwise, either she kept missing him or something horrible had happened. Lu counted and recounted how many vials of healing plants they had and used the monotony to sear her mind. He would be fine. He was smart. Likely he had to stay silent while searching for Teo—but he was fine.

Two days after they sent the message to Elazar, Ben came to see Lu. The messenger had returned. Elazar's reply was simple. *"Praise the Pious God. I look forward to our reunion."*

Ben held out his hand to Lu, and she took it, fingers tight around his.

"Together," she told him.

Ben squeezed her hand. His eyes glistened. "Together."

❊❊❊

The steamboat's engine hummed under Lu's feet. She stood at the bow, drawing Lake Regolith's crisp air into her lungs. The evening sun was just beginning to fade, casting a hue of orange over the sky, and the water's glassy surface reflected it in a rebound of flame and night.

"Vex will be there," Ben said, standing behind her.

Lu's chin dropped to her chest. The peace of the lake shattered.

Nayeli still hadn't heard from him. He hadn't returned to the sanctuary before they left. It shouldn't have taken him so long. Something had happened, and Lu couldn't contain her panic in a safe, quiet little box like she needed to. It took all her willpower to not beg someone, anyone, to let her go find him.

"In Deza," Ben started, words as soft as the wind, "the Grace Loray holiday is celebrated with mass healing ceremonies. People pour out of infirmaries and line the streets as my father and his priests walk through the city, laying hands on them, *cleansing* them. Whether it works or not, I honestly can't say—disease does drop after this holiday. But Paxben"—there was a smile in Ben's voice—"one year, he convinced me to pretend we had both gotten a plague. We painted ourselves in bright red spots and intended to sneak down to the ceremony, to make my father heal us. I don't know what Paxben's plan truly was—he was laughing too hard to explain. We both looked absurd, covered in blotchy red welts."

A moment of silence, then Lu tipped her head, staring at Ben's boots. "What happened?"

"My uncle caught us. And it turned out that the paint Paxben had found was for touching up statues in the gardens, meaning it could withstand rain, snow, wind—"

"No," Lu breathed, and couldn't help but smile.

Ben nodded. "It took four weeks for the red spots to fade."

Lu laughed. It cut down to her toes. "He's still just as careless."

Ben shrugged. "But if there is a Pious God, I swear it must love him, for all he has survived. He will be fine. He's resilient. And—we are, too."

In the steamboat's pilothouse, Lu caught sight of Gunnar, watching them. Near him, talking with a Tuncian raider, Kari slid her eyes, occasionally, to Lu.

"I have to believe so," Lu whispered. "For all we have survived."

And all we have yet to overcome.

❖❖❖

Ben didn't know how many people populated New Deza—but he suspected all of them were at the wharf.

Kari assumed Elazar would be deep in the port to give himself an upper hand, and that defensors would escort Ben and Lu far from the waterways. But as their steamboat approached the city, it became clear that Elazar had set himself up here. People packed the wharf, shifting bodies that clogged every free space Ben could see between the docks and the anchored steamboats. All of it concentrated around the northern end—the military docks, Lu said.

The raider driving their boat plowed it down the second dock. At the end, a platform waited, wide planks of wood holding defensors along the back and priests in somber black robes. Banners and pennants fluttered in the evening breeze, carrying the navy and white of Argrid down the wharf and almost, but not quite, hiding the defensors lining the top of the tide wall.

Also on the platform, a line of Mecht raiders stood behind Ingvar Pilkvist. Ben hadn't known the man before those village parades, weeks ago now, but he recognized again the vacancy in his expression that came with Menesia. How many memories had Elazar taken from Ingvar to convince this mighty stream raider Head that he was loyal to Argrid?

It was only slightly less horrible than what Elazar had done to Cansu, making Menesia's effects delayed until triggered by his hymn. And then she had obeyed him. Utterly. She had murdered her own raiders at his feet.

What did Elazar have planned for the rest of this island?

Ben was so lost in searching for his father—Elazar was nowhere in sight, but he was here, he had to be—that Lu's clipped inhale had him grabbing for a nonexistent sword.

"Tom isn't here," she whispered. She turned to look at Kari in the pilothouse. The expression that passed between them kicked Ben in the chest—a deep, meaningful connection of parent to child that he couldn't remember ever experiencing.

As if dragged forward to cement the inadequacy of their relationship, Elazar ascended onto the platform, hands lifted to the heavens.

The steamboat shuddered to a stop. Raiders rushed to the railing, met by defensors with weapons out. Everyone hardened.

Ben had told Gunnar to stay in the pilothouse until things turned dire. He needed Gunnar here, but he needed Gunnar *safe*, somewhere he couldn't be used against Ben until they were all free to fight for themselves. But with his back to the pilothouse's door, Ben felt the temperature increasing, steady and sure.

"Benat," came Gunnar's voice.

Ben pivoted enough to send Gunnar a weak smile. He couldn't make himself meet his eyes.

"My son has returned to me," Elazar's voice boomed from the platform. The crowd was silent.

Velvet-soft peace fell over Ben. He took one step, another, crossing the deck to meet Lu, still at the bow. The defensors before them gave leery glowers, their pistols cocked at their sides, a few swords naked.

Ben grabbed the edge of the boat and leaped onto the dock. Lu followed, steadying herself on his arm.

Lu had made sure every pocket was stuffed with plants, small, discreet vials and pouches. Defensors searched them for weapons—they took a few vials of plants but didn't find all of them—and, hand in hand, Ben and Lu walked toward the platform.

All the raiders stayed on their boats. When the fighting started, Ben and Lu would be separated from any allies until they fought their way through, unless Nayeli's people had made it into the crowd.

Brittle hope and handfuls of magic were the only things that would keep them alive.

The silence held as Ben and Lu walked up the platform. When he stood on the wooden planks, able to see far across the crowd, unease drove into Ben's chest. Many of these faces had masks of blankness similar to Pilkvist's. Had they been in Argrid, Ben would have dismissed it as devotion—but had Elazar inspired that deep piety here? Or had he already given them Menesia? Were Ben and Lu too late?

Elazar moved to the front center of the platform, his body cocked slightly toward the crowd but his arms open to Ben. "Benat Gallego," he said, voice rising. "And Adeluna Andreu. The Pious God is eager for you to return to his fold. Kneel and offer your surrender."

Ben swallowed. He expected to kneel first, to have to pull Lu to her knees beside him, but Lu stepped ahead of him and lowered herself to the platform, back stiff and eyes on the wood.

"Benat," Elazar prodded, his arms still spread.

Defensors rimmed the platform at Ben's feet. They stood at the rear of the stage, by the steps, held pistols on the tide wall above—waiting on Elazar's orders, should Ben falter.

Elazar, though, was calm and sure. Joyful, even.

"No," Ben said.

Elazar's arms slid down. "No?"

Ben had been reciting questions for days, things he would ask his father to get him to prove his madness before the crowd:

You say I am impure—but I came from you, so does that not also make you impure?

When did my impurity start? Everyone I caught as an Inquisitor in Argrid—you should release them, for I captured them while under the Devil's hold, and their arrests were therefore to serve him, not the Pious God.

A dozen questions rolled through Ben's mind. But only one came out of his mouth.

"Have you ever loved me?"

Elazar's eyebrows shot up. The question was as unexpected for him as it was for Ben, who trembled in the wake of it, not realizing how desperately he had always wanted to ask that.

"Did you love my mother? Your parents?" Ben continued, heat rising in his chest. "Are you even capable? Am I a fool, to keep expecting something from you that you cannot give?"

For one shallow inhale, Ben saw hesitation on Elazar's

face. The corners of his mouth dipped downward, his eyes narrow, calculating.

Ben knew, if Lu had asked that question of Kari, she would have responded simply, but far more meaningfully: *Yes. Yes, I love you. Of course I love you.*

"You don't, though," Ben whispered. "You don't love me."

He was small again, a boy in awe of his father, the king, the Eminence. He was a child, and Ben staggered, facing the crowd.

"I trusted this man," Ben shouted, pointing at Elazar. "I was once every version of you—eager and hopeful and so in love with King Asentzio Elazar Gallego that every word from him sounded dipped in honey. But I promise you"— here was where bullets would fly, if Elazar wanted. Here was where he would realize his son had no intention of bowing to him—"I *promise* you that he is a lie. Everything about him, every word he says. *Lies.*"

Ben faced Elazar, vibrating in a lifetime of repressed actions, unspoken words.

And Elazar stood there, watching him, an unreadable face framed by waiting defensors.

"He killed my family," Ben said, the truth scraping up through his soul and falling out of him in a rush of breath and tears. "You—*you*—murdered everyone I loved and made me watch as they burned, *alive.* You let your monxes beat me—*you* beat me until my bones snapped. I lost myself in a dozen different vices trying to escape the things you did to me. You speak of benevolence as though you know it so well, and of mercy and love and honesty, and I believed you were those things. I don't believe anymore." Ben's tongue was aflame, his soul rapturing from his body. "I don't believe in you."

He waited, expecting gunshots.

The crowd murmured. A handful of people gaped at him, the weight of his words shattering what hold Elazar had had on them; others stared in that glazed unawareness, hardly having moved since Ben started speaking.

"I knew," Elazar started, and he faced the crowd, "that it was too much to hope that Benat had chosen to renounce evil. But I told you, Grace Loray—my son has returned to me. The Pious God makes a way, as long as the faithful remain true. And he has presented a way."

The adrenaline that had wrapped around every word from Ben returned on him tenfold, panic and dread a toxic brew. Elazar would force Menesia on him, like he had on Cansu.

Ben reached for the Bright Mint vial in his back pocket, fingers moving slowly—

"My son was taken years ago," Elazar said. Ben frowned, his body freezing. "Swept up in the war on Grace Loray. I admit before you now that he was the product of an illicit romance, an affair that speaks to the sinful nature at my own core. Yes, I am capable of being seduced by evil—but I repent my sins and strive, every day, for purity. My punishment for this failing was to lose my son. But the Pious God has seen fit to return him to me. My youngest son, a fresh start."

The declaration was so incredible that Ben's mind went white. He was vaguely aware of Lu shooting to her feet and saying a name:

"Teo."

The boy? Elazar's—

Ben's vision fogged. Gray clouds and a thrashing sea.

"Teo Gallego," Elazar corrected, giving Lu a sweet smile. "The Pious God has given me a new son to cement the rightness in Grace Loray's rebirth. He rewards his followers when the costs we pay are great."

"You're lying," Lu growled. She turned to Ben. Saw his blankness, his immobile panic, and he felt her fingers on his arm. "He's lying, Ben. Teo is too young, he can't be your—"

"You asked me, Benat, if I ever loved you," Elazar cut in. Ben glared at him, and Elazar grinned. "The truth is: not enough. For your sake, though, you should be glad— the Pious God requires sacrifices even from his staunchest children, but you never meant enough to me. No, Benat, there is a greater sacrifice. I told you once—the Pious God showed me what I have to do, once and for all, to resurrect Argrid from the poverty it has sunk into, and he has confirmed it by returning Teo to me—this boy, filled with power, who is worthy of my name."

It shouldn't have hurt. Ben was glad not to be worthy of

Elazar—but the look in his father's eyes, the direct nega-
tion of everything Ben had wanted, hoped for, dreamed of—

"We will turn this island against you," Lu snapped. "We
already have what we need to stop you from destroying
Grace Loray more than you already have."

Elazar's eyes widened in amusement. "Do you? With so
many raiders against you?"

Lu's shoulders leveled. "The Mecht syndicate doesn't—"

"Not those barbarians."

At the rear of the stage, Pilkvist looked up.

Ben stepped closer to Lu, taking her elbow. He didn't
dare scan the crowd, hoping for Nayeli's Tuncian raiders to
be nearby; he couldn't make himself look back at the docks
to see Gunnar, flames up his arms.

He waited, breathing only to fill the moments until the
storm broke.

"You provided the means to uncover Menesia's purpose
in the Pious God's plan," Elazar said to Lu. "Your father—
his brilliance on this subject has kept him alive, despite his
weakness over you. The Church's hymns, when sung after
the highest Menesia dosage, trigger utter obedience. Which
is what the Pious God rewards. *Obedience.*"

Lu staggered. Ben's grip on her arm pinched tighter.

"Many of the raiders on this island," Elazar said, "once
uncontrollable criminals, are now docile servants of the
Pious God."

"The missing raiders," Lu guessed.

Elazar's smile was steady. He tipped his head and lifted the fingers of his left hand, motioning above him—to the sky? No, to the castle, the one sitting on the cliff over Lake Regolith, night's black shadows curling around the towering stone walls.

Soft light emanated from it now. Ben's stomach twisted. What—who—was up there?

"The raiders, like the people of this island, refused to submit to purity," Elazar said. "But the Pious God is wondrous. Everyone is helpless when asked to play their role in his will, even those the Devil has ensnared."

"No," Ben stated. "We're done. This is *over*, today. We won't—"

"But you will, Benat! Don't you see? You came for war, didn't you? You have raiders lying in wait to attack. You have allies, weapons, all out for blood. Just as the Pious God wants!" Elazar's madness drew color into his cheeks. "*This island* is the source of all evil. It brought war. It brought division. It caused the ills that harm Argrid. To bring peace to our country—no, to the *world*—I must sacrifice Grace Loray. I must cleanse this island, in its entirety, and thereby destroy the source of all evil."

The crowd might have reacted with gasps, protestation. But Ben was beyond himself, watching as though above his own body.

"These people"—Elazar waved at the crowd—"even the ones who have not been given Menesia, they will not fight

470

back. They believe the word of the Pious God. And the villagers in the outskirts—they will receive with open arms the people my defensors arrested and are, even now, returning. People like your *missing raiders*, who are now wholly my servants."

"No," Lu murmured.

"Every soul on this island"—and Elazar didn't stop, *couldn't*—"every speck of corruption, every seed of evil— *everyone*, after tonight, will be given over to the Pious God, as I should have done long ago. This new son of mine, Teo—he is the beacon of Argrid's future. We shall leave this island, fresh and reborn, and Argrid will rise from Grace Loray's ashes, anew."

"You never wanted to convert Grace Loray," Ben said, breath escalating. "You're going to kill everyone."

"You're insane," Lu said. "This is barbaric—"

Pilkvist shot forward another step. He had a pistol out now, and Ben swung in front of Lu, a shield.

"Barbaric," Pilkvist echoed.

"Ingvar!" Lu shouted. "Elazar promised you support on this island. He promised to help your people and return New Deza to the Mecht immigrants. He's taken you—he lied!"

Ingvar launched forward again and aimed his pistol at Elazar's head.

Defensors swarmed the platform, weapons out. The crowd reacted, stifled screams and calls of alarm, the first beginnings of reaction through their confusion.

But Elazar smiled, one hand raised to stay his soldiers. His other hand he stuck into his robes and withdrew a vial.

Lu's other vial of permanent magic. Ben had the last one, which he had given to Gunnar before this so the defensors couldn't take it from him.

Ben instinctively reached for Elazar's vial. At a tip of Elazar's head, defensors pinned their weapons on Ben and Lu.

"Ah, Benat. I wouldn't. The Pious God has no use for you anymore. Adeluna, child—you have succeeded, I heard?" Elazar tipped the vial, admiring it. "Everyone on Grace Loray will die to drive out the Devil's foothold in this world. Argrid will rise. I will unlock the powers in my new son's blood, and he will reign unmatched over this earth. With this vial, I will pave the way, becoming the Pious God myself."

He uncorked and downed the contents before Ben could scream, *"Don't!"*

Coughing, Elazar doubled forward. Lu braced herself on Ben.

Pilkvist didn't pull the trigger. He watched Elazar sink to the ground, defensors doing the same, and Ben was reminded of a cell in Deza, Elazar and Jakes watching a sick man Ben had given healing potion. Not caring for the life or death in the balance—wanting the outcome.

After a lifetime, Elazar uncurled, straightened. His hair

was mussed now, wild around his face, and his deranged eyes focused on Ben.

"I am the Pious God incarnate," Elazar bellowed, and cupped his hands over his head in the Church's symbol. "And I will consume this Devil-touched island in fire and blood."

He began to sing a bellowing hymn that the defensors surrounding the area picked up. It reverberated through the docks, resonant and haunting, and when it ended, death followed.

A gunshot. Another. Ben grabbed Lu and hit the platform, arms thrown over their heads. Through the tangle, Ben watched spots of blood puncture Pilkvist's chest. Defensors fired again, and again, but Pilkvist snarled and forced his pistol to stay up—

Elazar didn't move, his focus on the sky, face utterly serene.

Pilkvist turned his pistol to his own temple and pulled the trigger.

A cry tore from Ben's lips. Lu scrambled closer to Ben, pushing him back, back—toward the edge of the stage.

Mecht raiders were interspersed with the Argridian defensors. On the stage, on the tide wall; everywhere, they saw Pilkvist's death.

"If you do not wish to surrender," came Elazar's voice again, "then, Benat, I suggest you head for the castle. My new son is undergoing his first task as Argrid's heir:

disposing of my errant nephew."

Lu spun around on her knees and screamed. "What did you do to them? What—"

Ben grabbed her, flattening the two of them as defensors started firing—at the crowd.

The defensors on the tide wall followed. The pop of gunshots fostered screaming, the crowd breaking awake in a frenzy of agony and attack. Within the crowd, citizens turned on their neighbors in snarling waves, fingers in claws, weapons made from stones or hidden knives. The vacancy in their eyes remained, Menesia triggered by the hymn.

Elazar was killing them. Everyone on this island. He *wanted* this bloodshed.

Chanting rose, the lull of voices fighting to break through the Menesia fog.

"Barbaric," the Mecht raiders said.

"Tell your raiders to attack. To slaughter without mercy." Elazar dropped a look at Ben. "This is Grace Loray's destiny. Do whatever you feel you must—but purity will come to this island, and in the morning, all evil will be crushed."

Ben and Lu rolled off the platform and raced for the docks as the Mecht raiders' chanting came louder over the gunshots, louder over the screams of death: "Barbaric. *Barbaric.*"

29

AFTER EVERYTHING THAT had happened—the lives changed, the plots unveiled—Vex had ended up right back in the New Deza castle's prison.

It wasn't the cell where he'd first met Lu. That'd been the high-security wing, for *dangerous* criminals—this wing had a door to the courtyard at the end, one Cansu had dragged him through. She'd tossed him into an empty cell despite his begging.

She hadn't reacted to Nayeli's name. Hadn't reacted to Fatemah's death, or Port Mesi-Teab being attacked. She'd just chucked him in the cell and left like she was some mindless defensor, not a vicious raider Head who could kick Vex's ass blindfolded, or the woman who drove Nayeli so crazy that Vex's heart was perpetually broken by extension.

The only thing she did before she left was rip the Budwig

Bean from his ear, drop it on the ground, and smash it with her boot.

Some part of her still existed. But no matter how Vex shouted, she didn't come back.

For days after that, the defensors left him alone. Occasionally someone brought him measly rations, and he'd scream at them for news of Teo, or to speak to Elazar—he didn't want to speak to Elazar, shit—or *anything* that might get someone to tell him what was happening. What the hell had been with all those raiders in the courtyard? *And where the hell was Teo?*

Vex's legs throbbed. He paced the length of his cell, trying to work out the spasms, but they came in tight, crippling waves that had him biting back sobs.

Lu'd be out of her mind with worry for him by now. Nayeli, too. Hopefully they'd be on their way to New Deza, ready to confront Elazar on their own and end this whole mess before Vex really did need answers to any of his questions.

Some rescue mission this had turned out to be. God. He'd been so damn certain he could do this, find Teo, solve *one* of these problems on his own. But Jakes had shaken him up. Vex hadn't been focused when he'd gotten here. He'd walked right into it.

Jakes. Vex hoped defensors would drag his sorry ass into this hall at some point. Maybe bruised or black-eyed. A broken rib or two. Yeah. That'd feel like justice.

Imagining Jakes with the shit beat out of him was the only thing keeping Vex upright.

Three days after Vex'd been caught, just as the sun was starting to set, the outside door opened. Four defensors marched down the hall and shifted to the side.

Tomás Andreu walked in behind them, hands behind his back, polished boots spotless.

Vex, who had been sitting against the back wall, didn't rise when Tom stopped in front of his cell. "Fuck you," he said in Argridian.

Tom ignored Vex's outburst and pointed at the doors behind him. "You will accompany me out those doors. You will not run. You will not fight. Though you may have forgotten, you are a Gallego, and you will accept this fate with all the grace and dignity befitting your station. Grace and dignity"—Tom paused, his lips twitching—"that I hear your father did not show."

That yanked Vex to his feet. "What?"

"Now, I understand you have little reason to obey any of the demands I have made. Let us call this . . . insurance, then." Tom snapped his fingers.

Two more defensors came just within the doorway, enough to frame them but not inside the hall. Vex moved to the cell's bars to see.

Between the defensors, Teo stood, hands clasped before him, eyes downcast and timid as though someone had ordered him to be still and obedient.

Vex yanked on the bars as Tom waved and the defensors pulled Teo out of sight.

"Son of a *bitch*!" Vex screamed. "Let him go!"

"You will not run," Tom said, speaking as though Vex wasn't swearing him into the afterlife, as though Teo wasn't a prisoner too. He seemed exhausted, if anything, worn out by the backbreaking work of destroying lives. "You will not do anything foolish. Understand?"

Sweat washed over Vex's body, his sight blurring in fury and horror.

Elazar's voice echoed from the cell in Deza, memories erratic with pain. *"Your son has one more eye, brother. Are you certain you have told me all I wish to know?"*

Rodrigu's desperate gulps of air still numbed Vex. *"Yes, I swear—stop hurting him—"*

"Yes," Vex told Lu's father. A piece of his heart shriveled up and died. "I understand."

Tom's focus slid to the floor and he absently motioned for defensors to unlock Vex's cell. Fuming, Vex kept his gaze on Tom's downcast eyes as defensors obeyed and snapped manacles around his wrists.

"She might have been able to forgive you," Vex told Tom. "But now? She'll *slaughter* you for touching Teo. If you think obeying Elazar is worth losing her, then you never deserved her in the first place."

Tom started to lead the way down the hall but stopped. His neck tensed as he considered something, and he tipped his chin over his shoulder, half turned back.

"The love you feel for her is a ripple," Tom said. "But the love of a parent for their child? You cannot fathom it. Everything I have done is for my children."

Disgust made an effective shield against any other emotions. Tom continued on, and Vex stumbled after him.

The defensors shoved him outside, back into the castle's courtyard. The high stone walls of the complex created a perimeter of light in the blackening evening sky, torches pulsing orange. The people crowding the area were the raiders who'd caught him, the ones from the Emerdian, Tuncian, and Grozdan syndicates who defensors had snatched up over the past weeks and pumped full of Menesia.

Distant gunshots made Vex jump. Farther out, was that—

"Screaming?" Vex twisted in the arms of the defensors. "What the hell—Andreu!"

Lu. Ben. Were they confronting Elazar? Was this part of their plan? God, he hoped so.

But the gates to the courtyard opened on a trumpet singing alarm. Defensors started belting a hymn, a low, melodic Argridian dirge that blanketed the area.

The crowd of raiders snapped upright. They drew their weapons. And, as one, they turned for the gate.

Who were these raiders going to fight? Their own people?

The yard emptied. Only a few raiders and defensors

remained, still looking ready for battle. One was Cansu.

"Cansu!" Vex shouted. He tripped and the defensors yanked him upright, whipping him around to face what they approached.

A platform sat where Vex'd last seen it, weeks ago. Tom stood on it, facing the single pyre arrayed before it.

Vex's throat swelled, and the pain in his legs flared so high he started to see spots.

A pyre.

More defensors stood at the back of the platform with Teo, eyes still downcast, mouth puckered in desperate concentration. Vex almost called out to him, but his throat was dry, and all that came was a gasp on the humid, rancid air.

A pyre.

More gunshots came from the city. Explosions now, too. Screams, war cries, various lilting, out-of-place hymns. Was Lu attacking? Kari? Maybe they'd get here in time. Maybe Vex wouldn't have to think about that damn pyre—

Defensors grabbed his manacles and heaved him at the wood post. He caught himself on it before he ripped back, a savage instinct tearing his soul in half.

His legs buckled. He couldn't be here—he *could not* be here—

The defensors hooked his arms and slammed his spine against the wood. One had a length of chain that he fastened around Vex's waist and chest, locking him back, secure and immobile. They left him facing the platform, and he looked up to see Tom—and Teo, at the head of the platform now, bloodshot eyes tearstained and furious.

Vex's horror redirected, briefly. What had they done to Teo?

Tom gave a slight bow and turned. "On your command," he said, hesitating. "Prince Teo."

Sweat slicked Vex's face, made the manacles grate on his wrists. "Prince?" he echoed. "What the— Teo! Teo, look at me—"

Teo's fury peaked. A tear slipped down his cheek, his rage bubbling to the surface. "You lied to me!" he shouted—at Vex. It stunned Vex silent. "You knew all along. You kept me away from my family. You, and—and *Lu*. And everyone. You all kept me away from my father."

Vex's mouth bobbed open. *What?* Oh god—Prince Teo. *My father.*

Elazar had told Teo that he was Teo's father. It couldn't be true—could it? Hell no. That kid had none of Elazar in him. Not that Ben did, either, but the image of Elazar being at all connected to Teo was revolting.

"Teo—I wouldn't do that," Vex tried. His voice scratched. "They're the ones who lied! Teo, Lu loves you. I love you. You can't believe—"

"*No!*" Teo barked, his little body trembling, his lips clenched tight. "I hate you, Vex."

He folded his arms and turned away.

Tom took that as a sign. He nodded at a def⟨

him, his movements slow and tired, as though some part of him had to detach from what was happening. The defensor had an unlit torch that he quickly set with flames.

In Deza, they covered the heads of condemned with canvas sacks to embody their shame. Vex wished for it now, for that one obscure Argridian tradition to make this fate easier. That had been the only solace he'd been able to find when he'd sat next to his father in the carriage outside the Grace Neus. *At least I won't have to see Ben watch me die.*

As if that would make the flames less painful. As if that would make his terror less nauseating. But then defensors had shoved Paxben back into the carriage while Rodrigu burned, and dragged out some other poor prisoner to die in Paxben's place.

Paxben hadn't seen any of it, but he'd heard it. He'd smelled it. He'd *felt* it, and canvas sack or no canvas sack, this death was incomprehensible.

"T-teo," Vex stuttered out. The kid was still facing away from him, shoulders jerking in sobs. He had no idea what was going on. "Teo, this isn't your fault—this isn't—your—"

"Pax, you didn't do anything wrong. You understand that, don't you? Your uncle—his defensors—they're wrong. I'm so sorry this is happening to you."

The defensor and his lit torch didn't approach.

away wanted Vex's death to draw Lu, Ben, everyone else

That was what those noises were. That was why Elazar had abducted and manipulated so many raiders—to turn them on the island. Elazar was killing everyone.

Vex sent out a silent, quaking plea that Ben and Lu wouldn't come for him. What did his life matter, if Elazar slaughtered everyone else on Grace Loray?

For six years, Vex had run from this fate. He'd hurled himself as far from it as he could get. He'd remade himself, done everything possible to be anything other than a charred corpse. And when it turned out he had Shaking Sickness, a part of him had been morbidly relieved. He'd prefer a death of bruises and broken bones rather than flames.

But he knew, standing there, his boots grappling for purchase on the shifting kindling, that this had always been his fate. This was the destiny he'd avoided six years ago, when Elazar had chosen not to burn him.

Paxben Gallego should have died that day. Rodrigu shouldn't have had to burn alone.

Vex closed his eye, a tear trailing through the grime on his cheek. If he held his breath, let the noise of the battle drone, he could almost imagine his father next to him after all.

30

LU RACED FOR the docks, Ben behind her, the two of them dodging defensors and the delirious crowd. The dozens of soldiers rimming the wharf continued to fire, pistols lighting the sky alongside torches and starlight. The only source of relief, a brief pocket of air in the rising flood, was the Mecht raiders—who continued shouting their reclaimed war cry as they turned on the defensors.

"Barbaric." Their voices carried, rising in speed and strength. *"Barbaric—"*

Lu broke through, boots thudding up the dock. Kari, Gunnar, and other raiders were off the boat already, welcoming them into a tight knot of return fire and swords.

Kari seized Lu in a hug, released her, and did the same for Ben. He went noticeably rigid in shock, but softened when Kari pulled back.

"All our people are moving," Kari said. "They are attacking *now*."

"To the castle?" Ben asked, his eyes going to Lu.

Yes, she wanted to scream, but the other screams of the crowd carried over her, and she fell apart into a dozen sharp pieces.

"Elazar," she gasped, and then, "Vex. Teo."

If they killed Elazar now, would his slaughter of this island stop? Would the people of Grace Loray turn against him, finally? With Elazar dead, Ben could step in as Argrid's commander and force his soldiers to stand down. Would the Argridians listen to him, though?

They had to try. They had to do *something*.

But if Elazar had Vex—or even Teo, god, no—killed while they fought . . .

He was forcing them to choose. Forcing *Lu* to choose. And where was Tom? What role had Elazar given him in all this?

"We can't leave Elazar unchallenged," Lu said. "We can't pull any of the raiders away from fighting him."

Kari nodded grimly. Beyond their group, defensors shot at them. Raiders returned fire. Up on the tide wall, a fresh scream came—but it was a war cry, a string of Grozdan phrases. Rosalia and her raiders had arrived.

"A small group?" Kari pressed. "You can be spared. Or—"

"Or," Ben cut in, his eyes on Gunnar, "we bring Elazar with us. To the castle."

Lu's lungs emptied on a rush. Before she could ask anything, Ben slid his hand into the pocket on Gunnar's shirt and withdrew a vial.

Her last vial of permanent magic.

"Elazar will want this," Ben said. He took Lu's arm, imploring. "Get to the castle. I'll be right behind you— with Elazar in tow."

Gunnar shook his hands, fists breaking into flames. "If I do not kill him first."

Ben smiled, feverish against the sounds of war, and closed his fingers around the vial. He nodded at Kari and met Lu's eyes one more time.

"Save him. Save them both," he told her. He broke through the raiders' line of defense, running hard for the wharf and, beyond it, one of the staircases that led up the tide wall, into the city. Gunnar followed, Ben's fire-wreathed shadow.

Lu's heartbeat thundered. Around her, the group of half a dozen raiders and Kari crouched lower, readying more weapons and plants.

She didn't want to be here. She hadn't wanted to be *this*, a soldier in a war, ever again; yet Lu found herself plunged without warning into a battle, surrounded on all sides by allies with weapons flashing and bundles of magic lighting, launching, exploding.

The last time, she promised herself. An empty promise. But on it, Lu took pistols from one of the raiders and filled her pockets with more ammunition.

Kari's smile in the rising twilight was soft and sad and just as destroying as the weight of this fight. "Use your Incris," she told Lu. "*Go.*"

Lu waited until Kari moved first. Then she ran.

Despite Kari's plea, Lu braced herself against her Incris, trying to keep pace with her mother. Defensors lashed out at anyone who came near—citizens, raiders, bodies moving on the poorly lit wharf. Their cries were more desperate than Lu had ever heard. She ducked around one such defensor purely on the delirium of his rage, his swords swinging over her head.

Croxy. The berserker plant, taken only by the truly desperate—or the truly destroyed.

Elazar had held nothing back from this fight. Not even his own soldiers were unaffected.

Ducking, stabbing, running—Lu slammed into the rough stones of the tide wall only a breath ahead of Kari, who led the way up a staircase, climbing hard for the road and the city.

Defensors waited for them at the top, swords and knives ready. Kari dove on them, twisting to parry, and Lu slid up behind her, ready to help—

"Elazar!"

The voice boomed across the wharf. The fighting didn't

stop; the hysterical screams of soldiers and civilians alike didn't break. But there—Lu spotted Ben down the tide wall, at the top of the next staircase, his hand lifted above his head.

"One last vial!" he shouted. "Permanent magic!"

And he was gone, Gunnar grabbing his arm and pulling him off the edge as bullets flew.

"Adeluna!" Kari drew her back. The closest defensors were dealt with. "He's heading for the castle—*come!*"

The last time Lu had seen the cobbled roads of New Deza, they had bustled with life, merchants and patrons and families, doors thrown open for inns and shops. Now the streets were as the rest of Grace Loray since Argrid's takeover—rolled up on themselves in terror. Boards covered the delicate glass of shop windows; a sign painted with a red cow and pig hung crooked from its bracket. Above, shutters slammed and someone cried out.

The most direct route would take them through the city. Kari sprinted north, Lu at her heels, the other raiders rushing behind them.

❈❈❈

The noises of the fighting drew closer to the castle's courtyard with every passing breath. Vex waited, the seconds dragging through his body and stretching his resolve. When it snapped, he didn't know what he'd do—dissolve, likely. There would be no body for the defensor with the torch to burn. He'd just disintegrate, float up into the clouds, and vanish.

Tom kept his arms behind his back, his focus on the planks under his boots. Occasionally he would look at Teo, then down again, eyes closing in something like pain. Vex hated him more—whatever internal struggle Tom was fighting, it made him way too human.

Next to Tom, Teo sobbed, facing Vex now, and that small spot of emotion was the only thing that kept Vex from begging for death.

A wail grew louder, coming up the road. Vex contorted to look over his shoulder. The raiders and defensors in the courtyard, three dozen at most, were focused on the open gate.

The attackers had made their way here after all.

Vex's stomach sank. Lu and Ben had chosen to save him over stopping Elazar? No. They had to have something else—there was another reason—

Tom looked up. His face was mournful, sad almost— "Burn him!" he shouted.

Vex swung back to face him, mouth open.

"No!" The plea came from Teo, his face purple with agony. "I didn't mean it—*stop!*"

Teo dove forward as if to leap off the platform. Tom grabbed his collar and yanked him back, slamming Teo to the wood planks.

Fury pierced Vex's chest so brightly he thought it might explode out of him.

Teo dropped, weeping and scrambling across the platform, into the defensors at the rear of the wood.

"Do not shame your father," Tom told him. "You have had many opportunities. Give in to your magic. Prove yourself. You can stop all of this! *Stop making me do this!*"

"I don't want him!" Teo screamed. "I don't want to be his son! Stop—*Vex!*"

The defensor with the lit torch approached Vex, flames extended toward the dry, eager kindling. Smoke streamed up from the torch. It smelled of death and ash and unadulterated fear.

"Teo! Teo, it's—it's okay—" Like hell was it okay, but god, what else could he say?

Vex slid on the loose wood, trying to kick the logs away while clawing himself up the pole. It was useless, but he fought, a frantic wail building in his chest as the defensor knelt, touched a log—and it caught.

Flames licked other logs, spreading around Vex in a hungry wreath. The wind shifted, whirling smoke into his face, and he gagged, unable to see or breathe and—

This was happening. This was what his father had gone through. A wall of smoke, a pause in which there was no sensation but sound, before . . . death.

Vex was going to burn alive, his death a means of bringing down Ben and Lu.

God. That really would be the only legacy he'd leave. Just Ben and Lu to mourn him, and mourn him for *what*? For the flippant jokes he'd tell, the useless way he'd follow them around?

When Rodrigu had burned, Vex had begged the monxes and defensors guarding him to stop it. *"We haven't done anything!"* he'd tried to lie.

Those words filled him again now, this lie that had become his truth.

I haven't done anything. I haven't helped anyone. Papa, you'd be ashamed of me, wouldn't you?

The fire found him, clawing at his boots with orange talons. Vex tugged fruitlessly against the chains holding him to the pyre. Tremors came and went in his frenzy.

He couldn't die like this. He couldn't die as *nothing*.

31

LU AND KARI reached the courtyard's main gate along with a wave of raiders joining them from side streets in a rising wail of battle and pain.

The gate to the courtyard was open for them already, welcoming.

Before Lu passed through it, Nayeli slammed out of the crowd and into her, hooking one arm around her neck. In comfort, and to press her lips to Lu's ear over the screaming, explosions, *noise*.

"Some raiders came out a little while ago," she told her. "Thought they'd be on our side—they're the ones we've been missing. But—"

"But Elazar changed them," Lu finished.

Nayeli pulled back, no spark of the vivacious girl visible in her rage.

Together, they broke upon the courtyard. Defensors

would be waiting for them, but raiders didn't fear defensors. They feared nothing.

Except their own people, a dozen or more clustered in the castle's yard, weapons out and ready. And Vex, tied to a burning pyre, Teo sobbing as Tom stood over them both.

Lu growled, and god, how she hated her father. Around her, the attacking raiders got no chance to rejoice that they had found the last of their missing people—the bodies packed in the courtyard turned on them, pistols firing and swords flashing and chaos descending as the attackers became the attacked. They hesitated—how could they attack their own people, friends, family?—and that hesitation cost lives in startled screams.

There was a scream from behind, the clash of battle, and Ben and Gunnar slid just inside the main gate, next to Lu. Gunnar immediately raced off toward Vex.

"Elazar's forces followed us," Ben told her, dirt smeared across his face. "But here—"

"We'll be surrounded," Lu finished. Dread settled in her as Nayeli screamed.

The scream became a name, pulsating with relief and agony. "Cansu!" Nayeli tore forward. "CANSU!"

Lu lost sight of her as people shifted. But Cansu whipped her head toward Nayeli's cry, her face that same vacant, disconnected sheet that everyone else wore.

Tom had used Menesia to turn all these people into Elazar's soldiers. Into defensors. He had forced them to surrender in the cruelest sense.

Nayeli stumbled out in front of Cansu. A space opened around them, the fighters giving them berth as other raiders struggled to reason with friends who beat at them.

Cansu ripped a sword out of her belt and swung at Nayeli, making her falter. Nayeli drew her own weapon and caught Cansu's blow, shouting at her, "This isn't you! Stop! Cansu—listen to me, *stop!*"

Everyone around them screamed the same thing. *Stop, this isn't you, stop, stop—*

"The Bright Mint!" Lu shouted, her voice breaking. "Try—give them the Bright Mint!"

How? Manic as they were, these people wouldn't willingly take it. And if Lu got to Vex and Teo, where would she take them? Out through this bloodbath of friends fighting friends?

Lu's eyes went to the platform. A cloud of smoke dissipated into the black night sky, and she couldn't see Vex now, but she saw bursts of flame—Gunnar.

Lu turned back to Ben. He nodded at her and together they bolted for the platform, Kari just behind.

※※※

All at once, the pain vanished. The flames, the orange and yellow fingers of light through the smoke—they were snuffed out. Was Vex dead? Had he passed out?

Grunting followed. A sharp yelp. Then a face burst through the smoke, a furious Mecht glare with blue eyes snapping from Vex to the chains.

"Gunnar!" Vex gasped. "BEN!"

"He is here" was all Gunnar said.

Vex shrank back as Gunnar grabbed the chains. A ball of fire surrounded his hand, singeing Vex's arm, and he cried out as Gunnar melted through the links. The chains dropped to the ground and Gunnar immediately spun away, sending blasts of fire at oncoming attackers.

With the smoke clearing, Vex could see the fight now. The courtyard was a mess of bodies and weapons and clashing raiders, defensors, *everyone.* More people spilled in through the gate, chasing others or running from pursuers, the yard swelling with bloodlust.

Vex stumbled forward and dropped to his knees, hacking for fresh air. Kindling scattered around him, charred and blackened, and Vex had a brief, terrifying realization that he must look like that, too. Soot covered and singed.

Shaking, he shoved to his feet. "Lu!" Where the hell had Gunnar gone? "Ben—"

Vex turned. He'd expected Tom to be cowering in a knot of soldiers—but he still stood at the front of the platform.

Only now, he had a naked pistol in his hand, the barrel pressed into Teo's neck.

�֍֍֍

Ben ran.

In his darkest nightmares, the ones that made him re-live Rodrigu and Paxben's burning, he'd tried to run. But

495

he'd been stuck in place, straining to get to their pyres as monxes with hollow black eyes swung lit torches toward their kindling. He could never make it, and many nights, Ben had woken himself up screaming for them.

Running now, dodging fighting enemies, pausing to evade blows—it felt like that. Moving but not moving, going but making no progress.

Gunnar had gotten Vex off the pyre. Ben pressed on, tasting salt on his lips, humidity and heat and the building storm of the courtyard making everything hot and unstable.

He slammed out of the fighting and into the side of the platform. There—Tomás Andreu still stood at the front, a gun now to Teo's head. Where was Vex? Gunnar? It didn't matter—

Ben braced his hands on the wood and got one knee onto it before something metal pressed the knot of his hair into his neck.

"Ben," Jakes said, "give me the vial."

Hands lifted more in caution than surrender, Ben eased off the platform and turned.

He had never seen Jakes so undone. His wide, dark eyes were entirely bloodshot, their color making the tears in them blend with the blotched redness of his face. He panted, each breath grating, and he seemed to be using physical effort to hold his eyes on Ben—and not look at Teo, just back on the platform, with a gun to his head.

Jakes cocked his pistol and refocused it on Ben's chest. "I

saw you reveal it to Elazar. Give the vial to me."

"Jakes—"

"We both know you aren't going to take it. He'll get it, and he already took the one—he's unstoppable now!"

A wave of fire shot from Ben's left. Jakes cried out and stumbled back, and it took all of Ben's fortitude to reach through the flames, grab Gunnar's arm, and yank him aside.

"Where's Vex?" Ben asked.

Gunnar blinked, his eyes darting back to Jakes. "Let me kill him. Let me—"

"*Where's my cousin?*"

Gunnar nodded over his shoulder.

Ben whipped to the front of the platform, the area cut off by the fighting crowd. More defensors and raiders alike poured through the front gate, Elazar's numbers adding in with Rosalia's, Nate's, Nayeli's—this area would be a graveyard in minutes.

In front of the platform, the area before the pyre, Vex stood, looking up at Tom and Teo. Back in the fray, Ben spotted Kari and Lu, fighting to get to Vex.

"Get to Teo," Ben told Gunnar.

"*Ben!*" Jakes screamed. It ripped each sound to pieces.

Ben spun around to see Jakes aiming the pistol again, his arm shaking, tears pouring down his cheeks. Gunnar lunged, and Jakes faltered back, pinning the gun on him instead.

"Don't make me do this, Ben," Jakes pleaded. "If everyone

had magic, if everyone had power, we wouldn't need to fight. My family wanted the world free. They wanted an end to these senseless struggles. They wanted—"

"What do *you* want?" Ben heard himself ask. The pistol aimed at Gunnar tapped an unknown well of calm, and Ben willed it to pour out of him.

An echoing trumpet cut across the yard. The fighting paused, but paused like someone ducking to avoid a stray bullet—it instantly picked up again, frenzied and bloody.

Through the gate, arms lifted, Elazar marched into the battle.

Ben heaved. His father didn't fight. His father let others die for him. This wasn't his—

Elazar walked up to a group of enemies and swung his lifted hands into them. Bodies flew through the air, tossed like barrels onto a ship. Elazar, his face glistening with righteous purpose, carved through the horde. Arms flew, his body twisted, strength and speed and—

Croxy. Pious God above. Lu had put *Croxy*, the rage-inducing plant, into her permanent magic tonic. And that was what had chosen to stick in Elazar—the plant that would give him not only formidable strength but unstoppable will and force.

Jakes saw it, too. "Ben—give it to me!" He shook the gun. "Don't make me kill the Mecht—*give me the vial!*"

✥✥✥

Kari took the brunt of the assault, batting aside swords and yanking Lu out of the path of bullets.

Vex was before the platform. Caved forward, hacking and covered in soot, but *alive*, and Lu shot through an opening between a defensor and raider engaged in combat. The Incris in her body sent her flying, and in a breath, she flung herself at Vex.

He turned, caught her, air leaving him in a cry of alarm and grief.

"Lu—" Vex was pushing her away. "Lu—*Teo*."

She spun, shoving Vex behind her.

Teo's eyes were pinched shut, his whole face wrinkled in terror. Tom held the gun to his neck, his expression drawn and mangled and *distraught*.

He had brought Teo here, amidst the guns and the people dying on swords and the friends slaughtering each other, just as he had forced him into the sanctuary slaughter. As though a child had any place here—

But Teo wasn't a child anymore, Lu realized with a heartbreaking cry. He was a soldier, as she had been, a weapon Tom had stripped of all innocence.

Defensors made a ring around her and Vex, blocking the battle from the platform. Kari was outside the ring, fighting to get in, her face livid at the sight of Tom and his gun.

Lu had two pistols at her thighs, pouches of explosive

and dangerous plants in her pockets. Could the Incris move her faster than bullets?

"Adeluna," Tom said. He didn't lower his gun from Teo, but his face softened as he looked down at her. "You will understand. It shouldn't have come to this, but—"

Tom cocked the gun. Teo sobbed, trying to stay immobile, his eyes pinched shut.

The world dissolved.

Lu held her hands out, aching and empty and more scared than she'd ever been in her life. "Stop," she tried. "Just let him go."

Tears welled in Tom's eyes. *Tears.* "Teo, you have to give in," Tom told him. He shook the gun against Teo's skin. "I know you have magic. You *have* to have magic in you. Too much is at stake. I've given everything, I've done *everything*— please, Pious God, please let him have magic. Don't make me do this, Teo. *Prove yourself.*"

Tom looked back at Lu and smiled through his tears. "Everything's falling apart, isn't it? My king forbade me to affect you while you were working on his potion, but I'll make you better after this, I promise. You won't remember it. I can fix us again, I'll fix everything—"

Again. The Menesia he had used on her.

Air knotted in Lu's throat. Vex said something to her, reassurances, but she saw only Teo, who managed to open his eyes.

When he saw her, every tight muscle released in sorrow.

"Lu, I'm so sorry, I'm sorry—"

"Teo, it's all right," she told him. "Teo—look at me—it'll be—"

Tom shook his head, a violent lurch. "*No! Teo*—you have to do this. You have to be a good boy, you have to be strong. You don't understand what I did to protect you. *Try*, Teo. Try to use magic."

"He doesn't have magic," Lu said. Her voice shook. "It's over, Tom. Let him go. Elazar already took the vial I made, anyway. You don't need Teo anymore."

"I didn't intend to sacrifice you," Tom blubbered. "I never intended to sacrifice either of you. You were meant to give Ibarra information in the safe house, not resist him to the point of torture. But when you did, when I saw the lengths the Pious God went to with the tools offered up to him . . . I couldn't stomach my children being used like that. I've sacrificed everything else. I have been loyal in every other way. I was wrong to keep him secret, wasn't I? I was wrong, Pious God forgive me—"

Lu had guessed, days ago, that Tom had given her Menesia to make her forget his involvement with Bianca and Annalisa, and to cover up Teo's role in Elazar's plans. Rage overwhelmed her now. She had never been more of a weapon than she was in that moment, and she would have charged the platform if not for Vex's hands on her arm.

"Who is he?" Lu demanded.

She knew, though. She knew in the way Tom sobbed

and begged Teo to try, he didn't want to kill him, but he couldn't fail the Eminence King, and people must believe that he was Elazar's son. They would believe if the Pious God blessed Teo with powers.

But Teo wasn't Elazar's son. He was Tom's.

A trumpet. There was a pause in the fighting, a gulp of breath, and Lu dared glance back.

Elazar had joined the attack.

She didn't let herself watch him long. Resolve tasted like iron and blood, and Lu's eyes scrambled to find a solution—

"Give it to me!"

The voice grabbed Lu. On the side of the platform, beyond a knot of clashing defensors and raiders, Jakes stood with a pistol aimed at Gunnar. Next to him, Ben had his hands out.

Lu had nothing but a wild, wicked hope.

She curled her fingers around a brown pod and pulled the Rhodofume from her pocket.

Guns fired. Her people, raiders, Grace Lorayans, were dying. Elazar was here now, enhanced with permanent magic, and there was no way to escape this courtyard without death.

Lu breathed, and leveled, and looked at Jakes.

"That's Bianca's son!" she screamed. Then, louder, over the death cries, "Bianca's son!"

And my father's. He's destroying him like he destroyed me.

Jakes spun to her, the delirium in his eyes slipping, if only for a moment.

Lu reared back her fist and smashed the Rhodofume pod on the platform.

32

SMOKE FILLED THE area in an explosion of gray.

Lu surged through it, toward the exact place she had seen Tom standing before fog shrouded them. She hit the platform, leaped onto it, propelling onward until she smashed into her father and the two of them flew back in a jumble of limbs and speed.

A single Rhodofume pod did not have an excess of smoke, nor did it last long. As Lu scrambled up onto her knees, the air had already started to clear—and she saw Tom, an arm's length before her, stumbling to his feet. He used the hand holding his pistol to wipe his mouth, smearing blood across his chin.

Distantly, Lu heard Kari cry her name. She heard the sounds of battle. She heard Teo weeping, but he wasn't near Tom, no longer close enough for that man to touch him.

That man. His father.

Lu tore away from him, across the wood, and threw her arms around Teo, around Vex too, burrowing Teo's face into her chest. She couldn't make a sound come out of her mouth, but she didn't need to—Kari was on the grass behind them with a look of horror on her face.

The noise of battle was starting to wane. People wept on the grass, holding their heads as friends tried to help them. Nayeli cradled a sobbing Cansu; Nate held his hands out as he cautiously approached one of his raiders.

They were fighting the Menesia, with grit and will and the small doses of Bright Mint.

The defensors still fought. Though their numbers were dropping, they rallied on, driven by the sight of their king—their god—tearing through the sobbing raiders as a sickle would cut through grass. Elazar had a sword now, his movements jerky and manic, blood spraying around him in a storm of destruction.

Kari's eyes moved past Lu, and her face set. "Tomás— don't."

Lu withered, spinning back to Tom as he took slow steps toward them.

He wavered.

"Of all the things I have done in the name of Argrid, to bring peace and healing to this island"—his eyes shifted to Kari—"the one I most resisted, the one that caused me to write to the Eminence King and dare beg him to choose another servant, was the task that made me unfaithful to you."

Lu gagged.

Her father had manipulated her. Tortured her. Lied to her.

And he didn't count that as his worst task?

Tom kept talking. "My king wanted to know the effects of Shaking Sickness on a child born to an infected mother. After Bianca had Menesia, she believed I had rescued her from Argrid. She fell in love with me. The task was . . . easy to accomplish."

"Stop." Kari lifted her hand, fingers shaking.

"But Teo was born, and Lu—Lulu-bean, God save me, the war ended, and what Ibarra did to you—I've tried to spare you from this pain, Lulu-bean," he told her. "You and your mother. This is why I used Menesia on you—you found out about Teo, and it nearly destroyed us. I've tried to keep you safe, but you refused to listen to me when I knew how close you were to permanent magic, and the whole of the *world* hung on your potion. Can you conceive of that weight? And I thought, maybe Teo truly did have powers. Maybe my love for him was a weakness. So I offered him up to the Pious God, as I should have—"

He wouldn't stop talking. Explanations, excuses, lies, horrors—Lu couldn't handle it anymore, couldn't take the fabrication he had sculpted.

Defensors reached them. Tears and sweat made Kari's cheeks shine. She drew knives and spun to fight off the defensors. Vex, his hands on Lu's shoulders, tried to pull her and Teo away—how far would they get? Where would they go?

"Lu," Teo sobbed against her. "Lu, I don't want to be here—"

Stiff, spent, Lu looked up at her father.

She still had weapons. She still had plants, and the Incris in her body.

"Lulu-bean," Tom said, reaching out to her. "Please, let me fix this. I can make you forget everything, and we can be happy again. Teo, too. I promise, my love. Please."

Lu faltered on the precipice of action. To kill her father. The man who had made her capable of killing at all.

She wasn't a soldier anymore. She wasn't a monster.

Lu slackened in Vex's hands. She shifted across the wood, toward the edge of the platform.

Tom tracked the movement. His lip curled. "No! Don't make me hurt you—"

A gunshot echoed.

Tom frowned, a crease dragging through his brow. His focus went around, searching for the source of the noise.

Jakes stood at the rear of the platform, his smoking pistol still raised. His eyes shifted to Teo and a look of awe passed over him, as though he had awoken from a long-held dream.

A thud yanked Lu back to herself.

Tom had fallen to his knees, hands to his chest. Jakes's aim had been true, straight through his heart, and Tom collapsed to his side before Lu.

She sucked in a breath, the air rank with sweat and iron.

He was dead. Like Milo. Two horrors in her life snuffed out.

This one brought a wave of emotions. Grief tried to drag her down, screaming sobs one breath from destroying her until Kari slid onto the wood and bundled Lu and Teo into her arms. Around them, the remaining defensors were either dead or gone, joining Elazar in his last stand against the raiders in the courtyard.

Lu clung to her mother. *Together.* They would deal with Tom together. She wasn't alone, kneeling by her father's corpse in agonizing solitude. She had her mother—and she had Teo.

"Lu!" Teo shrieked. "What's he doing? Stop him!"

Elazar? Yes, they would—but Lu needed this, a small moment of her mother taking her weight and Teo breathing, steady and sure, against her.

Teo. Her . . . brother. The thought felt disjointed, but Lu held it anyway—

Until Teo bucked against her. "*Stop him!* Don't go, Vex!"

✻✻✻

Ben wasn't sure what had pushed Jakes to act. The drawing out of the battle, the appearance of Elazar, the endless screams of people dying—it had a way of throwing the smallest of details into stark clarity.

For Jakes, that seemed to be Teo. He hadn't said a word to Ben or Gunnar before he'd dived past them, onto the platform, and shot Tomás Andreu.

Some settling in Ben's mind told him that the actions on the platform would be resolved, a calmness that centered him on the only detail, in this courtyard, that mattered to him: Elazar.

The vial of permanent magic sat in his breast pocket. Jacket tattered, shirt drenched in sweat, Ben removed the vial and stared at the liquid within the glass, the shifting rainbow of colors that caught the torchlight from around the yard.

"Benat," Gunnar said insistently. "Are you certain?"

No. Ben looked up. Elazar was in the center of the yard, a handful of defensors at his back, weapons bloodstained. A dozen or more raiders still fought, coming at the tight knot of resistance from all angles. Ben spotted Rosalia. Pierce, just there.

But Elazar was, as they had feared, unstoppable. His limbs and weapons swung in constant arcs, a flurry of redemption that would drown this island in death.

"Sinners!" Elazar bellowed. "You are defenseless against the Pious God!"

Perhaps Elazar was the Pious God now. Perhaps that permanent magic had given him and Lu and Nate and Rosalia all an unearthly level of power.

Ben stared down at the vial in his palm, hearing a dozen voices telling him that he needed this weapon. He couldn't fight his father without equaling him.

"This is—" Ben started, ground his teeth together. He uncorked the vial and held it ready. "This is Argrid's war."

His arm tensed to dump the potion into his mouth before he could reconsider—but a hand covered his.

"You aren't the only Argridian here," a voice said.

Ben blinked. Paxben was holding the vial now, his ash-covered face cocked in a sad attempt at a smile.

"Irmán," Vex said, and downed the potion.

Ben jolted. "No!"

Vex gave him another grin. Staggering, doubled in half, he turned and ran for Elazar.

"Paxben!" Ben screamed, and tore after him.

Gunnar caught him around the waist. "Benat—he can do this! You cannot face your father without magic!"

Lu bounded off the platform and landed next to Ben, her face drawn as she watched Vex race across the battle-field.

"What did he do?" It came as a whisper, the situation punching her in the gut.

Ben went slack in Gunnar's arms when Lu's eyes met his.

"He will be fine." Gunnar tried again. "He has magic. It may be enough to—"

Lu shook her head. "His Shaking Sickness. I tried to cure it, but—"

"—that much magic might kill him," Ben finished.

⁂

As he crossed the field, Vex didn't let himself think about each person he hurdled over—raiders, defensors, people he might've known on both sides.

God, the potion hurt. It felt like he'd swallowed a handful of nails. He staggered, faltering to his knees as a spasm grabbed every muscle and *squeezed*.

It took all his willpower not to scream. Hell, it'd taken all his willpower to grab the vial from Ben at all—just when Vex thought he'd hit the bottom of his strength, he found another layer, another, shocking himself with how deep his fortitude ran.

He'd never dug this deep, though. He'd never put himself in situations where he'd have to tap into some hidden reserve of strength since he'd gotten out of the Church's mission-prison.

Now it let him shove himself back to his feet. Maybe it was the potion he'd taken, or this new wash of tenacity—but as Vex stood on the battlefield, surrounded by the dead and dying, he faced Elazar, a dozen paces in front of him, still tearing aside any who approached.

And Vex felt *ready*.

He swiped a stray sword from the ground, the tip dragging through the matted grass. Step by step, Vex clenched and unclenched his free hand, waiting for some shock of extra speed or muscle power or berserker drive to slaughter people. How long had the potion taken to work on everyone else? What'd they do to figure out which magic had taken root?

Vex wavered. He probably should've known more about this magic before he'd snatched it from Ben.

He sucked in a breath and cut off his mind from the spiraling questions. Another step, boots slipping on the slick grass. Vex held other images at the front of his mind:

Edda. How she'd walk into a fight. Back straight, weapon ready, her face set.

Rodrigu. Every meeting with his allies, every solemn ceremony in the cathedrals—the same impossible mask had descended over him, a wall that refused to let his worries or misgivings break his concentration.

Paxben had practiced stoic expressions like that in the mirror. He'd thought of his father and puckered his face and laughed at the uselessness of something so *serious*.

There was no humor in Vex now, though. He set his features, brick by brick building a wall out of memories of Rodrigu, out of memories of Edda.

Elazar pivoted in the yard, a broadsword raising overhead as he swung to the next source of movement—Vex.

His fog of vengeance shifted. Through it came a long, slow smile of recognition.

"Paxben," Elazar growled, and charged him.

Paxben had trained alongside Ben when they'd been kids. He'd never been good at moving like this, his long limbs too lanky and uncoordinated, but some remnant of that training burst up through him, and Vex moved.

He caught the first of Elazar's blows. The force vibrated up Vex's arm and he cried out, the destructive power jarring every muscle, every bone, every sinew that for the past few years had slowly been deteriorating under Shaking Sickness.

Darkness wafted over him, the pain too intense. When it cleared, Elazar was pulling back to swing again—

Vex hesitated, his body recoiling from another shattering block, and that pause sent Elazar's broadsword slicing straight for Vex's neck. He faltered back and the tip of Elazar's blade sliced along his cheek.

"Coward!" Elazar screamed, eyes peeled wide, lips snarling spittle. "Just like your father! *Coward!*"

Elazar hefted the sword for an overhead blow. Vex caught it again, and the contact rang through him like the toll of a bell, each vibration darkening his vision more, more. . . .

He'd crawled up to the Grace Neus Cathedral bell tower with Ben. They'd made a secret hideaway of the little-used nook there, giggling about how no one would ever find them—until the bell had struck noon, and the incessant *dong, dong, dong* had deafened them for hours.

Vex shook his head, forcibly clearing his mind. Damn it—why hadn't the potion kicked in? Had it not worked on him? God, his body ached.

Blood gushed down Vex's face, warm and thick. He gripped his sword with both hands and tried to run, to put distance between himself and Elazar. Maybe he'd get Incris, like Lu, and be able to bolt away—

A hand seized Vex's shoulder and ripped him back. He slammed against the ground, something in his chest snapping in a burst of agony like a candle disturbing a peaceful night. Vex arched against the pain as Elazar loomed over him.

Elazar rested the point of his sword on Vex's collarbone. The weight of the broadsword alone was enough to puncture his skin. Vex cried out.

"Pathetic," Elazar snarled. "That you came from my line. Look at you! How your father would weep to see what a useless creature you've become."

Elazar raised his sword.

At the edge of the yard, Vex saw the faint outline of bodies running toward him. Ben? Lu? He couldn't twist to look, frozen on the ground in the heaviness of Elazar's gaze and the intensifying tremors that spread from Vex's torso, down his legs, out to his fingertips.

He shouldn't have taken that potion. He could feel it warring with the temperamental state his body had been in, magic heaped on too much magic already.

The image of Elazar, lifting his broadsword for a death strike, slowed. The shadows on the edges of Vex's eyesight, Ben and Lu racing for him, faded and rippled into the night.

Vex had been terrified during the first resistance meeting Rodrigu had brought him to. His father had noticed Paxben's fear, dismissed everyone, and sat with him on his lap for hours, until they were both giggling about nothing, about everything.

"Papa," Paxben had asked, his head tucked against Rodrigu's neck. *"What if I'm not as brave as you are?"*

"You will be one day. You won't even feel it happen—something will become more important to you than fear, and you will find yourself doing amazing things."

The world smelled suddenly like Lu's hair. Like salt and sun, warmth and honey. The hum of the battle sounded like the shushing wind when he'd been alone with Ben atop the cathedral, the whole of the world bowing before them.

Elazar's eyes leaped to Ben and Lu, gaining on him. His grin was beyond demented—it came from the very depths of whatever hell he so feared. His lifted sword shifted course, and Vex knew it would strike one, or both, of the people rushing to his aid.

Vex's body was broken. The muscles in his legs were unraveling, spasms stretching him thin and tremors coming one on top of the last. He couldn't move. Couldn't fight. Couldn't do anything but sit in that carriage and listen to his father burn to death—

Vex screamed. His soul cleaved in two, spilling the last of his strength.

He planted his palms and swung his legs in a spinning

arc that hooked Elazar's ankles. Elazar dropped to the ground, his blood-covered robes wafting around him as his head slammed back against the grass.

Vex panted, too high on possibility to let his momentum falter.

"Vex!" came Lu's scream. She was nearly upon him.

He ripped Elazar's sword from his grip, spun it around in both hands, and heaved all his weight into driving the blade into his uncle's chest.

The crunch and spurt of blood shook Vex head to toe. He wondered if Incris had taken him after all, for speed; and Powersage, for strength; and maybe he was just all of it, Croxy and Aerated Blossom and *everything*. He was flying and powerful, healing and destruction.

The world trembled. Beyond, defensors wailed, their words muffling so they sounded like "Our Eminence! The Pious God! Rise again, Eminence, you cannot be killed!"

Vex wavered, the hilt of the sword keeping him upright. He almost expected Elazar to obey the pleas of his defensors.

"Rise again, Eminence! Pious God, save you—"

Elazar's eyes, staring at Vex, dimmed. He looked shocked—that his useless nephew had truly killed him? Or that he had died at all?

The defensors' pleas faded. Faded more. Each second that passed without Elazar bursting up from the ground brought a deep, rippling sense of finalization across the courtyard.

Defensors lowered their weapons. Elazar's devoted servants stared in horrified wonder.

Vex fought to stay upright, to revel in their amazement, but his body had gone too far. He pitched to the side and curled inward, a tremor contorting him into an unyielding knot of limbs and bones and a stunted cry.

Hands on his face, smoothing his hair back. "Vex—can you hear me?"

He couldn't breathe without his lungs feeling like they'd catch fire. Even the act of closing his eye drove spirals of anguish down his bones, and he felt something crack in his leg, another, tremors shaking him apart from the inside.

"Heal him!" Nayeli, frantic. "You healed him once—heal him again!"

"I didn't heal him! That's why—oh god, he shouldn't have taken it—"

Vex bit down on his tongue and pried his eye open. He knew he was fading, fading fast—he scrambled through the delirium with one last, feeble grasp at the sights around him.

Lu, his head on her lap, tendrils of her hair flurrying around her face. Nayeli, over her, lips moving as she said something, or prayed maybe.

And Ben, standing halfway between Vex and Elazar—who was motionless on the ground, a sword sticking out of his chest, his eyes gaping up at the star-filled sky in a permanent look of surprise.

Ben's gaze followed Vex's. His lips parted. "He's dead," Ben said, an echo down a long tunnel as he took a staggering step back.

Lu and Nayeli whipped to him. Vex heard the words *dead, Elazar.*

Ben slid to the ground, on his knees.

Irmán, Vex wanted to say. *Irmán, he can't hurt us anymore.*

There was no strength left. Vex had reached the end of his possibility, drawn thin over pyres and magic and memories.

He closed his eye. He was so tired.

33

BEN SAT IN the castle's courtroom, a long space filled with wooden pews framed by marble columns. The vaulted ceiling towered up around a brilliant chandelier, and it was that glittering diamond light that Ben watched as a defensor knelt on the tiled floor.

"All Argridian forces are converging on New Deza," the defensor said in clear Grace Lorayan. "They sent me ahead to ensure you perceive no ill will from their arrival. They are coming peacefully to surrender to the new—"

The defensor paused.

Ben swallowed, still unable to look at the man due to the exhaustion and disbelief that muddled his brain. Or maybe it was that the battle had been only three days ago, and his soul hadn't had time to untangle itself.

Once news spread of Elazar's defeat and a Grace Lorayan base had been established in the castle, reports had trickled in of battles in other ports, other villages. Here twenty Grace Lorayans were dead by their own relatives, recently released from Elazar's prison; there, defensors had killed a dozen people. A stack of parchment sat on a desk in the rear of the courtroom, listing the lives lost from Elazar's failed attempt at slaughtering everyone on Grace Loray.

No one had had the fortitude to total the numbers yet.

But Elazar's death and the decimation of his forces in New Deza had sent a message to all his remaining defensors: Argrid had lost. Elazar's plan had failed.

The Pious God Incarnate had been killed.

What that meant for those who followed Elazar willingly, who believed in the righteousness of the Church, Ben didn't yet know. But this defensor, who had come as a messenger, had bowed his surrender into a castle crowded with raiders, defensors, and wounded, many struggling through the ebbing fogs of Menesia as they waited for Lu and others to prepare doses of Bright Mint to counteract the magic. It felt as though they were still on a battlefield, not reveling in victory and preparing steps into the future.

They had, in fact, won. But it felt as though they had just barely survived.

Ben sat on the steps of the dais, in front of the pews that had been turned into cots, listening to people moan and beg for water, food, more healing plants.

"They are coming peacefully," the defensor repeated, "to surrender to our new king-in-waiting."

"They will discard all weapons outside the castle grounds," Kari said. She had positioned herself on the dais behind Ben. How she was still able to stand after everything was beyond him. But she towered over the defensor, with Pierce, Nate, and Rosalia briefly leaving their people to stand with her.

A few other people joined them, too—councilmembers, Ben had heard someone say. Slowly, Grace Loray's government was coming back together. Or together in a new way.

"Of course." The defensor straightened. "They wish only to discuss terms."

Ben frowned. "Terms? They have conditions?"

The defensor shrugged. "They will explain."

And he turned, making his way back down the long courtroom, passing the wounded on the pews and the people aiding them.

In his wake, Kari exhaled. She looked at Pierce. "Can your people watch for them? We'll receive them in the courtyard."

Pierce cut a wicked grin. "The site of the battle. Subtle."

Kari lifted an eyebrow. "We don't have time for subtlety."

No. They certainly did not.

Ben stood, shoving his rolled-up sleeves higher. His legs took him by instinct toward a table at the side of the room, one overflowing with every piece of laboratory supply and botanical magic that had been found in the castle.

Lu was grinding Bright Mint in a mortar and pestle, as

she had been every moment since they had set up recovery here.

"Your army is coming," Lu whispered to him without turning.

Ben stopped, his hand outstretched over some as yet unprepared Bright Mint flowers. When he didn't respond, she gave him a tired look.

"This room echoes," she said.

Ben moved his hand from the table to her arm.

A flare of light caught Ben's eyes. The chandelier reflected light off a flash of blond where Gunnar tossed his hair out of his face, his arms burdened with rolls of cloth. He moved among the pews, letting those helping the wounded grab what they needed.

He felt Ben watching him. He looked up and smiled, the connection clearing a bit of the exhaustion in Ben's mind.

Lu worked the pestle harder, faster.

Ben's fingers tightened on her arm. "He hasn't woken up yet?"

"No. Nayeli's with him." Faster, faster, the stone clanking on itself. "I've started making him tonics a dozen times. But more magic? I don't know. I can't risk—"

"He'll be fine," Ben offered, his voice pinched. He said it to her, and to himself, a constant stream of reassurances so he wouldn't drown. *Vex will be fine. He'll wake up. He'll be fine.* "We've all been through more than we can bear. Likely his body is healing. He'll wake up."

Lu drew in a deep breath and nodded, but she kept grinding the Bright Mint, refusing to look at him.

Ben put his other arm around her shoulders, pressing a soft kiss to the top of her head.

She stopped. The mortar dropped to the table with a heavy thunk and she leaned into him, staying there for one second, two, before she sniffed and pushed away.

"Here." She handed him the mortar. Blue paste filled the stone bowl. "Should be three doses."

Ben took the bowl, grateful to work. To do something.

He kissed her head again and made for the section of pews holding those who had not yet received the Bright Mint cure.

As he worked, offering doses to raiders with sunken eyes, his heart broke a little more. Remembering was just as horrible as not knowing. Remembering brought images of fighting and sometimes killing loved ones.

One raider resisted Ben's last dose of Bright Mint, his face pressed into the corner of the pew. The man didn't move, his hands over his head.

He placed a hand on the man's shoulder. "I'll come back. Don't—"

"I'll sit with him."

Ben froze. In his peripheral vision, he saw Jakes, disheveled and covered in blood and sweat and dirt, like everyone else here.

"You shouldn't speak Argridian here," Ben whispered in

the Grace Lorayan dialect.

Jakes smiled, but the expression didn't reach his eyes. "My Grace Lorayan isn't very good," he said. "But I'll get better. Here." He reached for the bowl and the last dose of Bright Mint.

Ben hesitated. The only reason Jakes wasn't bound in the dungeon was because he, like the other defensors in this courtroom, had surrendered.

Lu had asked Ben to pardon him. To let him stay on Grace Loray, when the time came to leave, instead of sending him back to Argrid to face trial for all he'd done.

Weight upon weight strangled Ben's heart, things that had happened and things that hadn't and things to come.

Ben handed him the mortar. Jakes took it, their eyes staying locked until Ben turned, walked out away from the pew, and left to help other wounded.

❖❖❖

Dreams sucked Vex into a void.

He saw his father in moments he'd long forgotten, off-handed conversations from unimportant days that filled him with longing for simpler times. He saw Nayeli and Edda in discussion at the bow of the *Rapid Meander* while Lu sat atop the map table in the pilothouse, her smile so painless it flurried his chest like a hurricane. He saw Ben in front of the arched cathedral entrance, his face tipped to a cerulean sky, his hands out, open and welcoming.

Vex saw everyone he loved in a dozen situations—but

his mind stuck again and again on a conversation he'd had with his father.

It had happened long ago, after Rodrigu's allies had left following a discussion of how best to kill Elazar. The evening was late, Rodrigu's study warm and dim. Paxben had shifted on his velour chair and eyed his father.

"*Papa,*" Paxben had said, his voice brittle, "*are you afraid?*"

"*Of what?*"

"*Of dying.*"

Rodrigu had shoved up from his chair and curved around the table. Paxben leaned out to him before Rodrigu even opened his arms, his father taking him in a bent-over, twisted embrace.

"*Every moment,*" Rodrigu said, voice rumbling in his chest and deep into Paxben, who buried his face in the plush cotton of his father's shirt. "*But I think of you, and our country, and I know that no matter what happens, this is the right thing to do.*"

Paxben couldn't imagine being so certain about anything. He just wanted his father to be safe. He wanted them to be like they were now, together and happy.

Maybe that was what Rodrigu meant. Paxben expected belief like his father's to be an overwhelming feeling of righteousness. He had heard his uncle speak of belief at Church services, an invigorating wave, an all-consuming conviction.

But maybe it was softer than that sometimes. Maybe it was this, warmth in his heart, determination digging like roots into his soul. Maybe belief was strong no matter its form, vivacious sometimes, gentle and sweet others.

Maybe Paxben could be just as strong in his beliefs as his father, too.

"Papa." Vex's memory folded over on itself. *"Are you afraid of dying?"*

Sometimes Rodrigu answered. Sometimes he laughed. Sometimes he acted as though Paxben hadn't spoken at all.

Which was the memory? What had Rodrigu said when Paxben asked him that question?

"Papa, are you afraid of dying?"

Paxben was so tired. An ache he couldn't locate made his body throb and everything was cloaked in scarlet, a film of rose over his eyesight that dizzied him.

"Are *you* afraid of dying, Pax?" Rodrigu asked him.

"No."

"Liar."

Something cooled his forehead. A wash of relief fell through him. He faded into a respite of nothingness until his mind surged, his heartbeat racing.

"Papa, are you afraid of dying?"

Rodrigu was kneeling before him, hands around Paxben's bony shoulders. The firelight gushed orange and yellow, fending off the shadows around their chairs.

"Not yet," Rodrigu told him, giving him a shake. "Not yet."

Paxben felt his vision fading. "But I could come with you if I wanted?"

Rodrigu smiled, his eyes teary. "Yes."

"Why wouldn't I, then? I miss you."

A brush of fingertips on his cheek. "You're a fighter, Pax—your place is there."

"I'm not a fighter. I'm not brave like you are. I want to go with you, Papa."

When Rodrigu spoke again, his voice was choked. "My son. My sweet boy. You were always my source of bravery. You are fearless and loyal, and you have a joy that kept me going on days when all else seemed dark and dismal." He cupped Paxben's cheek. "I would like nothing more than to have you in my arms again, but you are not meant to be with me yet."

Rodrigu tipped Paxben's head down to him, planting a kiss on his forehead.

"Not yet," his father whispered against his skin. "Not yet, Pax."

Warmth brushed Vex's forehead. Was it his father? He tried to call out, but all was darkness now—had the fire gone out in the study?

A shifting, a lightening of awareness.

His body felt like someone had hung him on a line and beaten him with a spiked club. Injuries screamed at him, cuts and bruises, and something in his chest tingled with every inhale.

Wait. The last he remembered, he was lying on the

ground, next to Elazar's body—

Pious God above. He'd killed his uncle. He'd taken permanent magic.

How the *hell* was he not dead?

Vex's forehead was still warm. The sensation lifted—a damp cloth.

But he remembered his father's touch. Had it been a dream?

The question stabbed him in his broken ribs. *No*, he told himself at the same moment his reason said *Yes*.

His father had been there. Vex had been so close to death that he'd talked with Rodrigu.

Well, shit, no wonder he felt like death.

Vex realized, then, that his legs didn't hurt. He'd almost gotten used to the ache and the brittleness, but they were gone, and he didn't feel the encroaching threat of a tremor on the edge of his muscles. Everything else in his body felt like flame-kissed hell, but his legs *didn't hurt.*

Had Lu really cured him?

He grinned.

"HE'S AWAKE!"

"Teo—gods, kid—"

Vex opened his eye to see Nayeli sitting next to him on a bed. Teo bounced on the floor, flailing his fists up and down with his jumps.

"HE'S AWAKE! LU—HE'S AWAKE!"

Teo barreled out of the room.

Vex squinted after him. His squint shifted to Nayeli, then to the room around him.

Wherever he was, it was lavish. The walls were pure white with ornate trimmings along the ceiling. A desk sat in the corner, tucked under a shelf that spilled over with books and vials of plants. The bed was soft and plush, the light ivory blanket over him fluttering in the breeze from the open doors. Beyond, blueness stretched into the horizon. Lake Regolith?

"Lu's room in the castle," Nayeli explained. Vex looked back at her. "She wouldn't let us put you anywhere else."

Vex pushed his fists under him and started to sit up. His chest shrieked with pain at the same moment Nayeli swatted him back down.

"Stop, you idiot. You need to rest. Your rib's broken and you almost killed yourself."

He relented, landing back on the feather pillows. "Why is it still broken? Lu didn't throw some of that bone-healing Juviper into whatever potion saved my life?"

The question brought a stab of pain that had nothing to do with his injury. Elazar had almost killed him. And even though Elazar himself was dead now, Vex couldn't shake his fear.

Nayeli cocked an eyebrow. "Lu didn't give you magic at all. That permanent potion you took was part of why you almost died. More magic might've—" She stopped. Sobered.

Vex started. "Wait. I survived. I woke up. *On my own?*"

That brought Nayeli's grin back out. "Don't let it inflate your ego even more."

"Do I—do I have permanent magic?" Vex lifted his hand like the answer might be there.

"Not as far as we could tell while you were out cold," Nayeli said. "But you haven't had a single Shaking Sickness spell. Lu thinks the permanent potion might've had what you needed to wipe out your Shaking Sickness, rather than give you any epic powers. But hey, we'll see, won't we? Maybe try jumping off some buildings, check if you can fly."

Vex wanted to joke with her. He needed to, to stopper the emotions bubbling up in his chest like a rising wave.

He'd survived the battle. The tingle of healing in his chest, his wounds knitting themselves together, was his own blood and muscles and abilities.

He was alive because of himself. Because of his own body.

Tears welled in his eye. God, it was stupid to cry, but a dam broke open in Vex's heart and he pinched the bridge of his nose.

He'd hated his body for so long, every scar and weakness. But those very scars and weaknesses had saved his life.

Vex must've been healthier than Nayeli said, because she scooped him into a gentle hug. He coughed a laugh through his tears and hugged her back.

"Stop crying," she ordered. But she sounded choked up

too. A pause, and her voice dipped, muffled in his shoulder. "That was a stupid thing to do. You, of all people, should know better than to start chugging magic. But you were really incredible."

Vex laughed. "Thanks." He sobered, his eye going behind Nayeli, expecting Edda.

Nayeli must have felt the drop in their conversation. She drew upright, sniffing into the back of her hand.

"How's Cansu?" Vex asked, desperately needing some good news.

Nayeli grinned. "She's fine. They all are, actually—the missing raiders. Or the ones who survived, at least. Lu and Ben whipped up the counter plant to Menesia. It'll be a while before they recover from the battle—before we *all* recover—but they're safe."

Vex exhaled. "I figured we didn't do too bad in that fight if I woke up here."

"Not too bad? We *won* because of you." Nayeli squeezed his arm. "The raider Heads are staying here, in the castle. Kari set them up in rooms. They're gonna start meeting with the remaining councilmembers to plan out a better form of government. And the weird thing is, they're all *excited.* I heard Nate and Pierce talking about the effects of a democracy versus a republic versus—get this—a *monarchy.* Nate and Pierce. Talking politics." Nayeli shivered. But her smile was pure and bright. "Cansu's hopeful too. We had a long talk, and she's not only willing to join with the

Council, she's already making up a list of ways Port Mesi-Teab can help the rest of the island. Turns out she was worried I'd choose this new government over her and the Tuncian syndicate *like I did with the Council*, she said."

Vex frowned. "You never chose anything over her. You wanted the Tuncian syndicate to join up with the Council specifically *for* them. For Cansu. To help them all."

"I know. Cansu didn't know that. But she's better now." Nayeli smirked. "A lot better."

Vex dropped his eye from her to the bedding.

A dozen thoughts pressed against his brain. Were Edda here, she'd have voiced them all, or slapped him in the head to make him voice them. Things like *So you're a Tuncian raider again, huh?* and *I'm glad you're back where you need to be* and *Tell Cansu if she hurts you again, I'll kick her ass. Or I'll try, at least.*

Vex's face tingled. "Edda would be really happy you're finally where you belong."

Nayeli slid her hand into his. "You can always join the Tuncian syndicate too. Cansu'd make room for you."

Vex shook his head. "That's your place. But we better still go out and cause a little chaos from time to time. Even if Cansu's one of the people in charge of this government, we gotta keep it in check, ya know? Can't let 'em get too comfortable."

Nayeli grinned. "Deal."

"See? I told you!"

Teo burst into the room, hauling Lu behind him. She

faltered inside the threshold as Teo started jumping up and down again.

Vex straightened against the pillows. An absurd smile rolled across his face.

She was wearing a dress now, a long brown one covered in stains. Her golden skin was flushed, her hair loose and swept over her shoulder in a tangle of curls. She looked more her, more *Lu*, than she had in weeks.

Entirely because of her smile.

Nayeli cleared her throat and tapped her fists on her knees. "Well. Remember, Vex, your rib is broken, so no strenuous activities."

Vex bellowed a laugh and grabbed his side.

Way too pleased with herself, Nayeli stood and held out her hand. "Teo, let's go find that uncle of yours, yeah?"

Teo snatched her fingers. "Yeah! Do you like him? He knows a lot about Mama—"

His voice faded as Nayeli steered him out of the room. Lu shut the door behind them and Vex gawked at her.

"His uncle? Jakes is here?"

Lu leaned against the door. "After what he did, helping us in the end—" Her smile wavered but held. "We all deserve a fresh start. None of us chose this war. And Teo has been through a great deal—his life has changed more than he even knows. Jakes adores him. I have people watch him with Teo, of course. But so far, it's been good."

Vex swallowed his own feelings about Jakes. Jakome.

If Jakes stepped out of line at all, Vex would deal with it then. But for now, he watched the way Lu's hesitation hung on to her.

"There's more," he guessed.

Lu's eyes went teary, but she shook her head. "I'm not ready to talk about it. Someday. But today, I just want to—" Her smile softened. "You almost died."

Vex sank back into the pillows. He didn't know how to respond to that. Couldn't, really, with his throat swelling up.

Lu nodded as though silence was enough. And after everything, maybe it was.

Elazar had finally gotten what he deserved. Ibarra was no longer a threat. Lu's father was dead, too. And Edda. And Fatemah. And everyone they'd lost, all the destruction around them, and the possibility, too—the work still to be done.

Vex reached out to her. "Come here?"

Lu's smile returned. "I don't know if I should. Nayeli's orders."

He tipped his head, stretching his fingers as far as he could. "If you don't come here—"

"What?" A blush tinted her face. "What will you do to me, raider?"

Vex snapped his head back with a laugh. "That's it, Princesa."

He shoved onto his palms and pain seared his rib cage.

"Goddamn the *ever-loving* Pious God—"

"Down!" Lu chirped, and dove for him. "You'll hurt your—ah!"

Her chirp of concern broke into a giggle when he looped his arm around her waist and lowered her down on top of him.

The humid lake breeze pulsated through the balcony doors, fluttering the blankets and Lu's hair where it made a shield around them. Vex twisted his head to one of the hands she had planted on his pillow, his lips meeting the warm, sweet skin where her sleeve showed her wrist.

She lifted that hand, thumb trailing along his bottom lip. Her smile was soft and light, the innocent, worriless smile from his dreams.

He leaned into her laughter like foam rolling back into the breaking of a wave when she took his face in her hands and laid that smile on his lips.

❋❋❋

Lu stood on the steps of the castle and stared out at New Deza. Some parts of the city still smoked, but if Lu hadn't known there had been a battle, she could have dismissed them as steamboat trails. From this view, she couldn't see the damage done to the buildings and streets. The city looked whole and normal under the clear blue sky.

If it could pretend, so could she.

The gates to the courtyard opened. As Lu's eyes dropped

to the movement, the illusion wavered. The courtyard was still in ruins, the grass slicked and trampled. Gray painted the wall in streaks of ash. The platform had been dismantled, but it sat in a pile of wood planks next to the broken pyre. Two long lines of raiders lined the path from the gate to the castle steps, watching, waiting, ready for attack.

The wounded were still inside the courtroom. The dead had been taken to steamboats in the harbor, to be sailed out to the sea.

As a small procession of defensors entered the courtyard, Lu half wished that the bodies were still here. That these soldiers could see what they had done, the cost of the nightmare they had followed. But they were beginning to realize it on their own—it was why they had surrendered at all. Because their king was dead, their future uncertain.

Around Lu, the raider Heads straightened. Lu smiled to see Cansu in her proper place now, alongside Nayeli, Nate, Rosalia, Kari, and three councilmembers who had been under house arrest in the castle. The only person missing was a representative from the Mecht syndicate, which had yet to piece itself together after the devastating loss of Ingvar. But Kari had sent word to them, offering assistance in cleansing themselves of Menesia and hoping for a show of forgiveness so they might all move forward, together.

Off to the side of the Grace Lorayan group, Ben stood with Gunnar and Vex, something of an Argridian representation. Lu smiled to see Vex lean over to his cousin and whisper something that made Ben grin.

The type of happiness Vex showed when he was with Ben was different from all his other types of happiness. He looked utterly content.

The group of defensors—maybe three dozen of them, with more waiting out beyond the courtyard—stopped at the base of the steps. One stepped forward. His jacket was singed, a rip through one sleeve, but the markings on his uniform's chest signified him as an officer.

Lu wanted to be glad to see the Argridian army in a beaten, shredded state. But she remembered how unhinged Tom had been before his death, driven to madness by Elazar's doctrine and demands. She remembered the terror in Teo's eyes.

She couldn't be glad. She could only be present.

"King Benat." The defensor officer bowed, addressing him in Argridian. The man hesitated, clearly torn about his purpose here. *Surrender.* Surrender to the Heretic Prince.

Lu sucked in a breath. They wouldn't attack, would they? Not now, so soon—

Ben stepped forward, dropping down one of the stone steps. "My father's goals changed Grace Loray in an unspeakable way—but he affected Argrid just as deeply, over decades of rule. I know most of you chose to follow him willingly. You believed in his vision for the world. You believed in *him*, as you believe in our Pious God, and our Church."

He paused. Were Lu the one speaking, she wasn't sure she could be so calm. Ben's hands spread before him in a welcoming, open gesture.

"There is beauty in our country," Ben said. "In our faith, our cathedrals and hymns, in our stories and history and art. We have so much good in Argrid, and for too long we have focused only on the impure. I know many of you will expect Elazar's vision to carry over into my reign—and I tell you now that this War on Raiders ends with my coronation."

Ben turned and dropped to one knee, bowing before Kari, Nate, Rosalia, Cansu—the whole of the Grace Loray contingent.

"Argrid apologizes for what we have done to you," Ben said in Grace Lorayan now, his eyes on the stones under his knees. "We cannot express our sorrow in words. But know, when we leave your shores, we will return only under banners of peace and friendship."

He looked up, glancing at Lu with a smile.

Behind him, his army held. Many of them were slack-jawed. Whatever they had expected to happen, this had not been it.

Slowly, the officer sank to his knees, mirroring Ben. Another defensor followed. Another. It spread out in a fan, defensors lowering to their knees before Grace Loray.

Kari smiled. Lu felt a grin break on her own face too. She hadn't seen her mother smile in so long, and there was a glimmer in her eyes, a seed of happiness behind her grief.

"Thank you, King Benat," Kari said. She motioned at the people around her, the start of a new Grace Loray. Again. "We are one nation, but we are many peoples, and all of us look forward to stepping into a new tomorrow as Argrid bridges theirs."

Rosalia punched her fists into the air and bellowed a Grozdan war cry. Nate and Pierce joined her, screaming, and it spread—Cansu, the raiders who stood along the sides of the courtyard, Vex, even Kari, whose smile intensified.

The thunderous vibrations of cheering resonated in Lu's chest. They shook free the remnants of the battle screams, filling her and the courtyard with possibility. With potential.

With a swelling promise of unity.

Epilogue

BENAT GALLEGO WAS nineteen years old when he became the Eminence King of Argrid.

He sat in the king's quarters on the *Desapiadado*, the ship that had carried Elazar from Argrid to Grace Loray. The ship that had always been Elazar's, a large, sleek vessel for an opulent, vengeful king.

Ben felt utterly small sitting at the desk. The curved *V* of the Church stared down at him from the ceiling, taking up the whole expanse in giant white tiles. Shelves for Church tomes lined the walls, the books held in place by statues of the Graces. All of it watched Ben, and he watched it, in a tentative, awkward peace.

Returning to Argrid would be just like this, magnified by anger and confusion. The people there were devoted to the Pious God. They feared magic still. They had built their lives around Elazar's edicts.

How would they respond to Ben as king, the errant, traitorous son who had been paraded as a heretic? Would they surrender to him as the defensors had, willing to believe in his station as chosen by the Pious God? Or would they revolt the moment he set foot in Deza?

Ben closed his eyes, head dropping back against the chair as he pinched the bridge of his nose. The ship swayed beneath him.

He had two weeks until he reached Deza. Two weeks to figure out how to lead people who believed a king was more god than man.

That was where he should start, perhaps. In showing Argrid that he was a person. He was human and flawed, plus more. Would they revel in seeing their leader be humble? Would it only solidify their fears and fury? No matter what Ben chose to do, he risked uprisings and lost lives.

His heart tripped and he swallowed hard.

A knock on the door.

"Come in."

"This ship is too fancy. I do not like it."

Ben smiled. He dropped his hand and looked across the desk at Gunnar, who kicked the door shut behind him.

"On behalf of the Argridian crown, I apologize," Ben said. "I can arrange a smaller vessel, if you like? A prison transport, maybe. Remind you of the old days."

"The Argridian king-in-waiting has a sense of humor."

Gunnar blanched. "Wait. Does this mean I must call you *Elazar* when you are crowned?"

Ben recoiled. The name was as much a title as *King*, but his father had tarnished it. Maybe, with some distance, he could hear himself called that. But not now.

"No." Ben leaned forward, elbows on the desk. He knocked something to the side—a small metal tin.

Nayeli had given it to him as they'd embarked. She had given the other one to Vex.

Budwig Beans.

Ben hadn't expected Vex to come to Deza, but he'd offered. *"Maybe someday,"* his cousin had said, and hugged him for a solid five minutes.

Vex belonged in Grace Loray, but Ben couldn't stop the feeling of abandonment when he felt the ship carrying him farther away from the only family he truly cared about.

"I'll be king soon," Ben said, staring at his desk until he could compose himself. "I have the ability to fulfill my promise to you."

Gunnar frowned. "What?"

"I promised to help you with the Mechtlands. To bring peace there. You helped my—"

"Are you crazy, Benat?"

Ben jolted. Gunnar grinned and shrugged.

"Vex taught me useful Argridian words. *Crazy.* Anyway. No, Benat. Your country needs your focus now. Do not worry for mine. Seeing Grace Loray and Argrid coming together, it has inspired me that the Mechtlands have potential as well. There is hope."

Ben tried to keep his face impassive. "You do not wish to return to the Mechtlands now?"

"Why do you always try to send me back to the Mechtlands? Do you not want me here?"

Ben shot to his feet. "Of course I want you here." He felt his face flare red. "But I want—I want *you* to want to be here. I want you to—"

"You always try to put your needs on me. I am not you, Benat. I do not need to return to the Mechtlands to help it—I can help it at your side."

"Nothing is simple now," Ben said, his chest deflating. "Argrid is in ruins. I want to help you while I can, before we get to Deza and everything erupts. Let me help you."

"All right." Gunnar beamed at him, taking a step around the desk. "Help me. Marry me."

Ben actually wheezed, a cracked, garbled noise. *"What?"*

Another step. Closer. Ben felt a wave of Gunnar's heat, surging brighter when Gunnar's smile intensified. "Marry me."

"I'm—I'm *the king-in-waiting of Argrid*—"

"You say that as though I do not know. You haven't changed, Benat. Marry me."

Gunnar reached him. Ben was pinned in place by the question—demand?—and by Gunnar's smile and the warmth of his being so near.

In two weeks Ben would see his country again. He would plunge into a nation on the brink of collapse. He would get off this ship as a ruler who had a reputation for being a heretic and bedding his guard.

It really wouldn't be a surprise, then, if Ben married a Mecht Eye of the Sun warrior. It might not help his reputation or his station, but it would help *him*.

Ben launched himself at Gunnar and kissed him. He felt Gunnar smile against him, his arms pinning Ben to his body. For a moment, there was only *this* moment, Ben whispering, "Yes, all right, I'll marry you," between kisses that grew desperate with need.

In two weeks, Ben would get off this ship. But he wouldn't get off it alone.

❧❧❧

At seventeeen years old, Adeluna Andreu stood in a free Grace Loray.

The wharf market was one of the places in New Deza that had been most affected by the battle. The docks were dented, some completely sunk. The stalls and shops were torn to shreds. Shattered glass, rotten produce, and splintered boards covered the stones—garbage and debris, everywhere.

Lu swept glass onto a stretch of fabric Kari held for her. Other people did the same; some carried boards out of the way or rolled barrels to be filled with trash. The area hummed with conversation as raiders worked and scrubbed and cleaned.

But Kari's attention wasn't on the task at hand—it drifted up, to the wharf wall.

Above them, the citizens of New Deza had started to gather. They watched, children clinging to parents, men pointing, women shaking their heads, and everyone looking wary and distrustful.

"It's good they're here," Lu said as one man shouted about how raiders had caused this destruction, so they were right to clean it.

Kari stood, tying up the length of fabric so the glass pieces sat safely within. She dropped it at her feet. "We must earn back their trust. Village by village, if that's what it takes. We will not build this government on a foundation of hatred and fear."

"The people of this island will see," Lu whispered. A promise, a hope. "We'll be better this time. This government will be true, when it's done."

Kari hesitated, her head tipped skyward. The noon sun caught a flash of light that might have been from tears before she closed her eyes. "It won't be done. Not this time. We cannot make the mistake of thinking this government will ever be finished."

Lu leaned on her broom, eyes going misty as she watched her mother. Her strong, resilient mother, who, even after

Tom and the Council falling and the whole of the island turning on her, stood here, now, basking in the scorching sunlight.

It might have exhausted Lu once, to think of this island as never being finished. But Kari was right. Freedom like this, a country so complex, would need to be fluid. There would be no definitions, no lines drawn between right and wrong. They would have to weigh every issue that arose, no matter how dark or shameful, and decide, together, what was best.

In the three weeks since the battle, Lu had found it difficult to tell whether her thoughts were about Grace Loray or herself. The two things had always been inextricably linked in her heart, more so now that true potential lay around them.

Lu had done irreparable things to get here. She had lost more than she knew how to deal with. And sometimes, in the dark hours of night, she woke in a startled sweat, certain Milo hadn't died or the war hadn't ended.

Brick by brick. Stone by stone. Wave by wave, they would all move forward.

"Tío, Tío!"

Lu turned to see Teo racing across the wharf. Jakes had been teaching him Argridian, and Teo particularly loved that the word for *uncle* was so close to Teo's own name. *"It's like we're the same!"* he'd said.

If Lu had been unwilling to forgive Jakes before then, seeing him blush and tear up at Teo happily calling him

Tío would have soothed any lingering resentment.

Teo waved something he'd found in the debris—a small leather ball. Jakes, who had been stacking planks of broken wood, turned, beating dust from his pants.

Teo hurled himself at Jakes, who caught him and stumbled back with a smile. Teo waved the ball, talking high and fast in a mix of Argridian and the Grace Lorayan dialect, his smile impossibly large.

No. Not *impossible.* His smile was exactly as it should be.

Lu hadn't been able to tell him about Tom yet. She wasn't sure, at this point, how she ever would. For now, Teo had settled into the suite of rooms she shared with Kari in the castle.

"Do you hate him? Tom, I mean," Lu whispered.

A pause, and Kari dropped her chin, meeting Lu's gaze.

Those were definitely tears. A lingering grief.

"Nothing is that simple, Adeluna," Kari returned. "Especially not your father. But at the end of it all, he gave me you." She cupped Lu's face in her hands. "And that"—she inhaled, the breath tripping—"is all I need."

Lu smiled. She smiled through her tears. She smiled through the broken pieces of her heart that would never truly heal. She smiled through scars and memories and pain, through aches that were as familiar to her as her mother's face.

Lu smiled and, impossibly, her smile felt as large as Teo's.

Devereux Bell was nineteen, and he was happy.

"Here, help me lift this—*ohh*, that's right. You can't."

Vex shot Nayeli a look from where he sat on a crate, sorting through a stack of nets to find the ones that hadn't been damaged beyond repair. Ahead of him, Nayeli half lifted a broken barrel, and she sagged, overdramatically acting as if she'd drop it.

"Really?" He scratched at the bandages under his shirt. "Sticking with the injury jokes pretty hard, are you? You'll have to find something else to mock when my rib heals."

Nayeli shrugged and dropped the barrel into the pile of rubble she'd made. "Well, if you could handle your magic like a *normal* person, you wouldn't have to heal on your own. I have weeks of *poor broken Vex* jokes ahead of me."

Vex made an inappropriate gesture at her. But he smiled.

Yeah, he did have weeks of healing ahead of him. Weeks of what he felt now—itching along his nerves, wounds binding together.

His body, working to make him stronger. His body, doing amazing things.

"*What did she say?*" asked Ben, through the Budwig in Vex's ear.

"Ben's not yet to Argrid. He says he'll send his armada back to Grace Loray to kick your ass for me," Vex told her.

"*Don't promise things like that! It's too fresh still.*"

"Kidding." Vex waved his hands, looking around at anyone who might've overheard. But the only people nearby were other raiders, focused on cleaning the wharf. "You hear, everyone? *Kidding.* Ben has no plans to send an armada to Grace Loray. For now."

"Vex!"

"Seriously, what's with you?" Vex adjusted the bean in his ear. "Gunnar not calming you down enough?"

"Hilarious."

"Hey, you went six years without my delightful personality in your life. Gotta make up for lost time."

Cansu came up behind Nayeli.

Speaking of lost time.

The two of them talked, low and quiet; then Nayeli kissed her. Cansu blushed. Nayeli kissed her again, and again, until she was chasing Cansu across the wharf, shouting over-the-top declarations of love in Thuti.

"Oh, I thought of a great wedding present for you," Vex told Ben.

Nayeli and Cansu raced past Kari and Lu, who halted some conversation they'd been having. Lu laughed, the sound pulling Vex to his feet. He started forward.

"You don't need to send a gift—oh, Gunnar is informing me that it is rude to refuse gifts. I think being the king's consort is already going to his head."

"He'll like this gift. You both will, I promise." Vex grinned. "It's a crate of Extin."

Ben barked a laugh. *"The plant that makes its taker fireproof? You're awful."*

"Brilliant, you mean."

"*No, awful—Gunnar! Thank you for that, Vex, you've given him all sorts of ideas.*"

"My pleasure." Vex stopped behind Lu.

In front of her, Teo kicked a small leather ball back and forth with Jakes. Lu laughed again, her hand on Kari's arm, joy pouring out of her in a wave that drew Vex from shadows into sunlight.

Noises started coming through the Budwig that Vex might have joked about but didn't particularly want to hear.

"All right. I think I'm just gonna— You don't care. Talk to you soon." Vex pulled the Budwig out of his ear and stuck it in his pocket.

But he was glad Ben had someone, that he wouldn't have to take on the daunting task of Argrid all on his own.

Though Ben wouldn't be on his own, not anymore. Vex might be on Grace Loray, but part of him would always be in Deza. And when Ben needed him, he'd be there this time. No more hiding. No more running.

Vex closed the space between himself and Lu to thread his arms around her waist. She leaned back into him, looking up to press her lips to his cheek, a spot she could access more easily now that he didn't wear his eye patch.

Apparently, Ben's healing potion could smooth his scar away. But Vex wasn't sure he'd ever willingly take magic again, even to fix his mangled eye socket.

Which shocked the hell out of him, that he had gotten

to a point of . . . not confidence with it, but acceptance.

Jakes overkicked the ball to Teo and fell to the ground. Teo tackled him, rampant with joy as Jakes grabbed him back and tickled him all over.

Lu hooked her hand around Vex's neck. The lake water lapped at the wharf and Teo giggled, raiders worked to better this island around them, and its citizens watched in cautious hope.

They all had to change. They all had to make up for what had happened and the things they'd done. But as far as Vex was concerned, this was his redemption: happiness.

Acknowledgments

And with that, my loves, another series comes to an end! Thank you for following me through Grace Loray. Thank you for opening your hearts and bookshelves to Lu, Vex, and Ben. The only reason I get to make a living in fantastical worlds is because of readers like YOU, who so thoughtfully pour your hearts into these books right alongside me. Thank you from Grace Loray to Argrid and back!

I must specifically call out the many, many people who work just as hard on my books as I do. Kristin Rens, who continues to chip away the rubble from my work to reveal the glittering jewels beneath. Mackenzie Bray Watson proves with each new book that she is the Super Agent of all Super Agents, and this journey would be infinitely rockier without her. Actually, this journey would be a helluva lot rockier without the entire Balzer + Bray/HarperCollins Children's team as well: Kelsey Murphy, Michelle Taormina, Alison Donalty, Renée Cafiero, Mark Rifkin, Allison Brown,

Olivia Russo, Bess Braswell, Sabrina Abballe, Michael D'Angelo, Jane Lee, Tyler Breitfeller; and, always and forever, Jeff Huang, who makes the best cover art, and I will fight anyone who says otherwise.

Thank you to writer friends, near and far and on social media, who rally and cheer and comfort. Kristen Simmons (next up: OUR BOOK BABY!), Evelyn Skye, Lisa Maxwell, Kristen Lippert-Martin, Olivia, Danielle, Anne, Natalie, Claire, Akshaya, Janella, Madeleine, Melissa Lee, Rae Loverde, Margaret Rogerson, Vina (her generous donation earned her her name in this book!), and so many more, I am always petrified that I'll forget someone, so I will just say: if your name should be here and it isn't, I will properly grovel at your feet in apology, but know I love you dearly.

Five books in, and my family still gets excited for me. Kelson and Oliver, Doug and Mary Jo, Melinda; my delightful, supportive extended family—the love you give me is the greatest magic I could ever hope for.

(If you don't end your acknowledgments section on a sappy note, did you REALLY write an acknowledgments section?)